THE
APPOMATTOX
7
SAGA

GILBERT MORRIS

✦

Wall of Fire

Tyndale House Publishers, Inc.
Wheaton, Illinois

Library of Congress Cataloging-in-Publication Data

Morris, Gilbert.
    Wall of fire / Gilbert Morris.
        p.   cm. — (The Appomattox saga ; 7)
        ISBN 0-8423-8126-0
        1. United States—History—Civil War, 1861-1865—Fiction.
    I. Title.   II. Series: Morris, Gilbert. Appomattox saga ; 7.
    PS3563.08742W35   1995
    813'.54—dc20   94-43872

Printed in the United States of America

01 00 99 98 97 96 95
 9   8   7   6   5   4   3   2

To Cindy Morris
The closest thing to a daughter
is a daughter-in-law.
You have brought a new joy
to my life, Cindy,
and I thank the Lord
for you.

CONTENTS

Part One: Clash at Gettysburg

1. *A Difficult Choice* 3
2. *Kings Go Forth* 17
3. *Out of the Past* 33
4. *Col. Rocklin Meets the President* 45
5. *Mark Calls on a Friend* 59
6. *The Sound and the Fury* 71

Part Two: The Bargain

7. *"A Woman Should Be Gentle"* 81
8. *"I Didn't Know What Love Was!"* 97
9. *A Ball at Gracefield* 113
10. *"I'll Have What I Want!"* 129
11. *A Visitor for Col. Rocklin* 147

Part Three: The Bridegroom

12. *Death of a Ship* 161
13. *"Every Woman Needs a Man"* 175
14. *A Bold Plan* 189
15. *Store-Bought Husband* 203
16. *All Brides Are Beautiful* 219
17. *The Wedding Night* 235
18. *Another Wedding* 247

Part Four: The Last Chance

19. *"What Is a Marriage?"* 265
20. *Maiden Voyage* 277
21. *Noel and the Secretary* 289
22. *Action at Sea* 297
23. *A Desperate Venture* 319
24. *Homecoming* 329

GENEALOGY OF THE ROCKLINS

Noah Rocklin (1767–1842)
m.1797
Charlotte Minton (1780–1847)

- **Stephen** (1798–) *m.1816* Ruth Poynter (1797–)
  - **Gideon** (1819–) *m.1840* Melanie Benton (1821–)
    - Tyler (1841–)
    - Robert (1842–)
    - Frank (1843–)
  - **Laura** (1818–) *m.1839* Amos Steele (1816–)
    - Patrick (1840–)
    - Colin (1841–)
    - Deborah (1842–)
    - Clinton (1843–)

- **Thomas** (1800–1863) *m.1819* Susanna Lee (1801–)
  - **Melora Yancy** (1834–) *m.1863* Clay (1820–) *m.1840* Ellen Benton (1820–1862)
    - Denton (1842–) *m.1861* Raimey Reed (1843–) — Thomas (1863–)
    - David (1842–)
    - Lowell (1843–)
    - Rena (1840–)
  - **Amy** (1822–) *m.1839* Brad Franklin (1810–) *m.1835* Lila Crawford (1818–1842)
    - Grant (1840–)
    - Rachel (1842–) *m.1862* Jake Hardin (1836–)
    - Les (1844–)
    - Vincent (1837–)
  - **Burke** (1830–) *m. 1863* Grace Swenson (1836–)

- **Mason** (1805–) *m.1825* Jane Dent (1807–1833)

- **Marianne** (1810–) *m.1830* Claude Bristol (1805–)
  - **Paul** (1831–) *m.1862* Frankie Aimes (1844–)
  - **Austin** (1832–)
  - **Marie** (1837–)

- **Mark** (1811–)

THE YANCYS

Buford Yancy
(1807–)
m.1829 ———
Mattie Satterfield
(1813–1851)

- Royal
  (1832–)
  m.1854
  Margaret O'Hare
  (1835–)
- Melora
  (1834–)
  m.1863
  Clay Rocklin
  (1820–)
- Zack
  (1836–)
  m.1859
  Elizabeth Stuart
  (1841–)
- Cora
  (1837–)
  m.1855
  Billy Day
  (1835–)
- Lonnie
  (1843–1863)
- Bobby
  (1844–)
- Rose
  (1845–)
- Josh
  (1847–)
- Martha
  (1849–)
- Toby
  (1851–)

PART ONE
Clash at Gettysburg

CHAPTER ONE
A Difficult Choice

⭐

Allyn Griffeth knew the French Quarter of New Orleans very well, but as she made her way down a narrow street late one Tuesday evening, she felt a chill of fear. *Shouldn't have come this way!* she thought, and the faint sound of movement coming from an alleyway ahead gave her a warning as plain as the cocking of a gun. She whirled around and dashed back down the dimly lit street. The flickering yellow streetlights threw her shadow on the walls that lined the narrow corridor. Her feet made a quick patter on the cobblestones, and the shadow became a leaping gargoyle.

No good to scream, Allyn thought. The sound of pounding feet behind her caused her to turn her head. Two men were almost on her. She knew she could not outrun them—and she knew what terrible things lay ahead if they had their way. Young women disappeared from the streets of the Quarter—most of them sold into white slavery, chattel for one of the many brothels in New Orleans.

Stopping abruptly, Allyn rammed her hand into her coat pocket and whipped out the small revolver. She had never fired it—she wasn't even certain that it *would* fire, but as the two men converged on her, she lifted the weapon and pulled the trigger.

The explosion echoed through the streets, and both men stopped as abruptly as if they'd run into a brick wall.

"Nom de Dieu!" one of them gasped.

In a thick French accent the other cried out, "Do not shoot!"

Allyn leveled the pistol at his head and pulled the hammer back as she had learned to do. "Get out of here, you scum, before I put a bullet in your brain!" She held the weapon high until the two scurried frantically away. When they vanished in the fog, she lowered it and began to tremble.

A window opened over her head, and a voice demanded, "Who's doing the shooting?" Allyn hastily pocketed the pistol and hurried away. The police of New Orleans paid little attention to anything that happened in the quarter, but she didn't want to take the chance that they might investigate. Her breathing was shallow, and the narrow escape brought a weakness to her legs, but there was no time to linger.

Avoiding the side streets, she hurried to Bourbon Street. Though she knew she would be accosted by men, at least she was in no danger of being dragged away. Keeping her eyes straight ahead, she ignored the crude invitations from the men she passed. They all assumed, Allyn well knew, that a lone woman walking through the quarter was available.

This is an evil place, Allyn thought not for the first time. New Orleans seemed to be covered with some sort of dark presence, and all her life she had sensed the evil miasma that lay over parts of it—especially the French Quarter. She had learned to avoid the dangers of the narrow streets as a Cajun girl would learn to avoid cottonmouths and other deadly wildlife that lurked in the swamps.

As she turned into a saloon with the words *Gay Paree* painted in elaborate letters over the wide front door, she felt safer at once. The large room was filled with the odor of whiskey and cigarette smoke in addition to the smell of many unwashed bodies. A hand caught at her arm, and a short, round-faced man grinned as he said, "Hey, Allyn, you come and give me three or two dances, no?"

Allyn smiled briefly and said, "Some other time, Frenchie. I've got to talk to Sam." The man shrugged elaborately, and she made her way to the table along the back wall, where a very fat man with a gleaming bald head and a tawny mustache looked up from a game of solitaire. Allyn asked without preamble, "No word from Lucas, Sam?"

Sam Barker, owner of the Gay Paree, was a native of Virginia, and the soft accent of his boyhood still threaded his voice. "No, Allyn, I ain't heard a word." Barker laid his thick forearms on the table and studied the girl out of a pair of hazel eyes.

What he saw was a young woman of eighteen, taller than average, dressed in a worn, cheap, brown dress. The shapeless garment, however, failed to conceal the rich curves of her figure. Her face was squarish, dominated by a pair of aquamarine eyes that were large and well shaped. The structure of her face made a definite, strong, and pleasant contour often seen in Welsh women. Her hair was dark red and was bound up in braids that formed a corona that gleamed as the lamplight brought out tints of gold. She had a long, composed mouth and a temper that could at once charm a man or chill him to the bones. This was a competence a girl acquired in the French Quarter of New Orleans, the manner of a girl raised in rough circumstances.

Barker said, "Maybe he'll write."

Allyn met his gaze and shook her head, saying briefly, "I don't think so, Sam." There was a fatalism in her attitude, the reflection of hard lessons and many disappointments.

"Aw, Allyn, you know how Lucas is. . . ."

Her answer was short, and bitterness lay cold on her voice. "Yes, I know how he is. He's run from every responsibility that ever came at him. He won't be back this time."

Barker tossed his cards down and stood up. *She's right about him,* he thought. *Lucas Rawlings never had any backbone and never will.* Aloud he said, "How's your ma?"

5

"She's dying."

The bluntness of the girl's reply caused Barker to blink, and he shook his massive head. "Naw, maybe not, Allyn."

"Maybe not today, but she'll never get better, Sam. She knows she won't live long."

Reaching into his vest pocket, the saloonkeeper pulled out some bills. Peeling off a few of them, he shoved them toward the girl. "Get the doctor, Allyn. Buy some medicine."

Reluctantly Allyn took the bills. "I—I hate to take this, Sam. I'll pay you back."

Barker waved his thick hand, protesting. "No problem!" He wanted to say something to comfort the girl but knew that there was little hope. Beth Griffeth had been sick for some time—consumption, the doctor had said. Barker had seen her "husband" getting more and more nervous, for Lucas Rawlings was not a man one could lean on in a pinch. Barker laid his hand on the girl's shoulder and said in a kindly fashion, "Look, now, Allyn." She was a proud girl, and as her eyes fastened on him, he chose his words carefully. "None of us likes to take charity. But you've got to think of your mama. She's going to have a tough time, and I want to help a little. You stay with her and let me worry about the bills for a little while. All right?"

Allyn Griffeth was not a crying young woman, but the unexpected kindness on the part of the saloonkeeper brought tears to her eyes. She dashed them away and nodded, saying huskily, "Thanks, Sam!"

"Now, you go to your mama," Barker said quickly. "Wait—I better go with you. It ain't safe on the streets this late."

A touch of grim humor came to the girl's eyes as she said, "I'll be safe, Sam. I had to use the gun Lucas gave me." When she related the incident with the two men, he frowned angrily, then smiled.

"Next time, don't miss. Shoot one of them varmints and it'll get the rest of them to understand you're serious."

After the girl left, Barker sat down, his thoughts moody.

When a tall man in the garb of a gambler came up and asked, "What's wrong with Allyn?" Barker clamped his bulldog jaws together, then said, "Lucas—he's run out."

"Well, he's the runnin' kind, Sam."

"Never was no good!" Barker began to lay out a new game, then stopped and gave the gambler a sharp look. "Keep your eye out for the girl, Tom. She'll need all the help she can get. Her ma won't make it, and you know what a good-looking girl can expect at a place like this."

Allyn made her way through the quarter without further incident, coming to a small frame house set back between two large warehouses. The door was unlocked, and she pushed inside, thinking, *I have to get a lock—anybody could come in while I'm gone.* The house consisted of three rooms—one that served as a kitchen, dining room, and living area plus two tiny bedrooms. She lit a lamp that threw an amber glow over the shabby, makeshift furniture, then moved at once to one of the bedrooms.

"Mama? Are you awake?"

The woman who stirred and tried to sit up was thin, and her face was gray with strain. Only a trace remained of the beauty that had been Beth Griffeth's, for poverty and sickness had drained that away. "Yes, I'm awake." Her lips were pale, but she managed to smile, saying, "I've been thinking of making a pie."

Allyn came over and helped her mother into a sitting position. The birdlike bones of her mother and the shrunken frame frightened her, but she said cheerfully, "Now that's a good idea. We've got some apples—how would an apple pie go down?"

The women chatted as Allyn helped her mother get out of bed and supported her as they made their way to the kitchen. Allyn sat her mother down in the battered horsehide chair and said, "Now, you can direct this piemaking. Nobody can make pies like you, so you just give me the orders, and I'll do the work."

For thirty minutes, Beth Griffeth sat in the chair giving

instructions and listening as Allyn talked of small matters. From time to time a smile touched her wan lips, but there was a sadness in her eyes that she could not conceal. When the pie was in the oven, she said, "Come and sit down. You must be tired."

"Oh no, I'm fine, Mama."

But sickness had not dulled the mind of Allyn's mother. She studied the lines around the girl's eyes and the drawn appearance of the wide mouth. "That factory is too hard on you. I wish . . ."

Allyn saw her mother hesitate and said quickly, "It's all right, Mama. I don't mind it. Lots of jobs would be harder." Actually she despised the bottle factory, where her job consisted of putting tops on small glass bottles. It was monotonous work for long hours and a pittance of pay, but she'd taken it to help out with expenses. Now she knew that somehow she had to be with her mother until . . .

"I expect we'll hear from Lucas," Beth said. "When he gets work he'll send for us."

"Why yes, Mama. Maybe we'll hear this week."

Beth gave her daughter a glance and then shook her head in denial. She had lived with Rawlings for two years—the last of a succession of men she'd taken up with—and knew what he was. "No. He won't write."

"Oh, Mama!"

"He's been good to us. At least he never bothered you, like some of the others."

"No, he never did." Allyn leaned and took her mother's hand. "We'll make out, Mama. I don't want you to worry."

Beth seized Allyn's hand with surprising strength. "What will happen to you when I'm gone? You won't have anybody!"

It was the first time her mother had stated the possibility of death, and Allyn saw that she was terrified. Holding to the thin hand, she leaned forward and pushed a lock of hair from her mother's fevered brow. "I'm strong, Mama," she said quietly. "You mustn't worry about me."

"How can I help it?" Tears ran down the pale cheeks, and anguish came to the eyes of the sick woman. "You haven't had any life at all—nothing!"

"Oh, Mama!"

"It's true. I've given you nothing."

"We've made out. It hasn't been so bad."

"If I could have found a good man, things could have been different."

Grief seized the older woman, and when she began to weep the action brought on a paroxysm of coughing. Her frail body was torn with gagging coughs that went on without end. There was nothing that helped the sick woman, and Allyn could only watch helplessly. Great hacking coughs continued until finally the woman was exhausted.

"Come on, Mama," Allyn said gently. "Maybe you'd better lie down. You don't cough so much that way."

"It doesn't matter," Beth whispered. When she was back in bed, her face pale as paste, she looked up out of tragic eyes and murmured, "I haven't given you anything, baby, and I wanted you to have a good life."

★   ★   ★

"She's given up, I'm afraid." Dr. Kinsman shook his shaggy head, then added, "There's only one end to that, you understand?"

"I know," Allyn said, nodding. For two weeks she'd seen her mother go down steadily, and she knew what that meant. The two of them had stepped out of the sick woman's room, and the doctor had hesitated before speaking. Allyn looked tired, for she had been up all night trying to make her mother more comfortable. Now she brushed a wisp of auburn hair back with a weary motion and said bitterly, "She gave up a long time ago, Doctor."

Kinsman was a thin, bespectacled man in his forties. He stared at the young woman, then said bluntly, "She could go at any time. Can't you get someone to be with you?"

"One of the neighbors will come in later, but Mama gets restless if I'm not there."

Kinsman nodded, then reached into his black bag to extract a large brown bottle. "Give her all she needs of this to make her comfortable."

"Thank you, Dr. Kinsman."

After the doctor left, Allyn slumped down in the ragged horsehide chair and put her head back. Weariness washed over her, and she went to sleep almost at once. She awoke some time later, aware of the familiar sound of her mother's coughing. Quickly she rose and went to the basin to dash her face with cold water. Then she took the bottle of medicine and entered the bedroom.

Carefully she helped her mother sit up, then poured a large spoonful of the dark liquid. "Take this, Mama. It will make you feel better."

Beth took the medicine, struggled to control the cough, then lay back and closed her eyes. "You need to get some rest, baby," she whispered. "You were up all night again."

"I'll take a nap later, Mama."

"You're not eating right, either." Stirring slightly, Beth looked over at her daughter, who had seated herself beside the bed. For a long time she said nothing, and when she did speak, her speech was already beginning to slur from the powerful narcotic. She was nothing but skin, bones, and nerves, and as she lay there she was aware that the end was not far.

"I could—go easy, baby—if I wasn't worried about you."

Allyn said quietly, "I'll be all right, Mama. You mustn't worry about me." She went on speaking, hoping that her mother would drop off into a deep sleep. She gave such assurances as she could, but they had been over this many times.

"I wish you could have had a good home," Beth whispered faintly. "A nice house—a father to love you. You never had that."

"Lucas wasn't bad," Allyn said quickly. "He was never mean to either of us."

"No, meanness wasn't in him, but he wasn't a strong man."

"He taught me how to play cards," Allyn murmured. "I got good enough to beat him most of the time."

Beth shook her head faintly. "Gambling was his curse. He could have been a better man, but he wouldn't leave cards alone."

A silence fell over the room, the sounds from the street outside muffled. The sick woman lay so still that she seemed almost to have given up the struggle. Allyn studied her mother's worn face, remembering how pretty she had been years ago. Now little was left of that charm except the bone structure.

A thought came to her, and she let it lay in her mind for some time without speaking. Finally she said, "Mama? Can I ask you something?"

"Yes, baby." The voice was weak, but Beth opened her eyes and smiled slightly. "What is it?"

"Who was my father?"

The question was one that Allyn had asked ten years earlier, but her mother had put her off, saying only that the past was better left alone. Now, however, the shadow of death was on Beth Griffeth, and she knew there would be little time. Her lips were dry, and she said, "Give me some water." When she had swallowed some of the tepid water, she lay back and studied her daughter. "That's strong—the medicine," she whispered. Then she began to pluck at the coverlet with thin hands, her eyes dim.

"He was a gentleman, baby," she said finally. "A fine gentleman. We met right here in New Orleans. It was in April, and I remember the magnolias were filled with lovely white blossoms. And he used to bring me flowers—all kinds."

"Where was he from, Mama? What did he look like?"

"He was from Virginia, and he was a handsome man, tall

11

and dark—" She broke off and put her hand out to touch Allyn's cheek. "You look a little like him, baby."

"Did—did you love him, Mama?"

"Yes! And he loved me, too."

"Why didn't he marry you?"

Beth's eyes were cloudy from the drug, and she was fighting against the drowsiness. "He . . . came from a fine . . . family," she whispered. "I was nobody . . . and he was quality."

Allyn had to bite her lips to keep from saying, "He wasn't quality—not to abandon a girl who loved him and had a baby!" But it was too late for that. She spoke softly, getting as many details as she could. For years she had longed for a father, though she had managed to bury some of that desire. Now she knew that once her mother died she would have no one to ask.

But the medicine was powerful, and soon her mother was deep in a comalike sleep. Regretfully Allyn sat there, her eyes on the worn face. *I'll have to find out more about him,* she thought just before she dozed off in the chair.

But she had little chance to find out more about her father. Her mother was in such pain that it was necessary to keep her drugged, and her speech was incoherent most of the time. When she was conscious, she seemed reluctant to talk about Allyn's father—saying once, "If it would help, I'd tell you, baby, but it was all so long ago!"

The next day the end came. Allyn had been cooking some eggs over the small stove when she heard her mother call. Putting the pan off the stove, she hurried into the bedroom. Her mother was lying flat on her back with her eyes wide open. "What is it, Mama?" Allyn asked, going to stand beside her.

Beth Griffeth's eyes were staring at the ceiling, almost blindly it seemed. "Mama? Are you all right?"

"I . . . have always . . . loved you. . . ." The words were so faint that Allyn had to bend down to hear them.

Fear came to her then for she saw that the breathing was very shallow. "I'll go get Dr. Kinsman."

"Too late." The words were a gasp, and then the dying woman seemed to recognize that the time had come. With the last of her strength she reached up, and her words were almost inaudible. "His . . . name was . . . Mark!"

"My father?"

But the effort was the last. The pale lips formed the word *baby,* and then Allyn's mother relaxed in that terrible finality into the great silence.

★ ★ ★

"You want to do *what?*" Sam Barker had been lifting a beer to his lips when Allyn had made her request. Staring at her, he put the stein down and shook his head. "Why, not in a million years would I let you do a thing like that!" His bald head gleamed, and he brushed his mustache fiercely as he did when something displeased him.

"What's wrong with it?" Allyn asked quietly. She came into the saloon three days after her mother's funeral, and when Sam had seated her at his table, she said, "Sam, I want to deal blackjack for you in the Gay Paree." She had known he would say no, so she had sat there patiently, her eyes determined.

"What's wrong with it?" Barker shot back. "Everything! This ain't no place for a young girl." He reddened as Allyn looked at the women who were serving at the bar. He snapped, "I won't have no part in making you into one of *them,* Allyn!"

"Look, Sam, all I want is a way to make money. I can't go on at that factory. It's just another kind of death." She gestured toward the saloon girls, saying, "I know what they do, and that's not for me. But I can't get any other kind of work." Her eyes were enormous, and there was a fierce determination in her. "Won't you at least let me try it, Sam?"

Barker was a hard man, but he had a soft spot for this girl. He'd had a daughter himself once. She had died, but he had never forgotten her. He was honest enough with himself to admit that he'd spent considerable time worrying about the fate of Allyn Griffeth. Now he sat still, his agile brain working. Finally he grunted, "What makes you think you're good enough to deal for me?"

"Lucas taught me."

"He wasn't much good himself."

Allyn smiled. "Try me!"

Sam had always liked the girl's spunk. He grinned, picked up a deck of cards, and tossed them in front of her. Allyn picked them up, shuffled expertly, then dealt the cards. Ten minutes later, Barker laughed, "Well, you're good enough to beat me, I reckon."

"Can I do it, Sam?"

"We'll try it." He dug into his pocket and handed her some bills. "That's an advance. Go get some fancy clothes. You'll start tonight."

That night Sam was shocked when Allyn walked into the saloon. He'd never seen her wear anything but worn, drab clothing. The sight of her wearing an emerald green dress that was modest by the standards of the Gay Paree but still revealed her stunning figure hit him hard.

"You look nice," he said. "Never seen your hair like that."

Allyn's rich auburn hair was done up in the latest fashion, but two tendrils hung down in front of each ear. "I borrowed these jade earrings from Marsha," she said, touching one of them. Then she said, "Sam, I'm—I'm a little nervous, to tell the truth."

"Why, these high rollers will be standing in line to lose their money to you!"

"What if I lose?"

"You won't lose." Sam grinned as he added, "You're so good-looking they'll be watching you instead of their cards. Go on, girl, you'll be all right!"

Allyn said softly, "Thanks, Sam!" Then she moved to the blackjack table and soon had a lively group gathered around. The tall gambler came over after an hour to say, "Sam, I didn't know you were so smart." He nodded at the group of men gathered around Allyn, adding with a grin, "She's going to do all right."

After the saloon closed, Allyn said, "I didn't make your fortune, Sam, but I didn't lose nothin' either."

Barker was pleased but felt a warning was in order. "You did fine, Allyn, but this isn't much of a life for a woman. I know you think you can make out, but this sort of thing hardens a man—much less a woman."

Allyn put her hand on Sam Barker's thick forearm. "I've got you to look out for me. That's why I'm not worried."

Barker flushed, then nodded seriously. "I had a daughter once, Allyn. I—I wish you could think of me as sort of a father."

Allyn felt intensely the loneliness that had been with her for years. "I'd be happy to think of you like that. I don't trust men very much. I've had . . . some bad experiences."

"You never knew your father, did you?"

The words, he saw, seemed to harden her, and she said, "No—nor do I ever want to, Sam. He abandoned my mother and me!"

"Well . . . that happens, I guess." He had touched a nerve and wanted to change the subject. "You go get some rest. Then you and me will go out to Antoine's and eat a big steak—all right?"

"I'd like that a lot, Sam." She turned and left the saloon, and Sam sat down and began to deal solitaire. His thoughts were not on the cards, however, but on Allyn.

CHAPTER TWO
Kings Go Forth

✦

Melora awakened instantly as the mockingbird greeted the dawn. He and his mate nested in the wild hedge outside the cabin, and the pair carried on eternal warfare against a yellow tomcat who stayed in the small barn. He had a scarred hammerlike head and never seemed to learn that the mockingbirds would peck him bloody when he approached the hedge.

Cautiously Melora climbed out of bed and tiptoed toward the door. Looking back, she cast a loving glance at Clay, who was still asleep. Five days constituted her marital life, and she was amused that she experienced a shock at finding a man in the bed beside her each morning. *Just an eternal old maid— that's all you are!* she jeered at herself.

She let her eyes rest on her new husband's calm, strong features, admiring his hair, dark as her own, and tentatively put out a finger to touch the slight cleft in his chin. Then she stopped, not wanting to awaken him. They had stayed on the river running a trotline until nearly three in the morning, and Melora thought of the times he had taken her fishing when she was a child. *I fell in love with him when I was no more than ten years old.* And then the memories came rushing back to her—how Clay had come to fill her life when he was a grown man and she was still a little girl. She'd been the

17

daughter of a poor farmer while he'd been a member of the wealthy planter class—a monumental wall between two people. Memories flickered as she thought of Clay's hapless marriage to Ellen Benton. She had tricked him into marriage, and despite the four children that came to the pair, Ellen had led an immoral life and made a hell on earth for Clay.

You were faithful to her, Melora thought, looking lovingly at Clay. *Most men would have sought another woman, but you never did.* She had loved him for that, loved him through all the years that had transformed her from a leggy adolescent to a tall stately woman.

Now Ellen was gone, and Clay was hers. In a normal world they would have waited a year to marry, but the war had changed all sense of time. Clay would be marching off with the Richmond Grays under the command of Robert E. Lee and his Army of Northern Virginia. They knew he might never return, and Melora had said, "Let me have what time there is, Clay!"

"But what if I don't come back—and there's a child?"

"Then I'll have part of you to keep and treasure!"

Melora smiled at Clay. *Even if I never have more than these few days I'll have had more than most women!*

The mockingbird screamed, and Melora crept into the kitchen and peered out the window. The scruffy tom was retreating, head down and bloody from the lethal bills of the mockingbirds, who were swooping down in great dives and peppering the hapless cat mercilessly.

Melora was on the side of the birds. *Go get that worthless tom!* she urged. *Peck his old head off!*

And then she uttered a short cry of alarm—for a pair of strong arms suddenly wrapped around her from behind.

"Got you!"

"Clay! You let me go!"

Melora turned and put her hands against Clay's broad chest and shoved, but he held her easily, laughing at her struggles. She flushed, as she did every morning when he first looked at her and took her in his arms. A rich color rose to her cheeks, and she had no idea how attractive she was to him at that moment. "If you don't stop, I'll—I'll—"

"You'll go off into the woods and eat woolly worms?" he teased. Ignoring her protests, he pulled her close, and her eyes widened as he looked at her, then kissed her.

Clay was very tall, and even at the age of forty-three was almost as lean and strong as he had been at twenty. She ran her hand down his muscular back, delighting in his strength.

Clay held her in his arms, marveling at the silken sheen of her skin. She was twenty-nine now, a mature woman, with all the love she'd harbored for years overflowing as he held her in his arms. He said, "We've missed a lot of years, Melora."

Melora knew he still grieved over the past, and at once she pulled his head down and kissed him. When she pulled back, she whispered, "We have each other, so never look back, Clay. We mustn't do that!"

She was, he had long known, a woman who possessed a rare wisdom. Now he realized she was speaking the truth. "No—never that." He held her close, murmuring quietly, "I've got the whole world—right here in my arms!"

★ ★ ★

Clay soaked up the last of the sorghum molasses with a flaky biscuit half, placed it in his mouth, and chewed slowly. "Got to make the taste of this last," he said, shaking his head. "The Army of Northern Virginia doesn't serve breakfast like this." Melora had fixed all Clay's favorite things for their last breakfast—eggs, bacon, grits, hash brown potatoes, biscuits and sorghum, and a pot of scalding coffee. It was the last of the real coffee, for the Confederacy was cut off from that item. Melora had hoarded the precious grounds, knowing how Clay disliked baked acorns and other substitutes.

"Maybe you could take me along as your aide," Melora teased.

Clay examined her critically. She was wearing a thin robe

19

over a silk nightdress—and even with her hair slightly tousled from sleep she looked beautiful. "Nope, I don't think that would work." He shook his head regretfully. "You don't look like any aide I ever saw in the army." He sipped his coffee, eyes running over her curves, then added, "Gen. Lee wouldn't like it." He reached over and took her hand, a knowing smile on his lips. "Now *I'd* like it mighty well, myself—"

Melora slapped at his hand, then rose to clean the table. He helped her as he always did, and afterward they left the cabin and walked toward the small stream that led to the river. The hammerheaded cat slunk toward the hedge and was promptly bombarded by the dapper mockingbirds. Both of them laughed as he crept away with his head down in abject humiliation.

"He never learns, does he?" Clay remarked.

"I don't care if they peck his old yellow head off!" Melora snapped. She loved birds, and the thought of anything preying on them angered her. But it was only a passing anger, and she was soon holding Clay's hand and laughing as they made their way along the river. When they reached the bank they sat down on a grassy knoll, and after a while Melora said wistfully, "It's almost over, isn't it?"

Clay was thinking the same thought. "For a while, Melora." Regret came to his dark eyes, and he shook his head. "I wish we could stay here forever."

"Wouldn't that be fine?" She reached over and took his hand, stroked it gently, then said, "We've had only a few days, but I've learned something about being a wife."

Clay's eyes gleamed, and he closed his hand on hers. "Yes, I'll say amen to that!" he said with a sly grin.

"Oh, you!" Melora colored slightly, then grew still. He had grown accustomed to this from her. There was more life in this woman than in any he'd ever seen, but at times she would seem to withdraw, her mind and spirit moving in some realm that he could only imagine. Finally she began to speak, and there was a wonder in her still face. "I can't find words to say it, Clay, but it's like I'm lost without you—no, not lost—but somehow *not complete*. I guess that's what the pastor meant when he said we'd be one flesh. When you're not right with me I get a queer, strange feeling inside—"

A large fish came to the surface, a black bass, and she broke off, eyeing the silvery flash as he rolled over and took a bug that had fallen into the water from an overhanging branch. He sank back into the green depths, and Melora turned again to Clay. "Sometimes when you're just sitting by the fire or eating breakfast—or when I look at you when you're asleep—I feel like my heart's going to bust wide open! Just crack and run down inside of me. I'm so proud that you're my man, my bones just—just sort of turn to jelly and a shiver runs over me." She turned her face away from him and whispered, "And that's what love makes me feel like, Clay."

He was deeply moved, for she had never voiced her feelings so strongly. He put his arms around her and drew her close, savoring the clean smell of her hair, the firm curves of her body, and the sweetness that was part of her. "I wish I'd said that, sweetheart," he said quietly. "I feel like that, too, but a man—well, he can't seem to say those things so easy." Then he turned her around and kissed her. Drawing back, he smiled, adding, "But I'm going to learn how to say what I feel. I don't know much, but I know women like to be told they're loved."

Melora's eyes suddenly grew mischievous. "You can practice on me, Clay Rocklin. I'll let you know when you do it right or when I've heard enough!"

They both laughed and sat there making foolish talk, and finally Melora grew serious. "How long do you think the army will be gone?"

Clay picked up a flat rock and skipped it expertly across the water. As he watched it sink, he grew thoughtful. "Hard to say, Melora. But things can't go on like they are. The South grows weaker every day, and the North grows stronger."

"Do you think we'll lose?"

"If something remarkable doesn't happen, I think we will. It comes to this, either we draw our army around Richmond and stand a siege—which will end sooner or later in surrender—or we invade the North."

"Isn't that what we did when the army went to Maryland?"

"Yes, and we have to do it again." Clay's eyes grew sober, and he shook his head in a moody gesture. "We'll be taking every man that can be spared, and somewhere we'll have to meet the Union army. But I don't know how long we'll be gone—nobody knows that."

Melora felt a sudden stab of fear but knew that she must never show it to Clay. She changed the subject, and later that day they packed their things and left the cabin. As they left the clearing, Melora clung to his arm. "It was the finest honeymoon any woman ever had, Clay!"

He saw the sadness in her eyes and said huskily, holding her with one arm, "We'll come back here as soon as I get home, Melora."

They turned and walked slowly toward the river, clinging to each other with a desperation that each of them had to fight down. The bass rose to take a shining minnow, breaking the water with a loud splash, but neither of them noticed the sound.

★   ★   ★

Rooney Smith scooped off a spoonful of the steaming broth that simmered in the large black pot and carefully tasted it. "This chicken soup needs more of something, Dorrie, but I can't tell what."

"Gimme dat spoon!" The black woman who spoke had been kneading biscuit dough, turning it relentlessly. Tall and straight despite her sixty years, her face was barely lined, and there was a nobility in her features. She took the spoon, tasted it, then frowned as she said, "Needs mo' thyme—and mebby a little mo' rosemary."

Rooney shook her head in disgust. "I'll *never* learn to cook like you, Dorrie," she groaned. She was an attractive girl of seventeen with curly auburn hair and large blue eyes shaded by thick black lashes. "I guess Lowell will have to hire a cook when we get married."

Dorrie glanced at the young woman, and a smile curled the edges of her lips upward. "You doin' fine, Miss Rooney," she said. "Never seed a girl learn to cook as quick as you. Mr. Lowell, he's gonna git fat as a possum when you gits a chance to feed him." She went back to pounding her dough, asking, "When you and Marse Lowell gettin' married?"

Rooney gave her head a toss, saying as she added the ingredients to the broth, "As soon as the army comes back." An impatience stirred in her, for she was a quick-spirited girl. "Lowell was afraid something would happen to him in the army. But Clay and Melora got married, so I don't see why we can't."

"Humph!" The short explosion that issued from the lips of Dorrie expressed her disgust. "Miz Melora been a'waitin' for Marse Clay 'mos as long as you been *alive!* So you jis settle back—learn how to cook and how to treat a man!"

Rooney smiled at the older woman, mischief in her eyes. "How *do* you treat a man, Dorrie? You and Zander have been married a long time. Did he ever take after another woman?"

Again the explosion: *"Humph!"* Then Dorrie said, "I doan reckon you needs to know *everything* 'bout it—but he did git to looking at a little ol' yellow gal onst. I kotched him at it!"

"What'd you do, Dorrie? Take a broom to him?"

"No! I made him a pie every day and tole him whut a handsome man he wuz!" Dorrie tried to frown, but instead a smile came to her. "And I wuz nice in other ways, too. You gonna have to learn, honey, dat when a man git steak *at home*—why he ain't gonna be looking around to find chicken backs somewheres else!"

Rooney giggled abruptly and would have questioned

Dorrie more closely, but Susanna Rocklin entered at that moment. "What are you two plotting?" she asked, noting the merriment on the girl's face.

"Dorrie's teaching me how to hold on to a man," Rooney answered. "She says you make everything so nice he won't *dare* run away. Is that right?"

Susanna laughed aloud, saying, "It worked for me, Rooney. And Lowell is so spoiled already—mostly by me and Dorrie—that you'll have to treat him better than most new bridegrooms." The mistress of Gracefield was sixty-two years old and still had the steady blue-green eyes and trim shape she'd had when she'd come to be the bride of Thomas Rocklin years earlier. A faint shadow lay over her, for the death of her husband had left her lonely. *Now I've got two new daughters to care for,* she thought. *Melora and Rooney will need me more than they know.*

The three women talked for a time, and then Rooney said, "I've made some chicken soup for Mark. He's not been eating well."

Susanna shook her head, for she had been concerned for her brother-in-law. "He's lost so much weight—I'm worried about him. Maybe I ought to get Dr. Maxwell out to see him."

Dorrie gave her mistress a quick glance and shook her head. "He ain't done no good, Miz Susanna, not since he got shot in dat battle. I'm plumb worried 'bout Marse Mark."

"He was always your favorite, wasn't he, Dorrie?" Susanna asked gently.

"I doan know 'bout dat!" Dorrie spoke sharply, turned, and left the kitchen abruptly.

"She always loved Mark," Susanna said to Rooney. "Maybe it was because he was such a lost man."

"Lost? How?"

"Oh, Mark was always a rebel. Dorrie practically raised him, was a mother to him almost. Finally he left and became a Mississippi riverboat gambler—and worse, I suspect. He would come home from time to time, but he always stayed on the outside of our family." Susanna began to spoon the soup into a bowl, her brow drawn up. "He's not been one to share himself," she murmured. "He never married, and we've always known there was some kind of a tragedy, though he's never spoken of it."

Rooney glanced at Susanna sharply, hoping that she wouldn't be asked if she knew anything about Mark. But Rooney said only, "I'll take him his soup. I can get him to eat usually."

Susanna nodded, studying the young woman. "He thinks a lot of you, Rooney. What do the two of you talk about so much?"

"Oh, different things," Rooney evaded. She quickly prepared a tray, then moved out of the kitchen into the broad hall. When she got to the room at the end, she knocked once, then entered. "Now then, Mark Rocklin," she said cheerfully as she set the tray down on a small table, "You've got to eat every bite of this!"

Mark was sitting in a chair beside the large window that let in the bright sunlight. He was a tall man, but illness had drained him of vitality. His dark eyes were sunk into their sockets, and his hair was lank, having lost its dark luster. He smiled, however, saying, "Sit down, Rooney. I've been lonesome."

"I'll sit as long as you eat," Rooney pronounced and proceeded to practically force him to eat all of the soup. She was a clever young woman and had learned how to cheer the tall man. For an hour she sat with him, entertaining him with tales of her attempts to learn how to function on a large plantation. She had been a city girl, and her romance with Lowell had been stormy. Even now her mother, Clara, was just out of prison leading an immoral life, and this was a constant grief to Rooney and her younger brother, Buck.

Mark sat quietly, smiling at her sprightly accounts, careful not to let the pain that came to him show on his face. At least he tried to do this, but Rooney was very quick. "You're in a lot of pain, aren't you, Mark?"

"I can't complain," he said quickly, then added, "You've learned a lot about wounded men, working at the hospital. But I'm all right." He had little hope left that he would recover from his wound but wanted to go with as little trouble as possible. "Tell me about Lowell. Is he champing at the bit to get married?"

Rooney answered Mark's questions, but she was thinking of the time she'd cared for him when he'd been in a delirium. He'd spoken of a woman who died, a woman he was in love with named Beth. Rooney had never mentioned what Mark had said but had cautiously probed Dorrie—who knew every detail of the Rocklin family—and had discovered that even she knew nothing about this part of Mark's history.

Now as she finished feeding Mark the soup, she watched his drawn face and the pain behind his eyes. She thought, *He loved a woman once—and it ruined his whole life!* But she couldn't bring herself to ask about the woman or her daughter. So she said nothing, and when she left, there was a weight on her. As much as she'd come to like and respect Mark Rocklin, she could see no glimmer of hope for him.

★ ★ ★

On the morning of June 8, 1863, Maj. Gen. Jeb Stuart greeted his commander, Robert E. Lee. Stuart cut quite a figure, wearing a brand-new uniform and a slouch hat with a long, black ostrich plume fastened with a golden clasp. Stuart sat astride a horse decked with garlands of flowers, and one of Lee's staff quipped, "It's Stuart in all his glory."

Stuart was proud—and had reason to be. His command— now five brigades comprising nearly ten thousand cavalry-men—had demonstrated time and again its ability to ride rings around the Federal cavalry. Now as he and Lee took position on a hilltop at Brandy Station, a whistle stop on the

Orange & Alexander Railroad just north of Culpepper, Virginia, Stuart gave a signal.

Bugles blared as twenty-two cavalry regiments wheeled into a column four across. While three bands played, horses pranced as the troopers moved out beneath their flags, which waved with the blowing of the breeze. A large dust cloud billowed up from the grand parade.

As the parade moved by, Lee thought of the meeting he'd just had with President Jefferson Davis and his cabinet in Richmond. He had laid his plan for the invasion of the North before them and had seen that some of them disapproved. Quietly Lee had said, "Mr. President—and gentlemen—we have just won a victory at Chancellorsville. But we lost Gen. Stonewall Jackson—who cannot be replaced. Now we *must* force the action."

"Why, sir?" Davis had demanded. He was an impossible man. "We cannot leave Richmond unprotected."

Carefully Lee had given his three reasons for the proposed invasion. "First, there is the matter of supplies. We must have adequate food and clothing for the army and forage for the horses. An invasion of Pennsylvania would give access to that rich storehouse and would allow the people of Virginia to stockpile supplies. Also, sir, the Peace Democrats in the North will press harder to end the war under favorable terms to the Confederacy."

Now as the last of the troopers filed by, Lee felt the weariness that had come from that struggle to convince the president and cabinet of the necessity of the blow against Pennsylvania. He complimented Jeb Stuart, then turned the iron gray horse away from the field.

"Sir, we will whip the Yankees again!"

Lee gave the flamboyant Stuart a hooded glance, but said only, "It will be as God wills, General."

The bugles began to blow again, brazen and harsh to Lee's ears. He had heard many bugles blow in his time, but Lee heard an ominous note to the sound this time. . . .

★ ★ ★

The leader of the Union cavalry was Gen. Alfred Pleasanton—a small man who was addicted to straw hats and kid gloves. He was sick of getting whipped by Jeb Stuart and had determined to hand the flamboyant Confederate a sound thrashing. "If you do," he had been told by Hooker, "it will be the first time our cavalry ever did anything but run from Stuart! But go see what you can do with him."

Pleasanton had at his command some fine officers, but perhaps the largest asset to him, in this case, was the review of the Confederate cavalry, for Jeb Stuart was so elated over the affair that for once he let down his guard. Thus, for the first time in the war the Federal cavalry caught its enemy off guard. Pleasanton got his men down to the upper fords of the Rappahannock at dawn on June 9 and sent them splashing across the stream yelling like madmen. They struck the Confederate outpost line, pushed it aside, and drove from the riverside to Brandy Station—not far from where General Stuart lay asleep, as though the enemy was still in Washington.

Lowell Rocklin had risen before dawn, groomed his horse, then shared a breakfast of bacon and biscuits with Lt. Lafe Hebert, a dark Cajun from Baton Rouge. "Gimme three or two of them biscuits, Rocklin. I'm hungry as a bear, me!"

Lowell grinned and leaned forward to pick up the biscuits, but he stopped and turned his head to one side. "Hey—what's that?"

"I don't hear nothin'," Hebert said.

Lowell tossed his plate down and stood up, alarm on his face as he turned toward the east. For one moment the two men stood still, and then Lowell yelled, "That's a charge, Lieutenant! Hear that trumpet?"

"Wake the men! The Yanks are comin'!" Hebert cried. He rousted the drummer boy, and a sharp staccato brought the troopers out of their blankets. They were none too soon, for by the time the officers had gotten their men into the saddles a terrific roar of guns shook the woods to their left. "They're all along the river," Hebert shouted. "Rocklin—go tell Gen. Jones we got trouble!"

Lowell shot away from the camp and found Gen. Jones—called Grumble Jones by friend and foe—without difficulty. The general appeared barefoot, hatless, and coatless as Lowell tore into the command post. "What's going on?" the general demanded.

"Yankees are attacking, sir," Lowell said. "A big force. Sounds like they're spread out along the river—and coming hard!"

Jones and Stuart did not get along, but the general was too good a soldier to waste time blaming his superior. "Come along, trooper," he commanded Lowell. "I'll need you to take a message to Gen. Stuart when I get this sorted out."

Lowell followed Gen. Jones, who sized up the situation very quickly after arriving at the line of battle. The field was covered with a mingled mass, fighting with pistol and saber, and Jones immediately saw a weakness. "Go down there and tell Capt. Chew there's a big gap in those woods. They'll be setting up their artillery right there!"

"Yes, General!" Lowell spurred his horse and without a moment's hesitation drove into the center of the fight. He drew his pistol, and when a maddened Yankee drove for him with saber raised high, Lowell lifted it and shot the man out of the saddle. The battle was a wild, confused affair, not a simple charge where two lines of cavalry are clearly defined. Before he had crossed the field, Lowell had ridden past several Federals and had emptied his revolver, but he did reach Capt. Chew and gave him Jones's orders. At once Chew ordered his guns brought up, cutting down scores of Federals. But the Union charge powered on, and the Confederates were driven back.

Lowell carried messages for Gen. Jones several times, and when Grumble Jones saw the enemy flanking Fleetwood

Hill, he sent Lowell to find Gen. Stuart. "Tell him we've got more Yankee cavalry than I've ever seen, and we're about to get flanked."

Lowell rode away, managing to avoid the center of the melee. Stuart was not far away, and when Lowell rode up and gave him Jones's warning, Stuart said with irritation, "Tell Gen. Jones to attend to the Yankees in his front, and I'll watch the flanks."

Lowell wheeled his mount, and when he gave Stuart's reply to Jones, the crusty warrior glared toward where Stuart was located. "So he thinks they ain't coming, does he? Well, let him alone, he'll darned soon see for himself."

And Stuart did, for the flanking force appeared across from Fleetwood Hill and began shelling the hill.

Jeb Stuart had never been flanked—and even now found it difficult to believe that the Federals were at him in force. When he heard the shelling, he commanded James Hart of his artillery, "Ride over and see what this foolishness is all about." But before Hart could leave, a courier confirmed the news. It was then that Stuart decided to throw his entire force against the enemy. "Order every regimental officer to get to Fleetwood at the gallop!"

Lowell was with Gen. Jones when the order came, and he ignored the fact that he was a courier. He was one of those who made the charge. Later he wrote his father, saying, "It was a thrilling sight to see these dashing horsemen draw their sabers and start for the hill a mile and a half away. The lines met on the hill, and it was like what we read of in the days of chivalry—acres and acres of horsemen sparkling with sabers. The flags above the two lines were hurled against each other at full speed, and when we met the earth seemed to tremble!"

Stuart's chief scout, young Capt. Farley, was right in front of Lowell, and he went down, knocked from his horse by a shell. Lowell had gotten close to the man and pulled his horse up at once and dismounted. Kneeling down, he saw that Farley was hard hit. The captain's leg had been blown off above the knee, and Lowell at once put a tourniquet around the stump. Farley was pale, but asked, "Are we winning? Did the charge drive them back, Rocklin?"

"Yes, sir. They're leaving the field," Lowell said as he looked across the field. "Take it easy, sir. I'll get you a couple of stretcher bearers."

Farley looked down at the wreck of his leg and managed a grin. "I guess we'll be a matched set, won't we? Reckon you can get your man to make me a leg like yours?"

"You bet, sir."

Lowell found the ambulance wagon, and when he directed it to where the captain lay, he found Farley much worse. He had lost a great deal of blood, and when the soldiers picked him up to put him inside, he pointed to his leg, which lay ten yards away where it had been flung by the shell.

"Bring it to me, please," he whispered. Lowell was shocked but did what the captain asked. "It's an old friend, and I don't want to part with it," Farley said. Then he looked at Lowell and whispered, "I know my condition. Good-bye, Lowell—thank you for your great kindness. . . ."

Lowell mounted and rode toward the front, deeply saddened. *He's in love with a girl named Alice. He's going to marry her—if he makes it.* He was hoping that Farley would survive the wound but was not optimistic. After the battle ended and the Yankees were driven off, he went to the field hospital. When he asked about Farley's condition, the doctor shook his head. "I'm sorry. Captain Farley died an hour ago."

Stuart had lost over five hundred men, and Rooney Lee, the son of Gen. Robert E. Lee, had been badly injured. Later in the month, while he was recovering, Federals captured him. Stuart ordered his camp set up at the site where the battle had been, but when he got there he discovered bluebottle flies swarming over the bloody ground so thickly and bodies of men and horses covering the field. He chose another spot.

The battle of Brandy Station proved one thing: Federal cavalry *could* stand up to Rebel cavalry in open combat. As one Confederate critic put it, "It *made* the Federal cavalry!"

Jeb Stuart was criticized for his conduct. Charles Blackford, a member of Longstreet's staff, said, "The fight at Brandy Station can hardly be called a victory. Stuart was certainly surprised, and but for the gallantry of his subordinate officers and men, it would have been a day of disaster and disgrace. Stuart is blamed very much."

But the invasion of the North was underway, so Stuart led his men on a mission to screen the movement of Gen. Lee. As Lafe Hebert said to Lowell, "If we wasn't 'bout to get in a big fight, I reckon Gen. Lee would spank Stuart—but we gonna need every man we got!"

Robert E. Lee was a man of daring. One of his opponents had said of him, "Good Lord—Lee makes a Mississippi riverboat gambler look like an old maid! I've never seen a man with such nerve!"

And now it was time to gamble again, not for money but for a nation. And the table stakes would be not currency, but the rich, red blood of men. Men and boys. The Confederacy had reached the end of its resources. The bravest had gone first, throwing themselves into the Cause with reckless abandon. When they were gone, there were no others like them to fill the gaps. The draft now drew men of fifty and boys of sixteen. Men with white beards and boys with no beards at all.

It will be for everything—we will lose or win on this invasion. Lee reached down and patted the shoulder of the great horse, then said quietly, "Come, Traveler—it's the time when kings go forth to war."

CHAPTER THREE
Out of the Past

★

Robert E. Lee was poised to strike. The Army of Northern Virginia would be the weapon with which he hoped to demolish the Army of the Potomac. However, the death of Stonewall Jackson meant that the army must be reorganized.

The Army of Northern Virginia had been organized into two corps, one under Jackson and one commanded by Lt. Gen. James Longstreet. Each corps comprised about thirty thousand men—too many, Lee felt, for one officer to handle. He decided to divide his army into three corps.

The Confederate I Corps would remain under the command of Longstreet, the solid Georgian whom Lee fondly called "my old war-horse." In fact, Longstreet was opposed to the invasion of the North but agreed provided that it should be offensive in strategy but defensive in tactics, forcing the Federal army to give battle only when the Confederates were in strong position.

Lee selected Lt. Gen. Richard S. Ewell to take Jackson's place as head of II Corps. This was a gamble, for Ewell was not the same Ewell who had fought well under Jackson. He had lost a leg, and big wounds change men. All through the campaign officers and men noted that Ewell did not have the drive he once had—but Lee could not know this before the fact. Ewell had made two acquisitions prior to the invasion. One was religion, which tempered his whole outlook. Formerly profane, he was now mild in manner. The second acquisition was a wife—a wealthy widow who in her youth had rejected him to marry a man with the undistinguished name of Brown. Ewell could scarcely believe his luck and sometimes forgot himself so far as to introduce her as "my wife, Mrs. Brown."

The commander of the new III Corps was Lt. Gen. Ambrose Powell Hill, a fierce fighter indeed, but also highstrung and impatient.

Thus Lee launched his greatest campaign without the incomparable Stonewall Jackson. And of his three commanders, one was skeptical about the mission, while the other two were totally inexperienced as corps commanders.

Across the Potomac, the matter of leadership was even more confusing. "Fighting" Joe Hooker had fallen into general disfavor following his defeat at Chancellorsville. Although President Lincoln liked him personally, Secretary of War Stanton and General in Chief Halleck were determined to oust him. Their response was perhaps natural. After the defeat Lee and Jackson administered to the Army of the Potomac at Chancellorsville, Washington fell into deep dejection. Horace Greeley cringed in print that the finest army on the planet had been defeated by "an army of ragamuffins." When Lincoln received the bad news, his sallow face turned ashen-gray, and he muttered as if dazed, "My God! What will the country say?"

It was a turning point in the war—this terrible defeat of Hooker's army. Nobody consciously made any decision about anything, yet people began taking something for granted that they had not known before: The war would have to be fought out, no matter how many ups and downs it might have, that there would never be any turning back, that out of the horror of this lost battle in a forest fire there would come a renewed determination and an unutterable grimness. The high watermark of the rebellion had been left behind, though many would have to die before it was over.

Somehow in the North, except for the new graves and the thousands of maimed men in the hospitals, it was nearly as though Chancellorsville had not been fought. The battle had been almost totally devoid of results. The army had been defeated again, but that did not seem to matter.

Why this attitude in the North? Some said that the Army of the Potomac had come of age. It was a professional army now, built around the volunteers of 1862 who had come in singing songs and dreaming dreams. But the songs had come to be doggerel, and the dreams had been knocked out of the men.

And so the two armies moved toward each other—and they were not the same.

The spirits of the men in the Army of Northern Virginia had never been higher. They set out with a dream of defeating the enemy so soundly that the war would end. The men in the Army of the Potomac had no such exuberance, but they had a grim determination to fight until the South was back in the Union.

The Army of Northern Virginia moved north through the Shenandoah and into Maryland and then Pennsylvania— and the Army of the Potomac tarried. To the east, Hooker paralleled Lee's course but remained at least two days behind. There were a few skirmishes along the way, but it was at a spot far ahead that the two mighty armies would clash.

★ ★ ★

"Buck—you leave those chickens alone!"

Rena Rocklin aimed a warning kick at the big dog, who had been engaged in chasing a banty rooster. "You don't mind a thing I say," she complained, but then when the huge animal came to paw at her leg, she knelt and put her arms around him, whispering, "Buck, I wish the men didn't have to go to the stupid old war!"

Buck whined and tried to lick the girl's face, but she stood up and shoved him away. "Come on, let's get the worms dug before Josh gets here." She moved quickly away from the house, and when she reached the barn, she picked up a tin bucket and half filled it with dead leaves. She turned to go inside the barn, but someone called her. She turned back to see Josh Yancy come around the house.

"Josh, hurry up," the girl called impatiently. "Where've you been?"

"Had to go to the mill for your grandmother." Josh Yancy at the age of sixteen was fully six feet tall. He had greenish eyes—as had all the Yancys—tow-colored hair that fell over his forehead, and a few freckles across his tanned face. "You get the bait?"

"No, I just got here. Come on, I want to get a mess of fish before it gets too hot."

"Here, give me the bucket." Josh took the bucket and shot a covert admiring glance at Rena. She was wearing a pair of old overalls that had once belonged to one of her brothers. The legs were cut off so she wouldn't trip over the ends, and her youthful girlish figure was evident even though they were men's pants. She wore a light blue cotton shirt, and a tan straw hat covered her dark brown hair. Her eyes were so dark they appeared black, not sharp as were her father's and brothers', but gentle and kind.

The pair moved to the barn and began kicking a pile of dried manure and rotten leaves. "Gosh, they're thick today!" Josh exclaimed. Reaching down he made a stab and captured a long worm that wiggled frantically in its efforts to escape. "Never seen so many!"

Rena bent over and came up with a long worm in each hand. When she put them into the bait can, Josh grinned at her. "Remember the first time I brought you to get night crawlers? You screamed like a panther!"

Rena sniffed and kicked up the leaves, then when she'd come up with another wiggling night crawler, said, "Dorrie says digging worms isn't ladylike. She says I ought to be sewing and doing needlework."

"Not near as much fun as catching f-fish," Josh teased her. Rena noted that he stumbled over the word and glanced quickly at the tall young man. When she had first met Josh, he had stuttered so badly that he refused to speak. But as time had passed, he had lost most of the stutter, so that now only in moments of crisis was his handicap noticeable. Rena almost commented on this but caught herself in time, knowing that Josh didn't like anyone to mention it. Instead she said, "Let's go over to the big pool today. Maybe we'll catch that big ol' bass that got away last week."

"All right."

Thirty minutes later, the two were watching their corks in a large pool made in the bend of the river. The air was still and it was cool, though the rising sun would soon lay a baking heat on the ground. Soon the bluegills began to bite, and Josh spent most of his time baiting Rena's hook. She disliked the job, and he contented himself with sliding the hook into the frantically wiggling worms and stringing the plump redear sunfish that Rena brought in.

"You get as excited over a one pound bluegill as I would over a five pound b-bass," he said with a grin, extracting her hook from the mouth of a fish. Slipping the fish on the stringer, he replaced it in the water, rummaged in the bait can, and began threading a new worm on her hook. "I'm going to put this big one on. I'm t-tired of these little fellows." When the hook was baited, he nodded at a strand of willows that formed the boundary of the water. "Put this sucker right in them willows."

"I'll get hung up," Rena protested.

Josh grinned at her and leaned back on the grass. "Best way to catch a big bass is to get your bait in where you c-couldn't get it out no way."

Rena stared at him, then followed his instructions. The red cork bobbed on the small waves, and she watched it carefully. The sun turned the stream red, and they could hear the sound of a cow in the distance. The water gurgled over the stones at their feet, and Josh idly said, "Shore wish I could make a living fishing. Beats work all hollow."

"I guess so."

There was a note in the girl's voice that caught Josh's attention, and he swiveled his head toward her. She'd removed her hat, and he admired her hair—dark brown like walnut. He had learned her ways very well over the past weeks and now saw that her natural gaiety was subdued. "What's the matter, Rena?" he asked.

Rena bit her lower lip, then took her eyes off the bobbing cork long enough to face him. She had creamy skin, and her eyes were wide, shaded by thick black eyelashes that Josh admired. "I'm worried about Father—and about Dent and Lowell."

"Why, they'll be all right, Rena!"

"How do you know? Every day it seems like we hear about somebody getting killed. Yesterday the Baineses got word that their oldest boy was killed in Tennessee."

Josh picked up a stick and began to probe the sandy bottom of the stream. A silvery cloud of minnows fled as he raked the stick through the silt, their scales flashing in the early morning sun. He was troubled by her statement and finally nodded. "I know. Guess I worry about my brothers, too, especially since Lonnie got killed. But it don't do no good worryin', does it? If somethin's gonna happen, why, I guess it will."

"You don't believe that, Josh," Rena said sharply. "You wouldn't go to sleep on a railroad track, would you? God gave us sense enough to keep from doing foolish things!"

Something seemed wrong about this to Josh. He shoved his hair back from his forehead, thought hard, then shook his head. "It ain't the same thing. I don't *have* to sleep on no railroad track, but we *do* have to fight the Yankees!" He was pleased with this and added, "Anyways, it would be downright uncomfortable sleeping on a railroad track."

Rena laughed aloud, amused by his thinking. She reached

over and grabbed a handful of his hair. Giving it a sharp yank, she said, "You can't think—that's your trouble!"

"Hey—that hurts!" Josh grabbed her wrist, but she clung to his hair stubbornly. He was strong enough to have freed himself but feared hurting her. He grabbed her other wrist and rolled her over on the grass, but she fought back, squealing shrilly. Josh ordered, "Turn me loose, you crazy female!"

"No! What's going to happen is going to happen!" Rena said, panting. "So what's happening is I'm pulling your hair!"

Josh began to laugh and with an easy strength shoved her back on the grass. He clasped her dainty wrists with one of his big hands, then reached over and took a night crawler from the bait can. Holding it over her face, he grinned down at her. "All right, it's *supposed* to be that I put this ol' worm in your mouth!"

Rena struggled frantically, her eyes enormous as Josh lowered the wriggling worm. "No! Don't you dare, Josh Yancy!" she cried.

Josh held her easily and let the worm drop another two inches. "Why, I'm just trying to prove a point. My grandpa was a preacher, and he allus said 'What is to be will be.' Now, it's just *got* to be that this worm—"

But Rena suddenly stopped struggling and looked up at him piteously. "You're so mean to me," she whispered, and to Josh's horror, tears welled up in Rena's eyes.

"Oh, g-gosh!" At once Josh released his grip. He was horrified at what he had done and threw the worm away and pulled the girl to a sitting position. "I never m-meant—," he stuttered vainly, but Rena's shoulders were shaking, and her face was buried in her hands. "Oh, R-Rena—for gosh sakes, don't c-cry!"

But she was quivering now, and Josh felt terrible. Awkwardly he put his arm around the girl's shoulders and tried to apologize. "Aw, Rena!" he muttered and was thinking,

Now you done it, you big ox! That's all you needed, wasn't it—scare her to death!

But as he was muttering his abject apologies and begging her not to cry, she drew back—and she was laughing! Her eyes were clear, and her white teeth gleamed as she said, "There! Now I guess you'll keep your old worms to yourself!" Her dark brown eyes glowed with a merry light, and she held herself, giggling at the look on Josh's face.

Josh was thunderstruck. He stared at the girl in disbelief, then his face reddened. "Why—why you little—"

"What are you so mad about?" Rena jibed. "Maybe you'll keep your ol' night crawlers to yourself from now on!" But then she saw that she'd gone too far. Josh, she knew, was as sensitive as a human being could be, and he stared at her with a mixture of humiliation and shame in his eyes. At once Rena put her hand on his arm, saying contritely, "Oh, Josh—I was just teasing you—don't be mad!"

But her words seemed to make things worse, for Josh got to his feet and turned his back saying, "I d-didn't think y-you'd fool me like th-that."

Rena came to her feet, grasped his arm, and pulled him around. "Oh, Josh, I'm sorry!" She put her arms around him impulsively and buried her face against his chest. Her voice was muffled as she whispered, "I shouldn't have teased you like that. I'm truly sorry."

Josh had been angry, but now as Rena clung to him he felt the anger leave. She was pressing against him, and he was conscious of the pressure of her young form. Then she lifted her face and whispered, "I'm sorry, Josh."

He had kissed her once, and now he did so again. It was a natural thing, and her lips were firm and sweet under his. Then there was a splashing sound, and Josh looked down to see that Rena's fishing pole had been jerked into the water and was headed downstream.

"Hey!" Josh released Rena so abruptly that she almost fell. He took a wild leap into the river and missed his stab at the pole. Sputtering, he began to swim after it, calling back, "It's a big 'un!"

Rena stared at Josh as he thrashed the water and caught the pole with one hand. As the boy fought to get his footing, she saw that his face was alive with excitement, and she angrily kicked at the bait can. It sailed through the air, fell, and rolled on its side. When it came to a halt, she saw the night crawlers come boiling out and snapped, "Go on—all of you!" Then she looked back at Josh, who was fighting to land the bass, and slowly the anger left her. Her lips curved upward into an amused smile and she said, "Josh Yancy, only you would leave off kissing a girl to catch an ol' fish!"

★ ★ ★

"Look at that, Rooney—Josh and Rena." Mark Rocklin had spotted the pair as he sat in the scuppernong arbor, watching the slaves as they worked the fields. He had not felt much like coming outside, but Rooney had bullied him into it. The warm sun had felt good, and except for the gnawing pain in his stomach that never completely ceased, he felt good.

Rooney glanced up from the fabric she was stitching to see a pair of figures emerge from the treeline. "Those two have gotten close," she said. Biting her lip she shook her head. "It might not be a good thing."

"Why not?"

Rooney shrugged without speaking for a moment. Then she said slowly, "He's a poor boy, and she's a rich girl."

Mark put his eyes on her, understanding at once what she was thinking. "I'd have thought you'd know better than to think that, Rooney," he said quietly. "You and Lowell went through all that, didn't you?"

"Yes, but it's different, Mark. You know it is." Her thoughts troubled her, and she picked nervously at the cloth she was working on. Finally she looked up and said, "A rich man can marry a poor girl, but it doesn't work the other way around. The Rocklins are wealthy planters, and the Yancys

41

are poor farmers. You'd never have them in to have dinner with you."

"I'm not so sure about that," Mark mused. "Before the war, all the time I was growing up, maybe it was like that. It was one of the things I didn't like about the South—maybe why I ran away from it. But now it's different. And after the war, no matter which side wins, it'll never be the same."

"I guess it will, Mark," Rooney disagreed. "Money makes a difference—and the raising you get. How could a girl raised like Rena ever be happy in a shack with nothing?"

Mark lifted his heavy eyebrows but said nothing. Something about the conversation, Rooney saw, unsettled him. He sat in his chair, his hands clasping and unclasping nervously. *He's gone downhill so much*, Rooney thought. *And it's not all the wound, either. Something's bothering him.*

The two sat there letting the silence run on. It was one of the things that Mark had always liked about Rooney, her manner of falling into the quietness of a mood. Not many people could do that, he'd often thought. Now he seemed to forget her and, lost in his thoughts, let his eyes fall on the June landscape.

Rooney thought that he'd forgotten the subject, but to her surprise, he said abruptly, "You're right—about rich and poor."

"Oh, I'm not sure I was," Rooney answered quickly. "I'll learn your ways, and if Rena and Josh ever got serious Clay would take Josh in." She smiled at him fondly, adding, "When two people love each other, there's always a way."

"No!" The word almost exploded from Mark's lips, and he gave her a look that was filled with anguish. "That's the way it *should* be," he said grimly, "but sometimes a man—or a woman—doesn't understand that."

Rooney strongly sensed the emptiness in Mark Rocklin. *Why, he's so lonely!* she thought. *Something in him is crying out for help.* She was a compassionate young woman, and as she sat there she remembered how he'd spoken of a woman he'd once loved. *I can't mention it,* she thought, but looking at the pain in his eyes, she felt this was one time when Mark might need to speak of whatever it was.

"Mark, when you were in a coma—I took care of you." Rooney hesitated, on the brink of turning back, but then forged ahead. "We talked once about how you once considered marriage. Was her name Beth?"

"Beth? Where did you hear that name?" Mark anxiously asked.

"From you, when you were delirious. You said you loved a girl named Beth, and that she was beautiful. Was she the one you wanted to marry?" For one moment Rooney feared she'd gone too far because Mark Rocklin's dark eyes were fixed on her in what seemed to be anger. Gently she said, "I don't mean to pry, but I've wondered why you never married."

Now Rooney thought the silence louder than any battlefield could ever be. Mark, she saw, had dropped his head, and the muscles in his jaw were working tensely. But then he lifted his eyes to her, and she saw that they were filled with pure misery.

"It was . . . a long time ago," he whispered. A deep breath stirred his thin chest, and he shook his head, his voice frail in the stillness of the morning. "Her name was Beth Griffeth," he said.

When he said no more, Rooney asked gently, "Was she from around here?"

"No, I met her in New Orleans. She was . . . the most beautiful thing I'd ever seen!" Mark shook his head as memories came flooding back. "She was Welsh, and she had dark red hair and green eyes. And how she could laugh!" He stirred in his chair, adding, "We'd dance all night, then go have johnnycake and fried oysters at Antoine's for breakfast. . . ."

The singing of the men in the field floated to the arbor, slow songs in rich male voices. Honeybees made a lazy humming as they sought the sweetness of the clover, and from high in the sky came the plaintive cry of a distant bird. These sounds melded together to form a faint background for Mark's voice, and for a long time Rooney sat very quietly. She understood without being told that it was the sort of thing that Mark could not have easily shared with any of his family.

"She was not 'quality,'" Mark finally said, almost spitting out that last word, bitterness twisting his lips. "How I hate that word! She was from a poor family and had no education. As if that mattered! But it did matter—at least I thought it did. I should have married her, but I was a fool!"

Rooney asked gently, "What happened?"

Mark shook his head, and there was a bitter note in his voice as he answered, "I left her, Rooney. She cried when I left. I've never been able to get away from the sound of her weeping as I left the room for the last time!"

"What happened to her? Did you ever see her again?"

"No, never. Once I got a letter from a friend of mine who lives in New Orleans. He knew about us—Beth and me—and was against our marriage. He told me she'd never be accepted in the family. Well, he wrote a while later and said . . . that she'd gotten sick and died."

"How awful!"

Mark lifted his eyes and saw the compassion on the girl's face. "She was like you, Rooney," he said finally. "If I'd married her, we'd have been happy. Maybe I wouldn't have wasted my life. . . ."

Rooney wanted to say something to comfort him, but she could think of nothing. Mark Rocklin was a strong man, but he'd let his life be ruined by a tragic mistake. Finally she said, "I'm sorry, Mark."

"Yes—so am I, Rooney."

The two of them sat there, and neither of them spoke for a long time. Finally Mark said wearily, "I've never told my family about this, Rooney. Please don't say anything to them. Nothing they can do, and it would give them more pain."

"I won't say anything," Rooney agreed.

Mark turned to look at her, and his thin face was etched with grief as he whispered, "She was a lot like you, Rooney."

CHAPTER FOUR
Col. Rocklin
Meets the President

The calamity of the defeat at Chancellorsville had appalled the North. But two bitter years of war had made many callous. Business was good, factory wheels were turning, and there was wild speculation on the stock market. The humblest man could pocket a large bounty by donning the uniform of his country.

But the price was high. The wounded cumbered the Washington wharves. To Gideon Rocklin, who was now making his way past a large group of wounded who had been almost dumped off a stern-wheeler, the prostrate young bodies symbolized the very figure of the Union itself, and his spirit grew heavy at the familiar scene.

The compact caravans of ambulances had become a monotonous part of the pageant in the streets, but Gideon never got used to it. The procession of the maimed with their empty sleeves and trouser legs moved him no matter how many times he saw such scenes. Even death had become commonplace. Once the death of one man, Elmer Ellsworth, had thrown the entire capital into mourning. Now from the silver-mounted rosewood of the higher officers to the cheap pine slats of the ordinary soldiers, the business of death was plied like that of any other prosperous trade.

Gideon Rocklin left the wharf, swung into the saddle of a

mottled gray stallion, and headed toward the center of the city. The sun was hot on Washington, and he sweated through his wool uniform as he passed through a section of the city where the *rat-tat* of the coffin maker's hammers sounded from the open doors of the cabinet shops. Outside he noted stacks of long, upended boxes—coffins that were a grim fever chart of battle.

He arrived at the War Department thinking that the city had a surfeit of misery. But if the horror of blood beat like a wound in the back of every mind, the faces on the streets were smiling. The soft summer air carried the plaintive mechanical melodies of the organ grinders, and on the avenue, under a huge transparency that advertised embalming, the promenaders sauntered in the sunshine. Gideon threaded his way through the hack, the wagons, and the caracoling horses of the officers. Fashionable ladies drove in barouches with black coachmen and footmen. On the sidewalks, salesmen cried the merits of patent soaps, and the proprietors of telescopes and lung testing machines clamored for customers. Pineapples, oranges, and tomatoes were piled in colored pyramids, ice cream dealers were stationed in the shade of the trees, and Italians roasted chestnuts in little portable stoves.

It's like a carnival! Gideon Rocklin thought with disgust. *They don't even know the names of the battlefields, some of them! Men are dying, and they're parading like it was a holiday!*

He made his way down Pennsylvania Avenue, arriving at the President's Park. The White House was here, flanked by four massive buildings that housed the State Department, the Treasury, the War Department, and the Navy Department. He dismounted, tossed the reins to a private, then entered the War Department.

When he walked into the large office occupied by Gen. Halleck, the adjutant, Lt. Sellers, said at once, "Gen. Halleck wants you to come in, Colonel."

"Very well, Lieutenant."

"Sir, the president is with the general."

Gideon's hand was on the door, but he hesitated, giving the adjutant a questioning look. "What's going on, Sellers?"

"I don't know, sir—but the president is worried."

Gideon thought for a moment of the state of the country, then grunted, "Well, he's got plenty to be worried about, I guess." He knocked on the door, and when the general's voice said, "Come in!" he pushed it open and entered.

"Ah, Rocklin—come in, come in!" The general in chief of the nation's armies was a small man with the air of a snapping turtle. He nodded toward the president, saying, "Col. Rocklin, Mr. President."

"Yes, the colonel and I have met." Lincoln had a smile on his homely face as he came over to offer his hand. "How's that niece of yours, and the young private she was so fond of?"

"Miss Steele is fine, sir, and you may have read some of the reports Noel Kojak has written for the *New Review*."

Lincoln thought, then nodded. "I did read some of them. Sensible writing, very powerful."

"I thought they stressed the misery of our men too much," Halleck grumbled. He had been displeased, along with some other high-ranking officers, when the stories written by young Kojak had been published. Most of the reports up until then had been patriotic and filled with flag-waving. Kojak had told the story of the misery and terrible trials experienced by the common soldier. "We don't need the people reading that sort of thing!"

"The truth is always hard," Lincoln remarked, "but is usually best, I reckon."

"I'd argue that, Mr. President," Halleck shot back. "We're having a hard enough time filling the gaps in the army. When men read how terrible it is, why, it'll be that much harder."

Lincoln only gave a faint smile to Halleck. Gideon saw him often enough, but almost always at a distance. Now he saw that the president had aged. His face was lined with strain, and his eyes were sunk into craggy hollows. *This war's killing him,* Gideon thought, but then Halleck began to speak.

"Col. Rocklin, the president wanted to hear firsthand about the battle of Chancellorsville. You were right in the center of the action. Give us your report and leave nothing out—" Halleck paused, then added carefully, "even about the behavior of the commanders."

An alarm went off inside Gideon. *They want to know about Hooker,* he thought instantly. He was trapped, for he knew he could not give his commanding officer a bad report. But Lincoln said at once, "Gen. Halleck has told me of your loyalty to the army and to your fellow officers, Col. Rocklin. I appreciate that and honor you for it." The gaunt man looked straight at Gideon and said evenly, "But I must know the truth—how else can I make decisions?"

"It's—an awkward position for me, Mr. President," Gideon said. "I don't want to be thought of as one of those officers who is never satisfied with the men above him."

"Just give us your critical judgment of the tactics of the battle, Colonel," Lincoln said, nodding. "That's all we expect."

"Very well, sir." Rocklin knew as did every other officer in the army that Maj. Gen. Darius N. Couch had been so outraged at Hooker's vacillating conduct during the battle that he refused to serve under "Fighting" Joe any longer— and at least two other corps commanders were maneuvering to have Hooker replaced. As he began to give his report, Gideon knew that Gen. Halleck had never liked Hooker and was anxious to replace him.

With the two men listening to him carefully, Gideon traced the battle. He was unable to tell the story without placing blame on Hooker, but he said finally, "Gen. Hooker is a fine officer. He's done a good job of pulling the army together since the battle, but he found difficulty in dealing with Gen. Lee and Gen. Jackson."

"Name me one general who hasn't!" Lincoln exclaimed.

"We send out enough men to overwhelm the Rebels, and they come back whipped! Why can't we beat them?"

Gideon hesitated, then said, "Without any disrespect to former commanders of the Army of the Potomac, Mr. President, I believe you must find a man who is not . . . reluctant to close with the Confederates."

Lincoln stared at the officer, then nodded. "A man with a killer instinct—just what I've said. But who among our choices has such a quality?"

"It's not my place to say, sir—but I've always felt that you saw this sort of determination in Gen. Grant."

"Yes, Grant's a bulldog," Lincoln nodded. "But he's at Vicksburg. He'll win, but we've got to face up to this invasion, and—" The president knew that he could not ask a mere colonel for more than this one had given. He smiled, saying, "You'll be leaving with your regiment, Gen. Halleck has told me." He put out his big hand and when Rocklin took it, said warmly, "God be with you and all your brave men, Col. Rocklin!"

"Thank you, Mr. President—and my prayers will be with you as you carry this impossible burden." Gideon left the office, and when the adjutant probed to find out what the president and the general had wanted with a mere colonel, he said, "Oh, nothing much, George. He just wanted to know who to appoint as commander of the Army of the Potomac."

The lieutenant laughed at what he felt was a rebuff, but Gideon thought for the rest of the day of how difficult it would be to make such a choice. *McClellan, Pope, Burnside, and Hooker—they all were too timid to go after Lee. This time if the president chooses the wrong man, he knows that thousands of our men will die—and for nothing!*

★ ★ ★

Gideon arrived home after a long day and found that Deborah Steele and her fiancé, Noel Kojak, were there. "You're late, Uncle Gideon," Deborah scolded him. She came to kiss his cheek. "Come! Sit down to dinner. We've all been starving."

Gideon grinned at the young woman, admiring her fresh beauty as always. He'd longed for a daughter, but this niece was as close as he'd come. She had blonde hair and large violet eyes, and most men turned around to watch her when she passed. "You see what you're letting yourself in for, Noel? This woman will run your life worse than any sergeant in the army!"

Noel Kojak was no more than average height and was not handsome. He had the short nose and high cheekbones of his European forebears, and a pair of steady gray eyes. "I guess it's worth it, sir," Noel said.

Deborah pinched his arm, smiled, and said, "You have your moments, I guess. But why don't you say flowery things to me? You know, 'Your eyes are like sparkling pools; your lips are like rose petals'? What's the good of having a writer for a sweetheart if I don't get any of that sort of thing?"

Noel gave her a wry look, saying, "I'm a journalist, not a poet. Maybe I'll get a book of poetry and steal some of the best things for you."

"Why, that wouldn't be the same! I want something just for *me!*"

"You two stop arguing and come to the table." Melanie Rocklin appeared suddenly, came over to take Gideon's kiss, then started to scold them about letting the food get cold. But even as she spoke, a knock sounded, and when Gideon opened the door, they heard him say, "Why, Uncle Mason!"

"I'm late, Gid, as usual." A stooped man wearing the uniform of a major entered and, seeing the others, stopped and apologized. "Sorry I'm late, Melanie. I got tied up at headquarters."

"You're just in time," Melanie said and came forward to give Gideon's uncle a quick hug. Mason was a rare guest but a welcome one. "All of you come and sit down. Everything's ready."

Ten minutes later they were all seated at the round oak dining table heaped high with roast beef, new potatoes, green beans, and fresh bread. Mason tasted the meat, shook his head, and said, "Gid, you've got the best cook in Washington!"

"Or anywhere else for that matter," Gideon said with a wide grin. "I'm getting fat! When will your unit leave, Mason?"

"In the morning." Mason had been a Union officer for years, spending a great deal of time in the Far West. He'd served in Mexico with Gen. Scott and was a trusted member of Gen. Winfield Scott Hancock's corps. "What about you?"

"The regiment's ready. We'll pull out and join Gen. Hooker day after tomorrow."

Noel studied the two older men and said abruptly, "I wish I were going with you—in the ranks, I mean." Noel had served in the army, but a wound he'd taken had never healed completely. Now he stared down at his plate with a disgruntled expression on his face. "I feel like I'm pretty worthless."

"Don't be silly, Noel!" Deborah reached over and squeezed his arm. "You're doing your part with your writing!"

"Can't stop a Reb charge with a turkey quill pen." Noel shrugged. "And from what I can pick up, they're coming at us with everything they got this time."

"I think so." Gideon nodded. He chewed thoughtfully on a morsel of beef, then added, "Lee will have to win big this time, and he'll hit us with all he's got."

"And that's a lot," Mason put in. He was fifty-eight years old, and years of hard service had stooped his shoulders and lined his face. "We've got to stop them this time—or it could all be over!"

Noel looked up quickly. "How is that, sir?"

"The Peace party's looking for one more big defeat of the Federal army. If we don't stop Lee this time, I think the country could give it up—let the South go its own way."

"Why, that can't happen!" Deborah was the daughter of

Amos Steele, a strict abolitionist, and was herself a fiery opponent of slavery. "We can't let slavery go on!"

"I hope not, Deborah," Gideon said slowly. "But people are tired of losing. They're sick of their husbands and sons and brothers dying—and nothing happening. I think Mason is right. We've got to whip the Rebels soundly this time!"

Mason nodded, and as the talk flowed around the table he listened but said little. He was a widower and owned half of his brother Stephen's munitions factory. His wife had died in 1833, and he'd never remarried. His life was the army, and he was grieved over the war that had turned brother against brother. Having no children of his own, he was very fond of his nephews and their children.

"How are the boys?" he asked. "Are they all seeing action?"

Gideon shot a quick look at Melanie, then nodded. "Tyler and Robert are under Grant at Vicksburg. Frank will be with me, of course—my aide."

"What about your brothers, Deborah?"

"Pat is home on sick leave, but Colin and Clinton are with Gen. Hooker now."

Mason shook his head sadly. "All the fine young men—they ought to be going to college or making careers!"

"They will, sir, when the war is over," Noel said quickly. The strain in the dining room was palpable, and no more was said.

The next afternoon when he and Deborah were on the way to his family's house, Noel mentioned his feelings again. He shook his head gloomily, saying, "I can't help it, Deborah," he muttered. "Your brothers and Tyler and Frank—all fighting for the Union. And all I do is write stories!"

Deborah didn't argue, for they had gone over this many times. She was secretly relieved that Noel was not in the army and felt some guilt over this feeling. She thought of how she'd gone to Richmond and found him sick and dying in a Confederate hospital, and it had taken a miracle to get him out and back home. His recovery had been slow, and she knew that he was anxious to serve. But she said now, "Every man has to do what's best for the country, Noel. Right now, until you get well enough to go back into the army, that's writing. People at home need to hear about what's happening, and God's given you the gift of putting things down so that they seem real."

"It seems so—so *little* to do, Deborah!"

She took his arm and said, "Noel, let's get married."

"You mean now?"

"I mean right away. You were too sick when you first came back from the hospital, but you're fine now." Her violet eyes filled with humor as she added, "Maybe you can't march twenty miles with a full pack, but I expect you can take care of your husbandly duties!"

Her boldness shocked Noel, for he was a reserved young man. "Why, Deborah—I don't think——"

"Don't you love me, Noel?"

"Sure, of course I do! Great Scott, Deborah, I never thought to have a girl like you!"

"Well, you've got me." Deborah moved closer to him and whispered, "Now, what are you going to do with me?"

No red-blooded young man could have resisted a pair of lips so inviting! Noel held her fast, and there was such a sweetness in her that when he lifted his head, he gasped, "Deborah—I do love you!"

Deborah stroked his cheek, whispering, "I want to be a wife, Noel!"

As the carriage made its way to the section where Noel's family lived, they talked about getting married. Deborah steadfastly maintained that they loved each other—and that settled it.

Noel had led a difficult life, and as he drove into the Swampoodle district, the stench seemed to depress him. The section consisted of ramshackle houses with privies behind them. The visual impact of the area offended the eyes almost as much as the smell offended the nose. There was no beauty in Swampoodle, only line after line of shacks unpainted and scoured to a leprous gray-brown by wind and weather. There was almost no attempt at decoration—no flowers or fresh curtains, and all was crude and plain and depressing.

Noel pulled the buggy up in front of a frame house, got down, and helped Deborah to the ground. The door was open, and when he called out, a woman appeared. "Noel!" she cried out and moved to embrace him.

"Ma, how are you?" Noel asked gently.

"Fine, Son, and here's Deborah!" Anna Kojak was in her early forties but looked ten years older. Her brown hair was streaked with gray, and only faint traces of an earlier beauty remained. "Come in. Can you stay for supper?"

"No, we're going to a meeting," Deborah said. "Noel's going to speak to a group of writers, Anna."

"Well, ain't that fine!" Anna led the way inside, and when the pair were seated she said, "This place you helped us buy is so nice, Son!" She looked around the simple room with pride, and Deborah thought of the wretched shack the Kojaks had lived in when she'd first met Noel.

"Where is everyone?" Noel asked curiously.

"Bing won a fight last night," Anna said. "Nothing would do but he'd take the kids to a circus."

"I hate for him to fight, Ma," Noel said with a frown. "I wish he'd get a job."

"So do I, but he makes more money fighting. He won't hear to quitting."

The three of them sat there talking for half an hour, then they heard the sound of excited voices approaching. "That sounds like them," Noel said. He got up and looked out the door, then turned with a smile on his face. "Looks like they had a good time," he remarked, then the small room was filled with Kojaks.

Bing Kojak led the way, his eyes gleaming. He was twenty-one, a year younger than Noel, but much larger. He was tall and muscular, with a shock of wavy black hair and a bruise under his left eye. "Well, look who's here—the bride and groom!"

Noel took the hard handshake from Bing, and Deborah smiled as the big man gave her a rough kiss on the cheek. "Did you see the elephant?" she asked, and as the younger Kojaks began noisily describing the beast she mentioned, she studied the family.

Bing she knew best, for it was Bing who had helped her when she had gone to Richmond to get Noel out of prison. He was a rough young man who wanted much out of life and had found a way to get it with his fists.

Grace Kojak, age seventeen, was not pretty, but had a pair of sharp brown eyes. She wore a dress that could have used washing, and her hair was in the same condition. She was, Deborah had discovered, the smartest of the children—except for Noel.

Holmes, at the age of thirteen, and Joel, five years younger, both had fine brown hair and thin faces. They were loud and boisterous, and for the next ten minutes vied with each other in describing the circus.

Finally Noel asked, "Where's Pa? Did he go to the circus, too?"

Bing looked a little awkward, then said, "Oh, he stopped off on the way back."

This, Deborah had come to understand, was the usual way of describing Will Kojak's trips to the bars. He would come back dead drunk, or Bing would go find him and haul him back bodily. She had learned something of the class to which Will Kojak belonged, and it stirred her compassion for Anna and the children and even for the father himself. *He drinks to forget his poverty,* she thought.

The two stayed for an hour, and when they got into the carriage Noel said, "Bing, come and ride with us."

Bing, never one to refuse an invitation, climbed into the buggy. Noel slipped his mother and his brothers and sisters a little money. "Use it on something foolish," he jokingly said. They understood that to mean they were to use it for themselves, not give it to their father for drink.

As they moved along the street, Noel said, "Ma loves the house, Bing. It was a fine thing you did, buying it for her." Bing shrugged off the comment, saying, "Ah, you know me, both of you. I'd have blown it on foolishness. Anyway, I couldn't have done it if you two hadn't chipped in."

"Bing, I hate to see you get involved in fighting," Deborah said. "My uncle will give you a good job in the factory."

"Ah, Deborah, I can't stand that kind of work!" Bing protested. "I can make more from one fight than I can working for a month in that place."

"But you don't get your brains beat out at the factory," Noel argued.

"I don't get bored to death fighting." Bing listened tolerantly but shook his head saying, "Nope, I'll just keep on as I am."

"Ever think about joining the army again?"

Bing shook his head emphatically. "Nope, that's not for me." He shot a quick look at Noel, then nodded. "You'd like to go back, wouldn't you?"

"Yes, I would." Noel's eyes were thoughtful as he added, "I guess I'd like to do anything that would bring this country back together again."

"Lots of men in shallow graves in Virginia and other places," Bing muttered. "They had the same idea as you, but they're dead. And from what I hear we ain't much closer to gettin' this thing settled than when we started."

"But don't you see, Bing," Noel said quickly, "if we let it all drop—all those men really *did* die in vain. But if we win, why their deaths *mean* something!"

Deborah held to Noel's arm, and when she heard this, she knew that she was hearing the real reason for fighting the war through to the end. "Noel's right, Bing. We've got to go on. As Mr. Lincoln said, this nation can't endure half slave and half free."

Bing Kojak was a healthy young man with an appetite for life. He was not a coward, but he strenuously objected to risking his life—unless he was pretty sure that it was for something worthwhile. The steel-shod hooves of the horses clattered along the cobblestones as he sat loosely beside the pair.

"Well, you can let me out at the Palace Saloon. I'll hang around until Pa's too drunk to care, then I'll take him home."

Noel and Deborah knew Bing too well to argue, so they said no more to him. When Noel pulled the team up in front of the Palace, Bing leaped lightly to the ground. He looked up at them with a challenge in his bright brown eyes.

"If you find anything for me to do to end this war, let me know. But I've only got one life, and I'm not about to throw it away unless I know it really counts!"

Noel and Deborah watched as Bing passed through the swinging doors. Then as Noel spoke to the team, she said, "He could be something great, Noel. He really could!"

"Yes, he could," Noel said soberly. Then as the buggy clattered on down the street, he said quietly, "But he'll never be much until he learns what's worthwhile in this world and what isn't! And that's the hardest lesson for anyone to learn, isn't it, Deborah?"

"I guess it is, Noel."

CHAPTER FIVE
Mark Calls on a Friend

★

"Mr. Larrimore?"

Jason Larrimore looked up from the poker table and narrowed his eyes against the smoky atmosphere of the room. He saw a young man—a boy, really—who had entered the Golden Nugget and had come to stand beside him. Larrimore took in the plain dress of the young man and could not remember ever having seen him before. "Yes, what is it, son?"

"My name is Josh Yancy. Could I talk to you a minute, sir?"

One of the cardplayers seated across from Larrimore, a tall, sallow-faced individual with a bristly mustache, grinned suddenly. "What'd you do, Larrimore? Have it fixed up with this kid to come in and get you out of the game when you're ahead?"

Jason Larrimore smiled at the man and shook his head. "No, it wasn't that way, Simon, but I'm tired of taking your money anyhow. How about we break up and start in again tomorrow?"

The man named Simon and the other two were all weary, for the game had gone on for hours. "All right," he said. "You can't win all the time. Meet you here tomorrow. Same time?"

"You got it. Twelve noon on the nose." Larrimore raked in the pile of bills and coins in front of him and stuffed them into the pocket of the frock coat that hung on the back of his chair. Then, standing up and slinging the coat over his shoulder, he said to the young man, "Come along, Josh. Let's get a little fresh air."

"Yes, sir."

Larrimore led the way out of the saloon. He was very tall, almost two inches over six feet, but lean and very quick. His blond hair was worn long, and he had exceptionally light blue eyes, wide spaced and penetrating. He had a wide mouth and high cheekbones reminding his acquaintances of the Vikings that had stormed across the sea to conquer the world in earlier days. His hands were very strong looking, yet he had long fingers that had made him into an expert cardplayer. There was something in his face that revealed a little of the cynical nature that was a part of him. It was a rugged face with sharp angular planes, and the set of the mouth was firm. As Josh glanced at the man, he thought, *He looks like a pretty tough fellow. I'd hate to have trouble with him.*

Larrimore walked to a restaurant, where he was greeted by a waiter who said, "Ah, Mr. Larrimore, your usual table?"

"That'll be fine, Robert." He turned and followed the waiter down a line of tables and seated himself in a chair at one of them. Waving his hand he said, "Sit down, Josh. How about a bite to eat?"

Josh hesitated. He had traveled far and had had nothing to eat since early morning at breakfast. "Well, I guess I could eat a little bit," he said.

"Fine, bring us some bacon and eggs and some of those biscuits of Millie's, if there are any. Bring us a pitcher of milk and some coffee. That do you all right, young fellow?"

"Yes, sir. It sounds fine."

The waiter nodded his assent, said, "It won't be long, Mr. Larrimore," and then turned and made his way across the room.

Larrimore looked at the young man and said, "I don't know you, do I?"

"No, sir, you don't," Josh replied. "I was sent by Mr. Mark Rocklin."

The name caught Larrimore's attention. "Is that so? I haven't seen Mark in quite a while. How is he?" He leaned back in his chair, pulled a thin black cigar out of his pocket and clipped the end of it off. Inserting it between his teeth, he lit it with a match he drew from another pocket. Then, sending a puff of purple smoke into the air, he smiled. "We've had some times together, that man and me. I'd like to see him."

"Well, sir, did you hear about his trouble?"

"Trouble? No, I didn't hear anything about that." Larrimore removed the cigar and leaned forward slightly, his eyes narrowing. "What sort of trouble is Mark in?"

"He got shot," Josh said softly, "in the war."

Larrimore leaned back and said, "I never heard anything about Mark being in the army. I thought he was still up North somewhere. How bad was it?"

"Well, sir, it was pretty bad. They didn't think he would live for a while, but they brought him back home to Gracefield, and Miss Susanna and the other ladies, they been taking care of him." Josh gave the details of the wound and finally shook his head, saying, "I sure was plumb sorry to see how bad he's doing. He just gets weaker all the time."

Jason lost interest in his cigar and put it down. He probed at the boy in a way that was his manner, extracting every bit of information that he could from the young man. When the waiter came with their food, he continued to inquire about Mark and the situation while they ate. Josh ate quickly, for he was hungry, and he answered the questions the best he could.

"I hate to hear that," Larrimore said slowly, his mouth twisted. "Looks like there's enough scoundrels in the world to get shot without a good man like Mark taking a bullet." He shoved the plate back, then reached over and picked up the coffee cup. Sipping it, he shook his head. "That's the way it is with this blasted war. It takes the best of them and leaves the scoundrels like me."

Josh hardly knew what to make of a man who would call himself a scoundrel, but he said, "Yes, sir, that's the way it is all right, but I'm going in just as soon as I'm old enough."

Jason Larrimore gave the young boy a quick glance. *He's just like all the rest of them,* he thought bitterly. *Can't wait to get into a war that's going to get him killed. And for what? The South can't win, slavery's doomed, and this boy never owned a slave in his life. Well, I can't tell him that because he wouldn't listen.* Aloud he said, "What message did Mr. Rocklin give you for me, Josh?"

"He wants you to come and see him, if you can," Josh said quickly.

"And he's at Gracefield? That's the old family place, isn't it? How far is it?"

"Oh, not too far," Josh said quickly, "and I've got a carriage with me. Mr. Rocklin, he said I was to wait as long as I needed to and to bring you if you could come."

Jason thought quickly about his schedule and then nodded. "My ship won't be ready for a while. Let me take a bath, change clothes, and get a few things together."

Josh was surprised at the quickness with which the man made up his mind. "You mean—right now—today?"

"Sure," Jason said with a grin. "We don't know about tomorrow, do we Josh? Whatever we do, we better do it right now. I think that's scriptural, isn't it?"

"I guess so. I'll wait outside for you."

"Come on up to my room, and you can wait there, Josh. Won't take too long."

Jason rose to his feet, put some money on the table, then turned and led the way out of the restaurant. As he went, his brow was broken by a slight wrinkle. He was thinking, *Sure hate to hear that about Mark. From what the boy says, it doesn't sound like he's going to make it.* He was a man who was used to hard knocks and always expected the worst. He had pleasant memories of Mark Rocklin, and Rocklin was one of few men he respected wholeheartedly. As he was soaking in his bath, he said aloud, "Got to help Mark if I can. I've owed him a debt for a long time, but what in the world can I do for a man like him?"

★ ★ ★

The woman who met Larrimore at the door was very attractive, and Larrimore pulled off his hat at once. "I'm Jason Larrimore," he said. "Mark Rocklin asked me to come and see him."

"Oh yes, come in Capt. Larrimore. I'm Susanna Rocklin. Mark is my brother-in-law."

She put out her hand, and as he took it he was impressed by the firmness of her grasp. "Josh must have found you very quickly," she said as she led him inside the large foyer. "We weren't expecting you so soon. Josh only left this morning."

"It's a lucky thing he caught me when he did," Jason answered. "My ship is being refitted, so I have more time on my hands now than usual. I'm glad he caught me."

Susanna led him out of the foyer into a hallway, then turned to him, "Did Josh tell you about Mark?"

"Yes, and I'm sorry to hear it. He's been a good friend to me." Jason bit his lip, then shook his head. "This war is taking the best of them, isn't it?"

"Yes, it is."

"How badly is he wounded?"

"Very badly, I'm afraid." Susanna's eyes were cloudy with worry. She said quietly, "I don't think he can live, Mr. Larrimore."

Her words shocked Jason. Even though he was a pessimist, he hoped that the wound wasn't as bad as it had sounded. "That's tough, Mrs. Rocklin. Does he know it— that he's going to die?"

"Oh yes. Mark's very perceptive, and he's quite alert. Doctors say he might live for some time, but he's not hopeful."

Larrimore clenched his fist and struck his palm. "Blast this war," he exclaimed. "I hate it!" Then he blinked and shook his head. "I'm sorry, I get carried away sometimes, but it makes me angry to see this waste. I hate to see anything wasted—especially men like Mark."

A smile touched Susanna's lips. She said gently, "I feel exactly the same way. I always have." Then she said, "I have a room all made up for you, just in case you did come. I hope you can stay for a few days."

"I'll stay as long as I can. I've got a couple of weeks or so before I have to ship out. Do you think Mark will be awake?"

"He was thirty minutes ago. Come along—he's so anxious to see you."

Larrimore followed the woman down the hall. She turned to a door, knocked, then opened it when a voice replied. She stepped inside and said, "Mark, Capt. Larrimore is here to see you."

Larrimore entered and was shocked at the sight of his old friend. He was, however, an accomplished poker player and let none of this show on his face. "Hello, Mark," he said with a wide grin. He crossed the room with swift strides, put out his hand, took the thin hand of the sick man, and added, "I see you've found a way to get out of work and to get people to wait on you. You always were a lazy scoundrel."

Mark had been sitting in his chair reading the Bible. He had dozed off but now was awake, his drawn face showing excitement. "You're a fine one to talk about laziness," he said. "I never knew you to do an honest day's work in your life." He looked over at Susanna and grinned. "I guess you've got the two laziest men in creation right under your roof, Susanna."

Susanna smiled, glad to see Mark showing such life. "You two visit. I'll bring you something to drink. We have some things left over from supper. I'll heat a plate for you, Captain, and I'll bring you something, too, Mark."

When the woman left the room, Mark said, "Sit down,

Jason." He waited until the tall man had seated himself and said, "Josh didn't have any trouble finding you, I take it?"

"No," Jason said. "I was at the Golden Nugget taking some money away from some sorry cardplayers." He looked over and paused. "Sorry to hear about your bad luck, Mark."

Mark shrugged. "It happens," he said briefly. Mark had never been a complainer, Larrimore knew, and in that he had not changed. Larrimore was shocked, however, at Mark's appearance. He had been prepared for some changes, but the strong, healthy man he knew was hardly to be seen in the thin, pale man who sat quietly in the chair. Mark Rocklin had always been a man filled with life, had met it with a shout, throwing himself into whatever was at hand with all his strength. Now, Larrimore saw, that was over. Mark's eyes were sunk back into his head, and his cheeks were sunk in. Pain had given his mouth a pinched look, and there was a fragility about him that frightened Larrimore.

Mark caught his glance and said, "Well, as you can see, I don't have much time."

"Oh, you never know about those things," Jason protested.

Mark shook his head. "I know about myself. I've been around awhile, Jason. I've had some close scrapes, but this time my time's about up." He held up a thin hand, as if in protest. "I'm not complaining, you understand. No man likes to die, but I suppose I've had a better life than most."

Larrimore sat there unable to answer. He felt a pang of grief for his friend, but he recognized the truth of what Rocklin had said. Death was in his face, and now Larrimore could only say simply, "Whatever I can do, Mark, you've got it."

"That's like you, Jason."

"Well, I don't think it is, really." Larrimore pulled a cigar out of his inner pocket, then hesitated. "I guess I shouldn't smoke in here."

"It won't hurt my health much."

Larrimore grinned at the slight joke. He lit the cigar,

leaned back, and shook his head. "Mark, you know me better than most. I'm not much of a one for charities, but I owe you one for that time you saved my bacon when nobody else would, or could. I haven't forgotten it, you know."

"It wasn't that much," Mark said quietly. "I was glad to help you. I don't want to presume on that but—I don't have a lot of choice, Jason." He clasped his hands and sat there and thought for one moment, then said, "I don't have much to show for my life, Jason. I've got some money, sure, but that doesn't seem to account for much at this stage of the game. Looking back on it, I see some turns I made that were wrong."

"I guess everybody feels like that."

"Maybe, but there's one thing I want to see before I die, and I can't do it for myself. That's why I sent for you." Mark looked up quickly and said, "I loved a girl once, years ago. I was too blasted proud to do anything about it. Had some stupid idea about aristocracy and the gentry, nonsense like that. If I'd married her, I'da been a better man, but I was a fool so I let it slip."

Outside, the sun had finally set, the golden dusk replaced by the darkening night sky. The room itself grew dark as well, with only a single lamp lit in the corner. Mark said, "Light that other lamp, will you, Jason? My eyes don't see as well as they used to." He watched as Jason drew a match from his pocket, struck it, lifted the chimney of the lamp, and turned it up to a steady yellow flame. Then, when Jason sat back, he continued speaking softly.

"Her name was Beth—Beth Griffeth. We met in New Orleans, and I fell in love with her. She was young and beautiful, sweet, all that a woman ought to be. She loved me too, more than I deserved." He broke off suddenly and looked out the window. A bat fluttered by, shuddering in quick, ecstatic motion, and something in the movement of the flying mammal attracted Mark's attention. He was having difficulty speaking of his past life, for he was not a man to speak of himself. He had no choice now, he well knew, so he turned back from the window and said, "There was a child, Jason, a girl. But I didn't know this until a few days ago." A pained smile briefly crossed Mark's face. "I didn't even know Beth was still alive. Years ago a friend of mine wrote and said she died. But four days ago I got a letter from Beth. She said she was dying and she thought a man ought to know when he had a child. She also said she'd always loved me."

Jason sat there taking a puff from the thin cigar from time to time, studying the face of the man before him. Finally, he said, "What is it you want, Mark?"

"I want you to go to New Orleans and find my daughter and bring her here."

It took a great deal to startle Jason Larrimore, but Mark had succeeded this time. "Are you sure that's what you want, Mark? I mean, how old is the girl now?"

"She's eighteen."

"Does she know about you, that you're her father, I mean?"

"No, I don't think so. Beth said she never told her who her father was."

Larrimore was troubled. He stood up, walked to the open window, and looked outside. Holding the cigar out, he knocked the ashes on the ground below, then turned around and said abruptly, "What if she won't come?"

Mark shrugged. "If she won't come, she won't. That's not your problem, Jason. But I've got to try. I did her mother an injustice too many years ago. Now my time's running out. I've got to do something to right the wrong. Will you go?"

Jason shrugged. "Of course I'll go. I have two weeks before my ship's refitted. Of course I'll go." Something, however, troubled him about this whole thing. He wanted to say no, but not because he didn't want to take the trouble. He was afraid it might be a disappointment for this dying man that he respected so much.

"Things don't always turn out like we want, Mark," he said slowly, "except in storybooks. I'll go to New Orleans and find the girl. I'll do my best to bring her here, but there's always the chance that it won't work out."

Mark nodded. "I know that, Jason. I've thought about little else for the past few days. She may hate me. She may not like the life here. She may be married. But, whatever I can do, I want to do it." He looked up and said, "It's asking a lot. I know you're a busy man."

"Don't speak of that," Jason protested. "I'm glad to do it, Mark, and I'll give it my best effort—but I guess I'm not very hopeful about most things."

Mark looked at him and said, "You and I have always been a lot alike, Jason. Both of us have been pretty cynical about things, but when you come to the end of the road, as I have, you get a little different perspective." He reached down and touched the Bible that was on his lap. "Don't worry," he said, seeing the look in Jason's eyes, "I'm not about to start preaching at you, but I've found something in this that's been good for me. You met Susanna. She's one of those arguments for Christianity that I could never answer. I could laugh at the Bible and see the hypocrites in the church, but there was always Susanna and some others that I couldn't explain away."

"And you've found God, have you, Mark?"

"Yes, I have. Not much else to do here but read, and Susanna keeps a Bible in every room, it seems. Well, I got reading the Gospels and talking to Susanna about what I read. I realized the loneliness I felt could only be filled by Jesus. I'd spent my life wandering around trying to find happiness, and I wound up finding it lying in my room." Mark paused and grinned slightly. "I guess I was going to preach after all." There was a quiet assurance in the sick man's voice as he said, "I found God very late, but I'm glad that it's not too late."

"I'm happy for you, Mark," Jason said. "I'll go to New Orleans and find the girl. I'll leave first thing in the morning."

The two men sat there and talked, long into the night,

Jason listening as Mark told him what little he knew about Beth Griffeth. Susanna brought a plate in, and he ate a little. Then, seeing that Mark was growing tired, he said, "I'll say good-bye now, Mark. I'll leave early before you get up."

Mark put his hand out and when Jason took it, he said, "God be with you and help you to find my daughter."

CHAPTER SIX
The Sound and the Fury

★

The protection of Richmond was the major concern of the Army of Northern Virginia, but Gen. Robert E. Lee reasoned that to hold on to the Southern capital he needed more than a defensive position. After his victory at Chancellorsville, Lee decided not to wait. He chose to carry the war into the North, into Pennsylvania, hoping to draw the Federal Army of the Potomac after him and away from Richmond.

The high-spirited Army of Northern Virginia contained seventy-seven thousand men under three corps commanders. On June 3, the Confederates marched west, turning northward up the Shenandoah Valley. They crossed the Potomac River and headed toward Pennsylvania.

It took Maj. Gen. Joseph Hooker nine days to discover that his enemy had badly deceived him. Lincoln sent word to Hooker that his first responsibility was the protection of Washington and the pursuit and destruction of the Confederate army. Hooker's problem was that he did not know where Lee was. Nevertheless, he struck north, hunting the Army of Northern Virginia. Lee was as badly informed as his opponent, for he did not know where Hooker was. Jeb Stuart's cavalry had gone off on a raid, leaving the Southern commander without any notion of his enemy's presence. On

June 28 a spy named Harrison came to Confederate headquarters with the alarming news that the Union army was
very close. He also revealed that Hooker had been replaced
by Maj. Gen. George E. Meade.

Lee immediately recast his plans. He issued orders for his
three widely dispersed corps to concentrate at Cashtown,
close to Harrisburg, the Pennsylvania state capital. At the
same time, Gen. Meade began to pull his troops together,
and the gap between the two armies started to close.

Just outside of Gettysburg on the afternoon of July 1,
Brig. Gen. John Buford, Commander of the First Cavalry
Division, encountered Confederate infantry who were on
their way to commandeer some shoes that were reported to
be in Gettysburg. His two brigades were under strength;
nevertheless, they managed to delay the Confederates until
reinforcements arrived. Neither commander wanted to fight
at Gettysburg, but the two armies had accidentally collided,
and both commanders quickly poured troops into the area.

Confederate Gen. Richard Ewell failed to take the high
ground south of the town of Gettysburg, so it was Maj. Gen.
Winfield Hancock who formed a defensive line shaped like
an inverted fishhook two and a half miles long in this prime
position. The Federal right lay on Culp's Hill, and the line
curved through Cemetery Hill, extended down Cemetery
Ridge, then rested its left on two hills known as Little Round
Top and Big Round Top.

The battle of Gettysburg was actually a play in three acts.
On July 1, the first day of the battle, Confederate strength
on the battlefield was greater than that of the Union troops.
Gen. Jubal Early's division made a slashing attack that crum-
bled the Union right flank. This threw the entire line of the
Eleventh Corps into confusion, and the Union army beat a
path back to the town. Early pursued the beaten divisions to
the clogged streets of Gettysburg, capturing many. He then
stopped to reorganize and sent part of his troops out on the
York Road to protect his flank.

The heavy fighting that day left many dead and wounded

on the grass and in the town. The day's casualties amounted to ten thousand for the Union and seven thousand for the Confederates.

All day long and far into the night, the numerous divisions in blue and in gray, with their supporting artillery, had been snaking along the roads that converged at Gettysburg. The men of both armies were driven at a rapid pace by their officers to get there first—but without knowing just where they were going or what they would meet when they got there.

The men of the Richmond Grays saw no action this day, but when Clay pulled his horse up and spoke to one of the staff officers, he returned to say to Dent, "We're too late for action today, but no doubt we'll be in it tomorrow."

Dent looked at his father, his eyes alive with excitement. "We'll get them this time, won't we, Major?" He always used the correct military title when in situations like this. He looked around and said, "The boys are ready for a scrap."

Clay looked over toward the low-lying hills almost hidden in the darkness. He stood there quietly, listening to the booming of cannons still sounding and the far-off rattle of musket fire and then looked to Dent. "I think we're in for the biggest fight we've ever seen, Dent. Pass the word to the men. Have 'em carry all the ammunition they can, and see that they get a drink from the well. They'll be going dry almost at once."

★ ★ ★

At dawn the next day, Col. Gideon Rocklin led his Federal troops onto the field of battle. His men were well trained, he knew, but that day nothing seemed to work as planned. Gideon turned to his aide midway through the morning's fighting, saying soberly, "We can draw our plans on the maps—but once the first shot is fired, you can throw them all away!"

The biggest problem turned out to be a weakness on the left side of the Union line, Little Round Top, the Union anchor on the south. Gen. Dan Sickles moved his men to what he thought was a better position and sent out Berdan's sharpshooters to probe the Confederate position. Without securing Meade's permission, he moved his entire corps forward about 1:00 P.M. and took position in the Peach Orchard. Part of his troops were in the vicinity of the Devil's Den, an area of enormous boulders. As a result of Sickles' movement, Little Round Top was left unoccupied, and Meade's scheme of defense was sadly upset.

The Southern troops were about as confused as the Federals. They were slow to take advantage of the Union weakness. If they had captured Little Round Top it would have been possible to attack the Union line from behind, which would almost have assured a Confederate victory.

Longstreet, always slow to move, consumed more than three and a half hours marching and countermarching west of Seminary Ridge. It was four-thirty when he finally started his infantry attack, which was badly conceived. He found one of Sickles's divisions directly in his front. Furthermore, Hood was not permitted to work around the south of the Round Tops as he wished to do. This disposed of Lee's idea that the attack would be a flanking operation.

For four long hours the battle raged. Sickles's corps was so badly chopped up it practically disappeared. The bloody fighting spread over the landscape until it engulfed the Wheat Field, Devil's Den, and the slopes of Little Round Top.

"We're gettin' beat!" Maj. Summit gasped, coming back to report to Gideon. "They're driving us back."

"We can't fall back!" Gideon shouted. "Throw every reserve we have into the line!" He stood there tall, walking along the lines, listening not at all to the bullets that whipped by close to his head. Cannon exploded all around— from both the Federal artillery and the Confederate guns. Everywhere men lay shot to pieces, some of them lying in that eloquent stillness that death brings, others crawling along the ground, leaving their scarlet blood on the rocks, in the dirt, and on the grass.

By the end of the second day, both armies were bled dry. Every man, no matter what side he fought on, knew that the third day of Gettysburg would decide the fate of this battle—perhaps the fate of the entire war.

★ ★ ★

When the battle of Gettysburg broke out, twenty-year-old Jenny Wade was at the home of her sister, who lived on Baltimore Street at the foot of Cemetery Hill. There was a new baby in the McClellan home, and Jenny was helping her sister with its care.

There was no heavy fighting in the immediate area, but a Federal picket line did run behind the little brick house. There was intermediate skirmishing between it and Confederate outposts in the town proper. On the third morning of the battle of Gettysburg, while Jenny stood in the kitchen kneading dough, a bullet pierced two wooden doors and struck her in the back, killing her instantly. The cries of her sister and mother attracted Federal soldiers, who carried Jenny's body to the cellar. Later, she was buried in a coffin some Confederate soldiers had fashioned for an officer. Jenny was engaged to a Cpl. Johnson Skelly, who, unknown to her, had been wounded two weeks earlier in the battle of Winchester. News that he had died in Confederate hands came several days after the Southern army had withdrawn from the Gettysburg area. The death of the young woman was one of many that day of July 3, 1863.

Basically, the battle that day consisted of a charge led by Confederate Gen. Pickett with his Virginia troops. Longstreet had argued strenuously with Lee that no troops in the world could cross the long, level plain and survive the fire thrown down by the entire Army of the Potomac as it kept its position on top of the high ground.

Lee had been suffering from the heart problem that would one day kill him. He had also had a ferocious two-week attack of diarrhea. Added to this was the fact that he had lost Stonewall Jackson at Chancellorsville and had gone into battle without this favorite commander. For whatever the reason, Lee insisted on the charge. As Pickett rode back and forth in front of his troops, he called out, "Up, men, and to your posts! Don't forget today that you are from old Virginia."

Clay was one of the officers who lay in the woods with the commands. His company was finely trained, but as he looked up and down the line, then across that long field, he said to Bushrod Aimes, who was standing beside him, "A lot of us are not going to get back off that hill."

Aimes shook his head. "Gen. Lee knows we'll do our best. We've never failed him."

Suppose you placed infantry behind a stone wall and had one rank fire and then fall back to reload while a second rank instantly took their place. Then you had these men fire and repeat this action so a constant hail of bone-smashing minié balls ripped the air in front of that wall. Now suppose you gathered the finest soldiers to be found and marched them a quarter of a mile across a flat field then up a slope into the muzzles of those guns behind that wall. The result of this sort of fighting was proven conclusively at Gettysburg on July 3, 1863—it was a slaughter!

Not that the men of the South failed for want of trying. They marched in behind their officers, lined up as if on a parade ground. For almost two hours the Confederate artillery had pounded the Federals on top of the ridge. When Pickett led his men out, the long gray lines moved out from the protection of the trees and corrected their alignment as though on dress parade. A sudden dramatic hush fell on the battlefield. In three lines, the Confederates marched forward across the open field, their fluttering battle flags adding a brilliant touch of color to the impressive scene.

Watching the pageant from Cemetery Ridge and holding their fire until the enemy was in effective range, Gideon's troops paid silent, grim tribute to the magnificent courage of the Confederates as they marched steadily forward, the lines closing doggedly as the shells knocked out huge segments of the attacking force. Only a few of the twelve thousand who started the charge reached the Union position through the hail of cannon fire and musketry. Over the stone wall went that intrepid handful, but after initial success, they were either killed or driven back.

Sick at heart, Clay had watched his men drop and was fearful of the lives of the rest of them. They were driven back, and finally he gave the command to retreat. He picked his way back through the lines of the wounded, giving commands that as many of them as possible be carried back, when he looked up to see a small force of Union soldiers practically upon them. "Major! Pin those Yankee troops down! Form a line!" he yelled. He joined the line, and his men began to pick off the Union troops as they charged down the hill to capture them.

"We'll be cut off! Watch on the right flank!" Clay screamed over the rattle of musket fire.

And then it was that he saw something he could not believe. Clay had always had good eyesight, and when he looked up and saw the officer that had come out with the attacking force, he saw that it was his cousin, Gideon Rocklin.

Gideon had been given the order by one of the generals to lead a force to take as many Confederates captive as he could. At once he had gathered a sizable force and led the charge down the hill. Now, he was on foot and waving his sword, urging his men onward.

Clay stared at him. "Go back, Gid!" Clay whispered. "Go back!" But, the officer had no intention of going back. As Clay watched, Gideon leaned over, picked up a musket, then ran straight down the hill. But he had not gone five steps before a bullet struck him, turning him around. He slumped to the ground, but by his movements Clay saw that he was not dead. "He'll be a target for every man in this line," Clay yelled to Dent, who had come to stand beside him.

Something came to Clay then—a thought that seemed to explode in his mind: *That's why I'm here!*

The thought blazed through him, and he immediately ran forward. Without a backward look, he charged the enemy. He heard Dent shout, "Father, come back!" but he did not even slow down. Every soldier along the line saw the Confederate officer rush right into the guns of the Union foes, and it was then that Dent cried "Charge!" and led the Richmond Grays back toward the Union troops.

All the world was covered by a red haze to Gideon. The pain, however, did not block everything out. And he looked up to see an officer in gray, almost upon him. He tried to pick up the musket, but his fingers lost their strength. Then he heard a voice saying, "Gid!"

Gideon thought, *I must be dreaming!* when he looked up and saw the face of Clay Rocklin. "Clay—," he muttered.

The two men clung to each other as the battle raged around them. Dent dashed up to say, "We've driven them back. Let's get the prisoners out of here!"

Clay wanted to leave Gid, knowing the hard fate of prisoners, but the fire from his lines was strong. "You men, take this officer back to our lines," he commanded. As four privates picked up Gideon and carried him off the field, the battle raged on.

When they were behind the Confederate lines, Gideon awoke long enough to see tears running down the brown face of the man who held him. Memories came to him of the days when he and Clay had roamed the fields of Virginia as young boys, and later as young men. "Clay?" he whispered, and, as the darkness came up to envelop him, he whispered, "I've missed you, Clay." The warm darkness moved over him and Gideon Rocklin knew nothing more.

PART TWO
The Bargain

CHAPTER SEVEN
"A Woman Should Be Gentle"

The *Natchez Belle* rammed into the pilings so abruptly that Jason Larrimore grabbed at the railing to keep his balance. A tall man with a full beard standing beside him jostled against him with a shock. He looked at Jason saying, "Not much of a captain, is he? Next time he'll knock the whole blasted wharf down!"

Jason smiled and shrugged. "At least we made it. I was afraid a couple of times we would ram another boat." With a look toward the bridge, Jason agreed. "No, he's not much of a captain."

The whistle gave a piercing shriek, and at the signal the deckhands lowered the gangplank. Picking up his small suitcase, Jason joined the crowd that jostled one another to get ashore. He was sleepy, for he had stayed awake most of the night engaged in a ferocious poker game. He had come out a winner by a slight margin, but his eyes were scratchy as the bright New Orleans sunlight hit them.

Reaching the crowded dock, he shouldered his way through the crowd, trying to decide how to approach the problem that had been dumped in his lap by Mark Rocklin. He was not a man given to introspection, preferring to plunge into action at once. He had made his way to the top of his profession by following this method and now, as he strolled along the streets, decided that he had no time for fine intellectual thought.

"Must be over 150,000 people in this city," he murmured, dodging as a group of Union officers headed down the sidewalk toward him. "I can't go from door to door looking for the girl. I have to find a better way than that."

He knew New Orleans well, having spent much time there. It was the port where his own ship most often docked. However, since the Federals had taken the city he had not been back. Still, he had some fond memories of the place, and as he strolled along he enjoyed the polyglot of accents that he heard around him—the twangy nasal dialect of the officers from New Hampshire, Massachusetts, and other New England states. The soft murmur of the Southern peoples came to him. The almost unintelligible sound of the slaves chanting along the roadside, selling the wares of their masters. Above all, as he moved along, he heard the soft murmur of French, for New Orleans was French in nature, the only truly international city in the United States.

He was hungry as he made his way to the Majestic Hotel, where he had often stayed before. He was greeted by the room clerk, a small, round-faced Frenchman whose eyes lit up when he saw him. "Ah, Monsieur Larrimore! You are back!"

"Yes, François, I'll be here for just a short time. Do you have a room?"

"Ah, it is crowded, monsieur, but for you I will find something. How about the room over the courtyard that you always liked so much?" The Frenchman smiled. "You see? I still remember you."

"That will be fine," Larrimore said with satisfaction. "Please have someone take my bag up, and I'll go have breakfast."

"But *certainement.*" The clerk raised his eyebrow and a small Cajun lad appeared magically. "Take Monsieur Larrimore's bag to room 216," he commanded. Then turning to Jason, he said, "You're here on business, monsieur?"

Larrimore extracted a long cigar from his inner coat pocket, stuck it between his teeth, and lit it. Sending a haze of purple smoke upward, he eyed the clerk and said, "I don't suppose you've ever heard of a woman named Beth Griffeth?"

"Griffeth, is it?" François pondered the name, tasting it on his tongue, so it seemed, then shook his head regretfully. "But no, Monsieur Larrimore. I do not know the name, but I will ask around."

"Thank you, François." Larrimore nodded, turned, and walked at once into the café. He was remembered there by the maître d', who greeted him warmly and seated him at a table by the window. The warm yellow sunlight filtered in, and Larrimore sat back in his chair allowing the waiter to fuss over him. He ate a fine breakfast of eggs, pancakes, and toast with a rasher of bacon, washed down with café au lait, a drink of equal parts coffee and hot milk.

As Jason sat there, he thought about Mark Rocklin. He liked the man and owed him a debt—and Larrimore was a man who paid his debts. He believed in very little, but he did believe in honoring his debts. To him, a welsher was the lowest form of animal life. It was this ideal that had brought him back to New Orleans. His mind darted back and forth. The strains of Mark's talk came to him. *He said she probably would be in the poor section of town,* he thought. Sipping his coffee, he shook his head almost in despair. *I guess that would describe most of New Orleans. I won't have to filter through the rich planters, but that's not much help.*

Finishing his breakfast, he went into the barber shop, took a bath, got a shave, then went up to his room, where he put on his clean clothes. He was rather a fancy dresser when not on duty and slipped into a pair of fawn-colored trousers, a white shirt with a string tie, and a brown, brocaded waistcoat. He wore over it a light-brown wool frock coat. He paused long enough to look into the mirror and brush his blond hair back carelessly, then left the hotel room. Before leaving the building, he stopped at the desk. "I'm not expecting any visitors, François," he said, "but if anyone does come by, make sure you take a message."

His only idea was to start at the city hall. As he made his way along the streets filled with Union soldiers he noted that the citizens of New Orleans had lost their gaiety. *They don't like being captives of the Yankees,* he thought grimly. He remembered Gen. Ben Butler, probably one of the worst of the Union's generals, but so strong politically that Lincoln couldn't fire him. When Butler had come to New Orleans, he had been accused of stealing silverware from one of the fine homes and was called "Spoons" Butler for a time. Later he got a worse name. The women of New Orleans were fiery Southern patriots and took occasion to vent their hatred of the Yankees by insulting the officers. Butler had retaliated by issuing a special order that stated bluntly that any woman who insulted a Union officer would be treated as a prostitute. This order had caused Butler to be hated worse than any Yankee, and he was henceforth known as "Beast" Butler.

Arriving at the city hall, Jason found the usual bureaucratic snarl. After impatiently going through two clerks, he found himself talking to an older man with a pair of tired, gray eyes. "My name is Jason Larrimore," he said. "I'm looking for a woman who lives in New Orleans." He had decided not to give the full story and said, "A distant relative is seeking to find her. Her name is Beth Griffeth."

"You have an address?"

"No, nothing except her name. Do you think you can help me?"

The man, whose name was Jenkins, shrugged. "I doubt it. If some of her male relatives are registered to vote, we may have an address. I'll check for you."

He disappeared and did not come back for fifteen minutes. Finally, when he returned, he said, "We have no Beth Griffeth listed. We have seven Griffeths on the tax rolls. It is a rather unusual name, or there would be more."

"I suppose I'm lucky her name wasn't Bourdeaux," Jason said with a grin. He took the list the man handed him, studied it, and said, "Thanks a lot, Mr. Jenkins. I appreciate it."

Leaving the city hall he hailed a carriage, stared at the first name on the list, and asked the cabdriver, "Do you know where Alexandria Street is?"

The cabdriver was a small, dark Cajun with black eyes. "Why yes, I know that."

"Take me there."

The cabdriver took what seemed to be a circuitous route to the address, and Jason felt he was padding his pocketbook by making the trip last longer. However, he said nothing. When he arrived at the plain frame house that sat close to the street, he got down and said, "Wait here. I probably won't be long." He went to the door and knocked.

When a woman opened it, Jason removed his hat and gave his best smile. "I'm looking for a lady named Beth Griffeth. Would you know of her by any chance?"

"Beth Griffeth? No, I've never heard of her."

"I suppose you know most of the Griffeths here in New Orleans? It's not a common name for this part of the world."

"Yes, I think I know most of them, but I've never heard of a Beth. Why are you looking for her?"

"Just a business affair," Jason said. "Thank you very much for your time."

Going back to the cab, he picked the second name on the list, and again the cabdriver seemed to take a great deal of time. He was a small, well-built man who announced that his name was Louis Prejean. "I been driving a cab ten years, me," he said cheerfully. "Better than getting shot at in the army, no?"

"Much better." Jason grinned, and as the two crossed through the small twisted streets of New Orleans, he listened as Prejean gave him a rundown of his family life, which was in poor shape, it seemed. He listened as Prejean told about how his wife was never satisfied with anything he did and now, if he had it to do over again, he would never marry.

Finally, the cab drew up in a much more affluent section of town, in front of a brick building of French design.

"I will wait for you, yes?"

"Yes, Louis. It won't take long, I shouldn't think."

It didn't take long, for the large man who came to the door had neither heard of a Beth Griffeth and doubted that there was any such in New Orleans. "I know all of our people here," he said, "but I know of no Beth Griffeth. A rather unusual name," he announced proudly.

"If you think of anyone, I'll be at the Majestic Hotel. My name is Jason Larrimore. I would appreciate it if you would contact me."

Jason went back to the cab and for the rest of the morning and part of the afternoon sought out the names on his brief list. Finally, after the last futile call, he came back and sat down in the cab, feeling defeated.

Prejean turned and said, "We go now, monsieur?"

"Take me to the Majestic, Louis," he said. "I've run out of names."

"Oui." The small cabdriver spoke to the horses in French and for a while chatted as he had all day. When they drew up in front of the Majestic, Jason asked the fee and when it was given, paid it cheerfully, though it seemed a little large. He added a ten-dollar gold piece to the sum, saying, "You've done a good job, Louis. I appreciate it."

"If I can be of further service, you tell me, no?"

"Well, there's one thing you might do. I'm looking for a woman named Beth Griffeth. You might ask around among your people down in the Quarter. I'll be looking myself. If you hear of anything, there'll be a couple more of those gold pieces for you."

The liquid eyes of the small muscular driver grew wide. "Twenty-dolla' gold, you betcha! I ask plenty, me." He leaped into the cab and whipped the horses up, dodging through the crowded street expertly.

Jason turned and went into the hotel. He asked at the desk, but there were no messages. He had expected none so he went upstairs, undressed, and took a nap. He rested fitfully for a time, trying to think of some way to narrow the search but thought of nothing. Again he thought, *I can't go from door to door looking for the woman.*

Finally he awoke, dressed, went down to lunch, and spent the rest of the afternoon and evening wandering through the French Quarter. He was approached by many ladies of the evening taken by his tall form and fine clothes but shook them off. He went into businesses, shops, asked the police officers, but got no help from any of them.

Dejectedly he went back to the hotel, ate supper, and went to bed. "I'll give it three days," he said, "if I don't find her by then, I'll have to give up."

The next morning he was brought out of a sound sleep by a knock on the door. Startled, he slipped his hand under the pillow—where he always kept his pistol at night—and rose up on one elbow. "Who is it?" he asked groggily.

"It's me, Louis Prejean."

"Prejean? Wait a minute." Jason rolled out of bed, pulled on his pants, and went over to the door. When he opened it he saw that Prejean was grinning broadly.

"Beth Griffeth, you look for her, no?"

A shock ran through Larrimore, and he awakened fully. "Yes, did you find her?"

"I find where she usta was," Prejean said. "I think they don't like Cajuns much there, but if a gentleman such as yourself go, they might tell you something."

"Where is it, Louis?"

"A boardinghouse over by Lake Pontchartrain. Not a very nice place." He shrugged. "I ask around, and one of my friends, he know. He met a woman named that once. I think his wife did. Anyway, I chase him like a bird dog all night long, and there she is—116 Chartres Street. You find out something there, maybe."

"You're a fine fellow, Louis." Jason smiled, stuck his hand in his pocket, and pulled out two gold coins. He looked at them a moment, then added a third. "Here you are. Now, you wait until I get dressed and get something to eat, and you can take me out there."

"*Oui*. I do that, you bet."

Larrimore threw his clothes on, went downstairs and ate a quick breakfast, then went outside. Louis was waiting with the cab, and he quickly got in, saying, "Now we go."

Soon they were in a poor district on the north side of town, and Louis pulled up before a dilapidated two-story building. "This is where the woman lived," he announced.

"Wait here, Louis." Larrimore stepped down, went to the door, and knocked. It seemed like a long wait, but finally the door opened a crack. An older woman with her gray hair in disarray grumbled, "What do you want?"

"I am looking for a woman named Beth Griffeth."

"What do you want with her?"

"I'm looking on behalf of a distant relative. I think there's some kind of estate involved. Do you know her?"

"I did know her. She's dead now. Didn't you know that?"

"I did hear that," Larrimore said evenly, "but I understand she has a daughter."

"That she has."

When the woman stopped abruptly, Larrimore sensed greed almost palpable on the air. "It would be worth twenty dollars gold to me to find the young woman."

At once the door opened, and the woman mustered a smile. "Well, that's business. You'll find her in the Gay Paree dealing blackjack."

Larrimore was shocked, for he had expected almost anything but this. "Are you sure it's the same young woman?"

"Didn't I know her all my life?" she said. "Allyn Griffeth, that's her name. You'll find her there tonight."

"Allyn?"

"Well, she spells it *A-l-l-y-n*," the woman said and sniffed. "But it sounds like *Ay*-leen."

"Do you know where she lives?"

"No, I don't. She'll be dealing cards in that saloon. How about that twenty dollars?"

Jason handed her the money, which she looked at carefully and stuck into her pocket with satisfaction. "Tell her Millie sent you."

"Thank you very much." Larrimore nodded. He turned and went back to the cab with a sense of accomplishment and at the same time a sense of foreboding. When he got into the cab and had Louis drive back to the hotel, he thought, *Dealing blackjack in the Gay Paree? Doesn't sound like the kind of daughter Mark needs—but at least I found her.*

★ ★ ★

As soon as Jason stepped into the Gay Paree he spotted the object of his quest. Moving to the bar, he ordered a drink and turned to look at the woman who was dealing blackjack across the room. He had rarely seen a woman so attractive— and he had seen many. He asked the bartender as he paid for his drink, "I take it that's Allyn Griffeth?"

The bartender, a husky individual, gave him a careful look. "Yeah," he said briefly, "that's Allyn."

Jason turned and studied the young woman carefully. She was wearing a rose-colored silk dress overlaid with some sort of pink lace flounces. It was fairly modest for a saloon, but the girl had a fine figure he saw at once. She had dark red hair, and her green eyes caught the reflection of the chandeliers overhead. She had, he noted, a strong, squarish face and a creamy complexion.

Jason finished his drink, walked over, and stood watching as the man in front played cards. As soon as he got up Jason slipped into the seat, saying, "Good evening."

"How are you?" the young woman said. There was a watchfulness in her eyes that told him she would not be easy to fool, and he sat there for a while playing. He soon discovered she was a good player; she had a quick mind and handled the cards well. He lost a few dollars, then said, "Miss Allyn Griffeth, isn't it?"

"That's right." The answer was spare, but the watchfulness in the green eyes was even more pronounced.

"I'd like to talk with you for a few moments," Larrimore said.

"Go ahead and talk."

As they were talking two men had come over to watch them play. Looking at them, Jason said, "A little more privately than this."

"If you want to play cards, go ahead. Otherwise, I'll ask you to let one of these gentlemen have your seat."

Jason flushed at the hard tone, and his temper flared. "Look, all I want to do is talk—"

Jason felt his arm grasped as if by a vise. He was pulled to his feet and turned quickly so that he faced the giant of a man with a red face and blunt features who was holding him. A smaller man had come to stand on his other side and said, "I'll have to ask you to leave, sir."

Jason pulled against the grip, but the large hand on his arm simply tightened, almost cutting off the circulation.

"I only wanted—"

"I know what you wanted," the man said. "This is my place, and I'm asking you to leave. Take him out, Toby."

Jason glanced down at the girl and saw a small smile on her lips. However, he had no time to do more, for he found himself simply turned around and walked across the floor. He had an idea of making a fight of it but was fairly sure that there were others at hand as rough as the one who held him. He found himself outside, and the big man said, "I don't think I would come back if I was you. Good night, sir."

Inside, Sam Barker said, "Come on, let's take a break, Allyn."

Allyn smiled up at him and shook her head. "No, it's all right. Just another fancy man. Thank you, Sam," she said. "I'll be all right."

Barker examined her carefully, then nodded. "All right, I'll keep an eye out in case he comes back."

"I don't think he'll do that, Sam."

Allyn played the rest of the night, took a break occasionally, and put all thoughts of the tall blond-haired man out of her mind. Finally at eleven she said good night to Sam and started for the door.

"Toby, see Miss Allyn gets home all right," Barker called to the large bouncer.

"Sure, boss."

Allyn was accustomed to this, although she had often protested she would be all right alone. Tonight, however, she walked the two blocks toward her room speaking occasionally to the huge man beside her. He left her at the gate, and she said with a fond smile, "Thank you, Toby."

"Yeah, sure, Miss Allyn. Good night."

Allyn entered the courtyard, went to the stairs that led upward, then stopped on the balcony to fumble for her key. She had just inserted the key when a voice said, "Miss Allyn?"

She turned and saw by the streetlight the tall blond-haired man who had been put out of the saloon. She was not a fearful girl, but he loomed large in the feeble light. She had not heard him approach at all.

"What do you want?" she asked coldly "Go away and leave me alone."

Jason took off his hat and nodded. "I know this looks bad, but I have to talk to you. I mean no harm."

"Come back in the morning."

"I'll do that if you insist," he said quietly. He knew he had to calm her somehow and finally said, "You don't have to be afraid of me."

"I'm not afraid of you. I just don't want to talk to you."

"It's about your father. He sent me to find you."

Allyn had reached into her bag, where she carried a small pistol called a pepperbox. It would fire four bullets at the same time, and Sam had given her careful instructions on how to use it. She had been prepared to draw it, hoping that it would frighten him, but his words shocked her. She blinked her eyes and stared, trying to see his face more clearly. "My father? What are you talking about?"

"My name is Jason Larrimore. Your father asked me to

find you." He looked around the balcony and said, "I know it's late, and I'll come back tomorrow if you'd rather, but I think you'll want to hear what I have to say."

Allyn hesitated, then made a decision. "Come inside," she said. She turned, unlocked the door, and entered. She lit the lamp and turned the wick up. Allyn wheeled to him, her eyes large in the amber light, and said, "What are you talking about? My father? I don't have any father."

Larrimore was aware that the caution she exercised was habitual. He knew that his words had come as a shock and that her calmness had been broken. Carefully he said, "Your father's name is Mark Rocklin. Did you know that?"

"I don't—" Allyn stopped and then remembered her mother's words: *Your father's name is Mark.* Inexplicably she began to tremble, and her knees felt weak. Quickly she moved to a chair and waved to another, saying, "Sit down." When he was seated, she said, "Your name is Larrimore?"

"Yes."

She stared at Jason. "I never—my mother never told me about who my father was."

Jason nodded. "It's not up to me to go into the past, Miss Griffeth. All I can do is pass the message along." He hesitated, then added, "I *will* tell you two things. First, your father was not even aware that you existed. He got a letter from your mother saying she was dying. In the letter, for the first time, she mentioned you. Mark had no idea that he had a daughter."

Allyn stared at him with disbelief in her eyes. "What's the second thing?" she asked rather coldly.

"The second thing is that your father's a sick man. He was wounded in the war and—well, I don't think he has long to live."

Allyn had gotten better control of herself now. She studied the face of the man in front of her. She had been forced to learn men rather well during her brief life. She had learned that fine clothes and fine manners did not necessarily mean quality. The face of the man in front of her was strong and bold. There was a fearless quality about him that she had seen in a few men. His features were carved and strong, his wide-set eyes fixed on her. He had a broad mouth and a long English nose. Something about his bearing told her he might be hard, but there was not a viciousness in him that she had seen in other men. "Why should I believe you?" she said.

"I have a letter here from your father." He shrugged. "But since you don't know him, that doesn't mean much." He hesitated again. It was harder talking to this girl than he had thought. He tried to put the words together in his mind before he spoke them. "I know that this comes as a shock, but after you've thought it over, I think you should go see your father. I'll be glad to escort you there, if that's what you want."

"Why should I go see him? He left my mother. She told me that much."

"I can't go into that," Jason said. "It's not my affair."

"I won't go," Allyn said almost harshly. "He's had eighteen years to find me. If he was really interested, he would have done something before this."

Jason shook his head. "As I said, he didn't know you existed. In fact, he heard your mother had died long ago. But if that's the way you feel, then I suppose nothing I do will change it. But let me tell you a little about your father. . . ." He began to talk, relating the time that he himself had been destitute and had hit bottom. He told her how it had been her father, Mark Rocklin, who had reached out and single-handedly saved him from ruin. "He gave me a new hope," Larrimore added thoughtfully. "If it hadn't been for him, I think I would have killed myself. Can't tell you how low I'd fallen, but it was low as a man could get. Mark didn't have any reason for helping me. We were no kin, but we were friends. I know he hasn't been everything a man should be, but I haven't been either. I can tell you this: He is a man of honor, and if he tells you that he didn't know you were alive, you can believe that that was the way it was."

Allyn had listened to this recital carefully, watching the face of the man who sat across from her. Her heart was beating faster as she remembered all the years she had thought about her father, as a child how she had longed for a father and there had been none. Now she recognized the bitterness of those lost years and shook her head abruptly. "I don't need him now. He wasn't there when I did need him, so why should I go to him?"

Larrimore wanted to argue, but he saw that against this girl arguments would be useless. He leaned back in his chair and studied her carefully. She grew nervous under his inspection, and finally he said, "A woman should be gentle."

A flush touched her smooth cheeks, and she dropped her eyes for a moment. His words angered her, yet, at the same time, there was some justice in what he said. Only the ticking of a small clock on her dressing table broke the silence. Finally, she lifted her eyes and met his. "I haven't had a chance to learn how to be gentle. A young girl doesn't learn gentleness on the streets of New Orleans."

"I know," he said, "and I ask your pardon. I spoke too soon." He abruptly got to his feet and said, "I've done all that I can do. I'll be leaving New Orleans tomorrow." She rose at once as he added, "I wish you would think about this. I know it's a big decision—you'd be leaving your life here and joining a brand-new one. The Rocklins are a big family."

"I'm sure they'd be glad to see a saloon girl coming to join them," Allyn said bitterly.

"You'd have to know this family to understand. They're fine people, planters just outside of Richmond, most of them. Mark's one of the older members. The younger ones are fighting for the Cause. There are some Rocklins in the North serving the Union army, but let me tell you this, it's no shame to anyone to be a Rocklin." He saw the doubt in her eyes and added, "I think there's a good life for you there, Miss Griffeth. Without being judgmental, I'd say the one you have now probably isn't the best for a young woman. I'm no judge of that—but I can tell you you'd be doing yourself a favor if at least you'd go for a visit to Gracefield."

"Gracefield? What's that?"

"That's the Rocklin plantation."

Allyn struggled with herself for a moment, and as she stood there, a desire to see the man who called himself her father grew in her. Abruptly she made a decision, which was not unusual for her. She had been forced to make decisions all her life, and now she said briskly, "All right, Mr. Larrimore. I'll go with you for a visit—that's all, just a visit."

Larrimore took a deep breath and nodded. "I think that's wise. There'll be a ship out in the morning. We'll have to do some dodging to get through the patrols, but if you'll come with me, I'll be glad to see you to your father."

Allyn studied him and said, "I don't like to put myself in the power of a man, and I don't even know you."

Jason shrugged. "That's your decision. I can't change what I am, but I can give you my word that you'll be safe with me. Mark's my friend, and I wouldn't let harm come to his daughter for anything."

Something in his words assured Allyn, and she said reluctantly, "All right, I'll be ready to leave tomorrow."

He bowed and said, "I'll see about the passage. Shall I come back here?"

"Yes, I'll tell Sam tomorrow that I'll be taking a vacation. I'll wait here until you come."

"Good night, Miss Griffeth."

He turned and left quickly, and for a long time she stood staring at the door. Then she walked over to the bed and sat down, discovering that her hands were trembling. She could not think clearly, and for a long time that night she lay awake thinking of the man called Mark Rocklin.

CHAPTER EIGHT
"I Didn't Know What Love Was!"

The large four-story building that had been converted to Libby Prison loomed over the sluggish James River as Clay and Melora walked down the dock. Glancing with distaste at the structure, Melora said, "It's an awful-looking place, isn't it, Clay?"

"Yes, but then I guess all prisons are. I don't suppose there's a pretty one anywhere." They approached the two guards who stood outside the main door, and Clay pulled a paper from his pocket. "Maj. Rocklin," he introduced himself. "I'm here to visit with one of the prisoners, Col. Rocklin."

The guard, a man in his late fifties or early sixties, studied the paper carefully, then nodded. "Yes, sir. I'll take you to him myself." He turned to a fat young man who stood watching and said, "Corporal, you stand watch while I take the major inside."

As Clay and Melora entered the ancient building, they both gagged as they were struck by the rank smells of the bodies of unwashed men and human waste, all mixed in a nauseating way with the odor of boiled cabbage. The corridor led through the building to a stairway, and the sergeant led them up to the third floor. There he addressed a private who stood guard outside one of the two doors in the corridor and said, "Visitor for Col. Rocklin."

The guard, a very young man, no more than sixteen, saluted Clay and said hastily, "Yes, sir." He pulled a large iron key from his belt and inserted it in the lock. There was a clanking rattle as the door swung open. Clay stepped inside, saying, "Where'll I find the colonel?"

"Well, sir, we've got just one private room here. I guess you can use that." He pointed over across the wide-open crowded room that was filled with men sitting on the floor or milling about aimlessly.

Clay said at once, "Yes, we'll take the room, Private."

He led Melora along the wall, and some of the officers stepped aside to let them pass. When he opened the door, the two stepped into a ten-by-ten room. It was occupied with a desk, a chair, and several shelves filled with supplies.

"It's worse than I thought," Melora said, "and if the officers' prison is like this, think what it must be like for the privates!"

"Well, it's pretty bad." Clay nodded. "But maybe we can help Gid. We are allowed to bring in food, I suppose."

They stood there quietly, waiting, thinking of how strange the war was, that one cousin would be captured, another free. Finally, the door opened and Gideon came in. "Hello, Clay." He smiled. "You must be Melora! I'm glad to finally meet you, though I wish the circumstances were better."

Both Clay and Melora were speechless. Gideon was in terrible condition! His uniform, which was torn in several places, was unwashed and stiff with food and dirt. Noticing their glances, he shrugged. "Not much of a chance to keep very neat around here. You'll have to excuse the way I look."

"We'll do something about that, Gid." Clay stepped forward, put his arm around Gideon's shoulder. "By the good Lord, I hate to see you here like this!" he exclaimed. He was shocked at the frail shoulders beneath his grasp. Gideon had always been a strong-bodied man, heavily muscled, but already during his short time here, he had lost so much weight his uniform hung on him.

Melora moved forward, put her hands out, took one of

Gideon's in hers and said, "I'm sorry to see you here, too, Gideon. How have you been?"

"Well, I'm alive." Gid smiled slightly. His face was drawn, and his cheeks sunken from lack of good diet. His eyes were sunk back in his head and were bright with fever.

Clay could tell that his body was hot, and he said urgently, "You're sick, Gid. You need to be in a hospital."

Gideon shrugged and answered in a rather hopeless tone, "Hospital's full, Clay. To get in there you have to be almost dead. I'll make out all right here."

Clay felt helpless, and a burst of anger ran through him as he looked at the emaciated form of his cousin. He and Gid had been suitors for Melanie Benton when they were younger, and there had been a time when Clay had hated Gideon with all his heart. But that was all gone. Now he felt pity and love for the feeble figure that stood before him. "Here, sit down, Gid," he said.

Gideon sat down and said with a wan smile, "That feels good. We don't have any furniture, you know."

"No furniture!" Melora exclaimed. "Not any at all?"

"No, I guess the Confederacy hasn't gotten around to making beds and chairs for prisoners."

"That's terrible," Melora exclaimed. "Would they let us bring some in?"

"I don't know what they'd do," Gid said, shrugging. "You can try, I suppose. Sure would be nice to lie down on a good pad again. If you can't get a bed in, some kind of a mattress—even shucks—that would be better than that hard floor." He looked up quickly and said, "I don't mean to complain. I know it's not your fault."

Clay's mind was working rapidly, and he said, "This place is terrible, Gid! There must be some way to get you exchanged."

Gideon shook his head. "I had hoped for that, but exchanges move awfully slow. It has to go through both commands, you know—Confederate and Federal. So, somebody somewhere is sitting around figuring who to trade for who. But there's always hope."

"I'll write to Melanie at once," Clay said. "And in the meantime I'll pull all the strings I can to get you a better place. Now, what would you like us to bring you?"

Gid sat before them in the chair, his hands grasping the arms. He licked his lips, which were cracked, and shook his head. "I guess we need about anything you can think of—medicine, bedding, food." He looked up suddenly and said, "You know, Clay, I thought a lot about getting killed in battle, and I thought about getting wounded, but it never once occurred to me that I would be captured. That's funny, isn't it?"

Melora put her hand on his shoulder and said, "You just wait, Gideon. We'll be going pretty soon, but when I come back, you'll see what I have for you!"

"Thank you, Melora. I appreciate that." He looked up at Clay and said, "I've written to Melanie. Don't tell her how bad it is here. No point in worrying her. I'm sure I'll be all right."

"Of course you will! The good Lord's going to take good care of you," Clay said heartily. For twenty minutes the three talked. Then Clay, seeing that Gideon was getting tired, said quickly, "We'll be going now, but we'll be back this afternoon with some blankets—maybe a bed. I'll see what I can do in the way of getting you out of this place."

"Thanks, Clay," Gideon said. He got to his feet slowly, like an old man, and looked at them fondly. "We've come a long way since the old days, haven't we? We Rocklins go back a long way. I remember hunting for bear with you out in the Black River bottoms. You remember that?"

"Sure I do," Clay said. "We'll do it again one day, too, when this is all over."

Gideon looked at him but made no answer. He turned toward the door, and Clay stepped to open it. They watched as he went back through the crowded room toward a dark corner. Then Clay said, "Come on, Melora, let's get out of here. We've got things to do."

When they were outside, Clay took a deep breath and shook his head. "Awful! Just terrible! Look, you go start getting some things together—food, clothes, whatever kind of medicine you think might be good. I'll go talk to the commandant."

"Do you know him, Clay?"

"I know who he is. His name is Maj. Thomas P. Turner. He's commandant of both Libby Prison and Belle Isle. I hear he's a hard man, but I don't see how he could object if we feed prisoners. Come along—I'll get you out of here, and we'll do something about this!"

★ ★ ★

The coal-burning engine loosed a piercing blast as it pulled into the station at Richmond. As soon as the train ground to a halt, Jason rose to his feet and led Allyn down the narrow passageway. Stepping down, he reached back for her hand, took it, and as she stepped to the cobblestone pavement, he said, "We'll have to rent a carriage, Miss Griffeth. I think we'll find one down this way."

Allyn was tired after the journey that had brought them into Richmond. The coach had been hot, and cinders had flown in through the open windows so that she felt coated with soot. "Please," she murmured, "isn't there somewhere I could go clean up before we leave?"

"Why, certainly. As a matter of fact, I think I could use a little washing down, myself. Come along."

He led her to a line of carriages, helped her into one, and they drove to the Patterson Hotel, where Jason had a permanent room when he was ashore. Going to the desk, he spoke to the clerk. "I'll have a room for this lady, James. We'll be leaving early in the morning, so one night will be sufficient."

"Yes, Mr. Larrimore. Number 200 is vacant. Will that be all right?"

"Yes, and have a bath drawn up for her, if you please."
He turned to Allyn and said, "Why don't you go up to
room 200 and have a bath? We'll leave in the morning."

"That would be fine," she said gratefully.

He nodded and said, "I'll have your bag sent up."

She made her way to the room and soon was soaking in a
tub of steaming hot water brought by two tired-looking
maids. She scrubbed and scrubbed—grateful for the luxuri-
ous soaking. As she got out and dried off, she discovered the
journey had exhausted her. Slipping into a simple gown, she
lay down on the bed. The journey had been hard on her in
more ways than one. Physically it had been demanding, as
all travel was, but even harder had been her emotional
tension. She had felt ill at ease with Larrimore. After he had
made several attempts at conversation, to which she had
responded almost in monosyllables, he had taken a newspaper and spent most of his time reading or dozing.

Now as she lay down, sleep came to her quickly, but she
thought as she dozed off, *I almost wish I had never come here.*
I can't see what good it will do to see him. Still, I've always
wanted to see my father. Now's the chance.

The next morning she awoke refreshed. She dressed,
putting on a light-gray dress with white lace at her throat
and wrists. It was a simple dress with plain, clean lines that
fit her well. She put on a small fashionable hat, then went
downstairs, where she found Larrimore waiting in the lobby.

"A hot bath and a good night's sleep do wonders, don't
they?" he said. "Are you ready for a meal?"

"Yes."

After breakfast he led her outside, where he had brought
their carriage. He helped her inside, then drove the carriage
through the town. She examined the streets of Richmond
curiously, thinking how different the city was from New
Orleans. It was the busiest place she had ever seen. The
streets were packed with Confederate soldiers of all ranks, all
hurrying as if they had very urgent business. Intermingled
with them were tradesmen, clerks, businessmen, and poor

people of all sorts, all shoving and jostling each other. They passed by factories as they moved out of the city, one of them with huge smokestacks belching out large clouds of black smoke. "That's the Tredegar Iron Works," Jason informed her. "Makes most of the armament for the Confederate army."

"Richmond's a busy place, isn't it?" she murmured.

"Busiest place in the South, I suppose," he said.

He had discovered she was not a talkative woman. *She's either sullen or perhaps a little frightened of what lies ahead of her.* Choosing to believe the latter, as soon as they were out of the city, he tried again to carry on a conversation. As they passed through the open fields and she commented on the lack of crops, he explained, "The men are all gone to the army—most of them, anyway. Besides, about all people know how to grow around here is cotton, and there's already cotton enough to supply the world, I guess."

"Can't the slaves grow the cotton?" she inquired.

"They can do the work, but what will the planters do with it? It's stacked up on the wharves now high as a mountain. They could sell it if they could get it to England, but the blockade has stopped that." He thought about it for a while, then turned to her. He looked alert, and his light-blue eyes were almost electric. "One of your relatives, Maj. Clay Rocklin, has the right idea. He says all the farms ought to grow food to feed the army, not cotton to sit on some wharf somewhere. But as usual, a prophet has no honor in his own country. They laughed at Clay, but another year of this starving and they'll listen to him, I think."

"What do you think of the war?" she inquired suddenly. He had not said anything about his own feelings. Yet it was apparent that he was a man who could become a soldier. Allyn was accustomed to seeing healthy men in uniform. Even in New Orleans, during the early part of the war, men were jeered at and ridiculed who did not serve, and she was curious about this big, strong man who obviously was fit in every respect.

"I'm just an innocent bystander." Larrimore grinned at her. He seemed cheerful enough about the matter, but as the carriage rolled on through the fields, occupied by slaves who were working in corn fields, he added, "I didn't grow up in the South, so my loyalties aren't here."

"Then you're for the North."

"No, I don't suppose so, at least not enough to put on a uniform and fight."

"But what do you think about the war?"

"I think it's going to ruin the South before it's over. Already the best and finest of the young men have died. That's always the way in a war, I suppose. The best go first and get killed, then the second-rate men have to go. They've been conscripting men for a while. It's not very popular, but that's what it's come to."

The carriage rolled on, and Allyn enjoyed the beauty of the countryside. She was accustomed to the flat land of the delta—New Orleans itself being below sea level. She could see the rising hills to her right and far ahead a blue ridge of mountains. *It's beautiful here,* she thought, *but I wish I knew what I'd find at the end of this trip.*

Jason sat silently in the seat beside her. He was impressed by her beauty. And though he had known many beautiful young women in his life, never had he seen one quite as beautiful as this. She lacked the tenderness or gentleness he liked to see in a woman, but he could understand something about that. *Growing up on the streets of New Orleans must have been a hard thing for a young woman,* he thought. *Men must have been after her. For a young girl, it's either give in or build a wall, and I guess it's best that she's built the wall. I wonder how she and Mark will even talk to each other. I'm afraid he's going to be disappointed if he's expecting her to fall on his neck. I can see she won't do that.*

As they approached Gracefield, he nodded and said, "There's Gracefield over there, one of the finest plantations in the county."

Allyn looked up, startled at the large white house that sat

back off the road. As Larrimore drove the carriage around the large circular driveway, she was impressed with the size and the gracefulness of the house. Large white pillars rose on three sides of the house, and the sunlight struck the many glassed windows as they approached.

Jason stopped the carriage, and a slave came out at once to hold the horses' heads. Leaping down, Jason said, "I guess you can water them and give them a little grain, if you've got any." The slave nodded, and after Allyn stepped to the ground he led the team off.

Allyn felt more nervous than she ever had in her life. "Will you—will you be staying for a while, Mr. Larrimore?"

Glancing at her quickly, and understanding her nervousness, Jason nodded. "Why sure! I'm going to be around for a little while. Come along now. You'll like your father's sister-in-law. She's one of the finest women I've ever known. She lost her husband, Thomas, a short while ago. She'll be glad to see you."

Allyn took his arm as he held it out, and they climbed the steps that led to the large double doors. Before they got there, the door opened and a woman came out. Allyn was taken aback when she came over and held out her hands, saying at once, "You must be Mark's daughter. I'm so glad to see you, my dear! Come in! You must be tired after your long journey."

"Thank you," Allyn murmured. She was impressed with the attractiveness of Susanna Rocklin, who at sixty-two had lost little of her youthful beauty. There was a little gray in her auburn hair, but her blue-green eyes were as bright as ever and her skin still fresh and smooth.

When they were inside, Susanna said, "Why don't you come in the drawing room? We can have something to drink and talk." She gave Allyn another smile and said, "I'm so glad to see you. Come now." She led the way to an opulent drawing room, sat them down, and a black woman came in when she rang a silver bell. "Bring us some lemonade, if you have any of those lemons left, Dorrie."

"Yes'm, we got some."

Susanna turned to the man, saying, "I'm glad to see you again, Capt. Larrimore. Mark has talked about you so much since you've been gone that I feel like we're old friends."

"I hope he didn't tell you everything." Larrimore smiled. "Some of my escapades aren't fit for the ears of ladies, I'm afraid." He felt slightly uncomfortable and said, "If you don't mind, I think I'll walk around the plantation. Might even take a ride on that black horse Mark's told me about."

"Why certainly, you go right ahead, Captain." Susanna recognized the tactfulness of the tall man, and as soon as he bowed and left the room, she said, "He certainly is a fine-looking man, isn't he?"

"I suppose so."

The reply was spoken rather shortly, and at once Susanna put aside her light manner. "This must be very difficult for you, my dear," she said quietly. "Mark has told me a little of the story about your mother. It must have been very hard for you."

Suddenly Allyn wanted to pour out the whole story to this woman who seemed so gentle, so receptive. But years of habit kept her lips shut, and she said merely, "We made out, Mother and I."

Susanna read the face of the young woman, saw the tightness of her lips, and knew at once that there was bitterness in the young woman's heart. She also knew it was too soon for her to start giving advice, so she asked quietly, "Would you like to go up to your father's room now? He was awake a little while ago."

"Y-yes," Allyn said, "I suppose so." She looked at Susanna and asked, "How sick is he?"

"Very ill, I'm afraid. The wound he took has never healed, and the doctors are afraid it's not going to get any better. We're praying for him, and I believe God has done a work just keeping him alive this long." She hesitated, then said, "He's had a strange life, your father. I've never really understood him. He's been different from the rest of the family.

He's been grieving all his life over what happened between him and your mother. He said so to me, so I know you'll be kind."

Allyn nodded, but lifted her head in an impetuous gesture. "If you'll take me to him—"

"Of course. His room is right down the hall."

Allyn followed Susanna out of the room and down the hall, where she paused before a large oak door. She knocked twice, and when a man's voice said, "Come in," she opened the door and entered. When Susanna was inside, she stopped and nodded to Allyn. "Come in, my dear."

Allyn felt light-headed, and her knees were not quite steady as she entered the room. She was breathing rather shallowly as she stopped and faced a tall man who had been sitting in a chair beside a window. He got up rather painfully, and when he turned to Allyn, a shock ran over her. He was not well, she saw at once, but even though he was ill and drawn, she recognized what a fine-looking man he was. Even as this thought came to her, a bitterness touched her, and she thought, *He must have been very handsome when he left my mother.* She had come partly out of curiosity, but now the sight of the man who had deserted her mother brought a hardness to her. She stood there unsmiling as she waited.

"Allyn, this is your father," Susanna said. She hesitated and said, "I'll leave you two alone to get acquainted." She turned and left the room, and when she was outside, she shook her head. "She's bitter against him," she murmured. "I could see it in her eyes and in the very straightness of her back."

The weakness that swept over Mark Rocklin was hard for him to bear, for he was used to keeping himself under control. But now at the sight of the young woman, he felt utterly inadequate. Nevertheless, he forced himself to step forward and said, "My dear, I know this must be very hard for you."

When she did not answer but stood there staring at him with large green eyes, his heart sank, for he recognized the hardness that lay in the young woman. Desperately he said, "Sit down. You must be tired after your long trip."

"Thank you." Allyn sat down and waited for him to speak. She saw how carefully he moved, and as he seated himself in the chair, a spasm of pain touched his face. *He's very sick,* she thought, and then she said nervously in an artificial tone, "I was very surprised when Capt. Larrimore found me in New Orleans."

"How much did he tell you of—of your mother and myself?"

"Very little," Allyn said. She hesitated, then said, "I asked my mother several times who my father was, but she would never tell me anything."

Mark Rocklin sat back in the chair, tried to organize his thoughts. They ran through him riotously, and nothing that came sounded right. Finally he said in a weary tone, "It's too late to change the past. Nobody can ever do that, can they? But let me explain that I never knew you existed. If I had, things would have been different."

"Why did you leave my mother?" Allyn demanded suddenly. "Didn't you love her?"

Mark stared at her, then a smile pulled the corners of his lips up. "You're very like her, you know. You look like her, same eyes, same red hair. Have you ever seen this?" He reached inside his pocket and pulled out a locket of mother-of-pearl and gold. Unsnapping it, he opened it and handed it over.

It was a miniature of her mother. She had never seen it. Taking it in her hand, she held it and studied the young face, the wide innocent eyes, and the gentle lips. "I've never seen this," she said. "She was very pretty."

"You are very like her, Allyn," Mark said quietly. "And her ways, too. She was a strong woman. Much stronger than I," he added with a trace of disgust in his voice.

He took the locket when she handed it back and said, "You'd like to have this one day, and you will." He put the locket back in his pocket and then said, "Well, no time for defense—and I have none to make." He looked out the window, his eyes growing dreamy. "I was a much younger man than I am now and had little sense. I went to New Orleans to have a fling. I was looking for a good time. Instead, I found . . . your mother. . . ."

Allyn sat there, listening to him, feeling as if she were an onlooker on a scene rather than a participant. As he spoke of those days with her mother in New Orleans, she tried to go back and picture them. Her memories of her mother were of hard times when life had been difficult, and she could not imagine the young woman that Mark Rocklin spoke of.

Finally Mark said, "You ask if I loved your mother. I can only say I was a fool. I didn't know what love was. Maybe I still don't. I don't know if anybody does. But I can tell you this one thing—I never got away from her." He turned his eyes back on her, and she saw the pain that was in them. "I've lived to be an old man now, and I don't think a day has passed that I didn't think of her in one way or another. I never married because I never found a woman that could stand beside her in my mind." Suddenly he dropped his eyes, and his fingers tightened as he grasped them, and she had to lean forward to catch his words. "I didn't know," he repeated, "what love was."

A silence ran across the room, and for a time Allyn did not know what to say. She had come with a hardness in her, angry at this man who had deserted her mother. Now, seeing him sick and alone, some of that melted. Yet, it was too much for her, and she finally said, "I don't suppose I'll be staying long, but I—I'm glad that I got to see you at last."

At once Mark looked up and said quickly, "Allyn, I didn't send Capt. Larrimore to get you just so I could meet you." He hesitated, then added, "I didn't do anything for your mother—except bring her heartache. Let me do something for you."

"Something for me?"

"Why yes." There was surprise in his voice, then he

laughed shortly. "Well, I've thought about it so much somehow I guess I thought you knew what I had in mind." He
leaned forward then, and excitement came to his tired eyes.
"I don't know about your life in New Orleans. You may be
very happy there. Is that so?"

"You don't know where Capt. Larrimore found me," she
said evenly. Watching him carefully, she said, "I was dealing
blackjack in the Gay Paree saloon."

Mark blinked in surprise, then shook his head. "I'm not
your judge, Allyn. I know it's been hard for you, and you
have to do what you can to make it. It would be hard for any
young woman."

"After Mother died," she said, "Sam Barker was really the
only friend I had. He owns the Gay Paree. My stepfather
taught me how to play cards, so I went to Sam and asked
him to let me deal blackjack." She drew herself up, and there
was pride in her eyes as she said, "And that's *all* I do—deal
cards—as perhaps Capt. Larrimore will tell you."

"What happened?"

"He showed a little bit too much interest in me and got
thrown out of the place. Devil fly off!" she exclaimed.
"Probably the first time a rich important man like him ever
got thrown out of a saloon."

"I'd like to have seen that," Mark chuckled. "Imagine,
Jason Larrimore getting bounced out of a saloon." He
looked at her and smiled fondly. "'Devil fly off,' you said.
That's what your mother used to say."

"I guess I got some of my Welsh expressions from her,"
Allyn said. Then she straightened up. "Anyway, I can take
care of myself. It's not a very good life, but at least I can have
independence."

"Independence is a fine thing," Mark said, "but it's a
lonely thing, too." He ran his hand over his graying hair and
said, "I ought to know about that. I've been independent all
my life, so I know how lonely that can be." He suddenly
gripped his hands together and said, "Allyn, stay for a while.
There could be a good life for you here. I have some money

that I've been putting back. Never knew what I wanted to do with it. But we could buy a place, a plantation. They are cheap enough now that the war has come. You could be independent there, too."

"Me, stay in Virginia?" Allyn had thought about this, but now it seemed impossible. "What would I do here? I don't know anyone. My whole life is in New Orleans."

Mark had gained considerable wisdom over his years, and he knew that this proud young woman could not be coerced, so he did not try. "You may want to go back to New Orleans, and if you do, I'll help you so that you don't have to work at all, if you don't want to. I don't want to run your life, Allyn. All I want to do is help you." He looked out the window and swept his hands in a gesture at the gracious lawn outside. "But Gracefield is your heritage. Your grandfather was here. Your roots and your people are here." He looked back at her and said, "If you'd just give them a chance, they'll accept you."

"A blackjack dealer from a New Orleans saloon?" she jibed. "I don't think so. That's not the idea I have of Southern gentry."

Mark knew it was useless to argue, but he said, "Will you stay for a week? Just meet the family, then if you want to go back, we'll work out something for you there."

Allyn struggled for a moment, then finally nodded and said, "All right, I'll stay for a week. We'll see how it goes."

"Fine, fine," Mark exclaimed. He reached out, and before she thought, Allyn took his hand. He held it gently, put his other over it, and studied her face. A silence ran through the room, and finally he said, "You're very like your mother, my dear. Very like her."

CHAPTER NINE
A Ball at Gracefield

✦

Melora sat at the kitchen table peeling potatoes. When Rena came in, she looked up and smiled. "Sit down and help me peel these potatoes. I don't think I'll ever get through with them."

Rena was wearing her usual garb—a pair of old pants that were faded with many washings and a brown-and-white checkered shirt. "Oh, I *hate* peeling potatoes!" she complained, but nonetheless flopped down beside the other woman. Picking up a knife, she began spiraling off potato peelings. After the two women had talked for a while Rena said, "I don't know what's wrong with Mark's daughter. She just doesn't seem to fit in here, does she?"

"Well, she's had a different kind of life than you, Rena," Melora answered. "A harder life in a lot of ways. It will just take her a little time to settle down."

"She's not very friendly," Rena complained. "She stays by herself most of the time. I've offered to take her riding, but she says she doesn't care anything about horses."

"I wish you'd keep on making yourself available, Rena. Allyn needs a friend. She's at a critical time in her life right now, and she needs all the prayer and help and friendship that she can get. You can imagine, can't you, how it would be if you were plucked up out of Gracefield and plumped

113

down in New Orleans in the midst of that kind of life, without any family? Think how hard it would be for you." She looked across at the girl with a smile and said, "It's been hard for me coming to Gracefield."

Rena looked up with surprise, her wide eyes taking in her stepmother. "Hard for you? Why, you've been around Gracefield most of your life, and we've known you forever, it seems."

"It's not the same thing." Melora shook her head and placed the potato she had just peeled on top of the stack of those already completed. Putting down the knife, she wiped her hands on her apron, then leaned back in the chair, her eyes thoughtful. "I grew up in a world almost as different from the one you have here as Allyn's. I was the daughter of a poor farmer. Why, Rena, you can't imagine how I thought about the life here at Gracefield! To me it was like a fairyland where everybody wore pretty clothes all the time and nobody ever worked and life was just one constant stream of dances and fancy affairs. And all the time I was out feeding hogs and chopping cotton."

"Well, it's not always like that," Rena said rather indignantly. "We *do* work around here—as you've found out by now!"

Melora laughed. "Yes, I know now. I'm just saying it was hard for me to come here, and it's even more difficult for Allyn." She smiled gently, adding, "That's why we must be very kind and very open to her."

Rena picked up another potato. She thought for several minutes about what Melora had said, then murmured, "She's so beautiful, Melora, isn't she?"

"Yes, she is."

"But Uncle Mark doesn't seem happy at all. I thought he would be after he got her back again."

"Well, he doesn't actually have her *back*. She's just here for a visit. But I know he'd like for her to stay." She rose and picked up the potatoes, saying thoughtfully, "I suppose that's enough for now." Going to the sink, she put them down, poured some water from a bucket over them, then turned back to Rena. "I've tried and tried to think of some way we could make her feel more at home—perhaps persuade her to stay here. But she's built a wall around her a mile high."

Rena rose and shrugged. "Well, I don't—" She halted abruptly, a light coming into her eyes as she said excitedly, "I know what we could do, Melora!"

"Do? Do about what?"

"Do about Allyn, of course!" Rena's eyes shone, and she spoke rapidly as she always did when she was excited. "Melora, she's all alone out here—never meets anybody. Why don't we have a party—or even a ball here at the house? She would meet people, and I think that would bring her out of herself. She's so pretty, and the soldiers would swarm her like flies to honey! Now *that* would make her feel at home!"

Melora's first impulse was to reject the idea, but as she stood there she realized that Mark's desire was not likely to come to pass. "We do need to do *something*," she murmured thoughtfully.

"Oh, let's do it!" Rena said. "It'd be *fun*, Melora! We haven't had anything around here for so long, and after Gettysburg, it's been so miserable! Everybody's so depressed and downhearted. We *need* something like that!"

Rena was correct in her evaluation, for after the carnage of Gettysburg, the city of Richmond had become one huge hospital. The wagons had struggled home bringing thousands of wounded men. Almost every house contained at least one of them, and Chimborazo, the largest Confederate hospital, was packed to capacity. The defeat at Gettysburg had sapped the spirit of the Confederacy. When Lee had led his army forth, it had been with high hopes that one battle would convince England to come in and recognize the Confederacy as an independent nation. If that had been done, loans could have been negotiated, the blockade could have been broken, and the future of the South would have been bright indeed.

Now, however, after the debacle in Pennsylvania, as Lee brought the broken army of Virginia back home, the entire Confederacy seemed to be broken—almost as badly as the army. Life went on, as it had to, but the grief of thousands of families who had lost husbands and fathers and brothers hung like a pall over the land. Enlistments in the army practically came to a halt so that another conscription obviously would follow soon. The factories at Richmond continued to pour out the tools of war, but something had gone out of the Confederacy.

The high tide of the Cause for which the South had gone to war had been reached when George Pickett led his Virginians in the last futile charge at Gettysburg. A few had reached the summit of the hill, and for one brief moment it seemed as though the South would win—that Lee's forces would be victorious. But then, overwhelmed by the superiority of numbers, Pickett's men were driven back down the hill, leaving a carpet of blood shed by dying and wounded men. From that moment on, it seemed the South had lost that fervor that had led them into secession. Now, though Jefferson Davis tried to whip up excitement and patriotism, it was not the same as it had been during the early days of the strife. Most people knew the inevitable outcome of the war—defeat—but no one would speak the thought aloud.

Melora thought of this and nodded. "I think you're right, Rena. There's been so much grief, so much sorrow. Maybe what we need is a little gaiety in life. I don't know what Clay will say, though."

"Oh, Daddy will do whatever we tell him to," Rena said airily. She smiled suddenly, adding, "Ever since he came back again, I know how to handle him. He's easy, Melora! All you have to do is just hang on him a little bit and pat his cheek and tell him how nice he looks. Things like that, you know. Even if he says no, if you keep on, he'll always give in."

Melora laughed with delight, "You are a caution, Rena

Rocklin!" She stared out the window at the tall oaks, then nodded firmly. "All right, we'll have a ball. Come now, let's sit down and figure out how we can afford it and when it will be."

"Well, I know one thing," Rena said excitedly as she sat down with the older woman, "I'm going to make Josh buy a fancy suit. And I'm going to have the first dance with him and the last one too, maybe."

"That young man—" Melora shook her head solemnly— "will never know what hit him. Come now, let's make some plans. . . ."

★ ★ ★

As balls go among the gentry of the South, the affair held at Gracefield was not much. The large ballroom that occupied part of the lower floor of the mansion was comfortably filled, but not to overflowing as it had been during happier times. This was primarily because so many of the young men were away in the army, many of them in Tennessee—and even those in the Army of Northern Virginia were scattered out in a thin line to defend the city.

Nevertheless, when Josh Yancy rode up on his bay gelding, his heart almost failed him, for it looked like a fairyland to him. He arrived at dusk, when the lanterns had been lit and were casting their amber gleam over the outside of the house. He could see through the large windows the women in their colored dresses and the officers in their gray uniforms. It startled him, and he muttered, "Gosh, I won't fit in this place at all! I don't know why I let Rena talk me into this!"

He halted, pulled up the bay, and swung to the ground. Box, one of the slaves, came to him with a flash of gleaming white teeth. "Yes suh, Mistuh Josh, let me take that fine-looking hoss."

Feeling very awkward, Josh grinned. "I almost turned around and rode away, Box, when I saw all the fancy dresses and uniforms in there. I'm as nervous as a long-tailed cat in a roomful of rocking chairs!"

"Naw suh, you go right on in and find Miss Rena. She been looking fo' you. You look mighty fine, Mistuh Josh! You go right on in and have yo'self a fine time!"

Josh took some courage from the friendly words. He walked to the steps and joined those who were filing in. When he entered, he heard the sound of music and turned at once to the ballroom. He looked around with shock for he had never seen the ballroom decorated for a party, and he now studied it carefully.

Lighted prisms dangled below glass shades on the lofty ceiling. They cast miniature rainbows on the dancers who already whirled and glided across the glistening parquet floor of the ballroom. All around the walls, green velvet draperies framed the scene. Intricately wrought Spanish ironwork decorated a broad staircase that led to a second floor with a balcony that accommodated the musicians. It was really late in the year for flowers, but somehow some had been found, mostly wildflowers, and these filled vases, adding splashes of color to the room. Overhead on the small balcony nine musicians worked at sending out the music that floated over the room. There were two violins, a dulcimer, several guitars, and even an accordion and a couple of banjos.

Shifting his gaze to the dance floor, Josh saw that the dominant color was the gray of the officers' uniforms, set off by the black sheen of boots and the golden flash of brass buttons. But it was the dresses of the women that caught his eye, as they flashed to the strain of a waltz. Some of them were startlingly décolleté, glowing in brilliant colors of sapphire, yellow, pink, green, and white.

"Josh—I've been waiting for you!"

Rena appeared before him and took his arm possessively. She was wearing a yellow dress with puffed sleeves and tiny blue stripes on the skirt. Her hair was done up in a way he had not seen before, and for a moment Josh felt that she was a total stranger. "Gosh, you look . . . you look . . ."

"Well, how do I look? Tell me," Rena teased him.

Josh was not a young man with a free flow of words. He had struggled with a stutter most of his life, and now in this strange environment he knew he had to be very careful. "You look pretty as a wildflower," he said slowly.

Rena's eyes widened, and she said, "Why, Josh, you're getting to be a poet. That's the nicest compliment!" She stood back and looked him over. She had insisted he take the money he was going to spend on a new rifle and buy himself a new suit for the ball. She had not seen the suit yet, and now she examined him closely. "Why, Josh, you look so *handsome!* That's a beautiful suit!" She eyed the suit, which consisted of a pair of light-brown trousers, a fingertip-length dark linen coat, a wine-colored waistcoat, and a ruffled white shirt with a black string tie. He was a tall, lean young man, and in his new suit he looked very masculine and handsome.

Rena smiled and grabbed his arm. "Josh, you stay away from that Mary Wadsworth," she whispered. "She's already told me how handsome she thinks you are—but if she makes a move at you, I'll scratch her eyes out! Come on now, let's dance."

Josh blinked his eyes and shook his head. "Well—I don't know, Rena, I'm not much of a dancer."

"I've taught you, and I'm a good teacher," she said. "Come on now!" Soon he was moving awkwardly through the steps of the dance, and the two were chatting away.

"My brother and Rena make a nice-looking couple, don't they, Clay?" Melora and Clay were standing beside the refreshment table. He lifted his eyes to see the couple. "Yes, they do," he said. He looked at Melora and grinned. "Not as nice looking as us, though."

"Well, of course not!" she mocked him, and then she giggled. "We're so vain, aren't we? But we are nice looking for an old couple."

Clay looked down at Melora, who wore a green dress that

brought out the color of her eyes, and said, "You'll never be old. When you're ninety, you'll be as beautiful as you are right now."

Melora squeezed his arm. "I'm glad you think so, but you're going to have to put up with me, no matter what I look like."

Now they stood there chatting for a while. Finally, Clay said, "Look, there's Larrimore. I thought he had left on one of his blockade-running expeditions."

Melora glanced in the direction of his nod. "Why, I thought so, too. I'm glad he came, though. He seems to do Mark so much good. He always cheers him up."

"He's a strange companion for Mark, isn't he?"

"I don't think so. As a matter of fact, they are alike in a lot of ways."

"Alike? How?" Clay asked.

"They're both alone. I imagine Jason Larrimore is a lot like Mark when he was that age." She looked across at Larrimore, who was dancing with a young woman who was staring up at him with fascination in her eyes. Melora shook her head. "He's a handsome thing, isn't he?"

"Oh, I don't know about that, but he's a good captain— or so I hear. He runs through that blockade like he's going for a stroll in the park. He's probably the best blockade-runner the Confederacy has, and he's getting rich at it, too."

Melora glanced at the stairs and said, "Allyn hasn't come down yet. Let me go up. It would be better if I came down with her and introduced her."

"Well, you'll have to fight some of these officers off, I think. I don't believe their manners are as excellent as their shooting."

Melora left the ballroom and climbed the stairs to where Allyn had been given a room on the second floor. She paused at the door and asked, "Allyn, can I come in?"

"Yes, come in."

When Melora entered, she stopped abruptly and stared at the girl. "Why, Allyn, how nice you look!"

Allyn was wearing a ball gown made of fine silk. It was a delicate dove gray with rose stripes. Clusters of pink rosebuds gathered the fullness of her billowing skirt into festoons above a silken laced petticoat that rustled with the slightest motion. Her shoulders were exposed and looked creamy and smooth. Her auburn hair was done up in a graceful swirl, and her eyes looked enormous, though somewhat troubled.

"That's a beautiful dress. You got it in New Orleans, I suppose?" Melora asked, coming over to touch the material. "My, I've never seen a dress so pretty."

"Well, I don't know what made me buy it. I never thought I'd have anywhere to wear it," Allyn said. She seemed subdued and looked at Melora. "I feel so—so *strange,*" she said. "I wish I didn't have to go to the ball!"

"Why of course you're going—and you'll have a fine time, too. There are some of your family you'll have to meet—Clay's son Dent and some of the Bristols and the Franklins, too. Come along now."

"Well, I suppose I must." Allyn stood there diffidently and finally said, "I don't belong in this place. I feel like a total stranger. I—I just don't belong here."

"Well, neither do I," Melora said quickly. "You know, I've told you the kind of family I had, where I came from, but God's put me here."

Allyn's eyes narrowed, and her lips grew thin. "I don't believe in God," she said rebelliously.

If she had expected to shock Melora, she did not. Melora had already discovered that Allyn Griffeth was a girl who had been so hurt and bruised by life that she had closed her heart to all thoughts of God. Now Melora only smiled and said gently, "You may not believe in him, but he believes in you."

Her statement caught Allyn off guard. Her lips parted with surprise, but she could think of nothing to say and stood there examining Melora. Finally, she shrugged. "I've been talking to my father. He wants to adopt me legally, but I don't know what to do."

Melora felt a great urge to put her arm around the girl, but she knew that there was still a wall there. "Why, I think that would be wonderful, if you would agree to it, Allyn. Not that we would love you any less if you kept your mother's name. But it would make your father so happy—and all of us, as a matter of fact."

The gentleness of the woman took some of the rebellious light out of Allyn's eyes. She had not expected Mark's proposal of adoption, which he had made only the night before. It had disturbed her, and she could not understand why such turbulent thoughts came to her over this. For long hours she had lain awake wondering what to do, but when she had awakened early in the morning, she still was confused. All day she had kept to her room, except for one long walk through the woods that surrounded the mansion. Now as she stood before Melora, the decision was clear. "I think I will," she said. She twisted her hands nervously and added, "There's really nothing for me to go back to in New Orleans. I don't know how it will be here, but I'd like to stay for a while, anyway."

Melora then did move forward and kissed the girl on the cheek. "I think you're making a very wise choice," she said gently. "Your father loves you, and you'll have a family. Come along now, and I can introduce you as Allyn Rocklin, the daughter of Mark Rocklin."

Allyn moved along the hall, something like fear coming to her. She had made a decision that she knew would impact her whole life. She had no idea what the days to come would bring, but she had grown weary of life in New Orleans, of fighting off unwelcome advances, of the tawdriness of the life that she led dealing cards in a saloon. Some of the gracefulness of the life at Gracefield still remained, though scarred and battered by the hammering of the war effort. And she had seen in Melora, Rena, Rooney, and Susanna—the women of the plantation—a quality that she admired. She knew herself to be much harder than any of these and regretted it, but now, as she moved down one of the curving stairways, she thought, *No matter what happens here, it couldn't be any worse than dealing cards in the Gay Paree!*

When she reached the foot of the stair, at once she was met by Clay, who took her hand, saying, "You look beautiful, Miss Allyn. Come, let me introduce you to some of my officers."

They were surrounded instantly by a group of young officers. One of them, a tall dark-haired man in a captain's uniform, seemed to edge himself forward, past the others, and Melora smiled. "Gentlemen, I want you to meet the newest member of the Rocklin family, Miss Allyn Rocklin, from New Orleans. Some of you have served with her father, Mark Rocklin."

The tall captain bowed at once and said, "Miss Allyn, let me be the first to welcome you to your new home. May I claim the first dance?"

Clay laughed, "This is Capt. Will Farley, Allyn, one of our most dashing young officers. He is headed for promotion. You can see how he's outmaneuvered the rest of his fellow officers."

A groan went up from the other officers, but Farley simply stepped forward and held out his arm. "Come, Miss Allyn. As we dance I'll tell you about what terrible fellows these are so that you will be forewarned."

Allyn liked the look of the tall young man and said, "Why, of course, Captain, but then I'll have to ask Maj. Rocklin to tell me all about *your* shortcomings."

A laugh went up as the two moved off to a waltz, and Clay said, "You fellows will just have to wait your turn. Looks like you better form a line."

"Clay," Melora said, "why don't you go and see if Mark would feel like coming to the ballroom. I'm sure he would enjoy seeing Allyn dance."

"That's a good idea. I was just about to do that."

Clay moved out of the ballroom, walked quickly to Mark's room, and knocked on the door. When he entered he found Mark dressed and seated in his usual place beside the table.

"You feel like a little trip, Mark?" he asked. "Allyn's already got half the company ready to shoot each other. She's a beautiful young woman."

Mark looked thin, but there was a light of anticipation in his eyes. "I believe I can make it if you'll stick close beside me. I don't want to go in a blasted wheelchair."

"You'll do fine, just hang on to me if you need to," Clay encouraged him.

They made their way down the hall and entered the ballroom. Clay maneuvered Mark over to the line of chairs along one side of the wall and said, "Here, let's sit down and watch for a while."

Clay was concerned about Mark, for his face was pale, and pain drew his mouth into a thin line. They talked for a few moments, and several of the officers came by to express their concern and to see how Mark was faring. Mark only half paid attention, for he had eyes only for Allyn. He watched her as she danced with first one and then another young officer and said, "Clay, she's the prettiest thing I've ever seen!"

"Well, I haven't seen an ugly Rocklin woman yet," Clay said. "She is a beautiful young woman." He shifted his weight, wanting to ask a question but not knowing how. "How are you two doing?" he asked finally.

Mark rubbed his hands across his chin thoughtfully. "Better than I have any right to expect," he admitted. "But she's an unhappy young woman, and it's mostly my fault." Pain struck him along the side; he took a deep breath and tried not to show it. The pains were becoming more frequent now, more severe, and he knew that he could not conceal them from the sharp eyes of those who knew him. Taking a deep breath he said, "I've got to do something for her, Clay. I've failed her all my life, and now I can't let it go on like this."

"What do you want to do, Mark?"

"Why, I'd like to buy a place and have her be the mistress of it. Not as large as Gracefield, of course," he added quickly, "but I've been saving some money most of my life." He smiled at Clay, saying, "You didn't think that, did you? You thought I was the prodigal, throwing money away right and left. I guess I was for a few years. But then I got tired of that. I've been making a few investments."

"Not in Southern stocks, I hope."

"No, mostly in Northern railroads, and they're doing very well. I can cash in now and have enough to buy a nice place."

Clay said excitedly, "You know, Twelve Trees is for sale. Jennings is giving up."

Twelve Trees was a medium-sized plantation five miles away from Gracefield. It had a fine home, not elaborate, but well built and solid. The mention of it at once caught Mark's attention. "Twelve Trees—I've always liked that place. Not too big, just a nice size. How much do you think Jennings would have to have?"

"Well, it's a buyer's market," Clay said with a shrug. "You know how much plantations are worth as much as I do." He looked over and asked, "Would you like Jennings to come over and talk to you about it?"

"Yes. Will you go see him tomorrow?"

"Sure. That'd be a fine place for you and Allyn."

"I don't know about me, but I would like to leave her a legacy. If she doesn't want that, I'm going to leave her the money anyway. Somehow I think she needs roots, and her only family in New Orleans is gone. She needs a family, but I've robbed her of that."

"Mark, you've got to stop beating yourself up about this," Clay interrupted. "You did a wrong thing. All right, so have we all. Think about what I did; I forsook my family and left them to come up alone—and I knew about my children. You didn't. So, I've done worse than you, but God has given it all back to me."

The remark struck Mark, and he said, "You know, that's right, isn't it? Since I've started reading the Scripture and asked God to come into my life, I've found out that God can do anything he wants to."

"That's right. Now we'll just have to pray that Allyn will

find her way, that she'll accept us as a family, just like we accept her. And it'll happen, too, you wait and see!"

As the two men talked, Allyn swept around the floor. She was dancing with a rather overweight young lieutenant when she saw her father and said, "Oh, look. I really ought to go speak to my father."

"Why, certainly, Miss Allyn. Let me do the honors." Lt. Grigsby led her across the floor, disappointed at being robbed of some of his time with her, but hopeful that he would make it up on another dance.

"Don't get up," Allyn said to Mark. "I just wanted to come and say what a nice ball it is. Father, this is Lt. Grigsby. Lieutenant, my father, Mr. Mark Rocklin."

The two men shook hands, and Mark's face glowed with pleasure at her reference to him as "my father." He said, "You look absolutely beautiful, Allyn. Are you having a good time?"

"Oh yes. Lt. Grigsby and his fellow officers are all quite gallant."

"Well, you'll have to watch out for this one," Clay said. "He has a fiancée, you know."

"Why, sir, didn't I tell you," Grigsby said. "My fiancée and I—well, we decided to call it off."

Allyn was amused at the young lieutenant's agony and said, "Well, perhaps you'll make it up with her, Lieutenant." This did not seem to assuage Lt. Grigsby, but finally when Allyn allowed him to take her back on the floor, Clay smiled. "She has a real sense of humor. A fine girl."

"Yes, she has. But she's also hard, Clay, but what could you expect after what she's been through?" Suddenly Mark said, "Look—there's Larrimore. He's cutting in on that poor lieutenant of yours."

Lt. Grigsby felt a hand on his shoulder, and when he turned he found himself maneuvered out of position. The tall man asked, "Do you mind too much, Lieutenant?" Then, without waiting for an answer, he simply waltzed off with the young woman.

Allyn was startled by the sudden appearance of Jason Larrimore. She looked up at him and said, "I thought you were going off on a voyage."

"No, the ship wasn't quite ready, but I'll be leaving soon." He looked down at her and said, "You look lovely. Have you enjoyed your time here?"

Allyn nodded. "Yes," she said diffidently, "it's been very nice." A thought came to her, and she said, "I suppose now that I'm going to be a Rocklin, you've come to court me."

Jason grinned down at her. He was wearing a fine gray suit, and a large diamond stickpin glittered on the cravat at his throat. "Well, I'm not the marrying kind, Miss Allyn. Now, if you're interested in other arrangements—"

His words suddenly angered her, and she drew back. "No, Capt. Larrimore, I am *not* interested in your 'other' arrangements!" She turned and left him standing alone on the floor. He watched her go and shook his head, saying to himself, *You're a fool, Larrimore. Why'd you have to say a thing like that?*

Josh and Rena had been watching the pair, and as Allyn left the tall man standing alone, Rena said, "They've had a quarrel of some kind."

"Yep." Josh nodded. "She looks mad as a wet hen, doesn't she? Wonder what he said to her?"

"I don't know. Josh, you go dance with that girl over there, and I'll see what I can find out."

"You mean that ugly one?"

"She's not ugly. She's just plain."

"Oh." He sounded rebuked but said, "Well, I really would rather dance with that girl over there, the one in the green dress."

"No," Rena said firmly, "you wouldn't want to dance with her. Just do what I tell you. That girl is Mary Higgins, and she's a very nice young lady. Now, you go dance with her, and I'll go talk to Allyn."

She turned and walked away, and Josh shrugged. Melora came to stand beside him. "What was Rena telling you?"

"She was telling me to go dance with that ugly—I mean *plain*—girl over there in the red dress."

"Well, are you going to mind her?" Melora teased him.

Josh grinned at her and nodded. "Reckon I will. You always mind Mr. Clay, don't you?"

"He likes to think so," Melora said smoothly. She reached up, patted his cheek, saying, "Go along now and do what Rena told you."

As soon as he was gone, she made her way to Jason Larrimore, who had moved off the dance floor and was headed for the door.

"Are you leaving, Capt. Larrimore?"

Larrimore turned and nodded. "Why yes, Mrs. Rocklin, I suppose I am."

She said, "Please don't go yet. Go and sit with Mark awhile. He enjoys your company so much."

"I'd be glad to. I'll be leaving soon and won't get to see him for a while. But—" he shrugged as he spoke—"Miss Allyn is not too pleased with my company." He frowned and said, "I guess I'm just a rough sailor. I've hurt her feelings, I'm afraid."

"You've done her a great service," Melora said. "She'll recognize that. Don't mind if she gets upset."

He smiled at her and said, "All right, I'll go visit with Mark for a while."

He went over, and Melora watched as the three men sat there talking. Mark, as always, was glad to see Jason Larrimore, and Melora nodded with satisfaction. "I wonder how he hurt her feelings?" she murmured, then turned and went back to her duties as hostess.

CHAPTER TEN
"I'll Have What I Want!"

The day after the ball, Allyn slept until ten, then went down for a late breakfast. She found Susanna looking worried as Dorrie set the food on the table.

"That was a wonderful ball last night," Allyn said, as she ate the eggs the black woman put before her. "I suppose you've seen bigger ones before the war."

"Oh yes," Susanna affirmed.

Susanna seemed unusually quiet, unlike herself, and Allyn said, "What's the matter—is something wrong?"

Susanna sipped the cup of sassafras tea that she usually drank in the morning. The pressures of running the plantation were great, and she looked tired. "Your father's not well this morning. I suppose going to the ball was too much for him last night." She sipped the tea, made a face, and put it down. "How I'd love to have some good China tea again! They don't have room on the blockade-runners for luxuries like that. It's all bullets and gunpowder now." She paused, put on a happier face, and said, "I'm glad you've decided to become a Rocklin."

The simple sentence seemed to trouble Allyn. She flushed slightly and pushed the eggs around her plate with the silver fork. "I thought about it and decided that would be best, but I still feel strange here."

"Why, the family all accepted you. Surely you could see that after last night?"

"Oh yes, they were all very nice, but that's not like being a member of the family."

"Time will change things. You'll grow more accustomed to things here. Now, I think you should go see your father this morning. He wants to talk to you."

"All right, I will."

Allyn got to her feet and left the small dining room. When she reached Mark's room, she knocked on the door. After a brief silence, a voice said "Come in." She entered the room and saw that Mark was still in bed. Pausing she said, "Oh, I didn't know you weren't up." Turning, she said, "I'll come back later."

"No, come in, Allyn." Mark struggled to a sitting position and tried to arrange the pillows behind his back. Seeing that he was in pain, Allyn walked over and helped him adjust the pillows. "Thanks a lot," he said. "Sorry to be such a confounded baby."

"I took care of Mother a lot when she was sick," Allyn said. She sat down beside him and said, "I'm sorry to see you're feeling so bad today."

Mark shrugged his thin shoulders and said, "I can't complain. I get better care here than I would anywhere else." He looked at her and said thoughtfully, "It's good to have you here, Allyn. I watched you at the ball last night. I was very proud of you."

"I'd never been to a ball like that before. One of the things I missed, I suppose."

"Didn't you go to any dances, parties, or anything like that?"

Allyn leaned forward, her eyes thoughtful. "I can remember when I was twelve years old—Mother bought me a new dress. There was a party at our school. I know she worked hard to save the money for it. It was pink and had blue bows on it, I remember. We didn't have the money to get my hair fixed, so Mother did it herself. I remember how excited I was when I went to the party."

Mark, seeing that an unhappiness had come into her voice, said, "What happened?"

"Oh, it wasn't any good. I was an outsider, and you know how children are. Two of them get along very well, but you put three of them together, they'll shut one out."

Mark blinked his eyes in surprise. "Why, I never noticed."

"You never watched that with children?"

"I guess I haven't been around too many children. Is that really the way they are?"

Allyn pushed a strand of hair back over her ear and nodded. "Yes, most of them, and it doesn't stop with the children either. Most people are like that, I guess. They like to form little clubs where they can be at the top and close everybody else out."

Mark thought about it and nodded abruptly. "You know, that's right. When I think back on it, that's the way most of life is, everybody wanting to be at the top." He gave her a quick glance, adding, "I guess if everybody were at the top, there wouldn't be any way to be exclusive. You are a very bright young woman."

"Oh, not very," she said. She was uncomfortable in his presence. Somehow the very knowledge that he had sent for her disturbed her. She had been angry with him subconsciously all of her life and now found it impossible to simply say that all was well. As she sat there, the two of them talking, she noticed that even during her brief stay, he seemed to have gotten worse. His skin was a sallow grayish color, with very little color in it, and she could tell his eyes were filled with the same sort of pain her mother had had. *I wish I could like him better,* she thought. *But how can I after what he did to Mother and to me!* "Would you like for me to read to you, or play cards maybe?" She managed to smile, saying, "I don't think you could beat me, though."

"You don't? Well, we'll find out. I think there's a deck over in that bureau drawer."

Allyn got the cards, and for the next hour they played various games. They were pretty evenly matched, and Mark was surprised. "You're a good cardplayer," he said. "Better than any woman I ever saw, at least at poker and blackjack."

"I had a good teacher—" Allyn shrugged—"my stepfather. He wasn't much good for anything else, but he was a good cardplayer—but not good enough to stop losing all his money. If it weren't for him, though, I wouldn't have been able to get that job in the Gay Paree dealing blackjack. I don't know what I'd have done if it weren't for that. Nothing very good, though."

Mark's face grew more sober as she made this remark. He said, "I'm sorry I wasn't around, Allyn."

"Look, you don't have to apologize every time we talk. You've said all that before." Her voice was a little sharp. She said, "Let's don't mention it again, if you don't mind."

"All right, then, I won't." He sat there for a moment silently and then said, "I was talking to Clay last night. Something came up that I wanted to talk to you about."

"What is it?"

"It's about your future. He told me about a plantation called Twelve Trees. It's not too far from here, about five miles. It's a nice place, not big like this one, but it has a nice house on it. I've been there several times; our two families visited quite a bit. The owner's selling out now—going north, I suppose." He hesitated, not knowing how to say what was on his heart. He wanted more than anything else in the world to please this girl, to bring happiness and joy into her life. But somehow that had become a spiritual matter as well. Part of his repentance, he assumed. He needed to make things right, and now he said quietly, "Allyn, would you live there, if I would buy the place?"

"Live there?" She was taken off guard. "You mean permanently—from now on?"

"Yes." He grew eager and said, "We could find someone to help with the work there. There's a good overseer, an older man. He takes care of the place mostly. Too old for the army, and there are enough hands to keep things going. Oh, it'll never be a great plantation, but we could buy it, and it would be in the clear. No matter what happens with the war or whatever, you'd always have it."

He hesitated and dropped his head. He fingered the gaily covered quilt that lay across his lap, tracing the orange and red and green designs that had been made by his mother, and he'd always loved it. He asked for it every time he came to Gracefield—a touch of the past that always moved him. Now, he said, "It would give you some options. It would be yours, of course, after I'm gone, to do with as you please. If it didn't work, you could always sell it for what it was worth and do something else." He lifted his eyes, and there was a pleading in them as he asked, "Would that please you, do you think?"

Allyn stared at him for one moment, disconcerted by his offer. She had felt that he would make this sort of an offer, and yet it caught her off guard. "You mean you want to spend all your money and buy that place—just for me?"

"I want to make up for the pain I've caused you, Allyn," he said simply.

For one brief moment she wanted to break down her defenses, reach out, and take him in her arms. There was a gentleness in this girl, but she had buried it so deeply it could find no way of expression. Now she sat there in the silence of the room, watching this man who had suddenly appeared out of nowhere, emerging from a past that was so dim she had no inkling of what lay there—and she didn't know what to say. The long years of bitterness were too strong, and finally she heard herself saying, "I'll do it, but I want you to know it's just because I'm selfish. I'll have what I want. You and I can never be very close. Now, do you still want to do it?"

Mark studied the girl and said quietly, "That's what I did. I took what I wanted, and it's not wise. It doesn't bring any happiness, Allyn."

She lifted her chin defiantly. "If you want to buy it, I'll live there. I'll do my best to take care of you, too, but I can't forget all the years that you abandoned me. I'm sorry to talk to you like this when you're sick—but at least you'll know where I stand."

"You're an honest girl," Mark said evenly. "Your mother was the same. Nobody ever had to wonder what she thought." He sat there quietly, then nodded. "All right, we'll buy the place. I think we'll get a bargain." He hesitated, then said, "I hope as time goes by, we'll get closer."

She shook her head, saying quietly, "Don't hope too much for that. It's hard to forget the past."

★ ★ ★

The sale of Twelve Trees proceeded. Clay talked to the owner, and a lawyer came the next day to talk to Mark. They sat together talking for a long time, and later that day Mark said to Allyn, "I think it's going to go all right. He wanted more than it was worth, and I wanted to pay less, but it looks as though we'll own Twelve Trees before too long."

Allyn studied him carefully, then managed to smile. "If you're sure that's what you want, then I'm glad for you. Would it be soon?"

"I think within a week we could take possession. I made an offer on all the furnishings, so all we have to do is move in." He hesitated, then said, "I think we'll have to have one of the slaves come as a body servant, or hire someone. I take a lot of care, I know."

"Oh, I think I can manage," she said calmly. "There'll be some maids there, won't there?"

"Yes, I'm sure there will be. It's just a small place, as I said, but there's an older slave couple that has been there a long time. They have a daughter. They take care of the house, mostly, with some help from one of the younger girls. But I don't want to be a burden on you."

It disturbed her that he seemed to be giving up so much, but Allyn simply said, "All right. We'll manage."

The word soon spread among the family, and the slaves,

of course, knew everything that went on in the Rocklin family. All the others seemed pleased that Allyn and Mark would be living close, but Dorrie had no pleasure in the thought. She was one of the oldest slaves, and she had shared the responsibility with Susanna of managing the huge plantation for so long that she knew the family better than anyone else. It was this familiarity that brought her into conflict with Allyn.

Allyn had come in from the fields where she had been walking, her face flushed. She had picked a bunch of wildflowers and saw Dorrie standing there as she came in the back door. "Dorrie, I need a vase for these flowers. Aren't they pretty?"

Without a word, Dorrie walked over to a cabinet, pulled a large vase out, and handed it to Allyn.

Allyn took the vase and stared at the round face of the older woman. Allyn turned, filled the vase with water from a bucket, and began to arrange the flowers. She said quietly, "Well, Dorrie, it appears you don't like me."

Dorrie had turned to leave, but she stopped now and turned squarely to face the young woman. Her face was lined now, and her step was slower, but her loyalty to the Rocklin family was a fierce thing—after her church and her God, the strongest thing in her life.

"Dat's right," she said evenly.

Allyn looked up and met the eyes of the slave. "Why not?" she asked.

"Cause you doan treat Mistuh Mark right," Dorrie said firmly.

"Why do you say that?"

"He's sick. He ain't got long to live, and he need somebody roun' him with love—and you ain't got none of dat in you."

Startled at the black woman's declaration, a quick anger ran through Allyn. "How do you know that? You don't know anything about me."

Dorrie knew that most slaves would never be honest in a

face-to-face encounter with a white owner, but to her the Rocklin family was almost sacred. Now she faced the young woman fiercely, her lips turned down in a frown. "I knows love when I sees it, and I knows it when I *doan* see it. Mistuh Mark, I knowed him all my life. He's a good man. He ain't always done right. He caused lots of heartache for his family—fo' me, too—but he's good, and now he's done foun' the Lord."

When the older woman stopped, Allyn said, "I didn't ask to come here, Dorrie." She knew that most white women would have lashed out at the slave, yet the direct stare from the brown eyes of Dorrie intimidated her. "I didn't even know who he was. You can't expect me to just walk in and start loving somebody without even knowing them!"

Dorrie hesitated, not wanting to go too far, and yet it infuriated her when anyone mistreated one of the family. "Dat ain't all dere is to it. You're a pretty woman, but dey's a *coldness* in you. You is hard! Mr. Mark don't need dat! He needs someone dat will be good to him, dat will love him. I wish you hadn't never come to dis place!"

Again anger flashed in Allyn's eyes. "You don't know how hard it was for me to grow up without a father."

"Don't I," Dorrie snapped. "You think I had a father? I didn't have *nothin'*, but I learned to love people, and you ain't never learned dat and I doan think you never will."

Allyn could not meet the woman's gaze. She slammed the vase down on the floor so that it broke with a tinkling crash. "You don't know anything about it!" she cried angrily. "I don't have to listen to talk from an old nigger!" she shouted, then whirled and ran from the room and out the front door.

The sun was hot on her face as she left. She heard someone call to her, but she did not turn around. She walked quickly until she found herself back in the trees that bordered the east side of the plantation. A small road led to the summerhouse where Clay had lived when he came back. Rooney and her brother used it now. She had learned that much of the family history. Blindly, she walked down the road, shocked to find tears rolling down her face. She had not cried for years, and now she found herself trembling. "She doesn't know anything about it!" she muttered furiously. "It's none of her business, anyway!"

The August heat was cut off by the trees that arched overhead forming a cathedrallike atmosphere. The ground was soft from a rain that had come the night before so that she made little sound as she walked along the road. Slowly she began to regain her composure and was startled when a large dog came bounding from around the turn, saw her, and came toward her with his head up, barking.

Allyn had never been around large animals, and the dog frightened her. "Get away," she cried, and the dog circled her, barking loudly.

"Buck! Buck! You stop that!"

Rena had appeared, and she came running forward, saying, "Don't pay any attention to Buck. He's all bark and wouldn't hurt a flea."

"I'm afraid of dogs," she said. "I never grew up around animals."

Rena said, "Pet him on the head."

Cautiously Allyn reached forward and touched the animal's head. He licked her hand and barked a booming *woof!*

"He looks so fierce!" Allyn said, feeling slightly better about Buck.

"Well, I guess he'd bite anybody that tried to hurt me," Rena said. She thought and said, "You know, when Daddy first came home, I didn't like him at all because he deserted me and my brothers and my mother. At one time, when he first got here, Buck thought he was going to hurt me and he bit him, laid his arm open." She straightened up, her fine young eyes moody with the thought. "I think that's when I first began realizing that he really cared for me. He let me wash the wound out, and after that he showed me the books that he had brought with him. From that time on, it was all right."

"Must have been hard for you, being brought up with your father gone like that. It was for me."

"Oh yes." Rena nodded. Then she said quickly, "But it was worse for you, I expect, because I had brothers around to help me."

Allyn had liked Rena from the time she met her. She admired her trim young beauty, her enthusiasm. The two were close enough in age so that they could be friends, but when she looked at Rena and saw the innocence in her eyes and thought of her life, she felt almost like a mother to her. "Well," she said, "I guess I'll be going."

"I'll walk back to the house with you. Come on, Buck." The two young women walked back, and Rena chattered on about the ball. "Wasn't Josh fine looking in his new suit?"

Allyn smiled. "You're very fond of that young man, aren't you?"

"Oh, I guess so. You know, when I first met him, he had the most awful stutter. It was because he was afraid to be around people."

"Really? Why, he doesn't stutter at all now."

"No, and you know, I think I was able to help him with that. He was so bashful that he couldn't even look at me, but when we became friends and we fished together, he stopped stuttering so much. Now, it's only when he gets excited or angry."

"Are you in love with him?" Allyn asked.

Rena flushed. "Oh, I don't know. Maybe someday it'll come to that. He's the best friend I have in the world—except for Daddy, of course. Do you like him, Allyn?"

"Yes. I don't know him very well, but he seems like a fine young man."

"It's going to be so good when you and Uncle Mark get moved. Will you have me over to visit with you?"

"Why, I guess I will," Allyn said. She laughed shortly, "I'm not used to being mistress of a house. I don't know a thing. You know a lot more than I do. Maybe you could come over and teach me how to keep house, things like that."

"I couldn't cook an egg, I don't think."

Allyn laughed. "I can't either, but we can learn." Allyn hesitated, then said, "Dorrie doesn't think I'm good for my father, says I don't love him."

Rena halted, and the other girl halted as well. "You don't love him? Why would she think that?"

"I don't know. She says I'm hard—that I don't love anybody."

"Oh, Dorrie's just an old grouch." As she said this, Rena felt a streak of disloyalty, for she loved the old black woman. Now she saw the loneliness in the young woman and said, "She's just hard to get to know. You'll like her when you get to know her better." The two girls walked on toward the house, and Rena later told Susanna, "I'd better go and stay with Allyn when she and Uncle Mark move. I think she needs me."

★ ★ ★

Two days later Mark was pleased when he looked up and saw Jason Larrimore riding up to the house. "Look, there's Jason," he said to Allyn, who was sitting with him. The two were playing cards out on the veranda—a habit they had formed lately—and he said, "Hope he can stay for a while."

Allyn rose and said, "I'll let you two visit."

When she had left and Jason had come up on the porch, Mark said, "Sit down, Jason. Got some things to tell you."

Larrimore shook the thin hand that Mark extended, noting how it seemed to grow more skeletal each time he came. He had a deep concern and a premonition about this man that he was so fond of, but he let none of this show in his face. He sat down, and soon Susanna came out, bringing them some lemonade to drink.

As the two men sat there, Mark faced Jason with excitement as he explained the adventure of buying Twelve Trees. "I think it's going to work out fine, Jason," he said, nodding

139

his head. "It's not a big place, but it's going to be just what Allyn will like, I think. Of course," he said, "I don't know much about her. We'll be together all the time there. I think she'll learn to care for me."

"How have you two been getting on, Mark?" Jason inquired.

"Oh, you know me, Jason." Mark smiled, but there was strain in his face. "I always like to work and get things done. But you can't do that in a situation like this. I can't expect Allyn to just pick up and start being a daughter as if I've had her all my life. I've put her through a hard time, and now I've got to pay my dues—show her that I love her and want to take care of her."

"Well, you're already doing that," Jason said. "Twelve Trees is a nice place, I hear. When do you think you'll be going?"

"Oh, we should take possession within a week or so, but it will probably be a couple weeks before we move in. You'll come and see us there, won't you?"

"Why, sure I will. I've got to make a run now, but by the time I get back, you two ought to be all settled in."

The two men sat there talking, and finally Allyn came back. "Hello, Jason," she said as she put her hand out. He arose and took it. "It's good to see you again."

He did not remark on their last meeting and had been somewhat ashamed of himself. "Good to see you, too, Allyn. Your father has just been telling me about your new home. I know you'll be happy there."

"Thank you." The words were spare and rather short, but Jason paid no heed to that. He looked down at the cards on the table and smiled. "You two are a pretty good match, I would guess. How about a three-handed poker game?"

"Fine," Mark cried, "sit down. I need to take some of that cash away that you've been stacking up."

As they sat down and began to play, they talked amiably, mostly Mark and Jason. Allyn, from time to time, made a comment. When Susanna came out and saw them, she said,

"Well, looks like I've got a gambling parlor started on my front porch. You suppose I could play, too?"

"Why, you don't know how to play cards, Susanna. You never could," Mark said with a grin. "If you ever got in a game, I'd win this place from you."

"You probably would," Susanna agreed, smiling, "so I'd better not play. Jason, you'll stay for supper and stay the night, won't you?"

"Well, I have to sail in the morning, have to be back to the ship—"

"Why, a young fellow like you doesn't mind an early morning ride!" Mark said quickly. "I wish you'd stay."

Jason glanced at Mark and saw the desire there in the older man's eyes. "If you can put up with me, I will."

"Good, I'll go tell Dorrie to kill another chicken," Susanna said.

The three began to play again. It was a pleasant morning, but Mark grew tired quickly and went to bed. Jason spent most of the day riding over the fields. He had never had a home like this, having grown up roughly, but the sight of the rolling hills and the scents of summer, the odors of earth, the clouds rolling overhead—all of it pleased him. He paused on a ridge and looked down on the valley where the fields were ripening and said, "A man has this, he has everything. Makes a ship look pretty lonesome."

He was not a man to think of himself much. He was a man, basically, who demanded action. For that reason the sea satisfied him, for it was a hard, demanding type of life. He had learned his trade well. Now, however, as he rode the sleek, black horse he had taken from the stable at a swift gallop down toward Gracefield, he thought, *Maybe someday, when I get too old to captain a ship, I can have a place like this.*

He dismounted, and when the slave stripped the saddle off, he gave him a coin, saying, "Rub him down, will you? He's a good horse." Then he turned and went across the yard, entered the house, and went at once to his room, where he lay down for a while—an unusual thing for him.

Later he arose and found Mark awake and feeling well enough to come down to the supper table.

Jason had a good supper that night—fresh sweet potatoes, thin slices of Virginia ham, new potatoes, and carrots. "The best meal I've had in a long time," he said to Dorrie, who had come outside. "Why don't you leave this place and come and cook for me on board the *Eagle?*" he said. "I'll treat you better than these folks do."

Dorrie, who had learned his ways already, smiled at him. "You hush now, Mistuh Jason! You know I ain't gonna get on no old boat!"

"Well, I'll bring you a present next time I come, Dorrie. Pick you out the best silk petticoat I can find."

Dorrie glared at him, then sniffed, "I ain't studying no petticoats!" and turned around and walked off, her chin in the air.

"Don't make the cook mad," Mark laughed.

"Don't worry. I think I know women well enough to know she'll take that red petticoat, if I can find one."

"I didn't think you hauled petticoats much through the blockade," Susanna remarked. "I thought it was all medicine and ammunitions."

"Mostly it is, but I always bring back a few small things. Anything you'd like? French perfume? Something like that, Susanna?"

"Oh, what would I do with French perfume?" she scoffed. "You might bring some for Allyn and Rena, though."

"Oh yes, Capt. Larrimore," Rena said eagerly. "Bring me some of that!"

"Don't be a beggar!" Susanna said sharply. "You know better, Rena Rocklin."

"Well, you suggested it, didn't you?" Rena said innocently. "And I bet Allyn would like some, too, wouldn't you, Allyn?"

"I'm sure the captain has lots of demands more pressing than French perfume."

"Why, not at all." Larrimore smiled at Allyn. "After all, a

bottle doesn't take much room. Of course, you never know what we'll find, but I'll see what I can do."

Later in the evening, after the short game of cards that Rena joined in with much merriment, Mark went to bed early. It was Larrimore who said, "I think I'll take a stroll around." He glanced at Rena and Allyn and inquired, "Why don't you two young ladies come with me?"

"All right, we will. Come on, Allyn," Rena urged. "I'll show you the new foal down at the barn."

It was still early enough for light to cover the scene as the three of them walked along. Rena chattered on about the virtues of the new foal. She brought the animal out, and it was duly admired by Allyn and Larrimore. Finally, Rena said, "I've got to go down to the summerhouse. Why don't you come with me?"

"Not for me," Allyn said quickly. "Capt. Larrimore may want to go."

"No, I guess I'd better turn in early. I've got to leave before dawn. I'll walk you back to the house, Allyn."

The two of them turned and made their way back to the Big House. Allyn again felt the strange discomfort this man always brought to her. Perhaps it was because he had seen her in the saloon. *I wonder if he thinks of me as a cheap saloon girl?* was the thought that came to her. It was difficult to tell what Larrimore thought, for he masked his feelings carefully.

They talked idly about the foal, then as they approached the house, Larrimore said, "I want to talk to you a minute."

Allyn turned in surprise. "Yes, what is it?"

Jason Larrimore was better at commanding a ship than he was at talking to young ladies about serious matters. He had thought much about what he wanted to say, but now as she looked up at him, he found it difficult to put into words. Her face seemed carved out of old ivory in the fading light. Her eyes were large and luminous. Once again he was acutely conscious of how attractive she was, and this disturbed him.

"I don't know how to say this. . . ." He hesitated. "Don't take it wrong."

Allyn looked at him, wondering at his meaning. "Take it wrong? What is it?"

"Well, I've thought a lot about you and your father. I guess I think as much of Mark Rocklin as I've ever thought of any man. I'd hate to see him get hurt."

"And you think I'll hurt him, is that it?"

Jason hesitated. "I don't think you'd do so intentionally, but have you thought about what's going to happen if you let him buy Twelve Trees, then you decide to leave?"

Allyn had indeed thought of this, and it had troubled her. She had persuaded herself that it was the best thing to do. But now, his words stirred the earlier anxieties in her. She grew faintly irritated, for he had touched on the very thing that had troubled her, and she was aggravated to find that he was wise enough to see what was in her. "I don't think that that's any of your business, Captain."

Jason grew angry suddenly. "Yes, it's my business all right. Anytime a bad thing happens to a friend of mine it's my business." Jason saw that he had shaken and angered her. "I'm sorry to talk to you like this, but right now it wouldn't be much trouble for you to pull out. If you don't mean to stay with him, I think you ought to."

"It's easy for you to make that decision, isn't it? You've never had to do without anything," she snapped. The anger, which she recognized as irrational, rose in her and she said, "I don't need any help from you to make decisions, Capt. Larrimore!" She turned to go, but he grabbed her by the arm.

Now he was angry and said, "Why don't you go back to New Orleans and deal blackjack?" As soon as he had said it, he let go of her arm, and he could have bitten his tongue off. But now, he could only say, "Wait—I didn't mean to say that."

"Yes, I think you did," she said. "Let me tell you this. He owes me something."

Larrimore stared down at her. She looked rather small and fragile in the gathering darkness. He wanted to reach out and shake her, but she looked up at him with an indomitable look in her large eyes. "And you're going to collect. Is that it?"

"Yes, I'm going to collect! There's no reason why I shouldn't."

Larrimore knew that he had failed and cursed himself for approaching the matter at all, certainly as awkwardly as he had. But he was still angry with her and snapped, "Well, I've got to go run the blockade and get rich." He stared down at her again. He reached out, took her by the arms, and said, "I'm as selfish as you are."

Allyn opened her mouth to argue with him, but before she could he pulled her close against him. He was very strong, and though she struggled, it was hopeless. She found herself pressed against his body, and then his lips covered hers. She could not move away for one moment. He was so strong that she was like a child in his grasp.

And then, despite herself, the anger and rage that rose in her at his touch, something in his embrace touched some well deep down in her that she had not known existed. His lips were firm on hers—hard and demanding, and she found herself surrendering to his embrace. She had spent so much time fighting men off, and now this man, with all of his exuberance and love of life, held her tightly. She felt his strength and power, and perhaps it was all of the years she had spent fighting her own fights that suddenly caused her to crumble. She surrendered to his embrace and added a pressure of her lips to his. The moment flowed on, and then she realized that he had stepped back.

"Well," he said slowly, "I guess that was a good-bye kiss." Jason Larrimore had known many women and had kissed many, but somehow this young woman had stirred him as no other ever had. He had kissed her in anger to show her his contempt, but somehow as their lips had met and he had felt her stiff defenses surrender, something had changed in him. But he could not speak the words, could not say what he felt. He saw her looking at him with something he could not define in her eyes and said, "I guess we're just two selfish people. Good night, Allyn." He turned and walked into the house.

Allyn went slowly after him. She went to her room, donned a nightgown, and found that her hands were trembling as she prepared for bed. Finally, she stood at the window and looked out at the darkness. The swifts were darting—black aerial acrobats, making arabesque patterns on the night sky. Slowly, she reached up with one hand and touched her lips, remembering his kiss. The moment came back to her and she whispered, "What was I thinking of? What was in me to let me give in to him like that?"

But no answer came. As she lay awake that night, her thoughts centered on Capt. Jason Larrimore.

CHAPTER ELEVEN
A Visitor for Col. Rocklin

Robert Simms was a cabdriver who made most of his money by being able to spot good fares. He had decided long ago that the best possibilities were Yankees, and even though he himself was a rabid secessionist and had lived in Richmond all his life, still he had a living to make. "This Confederate money," he had complained to his wife, "ain't worth nothing. Takes a wagonload of the blasted stuff to buy a sackful of groceries!"

He spotted at once the well-dressed woman who stepped down off the car pulled by the ancient wood-burning engine and beat out two other cabbies by stepping forward and saying, "Yes, ma'am! Give you a hand with your baggage, ma'am?"

Melanie Rocklin was weary from her long journey from Washington. It had been a difficult task persuading her children that she had to go do what she could for Gideon. They had all protested that she had no business going to Richmond, but in the end she had simply ignored them and gotten on the train, leaving them notes saying she would be back when Gideon was exchanged or the war was over. "Yes," she said, "I have a small trunk also—that one right over there, the black one. Would you please get that for me?"

"Yes, ma'am." Robert grabbed the bags with alacrity and led her away with the small trunk over one shoulder and her valise in his other hand. All the way to the carriage he chattered, talking about the weather, the war, and what was wrong with the way things were going in the world. When he reached the carriage he plumped the trunk down soundly with a thud that made Melanie blink her eyes, tossed the bag in beside it, and then turned to her. "Let me help you in this carriage, ma'am."

"Thank you, Robert." She had gotten his name as they walked to the carriage and now accepted his aid. As she settled into the seat, her body was racked with fatigue. *I'm not as young as I used to be,* she thought wryly. Then, when he settled into the seat beside her and cocked his eyebrows she said, "Take me to the Majestic Hotel."

"Yes, ma'am. Majestic it is!" He spoke to the horse, whose ribs were rather prominent, and the carriage moved out with a jerk. "Hot weather we've been having, but it's good for the crops. I don't reckon you're from around here, ma'am?" he inquired.

Melanie concealed a smile behind her fan, amused by his curiosity. "I used to be," she said. "I grew up here as a girl. My family's name was Benton."

"Benton! Would that be James Benton, ma'am—Maj. Benton?"

"Yes, that's right. You know him?"

"Oh, well, we ain't personal acquainted, ma'am, you understand, but everybody knowed Maj. Benton. You been off on a visit, I'd say."

She saw him eyeing her fashionably designed clothes and decided that she may as well tell him the truth. *Be like putting it in the papers,* she thought. "I'm married to one of the Rocklins," she said. "Col. Gideon Rocklin of the Union army."

A change traced its way across Robert's face, but he concealed it quickly. "Oh yes, ma'am. That's been quite a spell ago that you married Mr. Rocklin. I still see Mr. Clay pretty often."

Melanie listened as he outlined the family history and realized he was a walking newspaper, knowing everything apparently about everybody. When they got to the Majestic she said, "Let me go in and see if there's a room available. If there is, I'd like for you to unload my baggage for me."

"Yes, Miz Rocklin."

Robert hopped down and helped her from the carriage. Going inside, she inquired at the desk for a room. The clerk looked doubtfully at her and said, "Well, we've got one little room, ma'am, up on the third floor. It's pretty small and nothing fancy."

"That will do very nicely," she said. "I imagine you're pretty crowded."

"Oh yes, ma'am, full to busting out. Would you sign the register?"

Melanie signed the register, saw him read it, and he looked up to say, "Why, Mrs. Rocklin, I remember you. I heard that your husband has been taken prisoner. You come to see about him, did you?"

Melanie saw there was no secrecy or privacy in this world. "Yes, I'll be staying for a while. I'll be wanting to visit him. May I have the key, please?"

Thirty minutes later Melanie was back in the carriage with Robert. She had had him wait while she washed her face, refreshed herself, and changed clothes. Now she had settled herself back, saying, "Take me to Libby Prison, Robert."

"Yes, ma'am, shore will. Is that where they got the colonel, ma'am?"

"Yes, it is."

Robert kept up his customary rapid-fire conversation all the way to Libby, and when they arrived in front of the large, three-storied brick building he leaped out to help her down. "Shall I wait for you, ma'am?" he asked.

"If you don't mind, Robert. I don't think I'll be too long this first visit."

"Sure, I'll be right here, ma'am. You just bet on it."

Melanie made her way to the entrance, where she was stopped by the two guards. "I'd like to see Col. Rocklin," she said.

The guards examined her papers and she wondered, *Maybe they think I'm a Union spy.* They did indeed give her strange looks but were accustomed to this sort of thing. One of them, who opened the door and let her inside, said, "We often get Yankee visitors coming to see their people, Mrs. Rocklin. Come this way, if you will."

Melanie followed him to the third floor and was appalled at the odor that struck her when he opened the door. It was fetid and nauseated her. There was no privacy whatsoever, she saw, just one large, open room with men sitting on the floor or lying down on old blankets. None of the prisoners were near the windows, which Melanie learned later was to avoid the risk of being shot at by the guards.

"Right this way, Mrs. Rocklin."

Melanie followed the guard to a corner of the room and at once saw that the man lying on the cot was her husband. Stepping forward, she said, "Gideon . . . ?"

Gideon's eyes flew open, and he batted them blindly for a few moments. Carefully he swung his feet over, rubbed at his eyes, then looked at the woman who had knelt beside him. "Melanie!" he whispered incredulously. He put his arms out, and she came to him, holding him fiercely.

"Oh, Gid! My dear!" she whispered. He was so thin, and she held him to her breast as a mother would hold a child. For a long time she could do nothing but fight back the tears that sprang to her eyes. Finally, she drew back and said, "I'm so glad to see you!"

Gid could scarcely believe it and said so. "I thought maybe," he said with a warm smile, "that I'd died and woke up in heaven. You look like an angel to me." He looked down and said, "I guess I look pretty bad."

She reached out and pushed a lock of his hair back from his face. It was lank and greasy. She knew how he liked to be clean and neat and always kept his hair washed better than any man she ever knew. An immense pity welled up in her, but she put a cheerful note in her voice and said, "I've come down to take care of you! I'll get to boss you like I've always wanted to."

Gideon smiled one of the few smiles since his imprisonment. "Well, I've got lots of bosses," he said. He looked at her, took in the smooth cast of her features, the wide eyes, and shook his head. "Mercy, you look good to me! How I've missed you, sweetheart!"

She reached out and held his hand, noticing how thin it was. "How are you?" she asked quietly.

"Oh, pretty well." He tried to appear jaunty. "Clay and Melora have been coming down and babying me pretty often. Rena and Rooney Smith, too. They bring groceries in here by the wagonload it seems." He waved his hand around, saying, "Of course, I can't eat before all these fellows, poor devils. So I share it with them. They've made this ward kind of their mission field, I guess."

"Well, I'll just have to join their ranks," Melanie said. "Now, how do you feel, Gid? How's the wound?"

"Oh, pretty well. Still a little infection, but I don't get the fever so much now as I did. That was what was so bad. I wouldn't be surprised if it wasn't a slight case of the smallpox, as it pops up here from time to time I'm told. Left me weak as a kitten." He shook his head, saying, "I don't want to talk about that. Tell me everything. How are the boys? Where are they?"

For the next forty-five minutes she sat there, straining to remember everything as he drank in her words hungrily. Finally, she said, "I have to go now, Gid. I need to write to the children—they're worried to death about you. I'll come back first thing in the morning and bring you something you'll really like."

"Just bring yourself. You're what I want most of all."

His broad face seemed very thin, and his eyes were sunk back in his head farther than she would have liked. She leaned forward, held him again, kissed him firmly on the lips, and whispered, "I'll be back first thing in the morning."

She stood up, left the prison, and discovered, when she got outside, that she was shaking. Robert at once saw her troubled face and said, "Well now, Miz Rocklin, let me help you back." He helped her in the carriage, got in, and sat beside her and spoke to the horses. Despite his garrulous manner, he was a kindhearted man. He knew a little something of the awful conditions that prevailed in the prison and, like most decent men, was unhappy about it. Finally, he said, "Not a very nice place, ma'am. It's all we can do in the Confederacy here to feed ourselves. We have to stretch it mighty thin to feed all these prisoners that we've took. Wish it was better."

"Thank you, Robert," Melanie said. "Nice of you to say that. I suppose we have prisons in the North just as bad. Just another horror of war, isn't it?"

"Yes, ma'am." He drove along silently for a few moments, then said, "Would you like to go back to the hotel now?"

"If you don't mind, Robert, could you go shopping with me? I want to find some nice things for the colonel, some food and maybe some fresh underwear and socks and clothes. I don't know Richmond anymore. Perhaps you could help me."

"Why, I'd be plumb glad to, Miz Rocklin," Robert agreed at once. "Just come right along with me now, and we'll get that man of yours fixed up like a Boston lawyer!"

Melanie moved among the stores and shops of Richmond, noticing how eagerly they snatched at the gold pieces she had brought from the North. She was forced to take Confederate money in exchange, knowing that it would be worth very little. Still, she had to have things for Gideon. Finally, she got in the carriage, and Robert drove her back to the hotel. He helped her out, and when she asked the price, he hesitated, then named a figure.

"Oh, it was worth much more than that!" She smiled and gave him an even larger amount. "I'll be wanting to take these things to the colonel in the morning early, if you'd care to come by. As a matter of fact, I'll be going every morning. Maybe we could work out a regular thing. You could go and leave me, then pick me up later."

"That'd be fine, Miz Rocklin," Robert said quickly. "I'll be glad to do it." He bowed to her and, when he went back outside, said to one of his fellow cabdrivers, "Wal, Ed, I hate Yankees, but that Miz Gideon Rocklin, now she's a real lady!" Then as if ashamed of showing such tender sentiments, he added quickly, "'Course— she's a good Southern girl to begin with, which accounts for it."

Melanie went to her room, which was indeed small. There was only one battered table inside, but it did for a nightstand and for a place to write. Sitting down, she quickly began to write to the children, telling them her news. When the letters were finished, she took them out and mailed them. Then as she walked back to her hotel she thought, *I've got to get word to Susanna and Clay. They'll be able to tell me more about Gideon than anybody else.* She went back to the hotel room and for a long time sat on the single chair beside her bed reading her Bible. Finally, she closed it and said, "O God, you will have to help us with this. It's too much for me!"

★ ★ ★

"Why this is terrible!" Noel looked across at Deborah, who had opened the letter. He had come straight to the house and found Deborah, and when she had come down, he'd given her the envelope. She had seen it was from Melanie and had torn it open and read it rapidly.

After her exclamation, she got up and began to pace the floor. She was a forthright girl, active and ever ready for any task at hand.

"What does it say? Is the colonel all right?" Noel asked anxiously.

"No, he's not all right! Here—read for yourself." Deborah thrust the single sheet of paper at Noel and, as he scanned it, continued to pace the floor. She twisted her hands, and when he'd finished she said, "There, you see? He's sick and wounded and likely to die in that place!"

"Well, maybe it's not that bad."

"You know it is! We hear all the time about our men dying in Confederate prisons. Noel, we've got to *do* something."

"Do what?" Noel asked in surprise. "Mrs. Rocklin's down there to take care of him. We couldn't do anything anyway."

Deborah looked at him, her eyes flashing. "Well, we've got to do *something!*"

Noel watched her carefully. He was accustomed to her ways and well knew there was no way in the world to stop her in her headlong rush. Once an idea possessed her, everything had to give way before her. He thought for a while, then finally said, "Why don't we go down to the War Department and find out who it is that takes care of prisoner exchanges? Maybe we can put pressure on him somehow or other."

At once Deborah halted. She turned to him, her eyes sparkling, and came over to give him a hug. "Oh, Noel, that's a wonderful idea! And I'll tell you what," she continued. "If he won't do it, you can tell him you're going to write a series of articles exposing what a worthless thing he is!"

"Why, I can't do that!" Noel said in alarm. "We don't know the first thing about this man."

"I know it, but you know how bureaucrats are. We just have to do something to get them moving. Come on, Noel—let's go right now!"

"All right," Noel said with resignation. He led the way out of the house. All the way to the War Department as they rode along in the carriage Deborah talked excitedly about how they could get some action.

When they got to the War Department, as Noel expected, they found it difficult to see anyone with any authority. They spent quite some time talking to a pompous captain who leaned back and assured them that nothing could be done that wasn't being done. "Why, my dear young friends," he said expansively, "you can't appreciate the magnitude of this task of working out exchanges." He had a full set of whiskers that wiggled when he talked and a set of small eyes that were almost hidden in the fat of his face. "It's a terrible task, I assure you, to work these things out. Those of us here in the exchange department work late into the night when you folks are all asleep. Why, it's worse than combat!"

"You've been in combat, have you?" Noel demanded, angered by the man's manner.

"Ah, well—no. That is to say—"

"Then how do you know this is worse?" Deborah demanded.

Angered by their attitudes, the officer said haughtily, "I'm sorry, but I have no time for you. You'll have to wait and go through the regular channels."

Deborah stared at him. "Well, that's it. We'll just have to go see the president."

The fat officer laughed at them. "Yes, you just go see the president," he said. Obviously, he'd had this sort of threat before and said, "I'm sure he's just *waiting* for you to come up and tell him how to run the War Department. Good day!"

Noel had to pull Deborah aside. She wanted to continue the argument, but he simply dragged her outside. When they were out of his office, Noel said, "You can't argue with a man like that. He's not in charge, anyway."

"Well, why don't we go see the president?"

Noel was aghast. "Why, Deborah, we can't do that. That poor man is burdened down with a thousand . . . a million details. He wouldn't have time for us."

"I'll bet he would," Deborah said defiantly. She lifted her chin and said, "Come on, we're going to his office."

Noel suddenly laughed, "You are *something*, Deborah Steele! Going to see the president!"

"Well, are you coming or not?"

"I'll come," Noel said, "but it'll be a waste of time."

So it proved to be. The president was out of town and would not be back for over a week. The secretary was kind when Noel explained their mission and said, "I'm sure the president would like to do something for you. He's a good friend, of course, of Mr. Stephen Rocklin. Perhaps I could put this in a note, and he could look at it and get in touch with you when he gets back or have one of us do it. Would that be all right?"

"We'd appreciate that so much," Deborah said. They turned and left the office, and her shoulders sagged. "Well, if he were here, I bet he'd do something about it."

"I don't know. He does the best he can," Noel said.

They moved on back to the carriage and drove away. As they drove along Deborah said, "I can't stand the thought of it—Uncle Gid being in prison."

Noel shook his head. "Me, too, Deborah, but I'm glad he's alive. He could have been killed—but those prisons are awful places. I guess all we can do is pray."

Deborah was silent for a long time. Finally, she looked at him and said, "We're going to have to do more than pray. Noel, you're smart, and I'm smart, too. When two smart people like us get together and we ask God to help us, we can't fail, can we?"

"Fail at what?" He stared at her with a puzzled light in his eyes.

"Can't fail to get Uncle Gid out of that old jail," she said. Then reaching over, she grasped his arm and squeezed it hard. "We've got to do it, somehow. So, start praying!"

Noel Kojak knew better than to argue with this girl. He loved her with all of his heart and realized if they ever married, she would run him half crazy—but that didn't seem to matter. Looking at her, he said, "You know, it's quite an education being around you, Deborah Steele. A fellow learns all sorts of things."

"Things like what?" she asked suddenly.

"Why, things like how to mind when you crack the whip." He grinned. Then, seeing anger come into her eyes, he said,

"Now wait a minute. I *like* it. So, if you command me to pray, so help me, I'll pray." Then he got serious and said, "And I will think on it. There's got to be something we can do."

"Will you, Noel?" She leaned forward and kissed him, oblivious to the people who had caught sight of her and laughed. "That's like you. Come on now. Let's go home, and we'll sit down and write down every possibility!"

PART THREE
The Bridegroom

CHAPTER TWELVE
Death of a Ship
⭐

At the very beginning of hostilities, Gen. Winfield Scott, commander of the Northern armed forces, had proposed what he called the "Anaconda Plan." Basically, this plan as implemented had two parts. The first was to gain control of the Mississippi River, thus cutting the Confederacy in two. The second was to blockade all the Southern coasts, cutting off all supplies from Europe. McClellan and others scoffed at this plan, saying it was too slow; however, after Little Mac had a taste of Robert E. Lee and the Army of Northern Virginia, the military had quickly learned that there was no quick and easy solution to the rebellion. Scott's plan, therefore, slowly became "the" plan by which the Union attempted to win the war. In July 1863, Vicksburg fell, which opened the Mississippi River to Federal control, splitting the Confederacy in half and barring shipments of goods from west of the river eastward.

The attempts at blockade went more slowly. At the beginning of the war, the North had a very small navy. Soon, however, shipyards were turning out ironclads and ships of all descriptions to throw a ring of iron around the Southern coast. Such a thing was not easy, for there were hundreds of harbors stretching all the way from New Orleans, at the mouth of the Mississippi, around Florida and along the eastern coast of the country.

One of these, Fort Sumter, at Charleston, where the war had begun, was the scene of a furious assault in August of 1863. Maj. Gen. Quincy A. Gillmore was assigned the task of subduing the major seaport of the Confederacy. This involved seizing Battery Wagner near the northern tip of Morris Island, which was defended by twelve hundred Confederate troops and several heavy guns. Gillmore was overconfident and, hoping to gain a quick strike with only two and a half regiments, advanced on the battery. He suffered a terrible defeat, the Seventh Connecticut Infantry losing 108 out of 196 men, while the Confederacy suffered only 12 casualties. Sobered by this defeat, the North began to throw added weight into the struggle, bringing the total to six thousand infantry. Though they tried hard, it was only after a long struggle that Battery Wagner was taken. Charleston, South Carolina, was all but lost as a Southern port. The Union dead, many hideously mutilated, littered the beach in front of Wagner. One Charleston journalist wrote that "probably no battlefield in the country has ever presented such an array of mangled bodies in a small compass."

Charleston had been the home port of Jason Larrimore, but with the attention the Federals were paying to the batteries at the mouth of the harbor, he avoided that city and chose a small, hidden harbor north of Charleston. He had run the blockade twice and had come back to unload his small ship into wagons, which he sent into both Charleston and Richmond. He arrived at the small town that marked the harbor and went at once to where the *Eagle* was anchored in a natural lagoon. He had been fortunate to find it, for the fingers that formed the lagoon were covered with palmetto trees that shielded the harbor from the eyes of lookouts on Federal gunboats. Dismounting from his carriage and walking out to the small wharf, he saw his first officer, Malcolm Davis, on deck. He quickly crossed the gangplank, stepped on board, and shook hands, saying, "Hello, Malcolm. Things going well?"

Davis, a short muscular man with reddish hair, had been an officer in the United States Navy but had resigned his commission, enjoying the freelance fighting for his home state of South Carolina and the Confederacy. He was the best sailor that Jason had ever seen and kept the *Eagle* as clean as a woman's kitchen. "Aye, sir, ready to go whenever you give the word." He gave a cautious look to the sky and said, "Going to have cloudy weather for the next night or two, I think. If you're ready, I think we ought to go tonight."

"I've got some supplies coming that we can sell on our trip over," Jason said. "As soon as they come, we'll load them and get underway."

He was glad to get back to the ship and spent the next two days anxiously awaiting the supplies. When they finally came and were loaded, he said, "I believe we'll go out at midnight, Malcolm. What do you think?"

The red-haired seaman chewed his lower lip nervously. "Our cloud cover was gone last night and probably won't be back tonight. The moon's a little bit full for my liking."

"Well, we'll chance it. I think we can outrun anything we're likely to meet." Jason smiled and clapped the shorter man on the shoulder. "The *Eagle*'s never been caught yet, has she?"

"No, that's right, but God's been with us so far."

"You always put everything at God's front door, don't you, Malcolm?" Jason smiled as he said this. He himself was not a believer, but he had come to respect Davis's religion. On shore or on board the *Eagle*, the first officer was always the same, a hardworking, hard driving man, but with a total commitment to the Scripture and to God.

"We're not alone, Jason," Davis said. "You'll find that out someday."

Davis had never attempted to force his belief on Larrimore, but there was something in his straight, direct gaze that caused the captain to fidget. "I hope you're right," he said. "I've seen a lot of hypocrites in my time, but I've seen enough of the real thing to know that there's something there that I'm missing." Quickly he said, "Well, get everything ready. We want to make a quick run. We ought to make a bundle this time. The Confederacy's starving to death. We could bring back a load of nothing but coffee and get rich off it." And then he smiled and said, "But I know you. You want to bring back shot and shell, something to win the war with."

"That's what I'd like," Davis said, "but we'll have to take what we can get." Davis was an ardent patriot, firmly believing in the rightness of his cause, and there was no hesitation as he said, "God will be with us."

At midnight, Jason stood at the wheel of the *Eagle*. The weather was clear, but there was a brisk breeze for which he was thankful. As the crew maneuvered the sails, he held the wheel firm in his hands, guiding the ship expertly through the narrow channel. As he kept his eye on the shoals, he thought of all the tricks and ploys that had been used by the North to stop the blockade-runners. In England, a reward of thirty pounds was offered to anyone who could supply reliable information concerning vessels leaving for blockaded ports. When the North learned that blockade-running ships used anthracite coal because it burned without smoke, all shipments of this fuel to foreign ports were banned. When the runners discovered that Federal ships were waiting to seize them, they learned to go to intermediary ports, such as Nassau and Bermuda, sometimes transferring their cargo to smaller crafts that could be sneaked into ports along the Southern coast.

As the sails caught the full breeze and the *Eagle* passed out into the open sea, Jason felt the ship tremble beneath his feet. There was always something miraculous about this to him, how the dead tons of wood lying in the water, almost like a log, suddenly came alive as the sails filled and the power of the wind lifted the ship out of the water and sent it flying along the surface. The wind blew through his hair, and he took a deep breath, inhaling the salt fragrance of the sea. The only sounds as they skimmed along were the hissing of the water along the sides of the ship and the harsh guttural cries of the seagulls that followed, as always, hoping for a free meal.

"Going to be a good trip," he said aloud, his eyes already scanning the horizon searching for those tiny dots or wisps of smoke that could mean disaster or even death. He was happy to be back at sea, as he always was. The land to him seemed to be a prison at times, and only when he stood on the deck of a ship and looked around at the limitless sea that surrounded him did he feel free.

He stood at the wheel for four hours, then Davis came and relieved him. "Not a sign of an ironclad," Jason murmured as he stepped back, giving the wheel to the first officer. "Maybe this will be one of those good ones that will be like a cruise on a ferryboat. I hope so."

"I've prayed to that intent," Davis said, nodding.

His simple words caught at Larrimore. He stood there moving instinctively to the roll of the ship and thought about what the shorter man had said. "How do you make it all line up, Malcolm?" he asked.

"Make it all line up? What do you mean by that, sir?"

"I mean, when you pray for something and don't get it. Doesn't that discourage you?"

"Why, not a bit." The ship gave suddenly under their feet, pitched down into a trough, then rose again like a bird. Davis planted his feet, held the wheel firmly, and commented, "We may run into a bit of weather—getting into some swells already." He had not forgotten the question, however, for he turned and gave his companion a steady look. "When you were growing up and you asked your parents for something, they said no sometimes, didn't they?"

"I guess they did."

"Why do you suppose they did that?"

165

Jason thought for a moment and said, "Sometimes they said no because they couldn't provide what I wanted, what I'd asked for."

"Aye, but that's never true with God, is it? He owns everything there is. His hand is not shortened. There's not a thing a man's mind could think of that God couldn't provide—if he wanted to."

"I suppose that's so. But still, you don't get everything you pray for, do you?"

Davis shook his head. "I'm afraid not, but if you'll stop and think, there were other reasons why your parents didn't give you everything. If you were like most boys—like I was for instance—you wanted some things that wouldn't have been good for you. I always loved firearms, and I asked my father for a gun when I was ten years old. Do you think he gave it to me? Not likely! I'd have probably blown my head off with it. So, you see, sometimes we ask for things, and God says no because he knows we're not ready for them."

Jason nodded. "I can see that, but I heard a preacher once in Montgomery, I don't know the verse or where the verse is found, but he preached for two hours on the subject 'Ask for whatever you want, and if you believe, you'll get it.'"

"Oh yes, that's in the twenty-first chapter of Matthew, verses twenty-one and twenty-two." He narrowed his eyes, thought for a moment, then quoted the Scripture, "'Jesus answered and said unto them, Verily I say unto you, If ye have faith, and doubt not, ye shall not only do this which is done to the fig tree, but also if ye shall say unto this mountain, Be thou removed, and be thou cast into the sea; it shall be done. And all things, whatsoever ye shall ask in prayer, believing, ye shall receive.'"

Jason stared at him with unconcealed admiration. "You must have the whole Bible memorized, Malcolm. You're just a walking concordance."

"Oh no, I wish that were true, but it's not."

Jason looked across the waters and thought he saw the first pale breaking of dawn. But he was not through yet with his questioning. "But what about when you ask and don't get what you ask for? That verse just says you'll get it. Doesn't that prove the Bible is wrong?"

Malcolm said quickly, "No, the Bible is God's Word. Sometimes it *seems* to be wrong, but it never is. What's wrong is our understanding of it. For example, many of us have struggled with the thing you have just mentioned. God seems to promise we'll get what we ask for. Sometimes we ask, we don't get it, what does that mean?" He gave a quick glance at his friend and said, "Why, it means we have misunderstood the Scripture."

"How have I misunderstood this one? It seems clear enough to me. 'Whatsoever ye shall ask, ye shall receive.'"

"Well, here is the truth of this doctrine, as I see it. When Jesus was about to be crucified, the last time he met with his disciples, he spoke of this very thing again. This is in the sixteenth chapter of John, verses twenty-three and twenty four, I believe. He said, 'Verily, verily, I say unto you, Whatsoever ye shall ask the Father in my name, he will give it you. Hitherto have ye asked nothing in my name. ask, and ye shall receive, that your joy may be full.'"

"Why that sounds like about the same thing to me as the other verse."

"Only one thing is different. Jesus said we have to ask in his name."

"Well, people do that, don't they? Usually people end their prayer by saying, 'I ask this in the name of Jesus.'"

"Oh, that's what we do, all right. But I think the Lord Jesus meant much more than putting a little tag on prayer asking for whatever we wanted. I think when he said 'ask in my name' he was really saying 'ask for the sort of thing that I, myself, would ask for.' Do you see the difference?"

"I suppose so, but it's a pretty fine distinction."

"Perhaps, but not when you think of it, Jason. Look, there are two reasons for men to ask things of God. One of them is selfish, and one of them is unselfish. If, for instance, I want to get a lot of money so that I can spend it on myself, that's selfish. Was that the sort of thing Jesus would do? Of course not. He said, 'I do always those things that please him,' meaning the Father. I think there is a point in a person's life when prayers become unselfish and we pray for things that would bring the kingdom of God to this earth in our own hearts. So that's the way I try to pray now."

Jason frowned and said, "I'm afraid I don't get it, Malcolm. Aren't we supposed to ask for what we need?"

Malcolm nodded at once. "Yes, what we *need*. But our needs are very simple. It's our *wants* that get us into trouble. That's why I don't pray for things until I've decided they're in the will of God. If I want a house, I wait until God tells me it's his will for me to have that house. Then I pray for it, and I always get it. Don't be too quick with your praying"— he grinned suddenly—"you might get what you ask for, and that might be the worst thing in the world for you."

Jason studied the face of the small, short, blocky man and wondered, not for the first time, how such a tough, hard-driving character could be such a devoted Christian. Finally he shook his head and said, "I guess my head is too thick for such things, Malcolm. I'll never get it."

Malcolm reached out and put his hand on his captain's shoulder. "It's not your head that's the problem. Not with you, Jason. It's the heart. One day, the Lord Jesus will come knocking at the door of your heart. You'll know it's him, and you'll have to decide who's going to be boss, Jason Larrimore or Jesus Christ." He took his hand away quickly and shook his head. "Didn't mean to preach, but I would dearly love to see you find God, Jason."

Jason turned and left somewhat embarrassed by the encounter. He had had many talks like this with his first officer and always, when they were over, the subject seemed to get stuck in his head and he could not escape it.

Dawn was approaching rapidly, and he began to walk around the deck, cautioning the hands from time to time, "Keep a sharp eye out. We may be encountering gunboats pretty soon." As the ship glided over the water, he went to the rail, put his elbows on it, and scanned the sky. Small areas of pale blotches appeared in the east, and he kept his eyes constantly in motion. At the same time, he remembered Allyn Rocklin. The memory came to him of their last meeting. He was disturbed and shook his shoulders restlessly as he thought of how her kiss had affected him. He did not like to be thrown off balance, being a self-sufficient man, and the thought of how the touch of her body against him and the firmness of her soft lips under his had shaken him bothered him. He pulled his cap down over his forehead with a half-angry gesture. "I'm not a boy to be set on my heels by a woman's kiss!" he muttered angrily.

He quickly shifted position, moving to the other side of the ship. Still the memory would not leave his mind. He thought over the entire history of his encounters with the girl and thought, *She's not a woman a man could get involved with. She's selfish to the core and will take poor Mark for everything she can get!* The more he thought, the more dissatisfied he became with his part in bringing Allyn to her father. "When I get back," he announced defiantly to the breaking waves that he stared at, "I'm going to talk Mark out of giving her everything. That would be a bad mistake!"

★ ★ ★

"Captain! Off the port! Federal warships!"

Jason, hearing the lookout's cry, whirled and threw himself around the superstructure. Gazing over the side, he narrowed his eyes. Sure enough, a tiny dot broke the clean edge of the horizon formed by the sea. At once he whirled and called Malcolm. "First officer, hang every inch of canvas!"

"Aye, sir." Davis had seen the sail as well and gave the orders that sent the hands scurrying up the mast to unfurl every sail available. He came to stand beside Jason and said, "It may be another blockade-runner."

"I don't think so—too big for that, and she's got the wind on us. Look." They stood watching for a time until half an hour later, Jason said, "She's Federal, all right." He put the spyglass down and said, "And a fast one, too."

Davis grinned. "Don't worry, sir. Those Yankees don't have a ship that can catch the *Eagle.*"

A premonition swept over Jason Larrimore. He did not believe in such things, yet a feeling such as he had never had came to him. "Wet the canvas down," he said, "it may get us just the speed we need to outrun that ship." Davis gave him an odd glance but at once gave the orders. By wetting the canvas down, the sails held the wind a little better. For the next hour they maintained this tactic, constantly dousing the sails.

Finally Davis came to stand beside the captain and said apprehensively, "You're right—she's a fast one, Captain, and she's got a bead on us."

"I think once we get clear of Pirates' Reef we'll be all right." He spoke of a range of the coast that had become a graveyard of many ships. It was a treacherous spot of water luring unwary captains into what seemed to be deep water, only to rip the bottoms out of ships.

Jason and Malcolm stood tensely behind the wheel, watching the enemy ship. Malcolm commented once, "That's only a cutter. Maybe we can put her out with the three-pounder."

"Give it a try, Malcolm," Jason said. "If you manage to dismast her, we could walk away and leave her."

At once Davis was yelling orders at the crew, who gathered around the small three-pound rifled cannon that was the single armament of the *Eagle.* Davis and the captain had had long discussions about how much armament to carry, and finally Jason had said, "We can never carry enough to fight off an ironclad. We'll rely on speed, which means getting rid of all the extra weight." Davis had argued and gotten his way in having the three-pounder mounted. It was only a small gun but was capable of piercing the side of a small vessel, such as the one pursuing them.

Soon the small cannon was booming regularly, and small dots of water showed that the shots were falling closer.

"That's it, Lieutenant!" Jason said with excitement. "You've got the range now."

During the next half hour, several hits were observed, but nothing stopped the other ship, which had now begun to answer with her own heavier armament.

A shot whizzed overhead, making a neat hole in the canvas. Larrimore looked up at it with alarm. "They've got our range, too," he said. He looked at the ship and shook his head. "We'll be at the cove in a moment, and she'll have to turn. We can outrun her on a straightaway. So just keep firing that pop gun, Lieutenant."

The enemy ship, a schooner, evidently constructed for chasing just such blockade-runners as the *Eagle,* had to turn, and as soon as she fell into the same parallel as the *Eagle,* it became apparent at once that she was no match in speed for the Southern ship. A cheer went up from the crew, and Davis turned and said, "There, you see. I told you no ship could keep up with the *Eagle.*"

Jason grunted, "Keep every sail full. I want to put her out of sight as quick as we can."

For the next hour they watched carefully as the Federal vessel fell behind. Jason finally drew a deep breath and was about to congratulate Davis on his gunnery, but a cry came up from a lookout, "Two sails off starboard!"

Whirling, both Jason and the first officer saw what they most dreaded—two sails in front of them spread out exactly the right distance so they could not hope to dodge them. "Those aren't schooners," Davis said. "They're ironclads."

Jason thought rapidly. "They'll blow us out of the water if we try to dodge between them. We can't fall away because of that fellow behind us." He said sharply, "We'll have to hug the shore. They can't come in close or they'll tear their bottoms out. They draw so much more than the *Eagle.* Hug that shoreline!" he commanded.

Davis rubbed his chin, shook his head. "You know what

Pirates' Reef is like," he said. "Seems like there's a devil down there that reaches up and tears the bottoms out of ships."

"I can't help that. It's the only chance we've got." He looked at the two ironclads that were coming steadily onward and said, "They'll take us into port. You and I'll probably land up in prison for the rest of the war. No, we'll make a try at it. Hard aport," he called, and the two men watched nervously as the *Eagle* wheeled over and headed for the shore.

The water hissed along the sides of the ship, and the mast creaked as the sails caught a full wind. "Could tear the sticks out of her," Davis said.

"We don't have any choice, Malcolm. Look, those ironclads are penning us in. They can't come after us, but their guns will be able to reach us if we don't get by in the next few minutes."

Like pieces on a chess board, the ships maneuvered along the narrow stretch of land. The two ironclads moved steadily to pen the smaller vessel in, while the Federal warship behind them plugged that area of escape. The *Eagle* headed straight for shore, heeling over only at the last minute when Larrimore gave the command. "I'm going forward," he said, "maybe I can spot the reefs. You stay here and follow the commands."

"Aye, sir."

Larrimore went forward and stood at the very prow of the ship. His practiced eye searched the waters ahead of him, and once he saw a finger of coral reef reaching upward he turned and yelled, "Hard aport—!" He watched, holding his breath as the *Eagle* heeled over and seemed to brush by the coral. "Straighten her up," he yelled when they were by.

All the time he was keeping his eye on the warships. Then suddenly he heard the booming of cannon. He waited, watching the ocean, and saw the shot send a small geyser of water into the air a hundred yards from the Eagle's starboard. There was nothing he could do. They would just have to stand the fire. Looking ahead, he was hopeful. *If we can just get past that reef, we'll have it made. They can't outrun us, and they can't reach us with their guns. Come on, Eagle—let's see you fly!*

The *Eagle* did seem to fly over the water, skimming lightly, and although the shells were falling closer to the ship, there was open water ahead. *I'll be able to turn soon,* he thought and quickly turned and raced back toward the deckhouse. He had reached the deckhouse when the shell struck. It was a single iron ball, but it tore through the wooden frame of the *Eagle*, sending splinters flying and then struck the mainmast. Already strained with the full sails, the mast broke in two and fell with a creaking, groaning noise, striking the deck with a crash and maiming one man who could not escape.

Jason was not aware of that. The same shot that had parted the mainmast had sent a flying splinter across the tiny wheelhouse and struck him high in the back. It drove him to the deck, and a searing pain raked along his side. When he tried to move, he cried out involuntarily. At once Malcolm shouted, "All you all right, Captain?"

Jason could hardly speak for the pain, but said, "Keep going, try to make it! We've got to get away!"

But it was hopeless. With the mainmast down, the two warships were catching up easily.

Malcolm Davis made a decision. "Get the lifeboats out! We've got to get off this ship!" he yelled. He stayed at the wheel while the men swung the two small lifeboats out, then said, "Get the captain into one. He's been hit."

Davis himself stayed at his station until the two lifeboats were well underway. Then he slapped the wheel with a hard fist. "Good-bye, my lady," he said regretfully, "you've been a good ship!" He turned the wheel toward Pirates' Reef, tied it there, and quickly ran and dove off the side. Swimming rapidly, he caught up with the boat that contained the captain and was heaved on board by the crew. He came up just in time to see the *Eagle* strike the reef. It reared upward like a deer that had been shot, then settled back.

"She's gone, sir," he said to Jason, who was being held carefully by one of the seaman. "Now, let me have a look at that splinter you took."

As Davis pulled off his shirt, pain raged through Jason Larrimore, but the pain of losing the *Eagle* was far greater than anything that could touch his body.

"There'll never be another one like her," he gasped, and then—as Davis opened his knife and began to cut the splinter out—he passed into a merciful oblivion.

CHAPTER THIRTEEN
"Every Woman Needs a Man"

Clay rode into the fields toward Gracefield after having been away for more than a month. The orange pumpkins dotting the fields brought good memories of the pumpkin pies that he had enjoyed in happier days. He was tired to the bone, and the horse he had finally scrounged was even more weary. Men and animals had been worn thin by the Gettysburg campaign, so that when they had reached the relative safety of Richmond, the army seemed to have simply given up. The rest of the summer had been spent regaining the army's strength and planning their next move.

As he rode slowly down the circular driveway that wound in front of the Big House, he saw Melora coming from around the house, and his gloomy mood lifted. Standing up in the stirrups, he lifted his hat and called, "Melora!" then spurred the tired animal into a gallop.

Melora glanced up and, seeing him, raised a hand to her lips. She ran forward to meet him, and when he came off his horse and took her in his arms, she clung to him fiercely. "Clay—Clay!" she whispered huskily. "I'm so glad you're back!"

He held her tightly, savoring the firmness of her body as he kissed her soft lips, then grinned down at her. "Nice to be welcomed home by such a beautiful lady," he said. Then with a glint of humor he added, "You sure look better than anything I've seen lately—of course all I've seen is hairy-legged, dirty soldiers."

"Oh, *you!*" she laughed. "Come on in the house and tell me everything." Drawing him into the kitchen, she sat him down at the table, saying, "Now, I've got a surprise for you." Turning to the pie safe, she opened the door and brought out a pie and set it before him. "Pumpkin pie—your favorite. Now you eat that, then you can tell me everything."

The two sat there, Clay wolfing down the succulent pie in huge bites. He related the details of camp life and assured her that his sons and her brother were getting along fine. When he halted she told him about Melanie, who had come to do what she could to take care of Gid. He nodded at once. "I'm glad of that. I'd hoped he'd be exchanged, but until then he needs her. What about Mark?"

Melora shook her head. "He's worse, I'm afraid—weaker than ever. He stays in his wheelchair most of the time and is in a great deal of pain."

"What about Allyn? Are they doing better together?"

Melora leaned forward, put her chin in her hands, a thoughtful look in her eyes. "I can't tell, Clay. She's a strange girl. She's built a wall around herself."

"She's had a hard life, I suppose, and this is all strange to her. She hasn't been here all that long, you know, only a couple months."

"That's true. She spends a lot of time with Mark and seems to cheer him up. But the two of them have never really gotten close. Allyn's hard to get close to. I've tried, and so have Rena and Rooney. Lots of the young men in the neighborhood drop by—those that aren't off in the army. She doesn't seem too interested in them, either."

"Well," Clay said, shoving the plate back and taking a long swallow of coffee from a thick mug, "it'll probably be all right. It'll just take some more time."

She leaned over, took his hand in hers, and caressed it, noticing that he had a fresh scar on the back of it. "It'll take time," she said softly. Then she added, "But that's the one thing that Mark doesn't have."

★ ★ ★

The day after Clay returned, Lowell rode in. Stepping off Midnight, his horse, he made his way up the steps limping slightly. The artificial leg that he wore was better than he ever thought such a thing could be. As soon as he stepped in the door, he shouted, "Hello! Where is everyone?"

His call brought Susanna and Rooney out of the kitchen. They both ran to him and smothered him so that he cried out, "Hey—wait a minute! You don't want to choke a fellow, do you?" He kissed Susanna lightly on the cheek, saying, "You're still the—" he paused, looked over at Rooney and winked—"the *second*-best-looking woman I know."

Susanna slapped him playfully on the chest. "Well, you've learned a *little* about women, I'm glad to say. Now, you two go for a walk while I finish cooking."

"Oh, I'll help you, Miz Rocklin," Rooney said at once.

"Lowell didn't ride in to watch you work. Now you two go on."

Lowell took Rooney's hand and nodded. "You always listen to your elders, young lady—and since I'm older than you, that means me. Come on, now." He led her outside, and the two strolled along the brick walk that led around the house. When they came to the east side of the house, Lowell grinned suddenly. "Come on, I know where we can go." He led her to the scuppernong arbor. The vines completely covered the latticework so that it effectively hid those who stepped inside. An ancient wooden bench was there, and Lowell pulled Rooney down so they were both sitting on it. "Here," he whispered with a grin. "Now I've got you where I want you!"

Rooney started to speak, but he threw his arms around her, drawing her close. She responded by putting her own arms around his neck, pulling his head toward her. She was an emotional girl and held him closely, savoring the touch of his lips on hers. Finally, he pulled his head back and said with a grin, "Well now, that was worth waiting for!"

"Yes, it was," she said demurely.

Lowell grinned at her. "Well, I guess it's time for me to get back to the war!"

He had started to get up, but Rooney pulled him back down vigorously. Rooney's eyes had an elfish light of humor. "Oh no you don't. Jeb Stuart's seen enough of you. Now it's my turn." With that, she kissed him again.

When their lips parted, Lowell stared at her. He was enjoying the fresh smell of her hair, the light that gladdened her eyes, the smoothness of her skin. He had missed her more than he knew, and as he sat there with his arm around her, he leaned over and whispered, "I feel it's time for us to get married, sweetheart."

Rooney lifted her eyes to his. She reached up, brushed his hair back off his forehead, then said, "Oh, Lowell, that's wonderful!" She paused. "Are you sure that's what you want, Lowell?"

"Of course that's what I *want*. But it may not be best for you." He took her hand, held it, stroked it gently, and said, "I may not come back, you know. You may be a widow—maybe even with a child."

"That's what your father told Melora, but they got married. I guess we can do what they did, can't we?"

"Yes, we can." He kissed her again, holding her longer this time.

She clung to him, enjoying his touch, then finally pulled her head back and said, "I think that's almost enough, don't you?"

"*Never* enough—I'll never get enough of you, Rooney."

Pulling away from him she stood up, and he saw there was a troubled light in her eyes. Standing quickly, he said, "What is it? Something's wrong."

Rooney shook her head. "Not between us. I love you so

much, Lowell, and you're the only man I've ever loved. But—I worry about my mother."

Lowell had thought about Rooney's mother. She was a common woman, and even now was only shortly out of jail and living a dissolute life in Richmond. Lowell disliked her but at the same time felt pity for her. But he knew he had to somehow convince Rooney that he was willing to accept that responsibility. "We'll help her, Rooney," he said quietly. "Perhaps she'd want to come and stay with you for a while."

The kindness of his offer touched Rooney. She knew that her mother would not fit at all in a setting like this. *Ma would never come here—she's too tied to the life she lives* was her thought. "That's sweet of you," she said. "She'd never come here, but I can go see her and spend more time with her."

"It's settled then. Let's seal the bargain with a kiss." He did so promptly and cocked one eyebrow. "You know what? This kissing could get to be a habit."

"Yes, I'll have to limit you. I'd say about three a day," she said mischievously.

"Three a day! That's no good for a man in my condition— in love so bad I can hardly walk!" Then he said, "I think the wedding should be late in October. Will that be too soon?"

"No, not too soon." She leaned forward and whispered, "You've already had your three kisses, but I'll give you an advance if you want one."

"I may be gone a long time," he said. "We'd better work our way forward a couple of weeks." Then he took her in his arms again.

★　★　★

Clay and Lowell's presence had brought a new sense of life to Gracefield. The first two days they were there seemed almost like an extended party. Underneath the gaiety, how- ever, lurked the knowledge that they had to rejoin their units. Fear would come like a cold hand to the women, an eerie whispering that these young men—so alive and vital— might lie in shallow graves very soon. They hid these fears, going out of their way to make the time as happy and meaningful as they could. Clay did not speak much of the war, nor did Lowell. It was as if they wished to close that part of their lives and take the few precious hours that they had, storing them up, as it were, against the lean, hard days they knew lay ahead of them.

Clay spoke of this once to Melora as they were walking through the leaves that had already begun to fall. "You know, all over the South—and the North, too, I suppose—men and women are doing just as we are."

"What's that, Clay?" Melora asked quietly.

He didn't answer for a moment. Finally he took her hand, and they ambled along under the shade of the huge walnut trees that lined the path leading to the small creek. "Oh, trying to forget about the war." A fox squirrel popped up over his head, chattering angrily. Clay picked up a stick and threw it. It missed, but the squirrel disappeared almost magically. They both laughed, and Clay said, "I'd like to have him in a pot with some dumplings!" Then he went back to his original thought. "After a battle, everyone's stunned, I think—especially after Gettysburg. It was as if we couldn't think or move or act. If it hadn't been for the timidity of George Meade, the war would be over. All he had to do was send a big force at us and the Army of Northern Virginia would have been wiped out. It's a good thing that Gen. Grant's commanding in the west! He'd have sent every man he had after us, and we'd have been helpless."

"It was very bad, wasn't it?"

"Very bad. The worst I've ever seen. Pickett's charge up that hill—" Clay shook his head—"I never saw anything like it! It makes you wonder what's in our men. They lined up like soldiers on parade and marched up that hill. When a man in front was shot, another one simply stepped in his place. It was the most devastating musket fire I've ever seen in my life!"

"Was it a mistake, Clay?" Melora asked gently.

"I think it was. It seems like our leaders just can't learn

not to march mass troops against troops that are dug in. It happens over and over again. The Yankees took about as bad as we got at Gettysburg when they tried it at Fredericksburg. Our losses at Malvern Hill were about as bad." He shook his head firmly. "We're still fighting European style, and it seems these new weapons have made that style obsolete."

They walked along, the leaves crisp under their feet, losing their brilliant yellow and orange and red. The woods seemed to be full of game, and finally he said, "I'll have to get Josh, and we'll take a gun and clean some of these deer and squirrels out—"

Even as he spoke, Allyn appeared, stepping around the pathway. Clay called, "Allyn!"

Melora looked up and called out, "Hello, Allyn." The two strolled forward to greet her. Melora said, "Come and walk with us."

Allyn was wearing a light-green dress that reflected the color of her eyes. Her rich, dark red hair caught the gleams of the September sun. She gave them a slight smile and shook her head. "No, I promised Father I'd play chess with him." Then she made a face. "I hate that game!"

"So do I," Melora said. "Clay makes me play with him, and I can never remember how those little men move."

Clay smiled at the young woman. "Try checkers, Allyn. You'll have a better chance at that."

"All right, I will. You two go on now, and I'll go see if I can do any better with checkers." She turned and walked away, but as soon as the two were out of sight, she thought of how awkward she had felt with them. *I should have joined them, but they need all the time they have together. When he's gone, I know she'll save all these times in her memory.*

She made her way down the road, enjoying the brisk wind that stirred the leaves and bent the dead grasses over. They seemed to bow in obeisance to the power of the breeze. She had come to love Gracefield and the country that surrounded it. All of her life she had been confined to the narrow streets of New Orleans, and now the freshness of the open countryside, the smell, the sights, the touch of raw earth under her feet had all come to be precious to her.

When the house came in sight, she admired as always the fine lines of the classic mansion. She knew nothing about architecture, but there was something about the mansion at Gracefield that was pleasing to the eye: the stately white pillars on three sides, the tall windows that caught the gleam of the late afternoon sun, the carpeted lawn that now was turning brown but was still evenly clipped and level. She thought of the mean, ugly streets of the section of New Orleans where she had lived—and dreaded the thought of going back to such a place again.

As she entered the yard, she spoke to several of the slaves, who grinned at her, saying, "How are you, Miss Allyn?" She wondered again about her feelings about slavery. She had grown up with it, and it had been a part of her world, so deeply entrenched she could not have imagined any other world. The war itself had not been as meaningful to her as to some, for she had not had a father, brother, or lover who was risking his life. Now, however, that she had come to know some of the Rocklin men, it gave her a chill as she thought that Clay, Lowell, or Dent in a few days might lie dead in some bloody field.

She entered the house through a side door, went at once to Mark's room, and knocked on the door.

"Come in."

She opened the door and entered, smiling at him. "I've got an idea," she said.

Mark sat in his wheelchair, as usual. He'd been waiting for her, as he always did. He'd noticed that he counted the hours until she came, and now he said, "Good. What is it?"

"I'll never learn to play chess. Let's play checkers instead."

Mark grinned at her. When he smiled some of the pain seemed to leave his face, and she thought, *What a handsome man he must have been when he was young—before he got hurt.* Moving to the cabinet, she picked up the board and a box containing some checkers. Placing them on a table she pulled over in front of Mark, she drew up a chair, set up the board, then asked, "How do you feel, Father?"

"Oh, very well today," Mark said. "Tell me what you've been doing."

Allyn knew he didn't like to talk about his illness. He never complained, and he always wanted to know all that she did. She began tracing her day for him, putting in the little things, and, as she spoke, she was unaware of how his eyes were fixed to her face. Her own eyes were fastened on the board as she studied the pieces.

Mark let her win the game and was pleased to see the delight that such a simple thing brought to her. Thoughtfully he said, "You look very like your mother, Allyn, when she was your age."

Allyn shook her head. "I don't think I'd ever be as pretty as that picture of her."

"You are, though."

His words pleased her, but she had been thinking of her position at Gracefield, and now she leaned back and stared at her father. "I can't go on forever like this," she said suddenly.

"What do you mean, Allyn?"

"Why, all I do is walk around and play games with you. I don't do any work." She moved restlessly. Some of the energy that was in her seemed to spill over. She got up and walked to the window and looked out briefly, then turned to him. "Everybody has work to do but me. I'm just a guest."

"Why, that's what you are, Allyn," Mark said. He was surprised at the girl and added, "You wouldn't want to do housework, or anything like that, would you? You'll have enough to do when we are able to move into Twelve Trees."

"I don't know. I just feel—oh, sort of useless, I guess you'd say."

"You're never that." He hesitated, then held out his hand. She came over and took it. He looked up at her and smiled again. "You've been a godsend to me, Daughter."

His simple words embarrassed her. She was not accustomed to being told things like that. His hand felt thin and fragile under hers, and she knew that if she squeezed it, he would not be able to withstand the pressure, he was that weak. He looked at her, then said quietly, "Sit down, Allyn. I want to talk to you."

She gave him a curious glance and then sat down. Folding her hands in her lap, she asked carefully, "What is it?"

Something, she saw, was troubling the sick man. Running his hand over his graying hair, he dropped his eyes for a few moments, seeming to study the intricate patterns in the carpet. In the quietness they could hear the slaves calling to one another outside the window out in the yard. It made a happy sound, and he sat there quietly trying to organize his thoughts. He finally lifted his eyes and said seriously, "Allyn, I'd like for you to marry."

"Marry!"

"Now wait—" He raised his hand to interrupt. "I know that sounds bossy, and maybe even crazy to you, but hear me out, will you?"

Mark's proposal had caught Allyn off guard. She had expected practically anything but this. Now she stared at him, her eyes wide with surprise, but she nodded and said, "Go ahead. I'd like to hear it." There was a wry tone in her voice that he did not miss. She leaned forward a little bit, her interest caught.

"Allyn, every woman needs a man. Don't you think so?"

Allyn seemed to get defensive. Her lips drew together, and she shook her head. "I don't need *anybody*—especially a husband!" she replied curtly.

"It's a pretty bad thing to be alone, Allyn." A bitterness came to his eyes, and he looked down again at his hands. "I guess I ought to know that better than anybody. I've been alone all my life. I've already told you how I made a fool out of myself about your mother. We could have had such a *good* life, but I didn't have sense enough to know it. I'd hate for you to make the same mistake I made."

Allyn shook her head stubbornly. "Why, it's not the same at all! You were in love with my mother, but I'm not in love with anyone."

"I don't know much about love," Mark said slowly. "I loved your mother. I see people like Clay and Melora that just seem to be meant for each other—and now, Lowell and Rooney. But this is a hard world, Allyn. I don't have to tell you that. A woman, I think, has a harder time alone than a man."

"I don't think that's so, not necessarily," Allyn said. "I can take care of myself. I don't want a man."

Her own words sounded harsh to her ears, but she was not ready to consider marriage. She had not thought that far ahead. She sat there as he began to talk, but there was a resistance in her that would not surrender.

Mark began to explain how he felt. "You know what it's like for a woman," he said gently, "but if a woman has a good husband, he can take that load off her. A woman has a difficult way to go in this society. She can either get married or teach school. There aren't many other options, are there?" He continued to speak, hoping to persuade her. But seeing that her back was straight, finally he said gently, "Allyn, you know I'd like you to have everything when I'm gone, but I want you to have a strong man to share it with."

Allyn shot him a glance that was almost harsh. "What do you want me to do? Advertise in the Richmond paper for a husband?"

"Why, you wouldn't have to do that," Mark protested. "I've noticed how many young men have stopped by. They have all kinds of excuses, but they come just to see you. Yet you won't have anything to do with them."

"I don't really want to talk about it," Allyn said shortly.

Mark leaned back in his chair and studied her. He put his fingertips together and formed a peak and let the silence run on. Finally he asked, "Did some man hurt you somewhere, Allyn?"

She gave him a strange, half-frightened look. "I've seen

the way that men have treated my mother over the years. Let's just say that I would rather do without what a husband can provide."

Mark saw that she was tremendously upset. He himself was shaken, for he had planned this carefully in his mind. It had been his concept that she would agree to marry and would begin to look around among the young men. He had been sure that, as beautiful as she was—and with some property—finding an acceptable husband would not be a problem. Now, however, he saw that she was both angry and frightened of the idea.

A weariness came to him, and the pain that lurked always just below the surface of his nerves suddenly attacked him. He sat there, enduring it, until finally it grew to a dull throbbing. Finally, he said quietly, "Allyn, I can't be around to help you, not for long. All I can do is be sure that you'll have someone who will take care of you."

"I can take care of myself!"

"You have a lot of determination. But a woman can be victimized—and I'd hate to see that happen to you. If I just handed you everything with no restrictions, I'd be afraid of what might happen."

"I don't want anything from you, Father," she said firmly. "I just came to meet you. Now I've done that . . . and I can . . . go back." This was not what she wanted, and she had to force the words out.

He saw that she did not mean what she said, and he reached out and put his hand on hers. "Allyn, until I can be sure, I can't sign the property over to you. Everything I have will be yours someday, but until you get married, we'll have to do something a little different."

Allyn felt a sudden burst of pity go through her. She had learned to respect this man. The antagonism she had brought with her when she came to meet him was now gone. She knew that he was telling her the exact truth, that he really wanted to help her. Nevertheless, she lifted her eyes and said, "Father, I'll never marry a man just to get a piece of land or money." A bitterness touched her lips; and she shook her head and said vehemently, "I've already seen too much of that."

Mark knew she meant exactly what she said. "Well," he said, as weariness marked his face with deep lines, "at least you're here and you have time—a little, anyway. I'll just pray that God will come into the situation." He looked at her and forced a smile. "I'm not much of a hand at praying," he admitted. "I came to it late in life, but somehow I know that God's got a man for you out there, and all we've got to do is find him."

Allyn didn't argue. Not wanting to give him more pain, she leaned forward, saying quietly, "It'll be all right. Now let's play another game of checkers."

CHAPTER FOURTEEN
A Bold Plan

The South was wearing down as the war ground on, and the North was also having serious problems. On March 3, 1863, the first Federal conscription act was passed. It stated that all able-bodied males between twenty and forty-five were liable for service. Prior to that the North had obtained its troops from volunteers and state militia called into Federal service. But when the conscription act was enacted in July, draft riots broke out at once.

Opposition to the act was widespread. Many were already lukewarm to the war effort. Secret societies for resisting the draft were formed, and in some areas draft officers were assaulted by mobs or run out of town. In almost every state there were protests, outbreaks of violence, and other forms of resistance.

By far the worst explosion took place in New York City in July 1863. New York had strong Southern sympathies, and its Democratic political machine despised Abraham Lincoln. The drawing of the first draftees' names touched off three days of rioting in which mobs roamed the streets and fought pitched battles with police. Several blacks were lynched, and the Colored Orphan Asylum was burned to the ground. Army units were rushed from Gettysburg to join the police and militia in quelling the riots, and the draft resumed in

New York. It was, however, a sign of the weariness of the North with the terrible conflict that drained it of young men and consumed all of its effort.

In Washington, with its still unfinished Capitol, the streets were filled with the crumbs of war, soldiers, clerks, all the baggage of war, veterans back on leave, recruits, spies, spies on spies, politicians, slackers, harlots, Negro boys who organized butting matches to please the recruits, tattooers, and fortune-tellers. All seemed to converge on Washington.

Perhaps the most lonely man in the entire city was Abraham Lincoln, who had lost a son but had no time to grieve him.

It was still hot in Washington that September. It was hot in the city, hot in the White House rooms, and sweltering hot in the office where Deborah sat waiting to see the president. The sentinel on his post clicked back and forth, and in the crowded bureaus the pens moved slowly as she sat there. The damp clerks, wet with sweat, watched the clock. Deborah mopped her brow with a handkerchief already soaked but stubbornly refused to leave. This was the second day she had sat in the office. The lieutenant in charge had done his best to persuade her to leave both days, but she had said quietly, "I'll wait, Lieutenant."

A short brigadier general exited from the door, and the lieutenant nodded to him, then stepped inside the office. He found the president standing at the window, staring out, and he said, "Sir, Gen. McCauley has been waiting all morning."

Lincoln turned and asked, "Who else?"

Lt. Smith shrugged. "The office is full, Mr. President, as it always is."

A smile touched the lips of the president. He stood there making a tall shape against the window, his coarse black hair awry, his body lank but muscular. He was weary and had to draw upon a tremendous energy, and now even that was growing weak. He was tired of the war, tired of the cabinet, tired of excuses, and weary to the bone of bearing the burden of this government. "Well," he said quietly, "I don't suppose it matters much. I guess I'll see the general—unless you have a better candidate."

Lt. Smith thought quickly. "Well, sir, there's a young lady out here. She's been waiting for two days."

"What does the girl want? Does she have a sweetheart she wants to get out of the draft?"

"I don't know, sir. She won't tell me, but I'll tell you one thing, she's better looking than anything else out there in the office."

Lincoln, always quick to appreciate a good joke, leaned forward and said, "Let's have her then, but don't tell my wife I'm seeing attractive young ladies."

"No, sir, of course not."

Deborah looked up with little hope when the lieutenant came out, but then he came over and smiled at her. "All right, Miss Steele, the president will see you now, but only for a few minutes. I put in a good word for you."

Deborah rose at once and gave the lieutenant a dazzling smile. She put out her hand and said quietly, "Thank you, Lieutenant. I appreciate it."

She moved inside at once, and the president came forward and put out his hand. "It is good to see you again, Miss Steele. How are you?"

"I'm fine, Mr. President. Thank you. I'm surprised you remembered," Deborah said.

"Yes. You're Col. Gideon Rocklin's niece."

"Yes, sir." She knew her time was short and said at once, "I'll try to be as brief as I can. Actually, Uncle Gideon is the reason I'm here."

He grew serious then and said, "I am sorry to hear of his being captured. That can't be very pleasant in those Confederate war prisons." His lips grew tighter, and he said, "Our own aren't much better, I'm afraid."

"I've come to see you, Mr. President," Deborah said, almost breathlessly. "I've tried everything I can to get my uncle exchanged, but it doesn't seem to have done much good. I've come to ask you if you could do anything to get him back."

Lincoln listened to her carefully, then nodded. "I'll write a letter, of course, but this thing has become very difficult, exchanging prisoners."

"How is that, Mr. President? We give them a man, they give us a man."

Lincoln shrugged. "Nothing seems to be simple in this war. In a bureaucracy I suppose, nothing ever is. But, I can tell you one thing," he added dryly. "If the Confederates knew for certain that the president of the United States wanted a certain man released, that would make it ten times as hard to get him. They'd hold out for the world with a fence around it in order to let him go."

"Oh," Deborah said in disappointment. Then she nodded, saying, "Yes, I can see that. But, we're so worried about him, I just thought that—"

"Of course, Miss Steele, we're all worried about our men in prisons. They're dying there at an awful rate. I will write the letter, as I said, and authorize the officer in charge of exchanges to exert every effort to get Col. Rocklin back, but we can't know how much good that will do. As I say, it is a confusing matter."

Deborah knew that she could go no further. "Thank you, Mr. President. I do appreciate it." She hesitated, then added, "I'll pray for you, not only for this but that you'll be able to bear this tremendous load that's on your shoulders. God bless you for what you're doing."

Lincoln's homely face lit up. He put his large hand out, which swallowed hers as he squeezed it gently. "Thank you, my dear," he said quietly. "Unless the Almighty sustained me, I could not go on for one day."

★ ★ ★

At the exact time that Deborah was speaking with the president of the United States, her fiancé, Noel Kojak, was in a much cruder setting. He had agreed—against his better judgment—to accompany his brother Bing to one of his bare-knuckle prizefights. It was not Noel's first fight. He had seen several others but never without a sense of disgust. Nothing could be much more depraved, he had thought, than watching two men beating each other into a state of insensibility.

The fight was held on a barge anchored offshore in the Potomac River. Noel had crossed over in a small boat along with Bing and his manager, a short, muscular man named Sam Phillips. Phillips himself had been a pugilist in his youth and now had found his glory in steering younger men down that same pathway.

"Cheer up, Noel. You look like you're going to a funeral." Bing Kojak grinned at his older brother, adding, "This is supposed to be entertainment."

Noel glanced at Bing, who was standing beside the referee in the center as he gave the instructions. "I wish you'd quit this foolishness, Bing," he said. But he knew that it was useless. He had talked to Bing so many times that now it had become automatic. He glanced at his brother, over six feet tall, strong and powerful with black wavy hair and dark brown eyes. He was very quick, which had saved his face from being marked in his fights. Even now there was a look of anticipation on his face, and Noel thought with amazement, *He likes it! I can't understand it.*

Phillips came over and massaged the thick muscles in Bing's neck. He was smoking a foul-smelling black cigar that seemed to be permanently attached to his face. Noel had never seen him without one and wondered at times if he smoked when he took a bath—if he ever took baths, that is. "You gotta watch this pug, Bing," he said, raising his voice above the noise of the crowd that lined the shore. "He's slow but strong as a bull. Just dance around him awhile. Let him wear himself out."

"Sure, Sam." Bing nodded carelessly.

The referee motioned to the two fighters, who went to the center of the ring. As he spoke to the two men, Noel looked over the crowd that lined the bank of the river. It was a male crowd, of course, composed almost equally of soldiers in the lower ranks and workingmen. Prizefighting was not a respectable form of entertainment, but no matter how many laws were passed against it, it appeared that people would always be willing to see two men come together to try to destroy each other. *I wonder why that is?* Noel asked himself.

Bing and Sam Phillips came back. Phillips jerked the robe from Bing's shoulders and growled, "Remember, don't let him catch you with that right of his."

"Sure, I'll watch it," Bing said with a grin. Then he moved forward, his left hand extended, his right cocked. He was wearing a pair of black tights and was naked from the waist up. He moved like a great cat, crossing the floor of the barge to meet the huge man that came roaring out like a mad bull.

"That fighter, he's pretty tough," Phillips informed Noel. "But Bing'll take him—if he don't get ideas of his own."

"What kind of idea?" Noel inquired. He watched Bing simply move to one side as Fred Cartwright sailed by. He was amazed to see Bing reach out and strike the big man on the neck negligibly. The blow did not seem hard, but the force of Bing's 190 pounds was behind it so it sent Cartwright to the floor, mostly as a result of his own momentum.

"End of round one," the referee announced. Every knockdown constituted a round, and there had been fights with as many as one hundred rounds. The fighters had thirty seconds between rounds.

Bing came back, took a swig of the water that Sam gave him, and said, "Pretty good crowd, eh Noel? We'll go out and celebrate after I've polished this bohunk off." Then he turned and saw that Cartwright had come back to scratch, standing in the middle waiting for him. The big man weighed well over two hundred pounds, and his face looked as if it had been battered by an ax handle.

"Stay away from him," Phillips warned. "That brother of yours, he don't think he'll ever get hurt. He could be champion of the world if he'd pay attention to me." He shifted the cigar around to another position, then shook his head. "Never saw anybody more stubborn in my whole life. Does it run in your family?"

"I don't think so, Sam," Noel answered. "That's just Bing."

Noel watched as Bing moved almost contemptuously around the bigger man. Cartwright bellowed and shoved and bulled his way toward the smaller man, but trying to hit Bing was like trying to hit a sunbeam. He simply was not there. Despite himself, Noel felt a twinge of admiration for his younger brother. *Well,* he thought, *I think it's a despicable way to make a living, but he's good at it all right.*

Time after time, Cartwright went to the deck but seemed to be indestructible. He had won most of his fights by the thick sheathing of muscle and bone that made him almost impervious to pain. He simply outlasted his opponents, soaking up whatever they had to give until they grew arm weary, then finally stepping in and battering them down.

After what seemed a long time, Bing came back after a knockdown and asked, "How many rounds is that, Noel?"

"I don't know, I've lost count. Aren't you getting tired?"

Bing shrugged. "A little, but he's slowing down, too. He's got a lot more beef to move around than I have."

This was true. Cartwright was moving slower. Now he simply plodded across the ring. Bing backed away most of the time, ignoring Cartwright's curses and jeers at his cowardice, biding his time. "He's doing fine," Phillips said, "if he just keeps on backing up—but look out, there he goes!"

Cartwright had propelled himself forward, desperately throwing a vicious roundhouse right that would have torn Bing's head off had it landed. Ordinarily, up until now, this was the sort of thing that Bing had dodged, but now that he was getting tired himself he decided on a new tactic. As Cartwright's fist whizzed by him, he blocked it with one forearm and threw himself forward. The force of his blow began with his right foot, traveled up his leg, then his torso. As his arm flashed out, his fist caught the bigger man coming

195

in. It was like being hit with a battering ram! The force of the blow drove Cartwright back, and his mouth was bloody as he hit the deck. He lay there, slowly moving his arms and legs as if he were swimming. Bing came back breathing hard.

"I told you to stay away from him," Phillips complained.

"Oh, that stopped his clock," Bing said. He watched the other fighter carefully and said, "I can tell. He won't be able to come back to scratch."

Noel watched as Cartwright's manager tried to get him upright. He poured water from a bottle over his face, hauled at him, but the bigger man's legs seemed to be made of rubber. After counting the thirty seconds between rounds, the referee said, "Eight seconds to come back to scratch."

Noel counted off the seconds, as did the crowd. Then a cheer went up as the referee came over and lifted Bing's hand shouting, "The winner: Bing Kojak!"

Bing laughed as Phillips reached up and pulled him down with a hard hug. Then Bing reached over and ruffled Noel's hair. "How about that, Older Brother?" he said. "Not bad, was it?"

Noel managed to grin. "Well, it's a good thing he didn't catch you. I believe he would have put you in a grave if one of those blows had struck."

"He didn't, though." Bing laughed, and his white teeth flashed in the light of the setting sun. "Let me get cleaned up, and we'll go out and eat."

Bing had brought extra clothes, and after he took a quick wash at a rooming house where he stayed sometimes he put on a new suit and came out looking fresh as a daisy. "I'm starved," he said, "let's go eat."

"I told Deborah I'd pick her up."

"Good, we'll take her out. She'll give us a touch of class, eh Noel?"

★ ★ ★

Deborah glanced across the table at the two brothers, thinking, not for the first time, how dissimilar they were: Noel,

with his light brown hair and gray eyes, was not over five ten
or 160 pounds, while Bing was over six feet and exuded raw
strength. He was much better looking than Noel with his
black wavy hair and dark brown eyes. Noel was not handsome. His features were regular, with a short nose and a wide
mouth. It was something on the inside that drew her to the
smaller man.

"Tell me about the fight," she said after they had ordered
their meal.

Bing said, "Oh, it was easy, Deborah—like taking candy
from a baby."

"It wasn't all that easy," Noel said. "If that big brute had
hit you, you'd have been in the hospital."

"Don't ever worry about what might have happened,"
Bing said airily. "That's my philosophy. There's something
like that in the Bible, isn't there?"

Deborah smiled at him. Bing was a good-natured young
man, wild and undisciplined yet devoted to his friends. She
had learned to trust him when they had worked together to
get Noel out of a Confederate hospital. Now she smiled at
him, reached over and patted his large hand. "I wish I could
have seen it," she said. "Next time I'll go along with you."

"You can't do that, Deborah," Noel gasped. "There are
no women at prizefights."

"Then it'll be a first," she said. She enjoyed teasing Noel,
who was far more straitlaced than she. Catching the look on
his face, she laughed delightedly and said, "Would I be an
embarrassment to you, Noel?"

"You certainly would!" he said. "I wouldn't permit you
to go to a thing like that!"

"Why, there are worse things than prizefights," Bing
protested.

"I'd like to know what!" Noel growled. "Two men beating each other into unconsciousness is barbaric."

"Unconscious?" Bing frowned. "Why, I'm about as conscious as a human being can be. Anyway, it'd be educational
for you, Deborah." He winked at her and grinned. "You and

I'll sneak off and go next time. We won't tell the preacher here."

"It's a date," Deborah said. She had no intention of doing such a thing, but she liked to tease Noel, who sat there looking disgusted with the conversation. "After all, Queen Elizabeth loved bearbaitings," she said.

Bing asked, "What's bearbaiting?"

"Oh, back in the days of Queen Elizabeth it was considered great fun to chain a bear to a tree and then turn dogs loose to kill it."

Bing's jaw hardened and his eyes narrowed. "Now that's what I call barbaric," he said. He looked at Noel, saying, "I'd be against a thing like that—but fighting, why, it's a test of skill."

Noel sat there, really enjoying himself. He knew the two were making fun of him, but his nature was such that he didn't mind it. Somehow Noel Kojak had risen amidst some of the worst circumstances in the world to become a scholar of sorts. He had never attended school, having been taught by his mother to read. He wrote poetry—which he was ashamed of and would let no one see—and had become a respected writer for several Northern newspapers. He had a gift, a flair, for describing a scene so vividly that the readers could sense the sights, smells, and color of the event.

Now as he looked across at Deborah he thought about their history—how she had befriended him and his family when he had never thought a young society girl would do such a thing. To him, she was the most beautiful woman in the world, and he never ceased wondering why she had chosen him out of all the men she knew. *She could have anybody,* he thought and was fiercely proud that she had agreed to marry him.

They talked cheerfully until their steaks came, then ate the food with the appetite of youth. Afterward, they ordered ice cream, cake, and coffee. After the meal, Bing patted his stomach and said, "I couldn't eat another bite! Now, I'll have to do a lot of roadwork to get rid of this paunch I've put on tonight."

"It was good, wasn't it?" Deborah said.

Then, as the two men talked, she fell into a silence that did not go unnoticed by Noel. He turned from Bing, asking, "What's wrong, Deborah?"

"I can't hide anything from you, can I? After we get married, how will I manage that? Women are supposed to have some secrets."

"Are you worried about something?" he asked, ignoring her joking.

Deborah bit her lip and said, "I finally got in to see the president this afternoon."

The two men stared at her, and it was Bing who exclaimed, "You mean—President Lincoln?"

"Yes, I've been sitting in his office for two days."

"I can't believe it!" Noel exclaimed. "I thought you were joking about going to see him."

"No, I wasn't joking. I haven't been able to think about anything except Uncle Gid and that awful Libby Prison."

"What did he say—the president?" Noel asked eagerly. "Did he say he'd help?"

"He said he'd write a letter, but he said if the Confederates found out that the president wanted Uncle Gid out, they'd ask for the moon and the stars for him."

"I expect that's right," Bing said. "Didn't he give you any hope at all?"

"Not much. He said he'd write the letter, as I said, but I could tell he didn't expect it to do much good." She leaned forward and put her chin on her fist and said, "President Lincoln is so tired. I don't see how he stands it. The office was full of people, every one of them demanding to see him, and that goes on every day." She shook her head almost angrily. "I felt bad taking up just that much of his time. But he was so kind."

The three sat there quietly. The two men respected Col.

Gideon Rocklin deeply and, of course, he had been Deborah's hero since her childhood, spoiling her completely.

"I wish I could help," Noel said heavily, "but I don't see any way."

Bing said suddenly, "You remember once I said I wouldn't risk my life for nothing, but if you ever found anything I could do that had some meaning to it, why, I'd go for it?"

Both Noel and Deborah looked at the large young man. "I remember," Noel said. He looked at his younger brother curiously. "What are you thinking, Bing?"

Bing leaned back in his chair. As they had talked of Deborah's uncle, an idea had come to him. Now he said casually, "Well, I think I'll go down there and bust Col. Rocklin out of that jail."

Deborah's eyes flew open with surprise. "Bing!"

"What are you talking about, Bing?" Noel exclaimed. "You can't do a thing like that."

"Tell me why I can't." Bing had spoken half in jest, but now he saw the expressions of the others and grew excited. He had hated his short stint in the army—the discipline, the lack of freedom—but he had looked back often and thought of the excitement that had been in him when he and Deborah had worked to get Noel out of the prison hospital. Now his face grew flushed as he leaned forward, saying, "Aw, it's just one prison, ain't it? And they got all the tough guys fightin' the war. Bound to be a bunch of old men and young kids serving as guards. Why, that's the way it was when you was in the hospital. Don't you remember, Noel?"

"I remember how we could have all gotten killed getting out of that place," Noel said in rebuke. "But, he's not in a hospital—he's in a prison. And from what I hear, in those prisons they shoot people who even *look* like they want to escape."

"Ah, you're just a worrywart," Bing said, dismissing Noel's concerns. He was enjoying the sensation his announcement had made. Leaning forward, he said, "I don't have another fight for a few weeks. I think I'll just go down and bust him out. Be some excitement in that, I reckon."

Deborah said clearly, "That's fine, Bing, and I'll go along with you."

Now it was Bing's turn to blink in surprise. "Why, you can't do that, Deborah!"

"Tell me why I can't," she echoed his words. A rash grin touched her lips as she said, "You've got to get him out and get him back into the North, and it's going to take more than you to do that."

Noel felt this was getting out of hand. "This is crazy! Both of you are crazy," he said. "Don't you know that that's about the same thing as being a spy? They hang spies down there pretty often, you know."

"They have to catch us first," Bing said. He was now totally enamored with his proposition. He knew that Deborah was smart enough to do the thinking and said so. "You do the planning, and I'll do the busting, Deborah." Then he looked over at Noel, slapped him on the shoulder, saying, "I'll just have to borrow your fiancée for just a little while. You don't mind, do you, big brother?"

Noel understood that these two could not be stopped. Both of them had an excitement in their eyes, and their whole faces were lit with the thoughts of what was to come. Heavily he drew a breath, then shook his head. "No, I won't lend her to you—but I'll go along with you." He grinned as the other two suddenly grabbed at him and pounded at his shoulders. "Hey!" he said, "don't beat me to death! Somebody with some brains has got to go along to be sure you two don't go to jail."

"We'll do it! We'll all three go," Deborah exclaimed in delight, "and we won't tell anybody. We'll just go get Uncle Gid out, and then you can write a story or a book about it that will make us rich and famous."

The three talked excitedly until the restaurant closed for the night. None of them had the vaguest glimmer of an idea about *how* to get Gideon Rocklin out of the prison, but they were all totally committed to the task and pledged themselves to do whatever necessary to get the job done.

It was Bing who said, "Why, it'll be a piece of cake!"

CHAPTER FIFTEEN
Store-Bought Husband

★

"You wait right here, Sonny," Allyn said to the tall young slave who had driven her into Richmond for supplies.

Sonny looked around apprehensively and said, "I'd better comes wif you, Missy—you don't know dis heah place. Dey's lots of bad folks here!"

Allyn laughed. "Don't be silly. I'll go make my purchases, then you can come bring the wagon around and pick them up." She stepped down, ignoring his protests, then made her way along the street that seemed to be more than unusually crowded.

For thousands of Southerners Richmond had become a city of refuge. Runaway slaves, destitute soldiers' wives, and army deserters all flocked to the capital, along with loyalists ejected from Federal occupied zones. Largely as a result of this migration, the city's population had trebled to 128,000. As the diarist Mary Chestnut put it, "Richmond was filled to suffocation, hardly standing room left."

For an hour Allyn moved among the stores, but most of them had bare shelves and demanded exorbitant prices. When she got home, she sat down and talked to Mark about it.

"Well, it's bad, and it's going to get worse," he said. "In April there was a bread riot in Richmond. A group of angry women led by a woman named Mary Jackson cornered Governor Letcher."

"What did he say?"

"Nothing much he *could* say—and not much he could do, either, when the women went on a rampage."

Allyn stared at him wide-eyed. "But—what did they do?"

"They raided the stores," Mark answered. "Just swarmed in brandishing knives and hatchets. Wrecked the stores and came out with food and whatever else they could lay their hands on."

"How awful!"

"Well, it was. But it didn't go on long." A thin smile came to Mark's lips, and he added, "President Davis stopped it. It was something to see, according to what I heard. The president reached into his pockets and gave them all his money. But when that didn't satisfy them, he took out his watch and said, 'I don't want to see any of you harmed—but this must stop. If you don't disperse in five minutes, you'll be fired upon!'"

"Did they leave?"

"Oh yes. I think they believed the president."

"Do you think he would have ordered the soldiers to fire on civilians?"

Mark gave her a thoughtful look and then nodded. "I think he might have done it, Allyn. He's a compassionate man at heart, but he sees everything in terms of war. Of course things are getting worse every day."

"Well, I don't know about everything," Allyn said, "but I know grocery prices are terrible! Soap was only ten cents a pound, Susanna said, but now it's a dollar ten a pound. That's one tenth of a soldier's monthly pay. Half a pound of green tea costs sixteen dollars."

"I know. I feel so sorry for the families of the soldiers who are fighting. I know they're suffering at home, and I fear it's only going to get worse."

Allyn had sat down across from Mark. She had taken him in his wheelchair to the porch, where they were watching a grouping of low-lying clouds skim along. The moon was yellow as old cheese as they sat drinking in the beautiful, dark scene. Far away they could hear the sound of singing from the slaves' quarters, and now the cry of a lonesome, mournful dog somewhere floated to them on the cool September breeze.

Mark looked up and said, "Look, those clouds are going to hit the moon." As they watched, the clouds blotted the moon momentarily, then slowly unveiled it so that the pale silver rays fell on the earth again, casting their gleam on the dead fields that surrounded the mansion.

"Have you heard about Jason Larrimore?" Mark inquired.

"Why no, I haven't heard anything. What happened to him?"

"Bad news, I'm afraid. Something I've been afraid of all the time, I suppose. The Federals penned his ship along the coast. Too bad!"

"Did they capture him?" Allyn asked quickly.

"No, he was wounded, but he and all the crew got away. They had to scuttle the ship, though, and everything he had was in it."

"Why, I thought he was rich. I thought all blockade-runners were rich—the successful ones, that is."

"He put all his money in that ship. It cost a fortune. He told me he had put all he could get his hands on, but he thought he would make a profit with this run through the blockade and back. He could have, too," Mark said regretfully.

The silence ran on, and Allyn asked finally, "What will he do now?"

"I don't know. He's in Richmond trying to raise money for another ship, but he won't have any luck. Money's hard to come by these days."

"Why don't you help him, Father?" Allyn asked.

"It's too risky," Mark said quickly. "It would cost all I have to get a ship like he needs, and the same thing could happen to it that happened to the last one. It's a dangerous business. No, I can't do that."

"I feel sorry for him," she said. "He's a little arrogant, but I suppose most captains are that way. I guess they have to be."

"Jason has had a tough life, Allyn. His parents died when he was fourteen. He went to sea as a cabin boy," Mark said quietly. "He rose all the way to captain on the strength of his fists and his quick wits. He bought a piece of a ship that had been condemned and kept it afloat somehow. He told me that he ran slaves once, but it sickened him."

"He's very cynical, isn't he?"

"Well, he doesn't believe in much. I guess he's had enough hard knocks to convince him there's very little honesty and kindness in this world." He stared across through the moonlight at her and said, "You didn't like him, I could tell. Did he mistreat you in any way in New Orleans or on the way here?"

"Oh no," she said quickly. "It's not that, he's just—oh, I don't know."

Mark let the silence linger and then said, "The papers are ready for signing. Twelve Trees is a wonderful place," he urged gently. "You and I could go there, and we could have some peace for however long I've got left. It's a little isolated, but I wouldn't mind that."

Allyn shook her head. "I'll go with you, but I won't marry." She saw that her answer disappointed him and wished that it were different. She found herself growing fonder of him and knew that except for that hard streak that had built up in her during her childhood and adolescence, she would have felt this affection even more strongly. She could not free herself from the resentment. She knew that was wrong, but that was the way she was.

"I'll have the papers anytime you are ready," Mark said quietly. "I'll go ahead and buy the place, but it'll stay in my name. Then, if I die, I'll leave Clay as the executor. He'll be that until you marry, then he'll sign it all over to you."

A lump came up in Allyn's throat and she said, "I—I don't want you to think I'm ungrateful. It's not that, but I've not been able to get very close to a man. Maybe I don't have any love in me. Sure, I loved Mother, but as for men . . ."

At once Mark said, "I won't rush you, Allyn. Maybe it's best this way. And who knows? I'm a tough old bird! I might live a long time."

"Yes," she said quickly and reached over and patted his hand. "You probably will. Let's do it. You buy the place, and I'll go there with you and you can teach me how to play chess. That ought to take a lifetime, at least." Neither of them referred to the subject again, and for several days she seemed unusually quiet. Early one morning she came to him and said, "I'm going into Richmond. I want some time to think. I may stay for several days. Is that all right?"

"Why, of course. Here, take this money. Rooms will be high in the hotels there, if there are even any vacancies. Have a good time." Secretly he hoped she would meet some young man and fall in love with him. "Go on now, bring me something back, maybe Dickens's latest novel if you can find it."

He watched as she left the room, then later spoke with Susanna about it. "I wish she'd meet somebody, but I don't think she will. She's afraid of men, I think."

Susanna said quietly, "A lot of women are—and some of them for good reason." Warmly she smiled at him and said, "But there's a man for her somewhere. You and I, we'll just beat on the gates of heaven until the Lord hears our prayer and gives her just the one she needs."

★ ★ ★

"Why, I'm sorry, Capt. Larrimore, but you must understand that the money in this bank doesn't belong to me. It belongs to the depositors, and I can't take risks with it. I have to put it into sound ventures—and buying a ship to run the blockade, why, that's about as risky a venture as I can think of!"

Jason had expected little from Giles Goodman, the president of Planters' Bank. He rose to his feet and said quietly, "Well, I didn't really expect you could, Giles, not after I just lost one ship."

Goodman rose at once and protested. "Now wait, Jason—" He was a tall portly man with muttonchop whiskers and a head of bushy white hair. "I think something might be done in time, some private subscriptions maybe. Let me talk to a few of my friends. But, as for a bank loan"—he shrugged his big shoulders expressively—"I'm afraid that's just out of the question."

"Sure, I'll be around," Jason said. He shook the big hand and, turning a little too quickly, felt a twinge in the wound in his back that had not completely healed. He left the bank, stepped outside, and blinked in the bright sunlight. The streets, as usual, were crowded, and he walked carefully to avoid being jostled by the many soldiers who hurried busily along. For over an hour he walked the main streets of the busy city and finally went back to his hotel and started to go to his room.

"Ah, Capt. Larrimore?"

Jason turned to see the clerk, a small man named Robbins, looking at him. Moving to the desk, he said, "Yes, what is it?"

"Well, I hate to mention it, Captain, but . . ." Robbins seemed embarrassed. He tugged at his collar and let his eyes drop to the register. He fiddled with it with his hands, then finally lifted his eyes and shrugged his thin shoulders. "The fact of the matter is, Captain, if you could pay just a *small* portion of your bill?"

Jason had already spent a small fortune at the hotel. He stared hard at the clerk, then shrugged. "How much is the bill?"

"It comes to a little over $170, Captain."

Jason reached into his pocket and pulled out a thin roll of bills, peeled off half of them. "There's a hundred—I'll pay the rest tomorrow."

Robbins took the money and said regretfully, "You know,

I hate to ask. You've been such a good guest, Capt. Larrimore, but the owner—"

"I know, Robbins," Jason interrupted, "it's not your fault. Don't worry about it."

He turned and walked back outside. As always, when there was trouble he liked to be near the water. He walked down to the James River and watched the deckhands on the small boats. Finally, he talked with one of the captains and found himself almost asking for a job. But then he knew he would never be content on a small riverboat. He bid the man good-bye and turned back toward his hotel.

"I'll have to go to sea," he muttered. "Ought to be able to find some shipping company that needs a good captain."

But he was not happy with the decision. Having been a ship owner had spoiled him for anything else, and he knew it. But when he ran over the possibilities in his mind, he found there were none. He had no way of raising the money to buy another ship except by a stroke of luck. He might take his remaining small roll of bills and win big in a poker game, but in his experience the very time a man needed to win was the time he usually lost. Quick and impulsive, however, he decided, "I might as well try it." He moved to a saloon nearby and soon was sitting in a game. He ran his stakes up to over three hundred dollars, then lost it all on one hand.

When he left the saloon he was as broke as he'd ever been in his life. He rammed his hands down in his pocket and came out with a coin. "Ten cents," he muttered. "That's my bankroll." His lips drew into a thin smile, and he shook his head. "It looks like I'm going to have to go to work. I hate to work for anybody! I guess I'm just too independent for that."

He did not even have enough money for supper, so he went to his room, lay down on his bed, and stared at the ceiling. He was essentially a man of action. If there was a job to be done, a risk to be taken, there was no hesitancy. But waiting was a different story. Now there stretched out before him a time of inactivity or of boring work. The truth was that he was enamored with running the blockade. There was enough risk in it to whet his appetite for adventure and enough profit to bring in the money to follow the kind of life he wanted to lead.

Now that was all gone, and he could think of nothing but leaving the next day and going to the coast. *Probably go back north—more chance of getting a ship there than in the South with this blockade.*

He dozed off and started when a knock at the door awakened him. "Who is it?" he called out, sitting up at once.

"Capt. Larrimore?" Jason advanced to the door, opened it, and saw Robbins there. "Captain," he said, "there's a young lady downstairs that wants to see you."

"Young lady? What's her name?"

"She didn't give it, Captain." Robbins smiled. "She's a fine-looking young woman, though. Dressed real nice. I offered to let her come up to your room, but she wouldn't do it. Shall I tell her you'll be down?"

A few possibilities ran through Jason's mind. He did know several attractive women in Richmond, but none would be coming to seek him out at his hotel. Or if they were such, he was not anxious to have them come up. "All right, Robbins, I'll be right down," he said.

Quickly, he washed his face, combed his thick blond hair back, and put on his coat. Leaving the hotel room, he started to lock the hotel door, then smiled grimly. *I don't know what they could get except my clothes.* He went down the stairs and looked around the lobby. Quickly his sharp eyes caught the woman who was standing beside a large potted plant over to his left. Her back was to him. He walked over and said, "Hello, I'm Jason Larrimore."

And then the woman turned, and he saw, with a slight shock, that it was Allyn Rocklin. "Hello, Captain," she said unsmilingly. "I'm sorry to disturb you like this."

Jason shrugged his shoulders. "I wasn't doing anything." He stared at her and asked quickly, "You wanted to talk to me?"

She glanced around at the busy hotel lobby. "Can we go somewhere and sit down?"

Jason looked over at the door to his left and said, "We can go into the restaurant. It's too early for most people to eat. I expect that'll be quiet enough."

When they entered Jason saw that there were only a few tables occupied. A waiter came at once and showed them to a table off in the corner of the room. Jason asked, "Are you hungry?"

"I suppose I could eat a little something." She listened as the waiter rattled off the entrees and then gave her choice. Jason shrugged, saying, "I'll have the same."

The waiter wheeled and left the table. Jason leaned back in his chair and waited for her to speak. She seemed nervous and was pale. *It must be about Mark,* he thought. *I wonder if he died? No, she would have told me that right off.* Aloud, he said, "How's your experiment turning out?"

"Experiment?"

"Why yes, I thought that was the idea, your coming to Richmond, to Gracefield, to see if you could become a part of the Rocklin family. Wasn't that the idea?"

Allyn nodded but said nothing. She seemed to have trouble concentrating, and for a while she stumbled over her words, giving him some of the details of Mark's illness. She talked about the family there and seemed very interested in the coming marriage of Rooney and Lowell Rocklin.

"Women always like weddings," Jason remarked. "Tell me, why do they always cry?"

"I don't know. I've never been to a wedding," Allyn said simply. "Not a fancy one, anyway. A girlfriend of mine got married once, but it wasn't very impressive, and I didn't cry."

"I don't suppose you cry about much. You're not a crying woman, are you?"

"Is that a way of telling me I'm hard and unfeeling?"

"Why, not at all. I don't cry myself, but I'm not hard and unfeeling. Matter of fact, I think we're alike, you and I."

"No, we're not alike," Allyn spoke abruptly.

"I think you're wrong, but we won't argue about it." He knew that she had not come to see him to talk about anything as trite as women crying at weddings—but whatever it was, he would have to let it come out. When the meal came, he ate slowly and watched her closely, thinking all the time what a fine-looking woman she was.

Finally, she pushed her plate back and said, "I have to say what I came to say." She'd eaten almost nothing, and he noticed that her hands were fidgeting nervously with the napkin.

A thought came to him. "Are you in some kind of trouble, Allyn? If that's it—"

"I am in trouble, but not like you think." She raised her eyes to his and waited for a moment, then said, "My father wants me to get married."

"Married? Married to whom?"

"He hasn't said," Allyn said wryly. She shook her head. "I don't think he's thought about it. He has this idea that a woman's not able to take care of herself, that she needs a husband."

"Well, that's true, isn't it?"

"Not always, but that's what he thinks. Anyway, he's been having trouble getting his money out of the Northern banks, so the sale of Twelve Trees has been delayed. While he's been waiting he decided that he'd keep the plantation in his name until I got married, then it would be placed in my name."

The waiter came back to refill the coffee cups, and they waited until he was gone to resume their conversation. There was a desperation in her that Jason had not seen before, a vulnerability that he had not suspected. She seemed younger, more vulnerable. Larrimore asked carefully, "Surely he must have some candidate. He wouldn't want you to marry just *anybody.*"

"I think he'd take any man who was decent and respectable. He's got this fear of a woman being preyed upon if she doesn't have a husband. He's afraid that'll happen to me."

"Well, I've seen it happen to others." He studied her carefully, then shook his head. "I don't think any man would take advantage of you. I don't think he'd have the chance."

She lifted her head impetuously and demanded, "What do you mean by that?"

"I mean you're pretty and look soft and gentle—but inside there's a hard streak in you, Allyn. That's what I meant when I said we are alike. I've got the same thing in me." He drank the coffee slowly and looked at her. "Both of us came up the hard way. That does something to a person—being poor, having to learn to fight to survive. Most of the Rocklins don't know anything about that. They're good people, but they always had money, family, someone to lean on." He leaned back, half shut his eyes, stirred the coffee gently, then said, "Sometimes at night I go by houses that are lit up and know there are families inside. Those people have everything."

"Why, I've thought that myself," Allyn said in astonishment. She had not considered this side of the tall man, for he had never revealed the softness or gentleness that she saw now.

And then he looked up and said, "Well, are you going back to New Orleans, or are you gonna get a husband and stay here? It's that simple, isn't it?"

"I could stay here with Father. When he dies, Clay will be the executor. But that's not what I want." She hesitated, then said, "You've been independent, Jason. You had a hard time, as you said, when you were a boy and you've had to fight your way. But you had the one thing that most women can't have—you had freedom and independence."

"I had that all right." Jason shrugged, a slight smile pulling the corner of his lips up. "Sometimes I wish I had somebody to run to, but there's never been anybody like that."

"That's what I want—independence," Allyn said firmly. She hesitated for one moment, gathering her courage, then said, "And I can think of only one way to get it."

Jason Larrimore looked at her curiously. "How are you going to accomplish that? Mark insists on you getting married. Are you just going to wait until a husband comes along?"

"That's—that's what I came here for, Jason." She took a deep breath and said, "I've heard about your misfortune with your ship." She saw his lips tighten, and she nodded slightly. "I'm sorry for it."

"I've been broke before." He looked around, and a whimsical thought came to him. "I hope you've got the money to pay for this meal," he said, "because I don't."

What he said seemed strangely to encourage her. Allyn leaned forward, her green eyes glowing. "Jason, you'll probably think I'm crazy, but here's why I came: You need a ship, and I—I need a husband." She smiled at his sudden reaction, for his mouth parted, and his eyes blinked. "Yes, we both need something, and I know I'm willing to do my part to see that you get your ship if you're willing to help me get what I want, which is freedom and independence."

Jason Larrimore had known many women and heard some strange proposals. Carefully he asked, in order to clarify things, "Let me get this straight—we get married, you buy me a ship, and you get Twelve Trees. Is that it?"

"Yes, that's it."

Larrimore smiled broadly, leaned forward, and shook his head. "I think you're crazy," he said amiably. "I never heard such a wild scheme in all my life."

Allyn's face flushed a rich red. She felt the heat rising to her cheeks, and she said harshly, "If that's the way you feel about it, then that's all there is to it."

She started to rise, but Larrimore reached across the table and pulled her down. "Wait a minute," he said. "I didn't mean to hurt your feelings, but you've been thinking about this for some time, haven't you? Now you just tossed it at me. Give me a minute to think."

Allyn said, "What I'm proposing is not a real marriage. You can buy your ship, and I think you could make your fortune with it. But Twelve Trees will be *mine.*" She hesitated and said in a lower tone, "And my life will be mine." A sudden color suffused her cheeks, and she gave him a direct stare as she said, "I don't want you in my bed."

Larrimore stared at her bluntness. "That's plain enough," he said. "Speaking right out, aren't you?"

"I don't think I'll ever love a man," she said quietly. "But I would love to have a place, and I would love to have the freedom to do what I please. Those are the things I want. You probably don't want to even think about this. I know men want a wife in—in every sense of the word, and there's no reason why you should be any different." Allyn shook her head in resignation. "Oh, why did I come? It's just a crazy idea!"

Once again she attempted to rise, but he said, "Wait, Allyn—" When she paused, he said, "I don't think you know what you're asking. Marriage is for a long time. If we got married, I could never have anybody else, neither could you. Divorces are hard to come by, especially in the South."

"I don't know how much time I have, but I want to do something more than just be a slave to some man," she said coldly. His refusal or semirefusal had angered her. She was embarrassed and humiliated that after steeling herself to make such an offer, he was turning her down. She said abruptly, "Forget that I even mentioned it!"

Larrimore leaned back and looked at her. He thought about the long days ahead, about his penniless condition, and as the silence ran on his choice became clear. "I think it would be a mistake," he said finally, "but I want a ship more than I want to live. I'll tell you what—give me a day, and you take a day, and we'll think about it. I'll meet you here tomorrow at two o'clock. If that's what you want and that's what I want, we'll do it."

"All right, I'll see you tomorrow at two o'clock. Come to my room at the Patterson."

She arose and started to leave. He called after her, "Didn't you forget something?"

"Forget what?"

"You didn't pay for the supper."

Allyn flushed, reached into her purse, and put some money on the table.

"You'll have to give me enough to pay my hotel bill," he said, "and I need a shave and a few other things. A hundred dollars ought to tide me over." He smiled and said, "Until we get married, that is. Then you can tell me what my allowance will be. I'm not up on the rules of being a kept man."

Allyn saw that he was not serious. She handed him a few bills, then turned, saying, "I'll see you tomorrow, but I can tell you right now, I won't change my mind. I'll keep my part of the bargain." She gazed at him and said in a steady tone, "And if we do this, you'll keep your part of the bargain—*all* of it."

"Or what?" Larrimore demanded in an innocent tone. "Will you shoot me if I try to break into your bedroom?"

Allyn Rocklin stared at him thoughtfully, then nodded and said, "Yes, I will shoot you." Then she turned and walked away.

Watching her go, her answer had delighted Jason Larrimore. "By George, I think she'd do it!" he muttered. He got up and left the room wondering what his decision would be. When he was back in his room he thought, *I want a ship, but do I want it this bad?*

★ ★ ★

At two o'clock the next afternoon a knock came at the door of Allyn's room. She had dark shadows under her eyes, for she had not slept at all well. She had risen at daylight, dressed, and had gone for a long walk, but had eaten nothing.

She stared at the door almost in fear for a moment, raising her hands to her breast, her eyes wide with anticipation. Then she straightened her back, walked over, and opened the door. "Come in, Jason," she said calmly.

Larrimore entered, pulled off his hat, and turned to Allyn. For a moment he said nothing and then murmured, "I didn't sleep much last night."

"Neither did I."

Larrimore considered her carefully and then said, "You know, I said yesterday that we were alike. You were angry about that."

"I remember. I still don't agree."

"Well, we're alike in one way. We both mean to have what we want no matter what it costs to get it."

Allyn raised her hand to her throat and for one moment could not think of what to say. Finally, she said, "Does that mean that you'll go through with it?"

"Yes." A calculating look came into his eyes. "You remember, I kissed you."

"Against my will," she reminded him quickly. She had been ashamed ever since that kiss at her response to his touch. And now she stared at him and said, "Don't start this way. I've told you my terms. If you're not willing to meet them—"

"You don't have to worry about my keeping the bargain," Jason said at once. "Let's be agreed. You buy me a ship, and I satisfy the requirements for your getting the money and the property. We live together, but as you put it, we don't share the same bedroom. But what about other women I might see?"

A flush came to her cheeks, and she held her head high. "I'll never ask you about them. I don't want to hear."

A smile touched his lips, and he asked almost idly, "Well, what about your men friends? Am I supposed to ignore them?"

"You don't seem to understand, Jason," Allyn said. "This is a business partnership, nothing else. What you do with your life is your own business—what I do with mine is none of your business." She halted, then said, "I think both of us are crazy for even thinking about it."

"You're probably right." He hesitated, then put his hand

out. She took it, and he held it tightly for a moment. "These are insane times we're living in. It's infected everybody, I think." Her hand felt fragile in his, soft and defenseless. He'd thought about this long and hard and now he said, "Make sure this is what you want, Allyn."

"I'm sure," she whispered, then pulled her hand back. "Like you say, you'll get what you want, and I'll get what I want."

"We're probably both fools, but I've been a fool about other things," he said. He stood staring at her, then said, "We'll have to put on some sort of a masquerade, I suppose, for Mark and your family."

"I suppose. I'll go home today. You come tomorrow, stay a couple of days, then we'll tell my father."

"A whirlwind courtship! Sorry I don't play a guitar and can't sing love songs."

"That won't be required," Allyn said. Now that the thing was settled, she had to fight down the feelings that seemed to close upon her throat tightly. "We'll just each remember our part of the bargain."

"All right, it's settled then." He turned to the door, opened it, then stood looking back at her. He started to speak, and she waited. But whatever it was he intended to say, he changed his mind. "I'll see you tomorrow," he said quietly and turned and shut the door.

Allyn walked over and sat down on the bed. She found she was trembling so much that her knees were unable to hold her up. Finally, without explanation, she turned over and buried her face in the pillow and began to weep.

CHAPTER SIXTEEN
All Brides Are Beautiful

★

"I'm surprised that Jason has stayed so long, even though it's only a couple of days." Mark Rocklin was sitting in his wheelchair looking out the window of his room as Susanna made his bed. Below him he watched as Allyn and Jason Larrimore strolled past. "Jason's not a man to waste time. He's always been active, on the go."

Susanna patted the pillow in place, then turned to come over and stand beside him. She too watched the pair, silently for a moment, then expressed her thoughts, "I don't know him as well as you do. He's restless, though, anyone can see that."

Mark looked up at her and said, "You know, everything that Allyn could wish lies ahead of her. All the good things."

Susanna reached out and touched his hair, saying, "I've got to cut your hair, you're getting shaggy." She considered his words and finally said, "Everything that lies ahead of her probably won't be good. It never is, is it? We have to learn to take the good with the bad." They both remained silent and she finally added, "I've prayed that the good things would come to her, and I know they will. God will hear us." She looked at him fondly and said, "You've come a long way in a short time, Mark. Not many men, or women, learn to know God as quickly as you have."

He shook his head. "I'm a child," he said. "If I'd found God years ago . . ." He stirred his shoulders restlessly, then smiled at her. "You can't go back, can you? None of us. All you could do is accept where you are, live in the time that God's given, and maybe try to make up for lost time."

The two sat there talking for a little while until Susanna rose and left the room, giving him a cheerful word. Again he turned and saw that his daughter and Larrimore had moved over to the line of trees. As he watched, they sat down on an old log, appearing to be engaged in some sort of earnest conversation. Mark thought about the things that can come into a person's life, the sounds of a family through a house, the deep midnight silence of that house when people slept in peace, the first stirrings of spring, the smell of hay rising from a sickled meadow, the voice of one you love calling to you fresh and clear. These were the little experiences that when put together made a life. If a man took them as they came and stopped for them and lived each good moment of them, he was a rich man. He realized, with a deep grief, that his own failure had been the failure to stop. Somehow he had lived for the future and had been impatient for today. So he had hastened through the day and lost the wonder of these full moments. Now he realized that over the years he had starved himself. He stirred, put his hands out on the windowsill, and said aloud, "On this earth there's only one moment in which to live—that little bit of time we call *now!*"

Later in the day Allyn came to him. She said at once, "Jason went out for a ride. He loves horses, doesn't he?"

"Yes, I think if he hadn't been a seaman, he might have turned out to be a jockey, although he's too big for that, of course." The light filtered through the window and fell on her, sending golden glints dancing in her hair. "You look very nice today," he said. "Is that a new dress?"

She was wearing a blue dress with a white collar and cuffs that fitted her snugly. "Yes, I bought it when I was in Richmond. I felt like a fool paying as much as I did, but everything's so high there." She sat down beside him and talked for a few moments. Finally she said, "What can I fix you to eat tonight? Anything special?"

"Just whatever the rest of you eat." He had no appetite and ate primarily to satisfy the pleadings of the women, who somehow felt that food would solve all problems. "I'm surprised at Jason," he said. "He doesn't usually stay this long in one place—not unless there's a card table or horse race or some excitement going on. Pretty dull life for him." He fingered the coverlet over his knees, then asked, "Has he said anything about losing his ship?"

Allyn hesitated, then said, "It really tore the heart out of him, Father. He said once that he didn't care much about anything after he lost that ship. It was almost like a wife to him, he said." The thought amused her for a moment, and the corners of her full lips turned up. She made a fine picture as she sat there in the amber rays of the sun. There was a fullness and a spirit of life about her that pleased Mark as he looked at her. She caught his glance and smiled. "He said ships made better wives than women because you could control them better. Just a matter, he said, of putting the sails up and down and hauling the rudder around one way or the other. Not a very complimentary thing to women."

"Well, that's Jason's way. I'm not sure he means all he says. Sometimes I wonder if I've ever known him. He's pretty outgoing, but deep under all that talk I think there's a pretty sensitive fellow." He saw that she was restless and finally asked quietly, "Is something wrong?"

Allyn licked her lips and then said, "I've got something to tell you. I'm—I'm not sure how you'll take it."

Apprehension ran along Mark's nerves. He had suffered such terrible misfortunes that despite himself and his newborn faith he could not help feeling some dire portent in her words and in her demeanor. "What is it, Allyn?" he asked quietly, preparing himself for the news that she was going back to New Orleans. He hated to see her throw her life away in a place like that, and although he had already determined to help her all that he could, he longed for her to be with him for whatever time he had left.

"I—I've been thinking about what you said, about getting married, about a woman needing a husband." She hesitated for a moment, and he saw the uncertainty that lay over her. It was unusual, for despite her youth she had an assurance and a determination that flashed forth out of her spirit. It showed in the set of her back, the way she lifted her chin when she made statements. But now she was fragile and more vulnerable than he'd ever seen her. He could not imagine what she wanted to say. Finally she said it. "I think you were right, so I'm going to be married."

An alarm went off in Mark's mind, and he said abruptly, "Married? Why, Allyn!"

"I know you'll think it's rash, but it's what you wanted, isn't it? And I suppose you can guess who the man is."

At once all the pieces fell into place in Mark's mind. Surprise washed over him, and he exclaimed, "You can't mean Jason?"

"Yes, I do."

Mark suddenly realized he had done the girl a grave disservice. "I pushed you into this, Allyn," he said, regret and remorse marring his face. "I can see that now."

"No, you were right. A woman is alone in the world. She does need someone. That's the way the world is, so Jason and I have decided to get married." She lifted her chin in a gesture of defiance, but her eyes pleaded with him for understanding. "I know it's sudden, but we have big plans that you'll like. One of them is that we're going to take part of the inheritance that you're making available to me and buy Jason a ship. I think it's only fair for you to know, before we marry, that that's what we'll do. He's a seagoing man, and he needs a ship."

Mark was shaken by this disclosure. As she spoke on he tried to think of some way to prevent this girl from plunging ahead. "But you don't love him," he said finally.

"I—don't think I shall ever love any man the way the

books tell about it, Father. But we have an understanding. He is a good man, and I'll try to be a good matron of Twelve Trees."

"That's not much to build a marriage on."

"It's more than some have," Allyn said quietly. "Anyway, he'll be coming to talk to you. I wanted to tell you first, and I want to ask you not to worry. You and Jason and me, we'll go to Twelve Trees, and it'll be good." She got up suddenly and did something very unusual. She leaned over, put her arms around him, and held him tightly for a moment.

Mark felt the warmness of her body against him, then the soft touch of her lips on his cheek. Without a word, she turned and whirled away, and he could see the distress written on her face. The door closed, and he sat there unable to think clearly.

Five minutes later, when Jason entered the room, Mark said at once, "Jason, this is wrong. You don't love that girl."

Jason came over, moving softly for a big man, and sat down in the chair. He leaned back, his blue eyes fixed on Mark, and said, "I came to make you a promise, Mark."

"A promise?"

"I know this seems rash to you. It does to me, too." He looked down at his hands, spread them open, then closed them and looked up again. "You're a smart man, Mark. I've never known anyone that I admired more, so I just want to promise you that no harm will ever come to your daughter through me. I'll do the best I can to take care of her."

"There's one thing you can't do," Mark said, his voice grating. "You can't love her. That means you can't give her the thing that a husband ought to bring to a woman."

"In that, you are right," Jason admitted reluctantly. "I don't think she loves me either. What we have here, Mark, is a situation of two people who need each other. You know me, I've been one of the roughs. But I want you to know that I'll take care of Allyn. Twelve Trees is hers, and I know I can make it this time with a ship, so she'll be provided for." He leaned forward, intensity drawing his face fine. He was a powerful man, and strength seemed to flow out of him. "This country is going to the devil, Mark, and we both know it. The South's not going to win this war, and when it's over who knows what will come? Even if you gave Allyn a place, there's no guarantee she could keep it. She needs somebody to help her fight for it, and that's what I propose to do."

Mark sat there quietly as the big man spoke. Jason finally leaned back and shrugged, saying, "I hope you'll understand. It's something we want to do. When I made up my mind, I was thinking partly of you. I owe you a lot Mark. This is one thing I can do for you—take care of your daughter. And you never know, maybe we can come to love each other the way you feel we should."

Mark studied the face of the blond man, the sturdy shoulders, strong hands, the face like a Viking. He knew this man, his strengths and weaknesses, better than most, and finally did what he felt he must do. "All right, Jason," he said, "God give you the strength, you and Allyn both, to do this thing."

★ ★ ★

Rooney looked across to where Allyn was sitting in a chair sewing and said, "I declare, Allyn, I'm jealous of you."

Allyn looked up at the girl who was observing her and said, "Jealous? What do you mean, Rooney?"

Rooney put her own sewing down, flexed her fingers, and stood up, arching her back. Then she smiled at Allyn and said, "Why, here I'm the one that's had the wedding date set, but you and Jason are getting married before Lowell and me. It's not fair!"

Allyn put her sewing down and leaned back in the chair. She and Jason had set their wedding date only a week away, which had brought shock waves throughout the entire Rocklin world. Susanna had been disturbed when Mark had given her the news, more disturbed than Mark had ever seen her. The two had talked long into the night, and finally Susanna had said, "It's not right, Mark. No man and woman should try to live together as man and wife unless they love each other."

Mark had agreed with her, but finally after talking with Allyn, Susanna had seen the adamant quality of her spirit and had reluctantly agreed to do all she could. The wedding would be at Gracefield so that Mark would be able to attend, for he was too weak to make a trip even to the church.

The rest of the family had received the news with the same sort of sheltered amazement. They had done their best to welcome Jason, to make him feel at home, but still there was an air of unreality.

Now Allyn looked across and saw the petulance on Rooney's lips and smiled. "I know it's hard on you. A bride wants to be the center of attention, I suppose. But Jason's got to find a ship. Perhaps even have one built. We want to get started in a hurry on that project, then we've got to settle down in Twelve Trees and make a place for my father."

"Oh, I know, Allyn," Rooney said, and the smile softened her features. She said, "I guess I'm just nervous. I don't know the first thing about being a wife."

"I don't suppose I do either," Allyn said. "But don't worry. Why, you and Lowell are perfect for each other. Anyone can see that. He lights up like a candle every time you walk into the room."

"He's so—so sweet," Rooney said. She looked around cautiously and said, "Allyn, I hate to ask you this, but I don't know anything about—about . . ." She flushed richly and blurted, "Well, I don't know how to be a *wife*, do you know what I mean?"

Allyn knew exactly what she meant, and her own face suffused with color. Then she said, "Well, I don't know anything either." The humor of it took her, and she said, "Here we are, two brides-to-be that don't have the vaguest idea of what to expect. It's like shoving off to sea in a sieve, isn't it?"

Rooney giggled and hugged Allyn. "We'll make out all

right. I think I love Lowell so much that I'll be whatever I have to be to make him happy."

Her words struck against Allyn and brought a sudden halt to the light conversation. She got up at once and said hurriedly, "I—I think I'll go see how my father's feeling. We'll finish this sewing later."

When she left the room, Rooney stared after her. "That was odd," she murmured. She ran over in her mind what she had said, thinking she might have offended Allyn, and realized it was when she talked about loving Lowell that a door had seemed to close down and the light had died in Allyn's eyes. She hurried at once to Susanna, repeated the conversation, and asked, "What's wrong? Is Allyn just afraid of getting married, do you think?"

Susanna hesitated, not knowing how to answer. "I suppose most brides are that way, apprehensive. And after all, Allyn and Jason haven't had the opportunity of getting to know each other. But they'll be all right, I am sure."

Rooney left the room shortly after that. Dorrie, who had been standing at the other end of the kitchen mixing biscuit dough, turned and came over to say, "Humph! Dat ain't so, what you just said."

Susanna, accustomed to Dorrie's dire proclamations of gloom, looked up at her. "What's wrong, Dorrie?"

"Ain't nuffin wrong wit me. It dat woman—dat's whut's wrong."

"Allyn? She'll be all right," Susanna said quickly. "We'll have to help her all we can."

"Humph!" Dorrie snorted again, disgust filling her face. She shook her head and put her hands on her hips, saying, "Ain't no good gonna come outta it. You mark my words! Dat's a triflin' man, dat sailor! I guess I ought to know one when I sees one. I seed nough of 'em in my days. He ain't gonna make dat girl happy." She snorted emphatically, then turned, walked back, and began pounding the biscuit dough with short vicious jabs of her fist.

Susanna thought, *Dorrie knows more about people than*

most anyone I know, and she feels about this even more strongly than I do. She thought about the fragile situation—Mark's illness, the newly born relationship between the father and the daughter, and now this tall stranger who had come in and would be a part of that.

A pang of apprehension flooded Susanna. She sat there feeling helpless as a swimmer caught in a strong current, and all she could do was say, "O God, help us all through this! Don't let them make some terrible mistake!"

★ ★ ★

"It's a good thing this train is so crowded," Bing said as he helped Deborah to the ground. He leaned closer and whispered, "Nobody'll pick us out as spies out of this mob, will they?" His brown eyes sparkled with excitement as he turned to Noel, who was struggling off with two heavy suitcases. Reaching forward, he took them and said, "You get the rest of them, Noel. I'll find us a carriage."

He moved through the crowd that had disembarked from the train, using his bulk to force a way. He held the two heavy suitcases as lightly as if they were filled with air, and Deborah followed in his wake. Finding a carriage drawn by a lop-eared ancient mule, Bing tossed the suitcases into the back and said, "You two go on. I want to look the town over a little bit. I'll meet you at the Spotswood Restaurant for supper tonight."

"That might not be the best," Deborah said quickly. "I don't want us to be seen together any more than necessary. We'll meet you out on the docks about six o'clock."

"All right," Bing said cheerfully. He picked his suitcase out of the back of the wagon bed and moved away.

"It'd be all right for us, I suppose, to be seen together," Noel said, "since we're engaged and I'm here on official business." He helped her into the carriage and then climbed up to sit beside her. "Take us to the Spotswood, driver."

"Yes, sir!" The driver urged the weary-looking mule into a stumbling walk.

"I hope the mule doesn't die before we get there," Noel whispered into Deborah's ear. "That would call attention to us." He was sitting close to her and impulsively put his arms around her and kissed her cheek. She turned to him and opened her lips to protest, but he closed them firmly with another kiss. "That's the way to stop a woman from talking," he said with satisfaction as he sat back.

"Noel! You shouldn't do that—not in public!" She was actually pleased, for Noel had not been brought up in a demonstrative family. She had had to educate him. Now she was pleased with the gesture, for it was the first time he had ever kissed her in public.

"Shouldn't do it in public? Well, let's get somewhere in private, then," he joked. Noel was feeling better. He had been apprehensive about the project at first, but as they had made plans, he had grown more and more excited. Now that he was actually in Richmond, his dark eyes glowed with excitement. As they moved along the street toward the Spotswood, he thought over the plan. He remembered what he had said when he had sprung it on Bing and Deborah.

"What we'll do," he had said, "is march right into the lion's den. We've got to have some excuse for being in Richmond, and there's bound to be someone that'll remember you, Deborah. I don't think we can go around wearing disguises, but these whiskers of mine will be my disguise. Besides, I was almost a scarecrow when you and Bing got me out of that prison. What we'll say is that I'm your fiancé and you've come to visit your family. A lot of that goes on—people from the North coming South to visit those they've left behind here."

"Well, what excuse will you have for being here?" Deborah had demanded. "You've got to have some reason for coming along with me."

"Ah! That's the heart of my plan," Noel had said. "We'll let it be known that I'm a writer, and that I've come to write a series of stories giving the North a more sympathetic view

228

of what people in the South are like. The power of the press, you know. They'll put on their best faces for us—I hope!"

But as they trundled along, watching the crowds that thronged the streets of Richmond, Noel was growing apprehensive again. "I hope this scheme works," he murmured.

"It's the only game in town. I'm going by the newspaper office as soon as I get you settled and meet the editor. That way it will establish my credentials, and hopefully I'll get on the inside of things a little bit."

Deborah shook her head. "No Yankee's going to get on the inside of many things," she said. "Not here in Richmond. You know how they hate us down here."

"I know, but at least it's a way of explaining our presence. It'll be all right, you'll see."

They arrived at the Spotswood and rented two rooms. After depositing Deborah and her luggage in her room, Noel threw his bag in his room and went at once to the newspaper office.

The editor of the *Richmond Examiner,* a tall stooped man named Tim Franklin, greeted him with a great deal of suspicion. He leaned back from where he sat behind his desk and smiled frostily. "So, you've come to get a story on what wonderful folks we Rebels are, if I understand you, Mr. Kojak?"

Kojak saw the skepticism in Franklin's eyes and grinned brashly. "Well, I hardly think I could put it that strongly," he answered. "I intend to report what I see honestly—and if you think the South can bear the light of honest reporting, I'm your man."

Franklin shrugged his wiry shoulders. "I don't think you'd ever get anything printed in the North that smells of truth," he said. He was a rabid secessionist and despised Abraham Lincoln with all of his heart, but he seemed to see something in the young man that he found acceptable. "All right, make this your headquarters while you're in town, Mr. Kojak. As a matter of fact, I'm going out now to do a little investigative reporting, I guess you'd call it. Come along, I'll introduce you to some prominent Rebels."

It was a stroke of fortune, Noel found, going to the newspaperman. All afternoon he trudged along with the tall editor, and by the time he got back to the Spotswood, he was glowing with excitement. "It's going to be all right, Deborah," he bubbled over. "Franklin's introduced me to the mayor, to one of the generals, and they've all made me kind of a guest. I guess Franklin convinced them I was part honest—" he grinned—"as honest as a Yankee could be, so we're going to be all right."

"Oh, that's wonderful," Deborah said. They were in her room, and she went over and gave him a quick squeeze. "Tomorrow I'll go see Uncle Gid. I'll have to find Aunt Melanie, but she's here in town and shouldn't be too hard to find."

They went that night and met with Bing, who announced he had found a place in a rooming house. They set up a meeting place and a system of messages and then parted. The next morning Deborah found Melanie by going from hotel to hotel asking for Mrs. Melanie Rocklin. At her third attempt, the clerk said, "Why yes, Mrs. Rocklin's here." He gave her the room number, and she went up at once and knocked on the door.

When Melanie opened it, she stared at Deborah in astonishment. "Deborah! What in the world—!"

"Aunt Melanie!" Deborah flew into the room and grabbed her aunt, whom she'd always loved dearly. She squeezed her so hard the older woman gasped, then gave her a delighted grin. "I'm so glad to see you."

"What are you doing here, Deborah?" Melanie gasped. "How did you get here?"

"Got here on the train," Deborah said with a smile. Her eyes sparkled, and she suddenly realized the door was open. Turning, she closed it, then turned back and said, "Aunt Melanie, Bing and Noel are with me."

Melanie stared at her without comprehension. "Why,

that's dangerous for Northerners to come into Richmond at a time like this."

"Listen, here's the way it is. We're going to get Uncle Gid out of prison." Seeing the shock touch her aunt's eyes, she said, "Wait a minute! Come and sit down, let me tell you all about it. I know you think I'm crazy, but Noel and I have a plan. Sit down, and we'll talk about it. . . ."

★ ★ ★

The wedding of Jason Larrimore and Allyn Rocklin took place on October 10. Dorrie and Susanna had struggled to make the house a substitute for the church where Rocklins usually married. The family—as many as could come—were crowded into the rooms. Since the army was ensconced, for the main part, within Richmond, the house swarmed with Rocklins. Denton Rocklin was there with his wife, Raimey. Raimey was glowing with health as was her baby, Thomas.

Lowell, of course, was there, never getting more than two steps away from Rooney. Rooney's brother, Buck, was in and out of the festivities. He was only thirteen and had been brought up under a hard school, along with his sister, Rooney, but life at Gracefield had brought out the best in him.

As the morning of the wedding dawned, the family began to arrive. Clay was granted leave, and he and Melora were there to greet them. They greeted Amy Rocklin Franklin and her husband, Brad, who came from Lindwood. Two of their children were there, Rachel and Les, while the other two, Vince and Grant, and Rachel's husband, Jake, were gone on duty. Marianne Bristol and her husband, Claude, from the Hartsworth plantation were there along with two of their children, Austin and Marie.

It was a time of happiness for Susanna to see the children filling the house, and she said to Dorrie, "Isn't this wonderful to see so many of the family together again?"

Dorrie nodded grumpily. "If you has to cooks for dis army, it ain't so much fun!"

Susanna hugged her quickly and said, "You don't fool me, Dorrie. You love this as much as I do."

The day went by quickly, and at two o'clock in the afternoon the ceremony took place. Clay stood beside Jason as they waited nervously in an outer room for the music to call them into the large hall, the only place large enough for such a wedding. It was a ballroom, actually, but chairs had been moved in, and it was now packed. Jason tugged at his collar and said, "Maj. Rocklin, how does a man endure all this?" He glanced nervously at the door that led out to the hall, then at the outer door. "What I'd like to do is run right through that door, get on a horse, and ride away as fast as I can!"

Clay had learned to like the tall sailor, so he came over and clapped his hand on his shoulder. "A typical reaction. All bridegrooms are the same."

Jason gave Clay a look and shook his head. "I'll bet you didn't do that. Not from what you've told me."

Clay, realizing he had overstated the case, shrugged. "Well, I confess I didn't have any temptation to run away, but it's common enough to be nervous, I suppose. Like before battle—" he grinned widely—"once you get into it you'll be all right." He grew serious and said, "Listen! That's the music, come on."

Jason Larrimore pulled himself up straight. He was wearing a gray silk waistcoat with satin stripes over his pleated shirt with a turned-down collar and a starched bow-tied cravat. He wore a wool, frock-coated suit and looked very handsome, but his face twitched nervously as he passed through the door. Once he stepped into the large ballroom, the nervousness increased. It was filled with strangers, and he had had no real peace about this plan since its conception. *This is all a mistake!* he thought wildly. *If I had any sense I'd run away right now!* He knew he would not, so he stood beside Clay and the minister, his eyes fixed on the door through which his bride would enter.

Allyn had been assisted into her wedding dress by Rooney and Rena. They had fussed over her, and Rena had said mischievously, "I don't think you could even button your shoes, could you, Allyn?"

"I don't think I could," Allyn said faintly. She stood there, getting into her dress, which was a white silk satin overlaid with pale peach lace flounces. She wore a stole, a pair of white kid gloves, and carried a small bouquet. Some small silk flowers were pinned to her bosom. She glanced at herself in a mirror and saw that her face was almost dead white. Then the music sounded.

"Here comes the bride," Rooney said. "Come along, your father's waiting for you."

Feeling like someone in a vague dream, Allyn allowed herself to be escorted to the door. When she passed through it, she found Mark, wearing a brown suit, in his wheelchair. He reached up one hand and she took it and he felt it tremble. "Don't be afraid," he said, noting that her lips were tremulous, and her face was pale. "God will be with us."

He nodded, and Rooney stepped behind the wheelchair. They moved down the hall and then passed through the door that led to the ballroom. The room was packed with visitors, all of whom turned to look at her, and Allyn felt totally weak and inadequate. Mark squeezed her hand and said, "Come now, I'm proud of you. You look so beautiful!" He looked up at her, saying, "All brides are beautiful, but I've never seen one like you."

Allyn began to move forward as Rooney propelled the wheelchair, and then she looked up. All of the other visitors, the surroundings, the flowers, all faded when she looked into the face of Jason Larrimore.

She seemed to float down the aisle, unconscious of her feet—even of the steps she made, but she found herself standing in front of the minister, who began to speak. She was so frightened and overwhelmed by what she was doing that she could barely understand the words. Finally, he asked, "Who gives this woman?" and she heard Mark say firmly, "I give her," and then he released her hand and she found herself standing by Jason. She could not look up at him as the ceremony moved on. She heard the words *to love, honor, and obey—with this ring I thee wed—cling to each other as long as you both shall live,* but she was mostly conscious of his large hand as it held hers. As he slipped the ring on her finger, however, she looked up.

He was staring down at her with a strange expression on his bronzed face. His lips were tight, and his eyelids were half closed over his blue eyes. Studying her carefully, he seemed to be a stranger. *I'm giving myself to him—a stranger!* she thought wildly.

And then she heard the words "I now pronounce you man and wife." Jason's hands closed on hers, and the minister said, more lightly, "You may kiss your bride, Mr. Larrimore."

Allyn felt his hand on her back, and she was turned to face him. She lifted her head, and her lips were half parted, her eyes filled with fear as he bent over her. She felt the firm pressure of his lips, his arms drew her closer against him, and she thought for one flashing moment of the other time that she had felt his kiss.

And then, it was over. The pianoforte played the Wedding March as they exited in spirited fashion, and when they stepped out and were headed down the hall toward where the reception was to be, he suddenly stopped her and said, "Are you afraid?"

Allyn looked up at him and said quietly, "Yes. I am afraid."

Surprisingly he nodded. "Me, too. I guess it's like jumping off a cliff in the dark. You leap off and don't know how far you're going to fall or how bad it will be when you hit." Then he studied her face carefully and said, "Come along, we'll be all right."

It was not much consolation, but she followed him toward the reception room, where they were surrounded almost at once by what seemed like hundreds of people coming by to shake her hand, to hug her, to claim the traditional kiss.

But all Allyn could think was, *I've done a foolish thing!*

CHAPTER SEVENTEEN
The Wedding Night

After the noise and laughter and the happy talk of the reception, Allyn was glad to escape to the carriage. Her hand was warm from the many times it had been grasped, and she had felt strange about the Rocklin family who had come to her one at a time, the women kissing her cheek, sometimes the men also. *Nearly all of them,* she thought, *said something nice about my being a member of the family now.*

Soon she shifted her eyes to catch a glimpse of Jason, who had gotten into the seat and spoken to the horses. They started with a jolt, and the cries of those who'd come to say their farewells rose in the late afternoon air.

"Turn around, smile, and wave at them," Jason whispered. "Like this." He turned around, lifted one hand, gave them a broad smile, adding to Allyn, "A bride should be happy."

Allyn did as he urged. Her eyes ran over the crowd, picking out Susanna, whose eyes even now held some sort of reluctance. Behind her, on the porch, Dorrie glared at her in absolute disfavor, almost hatred. *She thinks I'm mistreating Mark,* Allyn thought, but quickly pulled her mind away from the black woman. Her glance picked up Rooney and Lowell waving, then Josh and Rena, the Bristols, the Franklins. As the carriage reached the outer road and turned right, she leaned back in the leather padded seat and gave a gusty sigh of relief.

Jason looked at her quickly. "I guess we're both glad that's over," he mused. "It never ceases to amaze me how much trouble people will go to to get married. If it had been my choice, we would have just gone to a preacher."

"No, Father needed this," Allyn said. "It was for his benefit, not yours, not mine. I guess it was partly for the whole family. They needed some kind of assurance, I suppose."

He gave her a cautious look. She had clean-running physical lines, and her face was a mirror that changed with her feelings. She took up the material of her dress now and let it slide through her fingers. Even in that small act, he noted, she was graceful. Then she turned to look at him, and he saw pride. Yet, something smothered this like a cloud. The horses clipped along at a fast gait, but neither Jason nor Allyn spoke. As they rode on the sun grew large and red on the horizon. Except for a few murmured remarks, both of them kept their silence, their own thoughts pressing in on their minds. Finally, after what seemed like hours but was only a short time, they pulled up to the driveway that led to Twelve Trees.

"Glad to be getting here before dark," Jason said as he guided the horses toward the house that sat back off the road half sheltered by a line of beech trees. They had been at Twelve Trees twice during their brief engagement, meeting the servants and slaves and moving a few things into their quarters. "It's a nice-looking place," Jason continued. "I never cared for the big, fancy houses, even like Gracefield. Something always seems too showy about it to me, but this place," he said, waving his large hand toward it, "it's got something about it that's more homey."

Allyn looked and saw what he meant. It was a small house, compared to Gracefield, at least, built in the manner of early Southern plantations, with a porch that spanned the entire front. The windows were evenly spaced, and on the second story lantern lights were already casting their glow out in the gathering darkness. It had a steep pitched roof broken by brick chimneys, and white smoke lifted gently out of them, curling in lazy spirals into the darkness of the upper air.

Jason pulled the horses up, and at once a muscular black man was there saying, "Yes, suh, Captain. Let me take dis team."

"Hello, Caesar," Jason spoke cheerfully. "How's everything?"

"Oh, fine, suh," Caesar replied. "Everthins ready in de house. You and Miz Allyn go right on in. Dey's waitin' supper fo' you."

Allyn took the hand that Jason extended, stepped to the ground, and moved toward the house. "I'll bring yo bags in, Marse Jason," Caesar called out, and he murmured their thanks.

They climbed the white steps, where they were met by the servants. Flossie and Ned, both in their sixties, greeted them at once. Flossie said, "You come on in now. We wuz afraid you wouldn't get here 'fore dark. We got a nice supper all fixed for you."

Ned bobbed up and down, his white hair catching the last rays of the lanterns on the porch. "Yes, suh, it's gonna be the best weddin' supper you ever had, I bet!" He grinned broadly, his teeth very white against his ebony skin.

Jason smiled at them, reached into his pocket, and passed some coins to Ned. "You take Flossie to town tomorrow and buy her something pretty. Get yourself something, too, Ned. Sort of a wedding present in reverse."

"Yas, suh! I'll just do dat," Ned said.

However, Flossie promptly reached over and put her hands out. "You give me dat money. You ain't got sense enough to spend it right."

She took the money that Ned surrendered reluctantly, and they stepped aside. Allyn walked into the house and, as nervous as she was, admired again the polished heart pine floors, the ten-foot ceilings, the walls covered with delicate paper, and the fine furniture—mostly of gleaming oak and walnut.

"You go to your room, missy," Flossie said, "and fresh up. Den you comes back and we'll have supper."

"All right, Flossie," Allyn agreed. She moved up the curving staircase, running her hand along the smooth oak stair rail. Everything was handmade in the house, created by craftsmen who took pride in their work. She moved down the hall to the room that they had chosen and entered. She stopped momentarily and stared around. Two lamps shed their pale amber light over the room. The large walnut bed was made with fresh linen and turned down carefully. She stared at the bed for a moment—then pulled her eyes away from it. As soon as Caesar brought the trunk in, she gave him his wedding present, saying, "Buy yourself something nice, Caesar. Thank you for your trouble."

"Yas, ma'am," Caesar said. "Anything you wants, you jest let me know."

Allyn changed at once out of her traveling dress, donning a simple blue dress of linen. After washing her face and brushing her hair, she went downstairs. When she entered the dining room, she found Jason already seated. He arose, motioned toward the place across from him. "A little lonesome in here," he said, "just the two of us. The Bennetts must have had lots of company, didn't they, Flossie?"

"Oh, yas, suh. Dey was entertaining folk—neighbors come from all around to eat wif de Bennetts." She had a broad face and deep-set, almost black eyes that caught the glint of the lantern. She smiled, revealing a gold tooth in front, saying, "Dey gonna come see you, too, Captain—you and yo' lady. It's gonna be happy times here at Twelve Trees."

"We'll be bringing my father here shortly. We'll have to make up the downstairs room for him. He's an invalid, you know."

"Yas, ma'am, I knows. We'll take good care of him, you don't worry bout dat."

The meal was excellent—chicken, potatoes, mushrooms, and a cut of meat that Allyn didn't recognize. "What is this, Ellie?" she asked the small servant girl who was filling the water glasses and doing the work of a waitress.

"Oh, that's coon, Miz Larrimore. Ain't it good?"

Allyn had always loved the sight of coons, thinking them clever animals. The idea of eating one was rather like eating a cat to her. She abruptly put her fork down and took a sip of water.

Jason grinned across the table at her, took a bite of his portion of the rich meat, and said, "Nothing better than coon—unless it's a nice, fat, greasy possum."

"You like possum?" Ned had come up to bring fresh bread. "Oh, dat's good, Captain, cause I know how to cotch 'em! And Flossie here, she know how to cook 'em. You take a nice juicy possum with a sweet tater in his mouth—ain't nothin no finer!"

"We'll look forward to it, won't we, dear?" Jason said, his lips turned up in a grin.

Allyn stared at him and then said reluctantly, "I think I prefer the chicken."

They finished the meal, except for Allyn's portion of raccoon, and afterward went into the drawing room, where Ellie brought them coffee in fine china.

Jason sat down, stretched his long legs out, and looked utterly at peace with the world. Sipping the coffee, saying nothing, Allyn, who was sitting at his right, had a chance to examine him. She noticed that he had a scar on his neck that ran into the thick blond hair, and she wondered where he'd gotten it. She discovered another scar on his chin; this one was less noticeable. He was staring at the books, which lined the wall, with a remote and angular smile. She saw behind the toughness the years had somehow beaten into him. He sat with a looseness, and she could not help but admire his strength. He was over six feet and didn't show the bulkiness of his two hundred pounds. It was a distributed weight lying in the muscles of his chest and upper arms, on the broad flats of his shoulders and the girth of his legs. He had big bones, she saw. His fingers were long and blunt at the end and looked very strong.

"I'll be leaving fairly soon." He broke the silence suddenly. "We'll make the arrangements for me to write a check for the ship."

"That's fine," Allyn said quickly. "I—I hope you get a good one. Tell me about your last ship."

Looking at her, he raised one eyebrow curiously and shrugged his shoulders. "Didn't know you were interested in ships," he murmured, then began to tell her about the *Eagle*. As he spoke, his voice made a pleasant baritone rumbling in the quiet room. He spoke almost lovingly of the ship he'd lost and finally gave Allyn a quick glance. "I guess I'll never find one I like as much as that one."

"Maybe so," Allyn said. "She'll be what you make her, won't she? I mean, don't the men who sail the ship pretty much determine what kind of a ship it is?"

He was impressed by her quickness. "I'm surprised that you'd know that, but that's the way it is. I've seen a few good hands and a good captain take an old tub and make a real clipper out of her." He spoke for a long time of ships he had sailed, some of the storms he had passed through, and some other difficulties. A large grandfather clock ticked the minutes away in the hall, and Allyn was acutely conscious of the passage of time.

Several times Ellie or Flossie came in to see if they would care for more dessert or more coffee. Finally, Jason yawned and said, "Well, I suppose I'm getting old." Flossie was picking up the coffee cups and deliberately not looking at them. Jason found this amusing, and he said, "Well, Bride, I suppose it's time for us to go to bed. Come along."

Allyn got to her feet, and Jason came over and took her arm. "Good night, Flossie. We'll probably sleep late in the morning and won't require an early breakfast."

"Yas, suh."

Allyn walked out of the room, aware of the touch of

Jason's hand on her arm. When they got to the hall, she pulled away deliberately, a gesture that amused him. Neither of them said anything until they had reached the landing and turned to go to the large bedroom at the end of the hall. When they got there, they noticed that the door was open. Stepping inside, Jason saw Ellie busy carrying fresh linens inside. "I brought you some fresh towels," she said. "If you wants any, I'll bring you some fresh hot water whenever you calls for it."

"Don't guess we'll require anything tonight. Good night, Ellie." Jason said. He waited until the small maid had left the room, then shut the door.

Jason looked very large and formidable to Allyn as he stood there. She had assmed he would simply find another room to sleep in. But now she didn't know what to do. Her mind moved quickly as she walked over to the wardrobe and opened it up, saying nervously, "I suppose I'll have enough clothes. I don't guess there's much social life out here in the country."

"Oh, we'll be going to Richmond since it's not too far. Got to show off my new bride, don't I?" Jason moved over to the window. He sat down on the sill, turning his back to the outer air, and pulled one of the thin cheroots from his pocket and lit it up. He tossed the match outside and crossed his arms casually. "You know how it is," he remarked, a glint in his eye. "People expect newlyweds to stay sequestered for a while, but after that they need to get out and be seen."

Allyn moved over to the mirror, sat down, and began to brush her hair. She could not think of a thing to say, and the silence began to be oppressive. Jason suddenly got to his feet and said, "I'll go down for a time. I need to talk to Caesar about a horse for traveling back and forth to Richmond."

He left the room, and Allyn put down the hairbrush with almost a violent gesture. As soon as she heard his footsteps go down the hall, she moved over and walked at once to the door and slipped the lock. Then turning her back, she leaned her head back and closed her eyes. She was incredibly weary;

she couldn't remember ever being so tired and exhausted in all her life. It was not, she understood, the physical exertion, but the emotional reaction to the whole thing had enervated her, drained her until there seemed to be no strength left.

For a long time she stood there, her head back against the door, her eyes closed. Then, finally, she took a deep breath, shook her shoulders slightly, and moved over toward the trunk. She stripped off the dress she'd worn for dinner, then the plain petticoat she'd worn under it. She glanced nervously at the door, then quickly sponged off with the tepid water in the large basin on the washstand, drying herself with a thick, fluffy towel. Moving to the trunk, Allyn dug through her possessions and produced a long, white cotton nightgown with green lace on the cuffs and collar. *This probably isn't what normal brides wear on their wedding night,* Allyn thought with dark humor, *but this isn't any normal marriage.* Then she sat down and began to brush her hair again.

The act of brushing her hair always seemed to calm her nerves. Her long cascade of auburn hair reached down to her waist, and there was a pleasure in running the brush and comb through it, feeling the shimmering mass beneath the ivory teeth of the comb.

Finally, her arm grew tired, so she put the brush and the comb back on the dressing table, then walked over to the window. Outside, the air was cold and biting, but she enjoyed the brisk wind as it came inside and touched her face. It made her flesh stand up in goosebumps. She rubbed her arms quickly but remained there, looking out across the yard. A pale moon threw its beams on the trees and the open spaces, and Allyn wondered, *How will it be here? What kind of life will I have?*

Allyn started to go to bed, but she found that as tired as she was, she was too nervous to sleep. So instead she went to the trunk, pulled out a thick, cotton robe, and put it on. Then she went back down to the kitchen to get another taste of Flossie's desserts.

"Why, Miz Larrimore! What you doin' down here? You'z s'pose to be wit yo husband."

"Oh, Flossie," Allyn said, surprised that Flossie was still up and about. "I guess it's just wedding night jitters." She moved over to the cabinets and took down a plate. "I thought I'd come down for another piece of peach pie. I've never tasted any so good!"

"Well, just doan take too long eatin' dat. You husband might get lonesome," Flossie said with a smile. "I see you folks in da mornin'." And she went off to her quarters.

Allyn did take her time eating the pie, savoring each bite. Eventually she cleaned the plate and couldn't think of another excuse not to go back to her room. Putting down her fork, Allyn stood up and walked out of the kitchen and toward the stairs.

As she aproached the bottom of the stairs, Jason walked in the front door and headed for the stairs. "I thought I put you to bed," he said lightheartedly.

She was startled at his voice, surprised that so many people were about this late at night. "Oh, I just wanted a little more pie," she said, explaining. "And what are you doing up and about?" she asked, with suspicion in her voice.

"I was just coming up to your room to—"

"My room!" Allyn had assumed that Jason had gone for the night. She stood there awkwardly and without thinking said, "Don't even think about going to my room. I don't want you in there."

Jason had come back to tell her that he would stay in the room until the house had gone to sleep, then would find another place. He tried to explain, but she wouldn't let him.

"Just because it says we're married on a piece of paper doesn't mean you can invade my privacy any time you want! You remember, we had a bargain. I thought you'd abide by it."

Jason had tried to be understanding, but her accusations enraged him. Without thinking, he stepped toward her and

243

firmly placed a hand on her shoulder. She tried to wrench free, but his grip held the robe tightly.

"Don't touch me!" Allyn ordered.

Jason looked at her. Her hair hung down her back, and her eyes, as she looked up at him, were large with rage. Jason thought of her as a mouse angrily glaring at the cat that has him in his paws. "It seems we need to get a few things clear, *Mrs. Larrimore!*" Jason said.

Her eyes narrowed. "I hate you!" she whispered. "You'll never know how much I hate you!"

Jason laughed at her. "No, you don't hate me. Or, if you do, it's only with your mind. I think your heart's saying something else." She tried to pull away, but he held her saying, "Look, Allyn, I promised your father I'd take care of you. I promised you that this marriage would be just a counterfeit thing."

"Yes, you did," she cried. "Now, get out of here and leave me alone. Don't ever come back."

He put his other hand on her other shoulder and held her, as if she were a child. "What a shame! There's a real woman somewhere hidden inside. All that beauty on the outside, and inside nothing but ice! You don't trust me at all. I'd thought that you might wake up, but it's like I said at the beginning—we're both of us two pretty hard people. We're alike, you and I."

"We're not! We're not!" Allyn denied vehemently. She wrenched away and stepped back from him. She held her hands tightly together and said, "Will you please leave?"

"All right, I'm going, but I hope I'm around when you decide to open up and trust someone, Allyn."

He spun and walked out the front door. Allyn ran up the stairs, into her bedroom, and quickly locked the door.

Turning, she looked in a mirror and saw herself. Her face was flushed, and her eyes were red and watery. She quickly removed the robe and crawled into the bed, hoping to take refuge there. She found she was trembling, and for a long time she bit her thumb to keep back the sobs that seemed to rise within her.

What's wrong with me? Why am I acting like this? she thought.

Finally, she went to sleep, but the night was interrupted by dreams. Once she awoke shaking, and when she remembered where she was and the scene that had taken place, she got out of bed and walked for a long time. Eventually she went back to bed but was racked by bad dreams.

She rose at dawn, dressed, and went downstairs. She met Flossie, who looked at her with astonishment. "Why, Miz Allyn, what you doin' up dis early? The captain, he say you sleep late."

"No," Allyn said, a flush on her cheeks, "I thought I'd get up early and take a walk. Is my . . . husband here?"

"Why, no, ma'am, he gone."

Allyn stared at her blankly. "Gone? Where did he go, Flossie?"

"I reckon he say in dis paper." Flossie reached into her pocket and handed a single sheet of paper to her mistress.

She looked at it and discovered the bare words: "Going to find a ship. Your loving husband, Jason."

Shock ran along her nerves, and she could not understand why. She managed to keep a straight face and then nodded. "It's all right. The captain will be gone for a few days."

Allyn turned and walked out the front door. She sat on the porch looking out over Twelve Trees, but the beauty of the autumn woods did not please her. She ran over the scene of the previous night, finding it was so vivid that she seemed to feel his hands on her. Gripping the top rail of the banister that lined the porch she whispered in an agonized voice, "It can never be right. Never!"

CHAPTER EIGHTEEN
Another Wedding

★

This was the third autumn of the war, and the South was still besieged but breathed a bit easier than during the disastrous midsummer. The Confederates had been successful at halting the drives on Charleston and Texas and had won at Chickamauga. On the other hand, the North was in Chattanooga, and troops were rallying to their relief. The most significant event went almost unnoticed. Gen. U. S. Grant was ordered to Washington, where he was given the command of the military division of the Mississippi. Lincoln had had practically no success in appointing generals. Hooker, Burnside, McClellan—all had failed him in the east. Lincoln now turned to the stubby, unobtrusive man who had failed at everything in civilian life, and placed in his hands the fate of the western theater. Meanwhile, in Washington President Lincoln issued a proclamation calling for 300,000 more volunteers for Federal armies.

Allyn lived through the days more quietly than she had dreamed possible. Twelve Trees was off the beaten track, and days went by when she would see no one except an occasional rider who would stop at the house asking for information. She formed the habit of rising early and walking in the woods, then coming back to have a late breakfast. Much of her time she spent learning the affairs of a plantation. She had seen some of this, of course, at Gracefield, but now, as the first week came to an end, she began to realize a truth. *This is mine,* she thought. *I've never had a place before, but now I can call it mine.* A love of the land was born in her, and she got Caesar to choose a horse for her. The tall black slave rode with her day after day, showing her around the place.

"She sho' do love this place already," Caesar said to Ellie, the small, black waitress with whom he was passionately and blindly in love. "She want to see ev'ry stalk of corn and ev'ry tree, I think. Gonna wear me out ridin' aroun!"

Ellie came over and pushed herself against him. "Never mind that," she said. "You pay attention to me." She was a born flirt, and this kept Caesar constantly on his toes to be sure that her eyes were for him only.

"Come here, woman, I'll teach you what a real man's like!"

Allyn had been watching the pair from where she stood. She smiled as the two romanced, then walked into the house through the back entrance. "Flossie," she said, "I want to learn how to make pancakes like you do. They're the best things I've ever eaten."

"Why, sho', Miz Allyn," she said, "you jes watch me, and I'll make you de best pancake maker in Virginia." She began to throw the elements together expertly, explaining the process. When the first pancake was placed into the pan she said, "You just wait until a little bubble comes up on the top, then you turn 'er over, you see?"

Allyn picked up the turner and stared down at the pancake. "You make it look so easy," she said. "I don't think I'll ever be able to cook like that."

Flossie grinned at her. "You don't have to, Miz Allyn, not as long as old Flossie's here to do de cooking for you!" She watched the young woman, who intently kept her eye on the frying pan and asked, "When Capt. Larrimore coming back? He been gone, seem like a long time now."

Allyn looked up at her and saw the wisdom in the old

woman's eyes. *She knows something's wrong with us,* she thought. *No man would run off and leave a bride unless there was something terribly wrong.* Aloud she said, "He didn't say, but he has to have a ship. That's—that's why he went off so suddenly, Flossie."

"I don't know about going off on no ship," Flossie declared. "I wants my foots on de *ground!*"

"I'll be leaving this afternoon, Flossie," Allyn said. "I don't know how long I'll be gone, but I've got to go to a wedding back over at Gracefield. When I come back I'll bring my father with me, so I guess Caesar better go with me."

"You watch out for dat worthless man! Any of them young gals wink at him over there, he go down like a tree! He thinks ever gal he sees is plumb in love with him." She looked over at her young mistress, who was now turning the pancake over. "We got de big room on de first floor all fixed for yo' pappy. We'll take care of him real good, Miz Allyn, don't you worry. The good Lawd's gonna take care of you."

Allyn had turned the pancake, and now she glanced up. "I don't know much about the Lord," she murmured. "I've missed out on that somehow."

At once Flossie shook her head. She had developed an interest in and a concern for the young woman. Her years had brought her a great deal of wisdom, and she had sensed at once the difficulties between the couple that now owned Twelve Trees. Her tone grew soft and gentle, and she wanted to reach out and put her arms around the young woman—but it was too soon for that. "Ain't none of us can do widdout the good Lawd," she said. "I been through some hard times, and if it wasn't for the Lawd Jesus, I don't know what I'd done!"

Allyn could not answer. She had felt an emptiness and a loneliness; although it had been a time of rest for her spirit, she realized it was only a stasis of peace. Soon Jason would return, and the very thought of that made her tense. She straightened up and asked quickly, "Is this pancake done? How can you tell when the bottom part's done?"

"You just has to know. Pick up the corner and peek at it, if you wants to." Flossie saw that Allyn was reluctant to talk about God. Later on she said to her husband, Ned, "That girl's running from God. Ain't no two ways about it. You and me, we'll have to pray that he'll catch her pretty soon." Then she added, "She got lots of misery, dat girl. Until she lets God get inside her, she ain't gonna do no good."

Allyn found Caesar at the barn later that day and said, "Caesar, I've got to go over to Gracefield. Mr. Lowell Rocklin's going to get married, and I have to be there for the wedding."

"Yes'm, I'll get the carriage ready."

"I don't think so," Allyn responded. "I'll be bringing my father back, and he won't be able to sit up for the journey, I don't think. We'll take a wagon and perhaps set up some padding so he can lie down in the bed of the wagon."

"Yes'm, I'll get a pallet, plenty of quilts from de house. We'll make him a fine bed, and I'll drive real keerful so yo' pappy won't be bumped."

"That's fine, Caesar. We'll be there overnight and will come back tomorrow." Her eyes sparkled suddenly. "You better be sure and give Ellie enough kisses to do her until then." She laughed at his startled expression, then shook her head. "When are you two getting married?" she asked.

"I don't know." He scratched his woolly head. "Dat's up to her, but I reckon pretty soon now. I be ready when you are, Miz Allyn."

Allyn went upstairs and chose and packed the dress she would wear to the wedding. She then put on a traveling dress of gray cotton and pulled out a cloak made of fine black wool. It had a hood, and she weighed it in her hands, thinking, *It'll be cold coming back. I'll have to remember to get plenty of blankets for Father.* She went over to the window and stared out at the trees that were stripped bare. They raised their naked arms to heaven, it seemed to her, in prayer.

A leaden sky overhead proclaimed the danger of bad weather. *I hope it doesn't snow,* she thought. *But I suppose it's too early for that. We'd better take an oilcloth cover in case it does get bad.* A dull spirit had come to her, and she realized she didn't want to leave Twelve Trees. It had been a haven for her, and now she was about to leave it. Finally she sighed and said, "I wish I could just stay here. When I get Father here, we'll pull up the drawbridge and not even know what goes on outside." She knew this was not possible, but it comforted her a little to think that once she got her father here they would be cut off from the world.

Later that afternoon when she left, sitting beside Caesar, she waved to Flossie and said, "I'll be back. Take care of things, Flossie. And watch out for her, Ned." She pulled the cloak around her and settled down for the long ride. Caesar chirped to the horses, who stepped out with a rapid pace. As they left the yard, the wind began to blow. It made a keening noise that blew her hair wildly for a moment, then she pulled up the hood, patted it into place, and tried to get comfortable.

By the time they got to Gracefield it was late in the afternoon. "Go right over there to the barn, Caesar," she said. "Get Box to show you where to put the horses." She stepped out of the wagon, saying, "Then come to the house, and I'll see that you get something to eat. I know you're hungry."

"Yes'm, I'll be there. I'll bring yo' suitcase up, too."

Allyn went directly to the house, where she was greeted by Susanna. The house was swarming with people. Susanna said with a harried look, "Allyn, I'm so glad you got here." She looked around and laughed ruefully, "Looks like everybody in the country's here for the wedding. Every bed's taken, and there are pallets all over the floor. Do you suppose you could make a pallet in your father's room?"

"Of course. Don't worry about it." Allyn smiled, then said at once, "I'll go to him now, then I'll come back and help."

She left Susanna and made her way through the milling guests, and several of them spoke to her. She stopped long enough to greet Lowell and asked, "How's the bridegroom?"

Lowell's face was flushed, and his eyes danced with excitement. "I've always heard bridegrooms are supposed to be scared, but I'm feeling pretty good right now." He looked over her shoulder and said, "Jason didn't come with you?"

"Oh no," Allyn said quickly. "He's gone to buy a ship. I don't know when to expect him back. Not until he gets one, I suppose." She answered that same question in one form or another many times in the hours that followed. Now, however, she hurried to Mark's room, where she knocked on the door and entered when he answered.

Stepping inside, she closed the door and threw off her cloak. Dropping it on the chair she went to him and sat down beside his wheelchair. He reached out his hands, and she took them and impulsively leaned over and kissed him on the cheek, saying, "I've missed you. I should have come earlier."

"No, you had to get settled," Mark said. His voice was thin and reedy, and she saw that his cheeks were even more sunken and his thin body more emaciated than when she had left. Her heart smote her when she saw how he had gone down, and she set about making amends. "You're going to have to put up with me tonight," she said. "Susanna says every nook and cranny of the house is full and that I'll have to make a pallet in here."

"You can sleep on the couch," Mark said. He sat there listening as she chattered, and he could tell that something was wrong. Finally, he asked, "Jason came with you?"

Allyn hesitated, then shook her head. "No, he left to go buy a ship." Defensively she added, "He said it might be hard to find just the right one." Again there was a break that revealed to the sick man that all was not well. "He—he said it might look odd for a bridegroom to leave so quickly, but these are not normal times, are they?"

"No, they're not. Now tell me about Twelve Trees."

Glad to get off the subject of her husband, Allyn spoke rapidly, stopping once to fix tea. As the two of them sipped the fragrant brew, she spoke with some excitement about her new home. "You'll love it, Father! We had a big room downstairs made up just for you."

"You like it, do you, Allyn?" he asked softly.

"Oh yes! It's so beautiful, and it's so private! I guess I've been with people in big crowds all my life one way or the other. When I'm there," she said, leaning back to sip her tea, her voice thoughtful, "it's like the world is somewhere far off, and I can just sit and let it go by." Then she smiled and said, "I can't wait to get you there. I'll have you all to myself then."

Mark looked down at his hands, then glanced up and smiled at her. "That will be good," he said, "but I'll be a trouble."

"How could you be that?" she said, rebuke in her voice. Then she asked, "It must be close to suppertime. Let me go get a bite to eat and see that Caesar is fed. I'll bring you back a tray."

She rose and left the room, and Mark sat there looking after her. He was tired and had no appetite, but when she returned shortly with food, he did his best to pick at it, to make some sort of a showing. She was aware of what he was doing and did not urge him to eat more, not wanting to become a nag. Finally, when he had eaten a little, he put the tray aside, and she took it away.

Then she came and sat down beside him, breathing a deep sigh. "I talked to Rooney for a little while. She's so excited." Her voice was thoughtful, and weariness had come to her. From different parts of the house they could hear voices speaking, and somewhere far away the sound of a fiddle came to them, making a happy, cheerful sound. "That's 'Dixie' they're playing. Wonder if they're going to have a military review?"

"I wouldn't be surprised." Mark smiled. "About half of

Lowell's company managed to get leave. I think they're camping out somewhere in the barn. When they leave, they're going to have to pass under one of those sword things—you know, where they form a canopy of swords."

"Won't that be nice!" Allyn exclaimed. "Something she and Lowell can remember for a long time." She grew quiet, and he could see that her mind was occupied. Finally, she said, "They're going to be very happy, aren't they, Father?"

"I think so. They're young and strong, and if Lowell's spared in the war, they'll be a fine family." Then he asked hesitantly, "I don't want to probe, but what about you, Daughter?"

She flushed, knowing at once that he was asking, as tactfully as he knew how, about her relationship with Jason. She dropped her eyes and traced the pattern of her skirt. The silence ran on for a time, and the fiddle ended the song and began a plaintive ballad. "Oh, we're fine," she said finally. She looked up at him, and his eyes were on her. *He doesn't believe that,* she thought. *I never was a very good liar, but how do I tell him what it's like when I don't even know myself?* Quickly, she said, "I'm tired. Would it be all right if I made up a bed and turned in a little early?"

"Sure. I'm ready myself."

She brought him his medicine to dull the pain and leaned over him. His hair had once been as black as a crow's wing, but now it was streaked with gray and lay lank about his head. She reached out and smoothed it, whispering, "When we get to Twelve Trees, things will be quiet. You and I can spend whole days talking and playing chess and just being together."

"That will be good," he murmured. He reached up and took her hand, then surprisingly kissed it. "You are very like your mother," he murmured, "very like." Then he closed his eyes and fell asleep so quickly that it alarmed her.

She placed his hand on his chest and moved over to fix a bed on the couch. She turned down the lamps until there was only a small light in the darkness. Then she lay down on the couch and pulled a blanket over her. It was rough and scratched her cheeks, but she was tired and for a short time lay there listening to the fiddle. The unknown player was a fine musician, and then she heard the sound of a clear tenor voice raised in song. She had heard the song before—everyone in the North *and* South had heard it, for that matter. It had a plaintive quality to it. As the words came to her they seemed to sink into her spirit:

> *Into the ward of the clean, whitewash'd walls*
> *Where the dead and the dying lay,*
> *Wounded by bayonets, sabres, and balls,*
> *Somebody's darling was borne one day.*
> *Somebody's darling, so young and so brave,*
> *Wearing still on his sweet, yet pale face,*
> *Soon to be hid in the dust of the grave,*
> *The lingering light of his boyhood's grace.*

A weight pressed on Allyn as the chorus followed:

> *Somebody's darling, somebody's pride,*
> *Who'll tell his mother where her boy died?*

The thought came to Allyn, *Why—that could be about Lowell!* She had grown fond of the young man, and the thought of his lying cold and dead frightened her. *What must Rooney think when she hears this?* she wondered. She hoped that the singer would break off—or choose a happier song—but it did not happen.

> *Matted and damp are his tresses of gold,*
> *Kissing the snow of that fair young brow;*
> *Pale are the lips of most delicate mould,*
> *Somebody's darling is dying now.*
> *Back from his beautiful purple vein'd brow*
> *Brush off the wand'ring waves of gold,*
> *Cross his white hands on his broad bosom now,*
> *Somebody's darling is still and cold.*
>
> *Somebody's watching and waiting for him,*
> *Yearning to hold him again to her breast;*

Yet, there he lies with his blue eyes so dim,
And purple, childlike lips half apart.
Tenderly bury the fair, unknown dead,
Pausing to drop on his grave a tear;
Carve on the wooden slab over his head,
Somebody's darling is slumbering here.

Somebody's darling, somebody's pride,
Who'll tell his mother where her boy died?

As the last words faded and seemed to drop off, the house grew quiet and Allyn lay still, thinking of the harvest of death that had fallen on the land. Then she thought of how Jason had stared down at her and accused her of being unwilling to be the woman she was meant to be. What if something happened to him after he found a ship and things were never fixed with them? *What if he died hating me?* She couldn't figure out why she cared about his feelings about her. Finally she dropped off into a sleep, Jason's strong, tan face framed by his long, blond hair recurring in her dreams.

★ ★ ★

Gideon lifted his head and stared fuzzily around. He had been half asleep and was startled when a voice said, "Uncle Gid?" He tried to sit up and found that he had trouble. *Weak as a blasted baby!* he thought. Then he felt a strong hand helping him into a sitting position. The light from the tall window struck his eyes, and he blinked owlishly and licked his dry lips. He coughed, cleared his throat, and then the face of the woman who had helped him swam into view. "Why, Deborah," he gasped. He could say no more for he was shocked to see her here of all places. He attempted to stand up, but she put her hands on his shoulder and held him down.

"Don't try to get up, Uncle," she said. "Here, let me get the chair." She reached over and pulled the folding chair close beside his cot and sat down. "It's cold in here," she said. "Do you need me to bring you more blankets?"

"No, Melanie got enough. I shared some of them." He waved his hand at some of the men in the vicinity.

He put his eyes on her, and she saw that they were sunk deep in their sockets. He'd gone down so much that she had to mask her true feelings, which raked against her nerves. Her uncle had always been so strong, and now he was as weak as a kitten. "I brought you something good," she said. She reached down to a large basket and opened it up to let him peer inside. "Some fresh beef and some pies that I had specially made."

Gid looked down into the basket, then looked up and smiled at her. "That sounds good," he said. "This is probably the best-fed ward in the whole prison, thanks to Melanie and the others."

"Can you eat something now?" she asked.

"Maybe a little later." He stared at her in the gloomy light of the room and asked, "What are you doing here, Deborah? Is something wrong?"

"No, not really," she said. She hesitated for one moment, then decided to tell the real reason for her coming. Leaning forward she whispered, "Bing and Noel are here with me, Uncle Gid."

The news surprised him, and he said quickly, "That's dangerous, Deborah. Neither one of them are in the army now, but they both were at one time. They could be arrested for spies. You don't know how bad the feeling is around here." He shook his head sadly. "Just last week a man who was just suspected of being a Union agent was pulled out of his hotel room and whipped, then tarred and feathered." He bit his lip and added, "The South is losing, and they're lashing out at anything that moves." He stared at her and said, "Why are you doing this?"

Deborah hesitated. It had all seemed so logical and so possible back at home, but now that she was here in this solid building with guards standing at every door, it did not seem quite so possible as it had then. Nevertheless, she reached out, took his hand, which she noted was very thin,

257

and whispered, "We've come to get you out of here, Uncle Gid."

He blinked at her, shock running across his nerves. "Why, that's impossible!"

"That's not what the Bible says—the Bible says that with God all things are possible!"

Gideon grinned despite himself. "That's what comes from trying to argue with a preacher's daughter. You've always got some sort of a text to throw at a man, haven't you?" He sobered and waved at the room. "There are escapes made from most prisons, but this is a tough one. Once someone gets outside, there is always a chance to break away. But I'm in such poor shape, I couldn't 'break' for anything. You've got to call it off, Deborah." He squeezed her hand and said, "You know what I would feel like if anything happened to you. That would be worse than being a prisoner."

Deborah had prepared all her arguments, and for the next fifteen minutes she sat there stubbornly refusing to be moved. Finally, Gideon said, "You're just like your mother—stubborn as a mule! Like all Rocklins, I guess."

"That's right, and you're as bad as any," Deborah said with a smile. She was glad to see that he had lowered his guard to some degree, although she knew the battle still lay ahead. "This was Bing's idea," she said. "I've never seen him so set on anything, except the time we were here to get Noel out."

"He's a rough young fellow, isn't he? But he's got a good heart." Gideon frowned and shook his head. "This'll be tougher than getting Noel out. This place is better guarded than Chimborazo was. There are guards around the clock, and they've got orders to shoot anybody that tries to make a break. So far nobody's tried it, for they know it would be the same as asking for a bullet." He leaned over and opened the basket, pulling out one of the pies. "Why don't you cut this up, and we'll divide it among ourselves here. I'm not hog enough to eat the whole thing."

"All right." She cut the pies into small segments and soon

it had been distributed. She saw how the men did not gobble it down, but took small mouthfuls and savored the taste of the fresh apple pie. They were all officers in here, most of them fairly well cleaned up and presentable, though their uniforms were torn and patched. Some of them had been here a long time, she had discovered. As she watched them eat, Gideon asked, "What's your plan?"

Deborah hesitated, then confessed, "Well, we don't have one right now, but we'll think of something." Then she smiled and said, "It's crazy, isn't it? Come down here without a plan. But really, Uncle Gid, we think the Lord's in it. Even Bing thinks so, and he's not even a Christian. But this is good for Noel. He feels useless not being in the army."

"He's doing his part, writing stories that help the war effort."

"I know, but he doesn't think it's a help. He always respected and loved and admired you, so all three of us feel like we are doing something if we can get you home again. Now eat your pie. I'll bring some more tomorrow. At least I can do that. I brought all the money I could get ahold of with me, and we'll do what we can for the men in here till we get you out."

Gideon sat back, nibbling at the pie, staring at the girl. She had a determined light in her eye, and he said quietly, "Well, I'm willing to be got out. I'll have to admit this isn't my idea of living, but don't take any chances. I'd rather stay here till the war is over than see any one of the three of you hurt." Then he began to eat the pie, and they spoke of other things.

★ ★ ★

"I don't think we can put this off much longer," Bing said morosely. He was slumped in a chair in the room that Noel had rented for himself and looked over to where Noel and Deborah were seated together on a couch. "I can't see that we're doing any good."

"You have to be patient, Bing," Deborah said. She herself was tired of the waiting. Two weeks had gone by, and every day she had gone to visit Gid. She had spent a lot of time with Melanie. She'd even gone out to Gracefield once for a quick visit with Susanna, whom she dearly loved. The time had passed, but almost daily the three of them had met. Most of the time they asked each other, "What do you think we ought to do next?"

Bing was worse off, for he was basically geared to action. He got up now and paced the floor back and forth, stopping once to look suspiciously toward the door. "Sooner or later," he said, turning to face them, spreading out his large hands in a gesture of impatience, "somebody's gonna catch on to the fact that we don't really *belong* here. We've gotta do something!"

"Do what?" Deborah protested. Her own temper was short, and she said, "If you weren't ready to wait, you shouldn't have come here."

"Maybe I shouldn't," Bing snapped. He stared at her angrily and would have said more, but Noel interrupted.

"Wait a minute! We can't afford to fight among ourselves." His calm voice seemed to bring a relief into the room, and he smiled. "I feel just like you two, but we can't just pick up guns and go charging into the prison, can we? That wouldn't do any good."

Bing cast an apologetic look at Deborah, saying, "Sorry, Deb. I'm just nervous."

Noel sat there, his chair tilted back. There was a quietness in him that the others did not possess. He was by nature reflective, and he had walked the streets of the city hours each day, circling the prison, considering every possibility. Like Bing, he wanted to take some action, but caution held him back. Now, however, he put his chair down and stood to his feet. "I've got an idea, but it might get us all killed."

Bing at once flashed a grin. "Well, they can't kill us but once, can they? What is it?"

Noel hesitated. The idea had come to him, not all at once but in bits and pieces. He had toyed with it as a man would play with a puzzle, trying to fit different pieces, rejecting those that wouldn't fit, searching for other parts. It was, he understood, a tricky and dangerous business. He had hoped for something better to come. Now he said carefully, "I'm not sure about this at all, but this is what I've put together. . . ."

Deborah and Bing leaned forward and listened as Noel spoke slowly. Both of them had come to appreciate this young man who had a calmer spirit than either of them. He had often served as a brake for their rather unbridled emotions, and now, as he spoke logically, taking point upon point, Deborah and Bing paid careful heed.

"That's it," Noel said. "It's not much, but it's all I've been able to come up with."

Bing leaped forward and pounded Noel on the shoulder. "That's it! Brother, you're a genius!"

Deborah came over and threw her arms around him. "We'll do it!"

Noel protested, "It won't be easy, and like I say, it'll be dangerous."

"Crossing the street's dangerous," Bing stated. "You can get run over by a wild horse. When can we start?"

Noel looked at the two and took a deep breath. "All right, we'll do it. Here's what we'll do first. . . ."

PART FOUR
The Last Chance

CHAPTER NINETEEN
"What Is a Marriage?"

★

Jason's homecoming caught Allyn completely off guard. She had not even realized he had arrived, but when she came back from a ride and entered the house, she found him standing in the foyer. He stood still, not coming to meet her, and she felt awkward. When she said inanely, "Why—hello!" she felt even more foolish.

Then he did come forward, pausing before her. "I just came in thirty minutes ago," he said easily. "You been out riding?"

"Yes. I'm not very good at it, but with some advice from Caesar I'm doing better."

At that moment Flossie came in and said, "You come and set down, Captain. I know you ain't had no fit cooking since you been gone, but I got some ham, and I battered you some eggs. Dey'll do till supper tonight."

Larrimore turned to smile at the heavyset black woman. "Thank you, Flossie, and you're right about not very good cooking. Those Yankees can build ships, but they can't cook a meal fit to eat."

"You come, too, Miss Allyn," Flossie insisted. "I'll fix you a plate."

"Oh, I'm not really very hungry," Allyn protested. Nevertheless, she entered the kitchen and sat down at the table.

Flossie kept up a constant stream of questions, for she was fiercely curious about the world of the Yankees. To her, they all had forked tails and carried pitchforks. She was rather disappointed at Jason's assurance that they were just men, no better or worse than the ones she knew.

"I can't believe dat!" she said emphatically, slamming a plate of biscuits down that she had taken out of the oven. "Why they coming down here with all their shootin' and killin' if they so good? You tell me dat!"

Jason grinned at her, then secretly winked at Allyn. "Well, maybe you're right, but I'm too hungry to argue the point."

He began to eat, and when Flossie had left the room, Allyn asked, "Did you get the ship?"

"Yes." He chewed thoughtfully on the eggs, sliced a biscuit open, and dipped a knife into the bowl of butter. Spreading it evenly, he took a bite of that, chewed on it for a moment, then nodded. "She's right about cooking, you know. Yankees can't cook." He took a swallow of coffee, then piled a heap of yellow eggs on his fork. Before he put it into his mouth, he said, "I got a good one. Didn't have enough money to pay for it, but the owner took a note."

"Tell me about it. How big a ship is it?"

"Different kind than I've seen, for the most part," he said. "She's built low and long, a rakish sort of craft, has short masts and convex forecastle decks."

"Why is that?"

"Well, a ship like that will go through the rough seas instead of bouncing along on the top. At least, that's the theory," he admitted with a grin. He put the eggs in his mouth, chewed on them, then swallowed. "The idea is that while the Yankee gunboats are bouncing around on top of the water, this ship will plow right through and outrun them."

"What color is it? White?"

Jason laughed at her. "Bless you, no! A dull lead color." Seeing her disappointment, he said, "If you want a pleasure ship, we'll try to get one and paint it red, white, and blue. For this business, the less visible a ship is the better."

"Oh, I see. I suppose that's so." Allyn knew nothing about ships and leaned forward as he described the vessel carefully. Finally, she said, "Have you named it yet?"

He grinned at her sardonically, a grin touching the corners of his eyes. *"The Last Chance,"* he said.

Allyn looked at him with surprise. *"The Last Chance?* That's the name of the ship?"

"Yes."

"But that's an awful name," she said. "Why don't you call her *The White Lily* or something like that. Anything but *The Last Chance."* She shook her head, sending her mass of curls bouncing. "Where did you get such an awful name?"

Jason put his fork down, picked up the coffee cup, and sipped from it. He was tired, and lines of strain showed around the corners of his mouth and the edges of his eyes. "Because that's about what it is, I suppose," he said quietly. "Can't afford to lose this one." He put the cup down and stared at her and said, "I've had second thoughts about all of this. It's not fair to you, Allyn."

"What do you mean, not fair to me? It's what we agreed on."

"I know it, but it doesn't seem right."

"The plantation's in my name. Even if you lose the ship, I'll have that."

"Yes, but it takes money to run a plantation. I don't know much about it, but every planter I know is head over heels in debt. He makes and spends all his money, uses all the credit he can, then when the crops come in, if they do, he pays it off. The trouble with that is," he said glumly, "crops aren't bringing anything. You can't sell cotton—no place to take it." He picked the fork up and pushed the eggs around on his plate, then he looked up at her, his blue eyes startling to her as always against his tan skin. "I guess I should have thought of all this before I plunged in and bought the ship."

She was pleased by his concern. "It'll be all right, Jason," she said. "I've heard of fortunes being made. Why you made a lot of money yourself."

"If I don't get caught, we'll be all right," he said. "But there's always that chance. It's riskier than a poker game, Allyn."

They sat there talking, and finally he stretched and said, "I think I'll go lie down awhile. I don't think I've slept a whole night since I've been gone."

She rose, asking, "When will you leave?"

"As soon as I can. I've got Davis getting the ship fitted out. As soon as it's ready we'll make our run. I've got to earn my keep around here." He glanced at her curiously and said, "What have you been doing with yourself?" A glint touched his eyes. "Explaining to people why your new husband ran off and left his new bride?"

Her cheeks flushed, but she managed to smile. "I just told them you'd gone to buy a ship. They seemed to think that was very patriotic of you. It's amazing how much everybody's depending on you and the blockade-runners."

He shrugged, saying, "No other way to get things, but we're not heroes, Allyn. We're in it for the money."

"I suppose so. After you rest awhile, maybe you'd like to take a ride around the place. You haven't seen it all."

"No, I left a little abruptly, didn't I?" He laughed at her, then nodded. "Yes, we'll do that." He turned and left without another word.

Later that afternoon when he awoke, they did ride through the fields. The early November wind was rough, but it brought a rouge to her cheeks that he found admirable and said so. "This country air is good for you," he said. "You're looking well."

"Why—thank you," she said, "but I've been busy taking care of Father. He can't get out much in this kind of weather."

"How is he? When I talked to him he didn't seem any better."

"No, he's not." She bit her lip. As the horses moved

along, she swayed easily with the movement of her animal. "I worry about him. He doesn't worry, though."

"No, he doesn't." A puzzled look spread across Jason's face, and he shook his head. "Mark's got lots of nerve. I never knew anyone with more. We've been in some pretty tough spots together, and he acted like there wasn't any such thing as fear. But this is a little different."

Allyn glanced at him. He was wearing a light-brown jacket over a white shirt, tight-fitting, fawn-colored breeches, and polished boots that came up to his knees. She thought he looked very masculine and strong. "What do you mean, different?" she asked.

"Well, when you go into a battle, you've got a chance of getting out of it, and that's what you always think about." He shrugged and added, "The fellow on the left of you or on your right, *they* may go down, but you don't think you'll ever be the one. But, in a thing like this, Mark knows he's going down, and he's not afraid."

Allyn thought about what he had said. She, too, had been impressed by the quiet and solid dignity that her father had shown. He bore without complaint the pain and the indignities that accompanied sickness, and he spoke of his death indifferently, expressing only the regret that he would not be around to help her. But as for himself, she knew he was absolutely resigned and had, as Jason had said, no fear.

"It has something to do with his belief in God," she said. "He told me that."

"He told me that, too," Jason said. He shook his head. "I'm a pretty sorry subject for a sermon. I guess Mark knows it, but I admire the real thing. I've seen it in a few—in Susanna and Clay, and now in Mark. That whole Rocklin family seems to have a hand on God somehow, don't they?"

"Yes, they do," she said quietly. They rode along a narrow trail with the leaves crisp beneath the hooves of the horses. The winds caught bundles of them and sent them in small whirlwinds over the ground, where they settled to fall back onto the earth. The clouds were white against the light blue sky. They skittered along, and Jason said, "They look like the sails of huge ships, don't they? I always did like clouds."

"So did I," she said in surprise. "Sometimes I get a crick in my neck from just walking along, looking up. Ran into a post once, and everybody laughed at me." He looked at her, admiring the color in her cheeks. He'd never seen anything like the satin silkiness of her skin, and there was a piquant quality in her expression. She looked, almost, like a very young girl. He almost told her so but felt it might not be wise.

When they approached the house, he said, "Well, I solved one problem for you."

"Problem? What problem is that?"

"I told Flossie that I wanted my own room." As he expected, she reddened, and he laughed at her. "Don't worry, I took all the blame for it. Told her that I talked in my sleep terribly. I don't think she believed it, but she didn't say anything."

"Thank you—that was thoughtful of you."

"Don't mention it. We husbands always want to be gentlemen and do the right thing by our brides."

She found no answer for that but sat in her saddle straightly, her body trim, outlined by the gray riding outfit she wore. She had left her hair loose, tied simply in the back with a single ribbon, and it cascaded down her back, catching the afternoon sun.

"Aren't you going to ask if I had any female companionship on my travels?" he said, a sparkle in his eye.

"No," she said shortly. "I'll never ask you anything like that."

"And I needn't ask you if you had any gentlemen callers, I suppose?"

She did not answer him but spurred her horse. His laugh followed her, and he came up alongside her. When they dismounted, he reached over and caught her hair for a moment. She gasped and turned to look at him, not knowing what he was up to. But he simply held it and said nothing. Then he dropped the strand and went into the house. "I'll spend some time with Mark before supper."

For two days Allyn and Jason kept an uneasy truce. Neither of them felt comfortable, and Mark was well aware of it. He knew, of course, that they were not sharing the same room, although he never spoke of it to either of them. It had been Flossie who had informed him of the fact. She had also said, "That ain't right, and you know it ain't right, Mistuh Mark."

"We'll have to let them work out their own problems, Flossie," Mark had said. Now, as Jason entered his room, he studied the big man and said, "Did you have a good ride? I saw you and Allyn through the window."

"Yes." Jason fell into a chair and tossed his leg over the arm. "She's a good rider."

"Tell me, what do you think of Twelve Trees?" Mark asked.

"Fine place. I've never seen better. Small, but I like that. I never did see any sense in having twenty thousand acres of land that you couldn't even walk around. Always felt the same way about ships, too," he said thoughtfully. "Take a man of-war, ship of the line, with a thousand men on them. Why, they're like towns, but small ships, small crews—you know, Mark, they're like family."

They talked on for a while, Mark listening mostly as Jason talked about the sea and about the blockade and how he intended to beat the Federals at their own game. Finally, when Jason got up to leave, he said, "Jason, I don't know how to say this."

Jason halted, cocked an eyebrow. "Why, just let me have it straight, Mark. We've always been that way with each other."

"All right, here it is: What is a marriage?"

Jason knew what his friend was getting at. He had not spoken of any of the intimate details, such as they were, but he suddenly was aware that Mark knew. He wanted to tell him more, to explain that this was Allyn's idea of a business

271

relationship, but he felt that that was her place to say. Now, he said, "Why, it's a man and a woman living together. I'm no expert."

"It's more than that," Mark said. "I missed it myself, but you've seen it haven't you? A man and a woman really one, both just one creature, almost, made out of two parts, the man and the woman. It always made me sad when I saw it because I knew that I had missed probably the greatest thing on earth, aside from God himself."

"You don't see it much," Jason muttered.

"It's there, though," Mark said. He leaned forward and said, "I can't interfere with you and Allyn. What's done is done, but—be gentle with her, Jason. That's all I ask."

Jason blinked his eyes, then nodded shortly. "You can believe that I'll do that, Mark. I'll not be the best husband in the world, but she'll never know meanness from me."

When Jason had left the room, Mark leaned back, fatigue overcoming him. The pain was worse now, and he bit his lip to choke the cry that would have escaped. Finally he whispered, "Marriage is more than not showing meanness to someone!"

★ ★ ★

Rooney and Lowell rode over the following day, arriving at noon. They were glowing with happiness and could not be separated from each other by more than a distance of two feet.

"They make me feel a hundred years old," Jason remarked as the two laughed and joked with each other. He was standing with Allyn, looking out the window where the new bride and groom were walking along, hand in hand, Rooney laughing at something Lowell had said.

Allyn came over and looked out at the young couple. She watched as Lowell reached down and pulled Rooney to him, kissing her thoroughly. She seemed embarrassed for a moment but then surrendered and put her arms around his neck.

"That's very sweet," Allyn whispered. "They're so in love."

"I suppose."

"You *suppose!*" Allyn looked up at him. "Can't you see it?"

"I see a lot of men kissing a lot of women, but that's not love." He gave her a straightforward look. "I guess I'm just not romantic. But then, you'd hate it if I were, wouldn't you?"

Allyn turned and left at once. He had a way of hurting her, whether or not intentional, she could not tell. She could not understand her feelings about him. Somehow she wanted to strike out, for at times he seemed arrogant or hard. Mark had told her that this was part of his rough upbringing, and she wanted to believe it. At times he was different. He seemed almost gentle. Certainly when he talked to the slaves there was an openness he never showed to her. *He's always got his guard up around me,* she said to herself as she went to Mark's room. Then she put her lips together firmly thinking, *But then, so do I.*

She entered Mark's room and saw that he was awake.

"I came to ask you what you want for supper," she said with a smile.

"Some of that squirrel and dumplings I think I could keep down," he said. "Jason went out and shot a bunch this morning, he told me."

"Yes, he took me with him. He's such a good shot." She laughed suddenly, a delightful sound. "He let me shoot, but only once. He was afraid I'd blow his leg off," she said.

"Tell me about Rooney and Lowell," Mark said. He lay there while she spoke of the young couple and finally, when she'd finished, he nodded. "They'll be all right."

"Yes," Allyn said, and then said more soberly, "if he gets home from the war. I don't know how Rooney would handle it if anything happened to Lowell. She's caught up in him so much. Why, she needs him just like she needs air."

"That's a poetic way of putting it," Mark observed. He

thought for a moment, then made a decision. "Sit down, Allyn, I want to talk to you."

Surprised, she looked at his face and saw that he was serious, so she slipped into a chair. "What is it?" she asked.

"I'm worried about you," he said. "I pushed you into this marriage and now, looking at it, I think I was wrong."

"I made up my own mind," Allyn replied at once. "You can't blame yourself for anything. Besides, it's going to work out all right."

"You think so? You really think so?"

Allyn said with much more confidence than she felt, "Yes, it will."

Mark had prayed much about the marriage of his daughter. He felt that it had been a mistake. It had never been part of his plan for her to marry a man like Jason. Now, for the last few days he had tried to find some way to make a contribution, but how do you pull a marriage together? How do you push a man and woman toward each other and make them care for one another? He had agonized over this and prayed about it. Only two nights earlier he had been searching the Scripture, praying, and an idea had come to him. The idea seemed so strange to him that he could not think it was from God.

But he carried it in his heart and meditated on it. More than once he whispered, "I wish Susanna were here to help me pray about this." But Susanna was not there, and now as he lay in the bed looking over at Allyn, he knew he had to at least try to make her understand.

He lay there, gathering his thoughts, trying to muster the strength and felt the weakness creeping up on him. *O God,* he prayed, *help me to help her make the right decision.* Then, he said aloud, "Allyn, I want to ask you to do something. You may think this is very strange, but I've prayed about it, and I think I'm giving you what God has given to me."

She stared at him blankly, then leaned forward. "Why, I'll do anything I can. You know that. What is it you think God has told you?"

"I think you should go with your husband on this trip."
Allyn stared at him, shock raking across her nerves.
"Why—why would you ask me to do a thing like that?"

"I'm not blind, Allyn," Mark said quietly. "It's obvious
that you two are not man and wife." He saw her eyes drop,
her long lashes falling on her cheeks. She could not meet his
gaze, and he said softly, "Don't be ashamed. I haven't given
up hope."

Allyn then lifted her eyes and licked her dry lips. "It's—it's
not a normal marriage we have, Jason and I. It's more of a
business matter. He needed a ship, and I needed a husband
to get the house."

Mark shook his head. "As I told Jason, marriage is more
than most people think. If it doesn't have love, it's nothing."

The silence ran on, and he waited for her to speak. He was
afraid for a moment that he had said too much. He saw that
she was vulnerable, her lips were soft and trembling. She
whispered, "You can't make people love, can you, Father?"

"I think," he said carefully, "you can put yourself in the
way of love. I don't know what's gone on between you and
Jason, but I do know you can't go on forty or fifty years the
way you're going now."

"But—but, how would going with him solve this?"

"I don't know. I do know it won't solve anything if he
goes off and leaves you here. You've got to be with him—be
together. Maybe on a ship. A ship's a lonely place. If you
seek the Lord and if you want to find love, Allyn, that might
be the place for it." He hesitated, then said, "Will you go?"

"I—I don't know if he'd let me."

"Will you try?" Mark urged. He lifted his hand, reached
over, and squeezed her arm with surprising strength. "It's
your life I'm talking about, Allyn. Go with him, open
yourself up to him. He's a good man—a little hard perhaps,
but a woman can do a lot to soften a man. Will you try?"

Allyn reached up, put her hand on his, and held it. "I'll
ask him," she said, "and if he'll have me, I'll go with him."

CHAPTER TWENTY
Maiden Voyage

★

As soon as *The Last Chance* slipped outside the small bay where it lay hidden from cruising gunboats into the moonlit waters, Allyn gasped. The bow rose, then fell, and she held onto the rail with all of her strength. She had never been in anything larger than a rowboat, and that on a still pond just outside New Orleans. Now the swells of the sea began to catch the long, low-lying craft as she steamed forward, the land rapidly falling behind. She had eaten a fish supper earlier—against the advice of Jason, who had warned her it was a rather heavy meal.

Now, as the ship dipped forward and rose again, her stomach seemed to do the same. A queasiness came to her, and for five minutes she stood there clinging to the rail, getting sicker by the moment. She decided to go below and lie down, but when she was halfway to the hatch that led below, she knew she would never make it. Staggering against the rollings and the dippings of the ship, she came to the rail, barely making it before she threw up.

Jason was standing in the wheelhouse and happened to glance down. He saw Allyn clinging to the rail and shook his head. *That'll get worse before it gets better,* he thought to himself. He could not leave the wheel at the moment, for the critical time of a blockade-runner was getting away from the shores. The gunboats lay offshore, cruising back and forth, and at any moment one or more might suddenly appear.

Malcolm Davis came to stand beside him, saying, "The engine's running smoothly, Captain." Then he stood there silently, the two of them sweeping the horizon carefully. There were lookouts posted on the tops of the masts to catch the first glimpse of smoke or enemy vessel.

For over an hour, Jason held the wheel. Finally he took a deep breath and said with relief, "I think we made it, First. I think we've passed through the net."

"God was with us," Malcolm said quietly. "He'll be there all the way to the pickup, too." They had an appointment to rendezvous at a port in the Bermudas to pick up the cargo that had been shipped from England. It would be a quick run.

Jason looked down and saw that Allyn was gone. "Take the wheel, Malcolm," he said. "I think my wife isn't going to be a very good sailor."

He descended from the pilothouse, went below, and made his way to the door of the small cabin that would have been his. Tapping on the door, he waited for a moment, heard a small moan, and stepped inside. Allyn, he saw, was lying on the bunk, her face pale and her eyes shut. "Sorry it took you like this," he said. "I'm hoping we'll get out of some of these swells when the weather lets up."

"I think I'm going to die," she whispered feebly.

He moved to her side and looked down on her. "Everybody thinks that, but I never saw anyone yet die of seasickness. Sometimes I've wanted to," he added. "Stay in your bunk. After a while, I'll bring you some hot tea."

"No—don't even *mention* it!" she moaned.

He grinned at her, shook his head, then said, "You'll be all right, Allyn. I'll be back soon."

For the next two days, Allyn kept to her cabin. The first day she took practically nothing at all except tea in small doses, which she threw up half the time. Once she had looked up at him as he held a towel in front of her and said, "I'm so much trouble. I should have stayed at home."

He had looked at her and said, "Well, you wanted a life at sea, and this is part of it."

He left the room, and she wiped her face with the wet towel that he left in the basin. As long as she lay still, it was not so bad. The weather had calmed, and *The Last Chance* was a smooth ride, all things considered. It was the sudden dips that brought the wrenches to her stomach, and she lay there praying they wouldn't happen again.

But on the third day she awoke in the morning to find herself hungry and without a trace of nausea. Getting up, she sat on the bed carefully and waited to see if it would return. When it did not, she took a deep breath and began to wash her face. She stripped off her nightgown, took a complete sponge bath, dried, and then put on a warm, blue wool dress. Her black cloak was hanging beside it. She fastened that about her shoulders and stepped outside into the passageway. Before she got to the ladder, she learned that she would be able to live with the slight motion of the ship and felt rather proud of herself.

She climbed the ladder and met the first officer, Malcolm Davis, whose name she remembered after a moment's struggle.

"Well, good morning, Mrs. Larrimore," Davis said with a smile. He touched his hat. "How do you feel?"

"Oh, much better, thank you." She gave him a wry smile and shook her head. "That's the sickest I've ever been in my life! Does it happen at the first of every voyage?"

"Well now, for some it does, but we'll pray that the good Lord will give you a better stomach and make a good sailor out of you." He smiled, his square face friendly and warm. "Being married to a sailor, a lady like you needs to have sea legs and be able to take a blow now and then. Why don't you go up and see the captain? He'll be glad to see you're feeling better. I know he's been worried."

"Thank you, Mr. Davis. I believe I will."

She made her way along the deck and climbed the ladder leading to the wheelhouse. Jason turned to greet her with a surprised look on his face. "Well, you're better," he said.

"Yes, it went away as quick as it came."

"You're probably hungry," he said. "Clinton, take the wheel, hold this course."

"Aye, sir."

Jason took her arm, moved her through a door that led into what seemed to be a small galley. "Sit down. I'll have the cook make you some eggs. They're usually the safest thing. Some toast and a little milk, perhaps?"

"That sounds good."

She sat there and he left, then came back after a moment to sit down across the table from her. "Ollie's making you something nice. Be sure you brag on him." He grinned, saying, "You don't want to alienate the cook on board ship."

She looked around and said, "It's not very ornamental, is it? I was on a riverboat for a few minutes once in New Orleans. It was all gold gilt and carpets and big chandeliers."

"No, you won't find any of that on *The Last Chance* or on any blockade-runner." He looked at the bare walls, the stark furnishings, all rough and slightly greasy. "This isn't a pleasure boat. We'll get that when we get our cargo back and sell it. Then we can take a trip on one of those fancy riverboats. Be nice to go all the way to New Orleans—but the Yankees are controlling the river now, so we can't do that."

"I'd like to do it sometime," she said. "I always wanted to ride on one of those big riverboats. They have music and dancing and things like that."

"Oh yes, they're floating palaces. I'll take you on one when there's time."

Jason studied her carefully, without appearing to do so, while they were waiting for the food. She was a little pale, but the sickness was gone from her eyes. She had shoved the hood back and now sat at the table, her hands in front of her. He was considering her offer to come. She had come to him saying, "I'd like to make the first trip with you." He'd argued against it, naming the discomforts on board a ship like *The Last Chance,* but when she had insisted, he reluctantly agreed. It had come as a surprise to him for he had not thought she would want such a thing. Even more surprising was the fact that he had agreed to let her come. Now, as he sat watching her, he wondered why he had given in.

A short, fat man with hairy arms came in bearing a tray and set it down before the couple. "I made you an omelet, missus," he said with a grin, exposing a line of gold teeth that glittered brightly. "If you've been seasick you wouldn't want some of the greasy food that we'll have at our regular meals. You can come to me, and I'll see that you get something good until you get your strength back. Me name's Ollie."

"Thank you, Ollie," Allyn said. She dug into the omelet and tasted it, then gave him an appreciative look. "Oh, this is *good!*"

"I'll make you another if that ain't enough. Captain, what can I bring you?"

"Just coffee, Ollie."

"Aye, sir, I'll be right back with it."

Allyn ate hungrily, and Jason watched her languidly. When she was finished, he said, "Like to take a turn on deck? Feel up to that?"

"Yes. I'm tired of that cabin." She rose, pulling the hood up over her head, then the two went out on deck. She walked the deck with him for some time, delighted with the passage of the ship over the gray-green waves. Finally they came to stand at the very prow of the ship, and she stood there looking down at the froth that the sharp cutting edge of the ship threw high in the air. "It smells good," she said, "crisp—different from the land."

"I miss the smell of the sea when I'm on the shore," Jason said. They talked for a while, and finally he asked, "Why did you want to come on this trip, Allyn? Were you just bored?"

The impulse came to Allyn to tell him what her father had said, but she knew she couldn't do that. Looking at him now, she studied the smooth line of his jaw, the strength that lay in his shoulders, and the light in his blue eyes. *He's hard and strong,* she thought. *I don't know how to get close to such a man.* Aloud, she said, "I just thought it would be nice to see what it is you do, Jason." She looked out over the sea and said, "I can understand a man wanting to be a sailor."

"It isn't always like this," he said. "Sometimes the storms come and throw us around like a ball. The food gets bad on long journeys, and the water's not fit to drink."

"I suppose so," she said. "But it's exciting anyway for someone out the first time."

After a while one of the sailors came and said, "The first officer asked me to tell you he wants you to come to the engine room, Captain."

"I'll be right there." Jason turned and said, "I'm afraid you'll have to entertain yourself, Allyn. I'll be busy most of the time, but we'll plan a good supper tonight. I'll have Ollie make something special."

"All right, I'd like that."

The rest of the day Allyn spent walking the deck. She never got tired of the endless stretch of the ocean. She was aware that the lookouts constantly swept the horizon looking for enemy ships, and she hoped fervently that they did not see any. Finally, she went to her room and rested. She woke up an hour before supper, washed her face, and sat down to pick up the Bible that she had brought with her—one that Mark had given her. She had grown interested in the Scripture, which was mostly Susanna's doing. For a long time she sat there reading. Then she closed the Bible and went to the galley, where she found Jason and Malcolm Davis waiting for her.

"No white tablecloth at this captain's table," Jason said, "but Ollie's got something you'll like, I think."

It was a fine meal, and Ollie outdid himself with grilled chicken, well-roasted beef, and fresh bread from the oven. There was fresh juice that tasted delicious. After the meal, the three of them sat around drinking coffee. The two men talked about other voyages they had made while Allyn listened. Finally she said, "It must be nice to have been with someone a long time. You two go back a long way, don't you?"

"Yes we do, Mrs. Larrimore," Davis affirmed. "And you're right. It is a good thing to have friends. The Scripture says that two are better than one."

A mischievous light suddenly glinted in Jason's eyes. He leaned back and said, "I know that one. I've heard you quote it enough. 'Two are better than one; because they have a good reward for their labour. For if they fall, the one will lift up his fellow: but woe to him that is alone when he falleth; for he hath not another to help him up.'" He looked over at Allyn and said softly, "'Again, if two lie together, then they have heat: but how can one be warm alone?'" A smile tugged at the corner of his lips, and he said no more.

Allyn felt her face grow warm, for she knew the way he had of using a barbed wit sometimes that hurt, and he was making fun of her.

Malcolm Davis missed that byplay, but he nodded seriously. "'Woe to him that is alone when he falleth.' I've thought about that verse a lot," he said quietly. "Nothing much worse than being alone in this world."

"Most of us are, though," Jason commented. He had moved a finger along his nose, scratching it, then dropped his hand. There was a thin veneer of cynicism that came to him often, and it seemed to be on him now. "Most of us live alone, even in the midst of crowds," he said.

At once Allyn lifted her eyes and stared at him. "Why, I've always felt that way!" she said.

"Have you? I wouldn't have thought it."

"Yes, I have. I've often wondered at people who have a lot of friends. I wish that I could have many, but I just haven't been able to make them."

"It costs to have a friend," Malcolm said. "The Bible says that if you would have a friend, you must show yourself friendly."

"You've always got a Scripture to fit everything, Malcolm." Jason grinned at his friend and said, "You should have been a preacher, not a sailor."

"I didn't have the call," Davis said. "They have a hard life, the ministers of God. I do all I can to help them. It's a glorious calling to have, to proclaim the glorious gospel of the Lord Jesus. I can't think of a higher one. Greater than an emperor, I think."

"That's nice," Allyn said thoughtfully. "Not many people speak that well of preachers."

They talked until Allyn got to her feet and said, "Well, it was a lovely meal. I really enjoyed it." She left and went to her cabin. For a time she sat reading, and then a knock came to her door. "Yes?" she said.

"It's me, Jason. Can I come in?"

Allyn put the Bible down and moved to the door. "Yes," she said carefully, "come inside."

He entered, having to duck his head. "These things were made for smaller-sized men, weren't they? Not for tall cranes like me." He studied her for a moment, then held up a bottle in his hand. "I found this wine when I was on shore. I'd forgotten about it. We haven't had our drink celebrating our first cruise together." He had two glasses in his pocket, took them out and handed one to her, then filled the glasses. "A toast then. Shall you make it or I?"

"I don't know how to make a toast."

"All right. Here's to a successful voyage and a safe return."

Allyn smiled and said, "Yes." She drank the wine, which she had never tasted before, and said, "I don't know whether I like this or not."

"The second one's always better. Can we sit down?"

"Yes. There's not much room, though." He took the chair and she sat on the bunk as he poured the glasses full again. "I don't drink, you know," she said.

"This is only wine. I didn't come to get you drunk."

284

She flushed, saying, "I didn't think you did. It's just that—"

"I know," he said, "you're afraid of me."

Allyn looked at him and lifted her chin and eyes. "No, I'm not afraid of you, not anymore."

"Then let's drink our wine."

They sat there quietly listening to the sibilant sound of the waves as the ship cut through them. She said, "I don't know much about you. Tell me about yourself, about your boyhood, things like that."

He shrugged and for a few moments spoke of his early life. He ended by saying, "Not a very interesting story."

Impulsively she asked, "Were you ever in love?"

He looked at her, the smile leaving his face. "Once," he said.

"Who was she?"

"Just a girl."

Noting his reluctance, Allyn said quietly, "If you don't want to talk about her, if it hurts that bad, then she's still inside you. I can hear the echoes inside."

Jason looked at her and said, "You're a very clever young woman, but you're not right this time. It's all over." He shook his head, took another sip of the wine, then said, "I was very young, and she was from a fine family—at least a rich family." A grimace moved across his face, and he said, "She married a son of one of the richest men in the state." He took a swallow of the wine and said, "I remember, she came to me and told me how it was, that she didn't want to do it, that we'd never be suited."

"Do you think of her often?" Allyn asked, almost timidly.

"Sometimes." Then he looked at her and said, "What about you?"

"No, there's been nothing like that in my life."

"Can't understand it, a fine-looking girl like you."

"Oh, there've been men enough chasing me, but I've never loved anyone."

Jason was interested. He leaned back, gazed at her and

said finally, "You know, it cut me pretty deep when she walked out on me, but something was even worse, at least it seems so now."

Allyn leaned forward. He was utterly serious, she saw. His lips were tight, and his shoulders moved with some sort of agitation stirred by an inner feeling. Something in him went very deep, and she asked, "What was that, Jason?"

"Well, it may sound funny coming from me, but I wanted to get married because . . ." He hesitated and seemed almost embarrassed. "I never had a family, so I wanted one. Most of all," he said, "I wanted a son."

From outside the cry of a lookout came. He straightened, listening carefully, then said, "No danger. But there's always a chance of a warship." Then he put the cork in the bottle and set it down along with the glass. Looking across, he said, "I still want a son."

Allyn grew still. She searched his face and saw that he had somehow changed. At once, she said angrily, "That's why you came here tonight, isn't it?"

The mood of the cabin suddenly became charged, and Jason stared at her. "Do you always have to have your guard up? You might as well get a suit of armor and put it on! You always think I'm after you."

Allyn rose and said, "I don't want to hear any more. We made a bargain, and I'm not ready to change. I've kept my part of it."

He got to his feet and stood, staring down. For a moment she thought he meant to put his hands on her, but he simply stood there, his eyes filled with regret. He did not seem to be angry, which surprised her. Finally he said in a clipped tone, "You know that verse of Scripture tonight, the one that Davis was quoting. I think you should have listened to it. 'Two are better than one.'" He waited a moment, then shook his head. "You'll never be 'two,' Allyn. You're too frightened of what you are and all the rest of it. You'll always be alone—and you'll always sleep cold."

He whirled, left the room, and slammed the door shut.

The sound seemed to hit her like a blow. She opened her mouth to cry, "No, that's not true!" but the words were muted. He had the power to shake her, and seeing that her hands were trembling, she clasped them together. She paced quickly back and forth in the confines of the small cabin, then sat down and buried her face in her hands. She thought of the words of her father, who asked her to open herself to love.

"I can't do it," she said between clenched teeth. "What's *wrong* with me? I *wanted* him to stay. Why did I act like I did?" And then she began to weep.

CHAPTER TWENTY-ONE
Noel and the Secretary

A chill hung over the large room that Gideon shared with the other prisoners. Almost all the men wore blankets over their shoulders to keep out the jaw-breaking cold. There was no stove or fire of any kind, and those men who had to sleep on the floor had trouble rising the next morning, so stiff and sore they were. They slept spoon-fashion, a line of them clutching each other for warmth, so that if one of them wanted to turn over, he called out, "Turn," and the whole serpentine row was forced to roll over.

"These blankets you've brought have been a lifesaver for us, Melanie," Gideon said. He was sitting on his bunk sipping a cup of lukewarm coffee that she had brought to him in a covered pot. "I don't think some of the men would have made it without your help."

Melanie looked over the men, whose faces were gray with illness, and shook her head. "I wish I could do more. It breaks my heart to think about the men that are in even worse shape."

"Yes, I hear they are dying like flies at Belle Isle and Andersonville. I'm thankful I'm here instead of one of those places."

"You're looking better," she said. She was seated across from him in a chair. Reaching forward, she put her hand on his as it rested on his knee. A smile lit her face, and she said cheerfully, "All you needed was a good nurse."

Gideon turned his hand over and clasped hers. "I'm not sure I would have made it if you hadn't come. I can face battle, but this—" He looked around the gloomy prison and shook his head. "It's the worst thing I've ever encountered. But you came. It's like you, Melanie."

"Oh, I haven't done anything," she said. She looked at him steadily and asked, "Don't they ever let you out for any kind of exercise?"

"No, I don't guess they have the manpower for that. I've been walking back and forth, getting all the exercise I can now that I'm up on my feet again."

"How's your wound?" she asked. "Let me take a look at it."

He put the coffee down, and she examined the wound, then said with satisfaction, "It's all knitted together. You heal quickly."

Again he said, "That's because of you and the good care you've given me."

The two sat there talking quietly, mostly about their boys. They got few letters, for communication between North and South was difficult. Finally, Melanie said with a puzzled look, "I can't figure out why Deborah came. Of course she wanted to help, but it seems strange she would just pull up, leave home, and come here with things as hard as they are. Also, why did she bring Noel and Bing along with her?" She stared at him and asked, "What's she up to, Gid?"

Gideon and Deborah had already agreed he would reveal nothing to Melanie about the plan, thinking it would be best if she knew nothing. "Well, for one thing, I guess Noel came to get a story. From what I hear, he's quite a celebrity—a Yankee in Rebel land. That editor from the *Richmond Examiner* has introduced Noel to every bigshot in the Confederacy, I think."

"Yes, Noel said that he'd met the president the other day, just for a minute. I'm surprised that they let him run loose."

"I asked him about that. He said that most of the stories he wrote about the North were pretty blunt and took a pretty charitable view of the South—for a Yankee, that is. I guess they figure they need all the help they can get along those lines." He leaned back, picked up the coffee, and sipped it. "He told me he was going to see the secretary of war today. I wish he'd talk him into exchanging me. I'd like to get home again. Get back to living."

Melanie smiled gently. "We'll get there, Gid, you just watch. God's going to do something for us."

★ ★ ★

Later that same day Noel was ushered into the office of the secretary of war by a lieutenant. He had been waiting in the outer office for over an hour, along with a crowd of people, and was surprised to be ushered in ahead of several high-ranking officers. When he entered, he said at once to the man behind the desk, "Secretary Seddon, I appreciate your seeing me. I know you're a busy man."

Secretary of War James Alexander Seddon rose and came over to offer his hand. A smile touched his lips, and he said, "I've been anxious to meet our visiting Yankee journalist, Mr. Kojak. Please have a seat."

"Thank you." Noel sat down and studied the face of the secretary carefully. "Sir," he said, taking out a pencil and pad, "I know how unusual it is for cabinet members to grant interviews to the Federal press, but I'd appreciate your views on the conduct of the war."

Seddon suddenly laughed. He seemed to be a pleasant man but one who was shrewd enough not to give away any vital information. "I don't think I'm much inclined to give you our strategy for winning the war, Mr. Kojak. However, if you'll ask specific questions, I'll be glad to answer them."

"Fine, sir. Now, are you comfortable with the conscription act, and is it working?"

"Yes to both. Of course, Mr. Lincoln has passed the same sort of act in the North." Seddon leaned back, picked up a short paper knife, and toyed with it as he said thoughtfully, "The volunteers came early and without pressure, but this war has gone on so long that those men were quickly used up. We went to conscription—as did the North—as the only way of filling the vacancies in the ranks."

Kojak kept the secretary's attention by his shrewd, often humorous remarks, and the two got along well. Finally, after nearly half an hour, Kojak said, "General, I know I can't take up any more of your time, but I do have a favor to ask."

A wary look crossed Seddon's face, and he asked, "What is it, Mr. Kojak?"

"I'd like to visit the troops in the west—in Chattanooga."

"I don't see any harm in it. Of course, we allow the British journalists to go right along with the troops. I'll have to ask you to submit the story you file with our authorities there, perhaps even Gen. Bragg or someone he designates."

"That will be fine, sir. I'd be happy to do that."

"I'll make you out a pass." Seddon picked up a paper and a pen. He dipped the pen in an inkwell, then stared at the paper. "I hate this grade of paper we're being forced to use."

"Well, the war has brought everything down some, I suppose," Kojak said. "I notice the newspaper's printed on wallpaper. I suppose all paper is in short supply."

"Yes, that is true." Seddon wrote a few lines on the paper, signed it with a flourish, then handed it to Kojak. "There you are, Mr. Kojak. Be sure you don't lose this. We are very careful about people traveling back and forth to the site of the action."

"I'll need passes for two men, General. I have a colleague who is traveling with me, another journalist."

When the passes were made out, Noel hesitated, snapped his fingers, and fumbled through the small case he'd brought with him. "Dash it all! I've come to the end of my paper!" He showed the general that he'd used the last page. He laughed with some embarrassment, saying, "I was going to get a few more interviews with some of your staff, but I'm out of paper. Could you spare a couple of sheets, sir?"

"Why, certainly. Help yourself."

Seddon picked up a small sheaf of papers and extended them toward Kojak. "Why, this'll be fine, sir," Noel said, taking a couple of them. He put them in the small case, along with his pencil, and put out his hand and said, "Thank you for your time. I appreciate it very much."

"I hope you will write honest stories, which I understand is your habit." The secretary of war rose, put his hand out, and said, "We in the South need the truth to get to the Northern people."

"I always try to be as honest as I can," Noel said. "Good afternoon, sir."

Noel was outside and walking through the corridor leading to the outer door. He passed outside into the cold air, muttering, "Well, that's a lie. Nothing very honest about what I'm doing right now. I hate to do a thing like this to the secretary, but that's the way things are."

★ ★ ★

"Getting colder out there!" Noel exclaimed. He moved over, putting his hands close to the small wood-burning stove that radiated heat. "Well, I think we're on our way."

Bing was eating a piece of beef, gnawing it hungrily, but he looked up at once and said, "What do you mean? Are we ready to bust Col. Rocklin out of that joint?"

"I think we've got a chance. Come along." He looked over at Deborah, who had poured a cup of coffee into a mug and handed it to him. "Thanks." He sipped it gratefully and said, "I'd hate to be one of those poor fellows in that jail with no fire at all."

Deborah asked quickly, "Did you get to see the secretary?"

"Oh yes." Noel sipped the coffee and grinned. "It was easier to get to see him than it was some of the underlings in our own War Department. "He seemed like a nice enough fellow. I liked him."

"Why did you want to see him?" Bing demanded. "Is he part of the plan?"

"Yes." Noel set the coffee down on the table, held his hands out and warmed them, putting things together in his mind. When his hands were warm, he picked up the cup, sipped the coffee again, and said, "All right, I've got it all now." A wry look touched his lips, and he shrugged, saying, "It'll probably get us all hanged, but it's the best I can come up with."

"Tell us about it, Noel. What are we going to do?"

Noel began to speak, slowly and distinctly. That was his way, to impose a solid methodology on anything that he had to do. He alone of the three was a careful planner, and he well knew that the burden rested upon him. Bing would be handy for the execution of the plan, but he knew his brother was no thinker, and Deborah was far too impulsive.

"We can't bust into that prison by force, we know that. We've got to use our heads. We've got to somehow get the colonel *outside* the building."

"I don't know how we'll do that," Bing complained. "They never take any prisoners out, that I can tell. They go in, but the only time they leave is when they take some out to be exchanged, and then there's a big guard—too many for us."

"That's right, Bing." Noel nodded. "Of course, if he were going to be exchanged, we wouldn't be here. What we've got to do is create a situation where they bring Col. Rocklin out all by himself."

"And this has something to do with your visit to the secretary?" Deborah asked. Her eyes were bright, and she leaned forward eagerly as she waited impatiently for his reply.

Noel reached over, picked up the small case, and opened it. "Look at this."

The two looked, and Deborah exclaimed, "Why it's passes for two men to travel by train to Tennessee."

"Yes, and the most important thing is that we have a

sample of the secretary's handwriting, and we have paper that came off of his desk." He held up the paper, which was a peculiar shade of brown and had the secretary's name printed across the top. "That look official enough?"

"What are you going to do with it?" Bing asked curiously.

Noel hesitated and said, "I'm going to forge an order. It's going to go to Maj. Thomas B. Turner."

"Who's he?" Deborah demanded.

"He's the commandant in charge of Belle Isle and Libby prisons."

She was very quick, this girl with the bright eyes and eager face. "I know, you are going to say something in that order that will get Uncle Gid out."

"That's right. I've been thinking about it a lot, and the order will say that the secretary commands that Col. Rocklin be brought at once to the War Department."

Bing exclaimed, "And while the guard's taking him, we hit them!"

"Well, that's pretty much the idea, but now that I think of it, it's got some holes in it."

"It can't be in daylight," Deborah said at once. "The streets are so crowded. You can't just stop a squad of armed men in broad open daylight, Noel. You'd be seen."

"We'll have to do it at dusk, but even that will be dangerous. There're only two of us to do the kidnapping."

"Three!" Deborah snapped.

"Well, three then," Noel surrendered. "But I've been thinking about this ever since I came back. Here is the final part of the plan—and the most dangerous." Bing was curious, as was Deborah, and the two stood there waiting until Noel had gotten the thing firmly in his mind. Finally, Noel said, "We'll procure a couple of uniforms—an officer's uniform for me and a private's for you. We'll deliver this order in person. Hopefully, they'll turn the prisoner over to us, and we'll just walk out of there and that's it."

"But what if they don't?" Deborah demanded. "What if they send a whole squad with you?"

"I don't think they have the kind of manpower for that," Noel said. "If they do, we'll just have to do the best we can."

They talked for a long time, picking the plan apart, finding every fault they could.

Finally Deborah went over and gave Noel a hug. "It's a good plan," she said. "I'm proud of you."

Bing said, "I ain't gonna hug you, but I think it'll work. You've given us the brains, and I'll do the rough stuff. We're gonna make it."

Noel shook his head doubtfully. "Well, lots of things can go wrong, but it's the only chance we have." He hesitated and said, "If we get caught, it could be rather—unpleasant. I want you to stay out of it, Deborah."

She smiled softly, saying, "You're going to learn pretty soon, after we get married, that we Steele women are used to getting pretty much what we want."

"I've noticed that," Noel said. He could not contain the smile that came to him as he said, "I guess I'll just have to get used to it."

"Good! You're learning!" Deborah smiled at him. "Now, let's go over it again."

CHAPTER TWENTY-TWO
Action at Sea

The light-blue skies began to change to a duller color and finally were transmuted into a dull leaden hue. The slight breeze that had barely filled the sails of *The Last Chance* swelled into heavy forceful gusts that sent the ship scudding rapidly through the water. In her cabin Allyn felt the entire ship shudder as it plunged into a trough. She grabbed hold of the edge of her bunk, and after what seemed a long time, the ship slowly recovered. Nervously she waited for a return of the nausea, but it did not come. "I guess I'm over that, for this trip anyway," she said.

The sailors had told her that once her stomach had become adjusted to a voyage, she was fairly safe. One of them had said, "Been at sea twenty-nine years, ma'am, and every time I go out I'm sick as a dog. After that, I'm all right."

There was no porthole in the small cabin, and when the ship began to plunge more sharply, Allyn put on her cloak and left the cabin. She made her way down the corridor, holding onto the walls. When she reached the deck, she was greeted by a fine drizzle that was sending slanted lines across the horizon, making dimples on the roiling billows. The waves seemed to rise like mountains, lifting *The Last Chance* high, then letting it slide down into the trough—only to rise again for the next wave.

Allyn was frightened by the power of the sea. She realized how fragile a thing the ship was; only a fraction of an inch, the thickness of the hull, kept her and the crew alive. She flattened her back against the bulkhead and watched as the rain swept across the deck. Seeking shelter to keep from getting drenched, she dodged into the hatchway that led to the galley. When she entered, Ollie saw her and called out, "Heavy weather, missus, ain't it now?"

"It seems very bad to me," Allyn said as she grabbed at the table that was bolted to the deck and asked, "Does it get worse than this?"

"Worse than this?" Ollie grinned. "Why, yes indeed, missus. But you just don't go wandering around on that deck by yourself. Many a man's been washed overboard by a wave, taken off in a moment to meet his Maker."

"I'll be careful," she said quickly. The ship took a nose-dive, and she lurched backwards. She made a grab at the table but missed, so she pitched back, falling full length on the floor.

At once, Ollie sprang forward, crying, "Watch out, missus—"

At that exact moment the door opened and Jason stepped in. He saw Allyn struggling on the floor and came forward to help her. He seized her arms and lifted her upright as he would have a child. "Here. Sit down," he said gruffly.

Allyn slid into the seat and held onto the table, whispering, "Thank you."

Jason paid her no further heed but turned to Ollie, saying, "Ollie, don't try to cook anything in this weather. Just serve the crew a cold lunch today. Maybe it'll calm down and you can heat the galley up tonight."

"Aye, sir."

Ollie dismissed himself, and Jason turned to put his eyes on Allyn. "Are you feeling all right?" he asked shortly.

"Yes," she said. "I thought I might be sick with the way this ship is pitching, but I think I'm all right."

"Good."

He turned and would have left, but she said quickly, "We're not going to sink, are we?"

Jason stopped abruptly, turned, and placed one hand against the wall to gain his balance. "No, not unless it gets a lot worse than this."

It was the longest remark he had made to her since they had had the confrontation in her cabin. For two days she had kept to her cabin, leaving only to go for walks on the deck or to take her meals in the dining room. She had talked to Malcolm Davis considerably and knew that the first officer understood that she and Jason were at outs—although he had said nothing. She had found that Ollie was an entertaining sort of fellow and had spent some time in the dining room and the galley listening to his exaggerated stories of sea life, but Jason himself had kept his silence.

It was the first moment she had had alone with him, and she forced herself to say, "Jason, I'm—I'm sorry for what happened in my cabin."

Surprised, he looked at her and studied her carefully. Ever since that incident he had been forced to keep his anger throttled down. He could not understand why he was being so sensitive and irrational. He had not revealed himself to many people, and he never told anyone about the girl who had touched his life in the past, who had been such an influence in making him reserved. When Allyn had taken his statement about wanting a son as an advance on his part, nothing had been farther from his mind. After he had stormed out of the cabin and tried to cool down, he had muttered to himself, *Why do I let her get to me like that? I knew what she was when I married her. I can't go the rest of my life with a short fuse, blowing up. I'll just let her go her way and I'll go mine.*

This had been the reason for his aloof behavior. He had deliberately cut her out, speaking only when necessary. But he had not been able to obliterate the thoughts that came to him, especially as he lay on his bunk at night, or stood the long watches behind the wheel. In the quietness of the wheelhouse he found himself thinking of her. Over and over again he went over his first meeting with her in New Orleans. He realized now that there was a strange attractiveness about her. He was accustomed to the favors of women, but there was an innocence about this girl that both drew him and baffled him. It was not her attractiveness, although her trim figure and beautiful features were enough to stir any man's blood. Nor was it the fact that she was virginal—although this piqued his curiosity and caused him to behave rather stiffly toward her. He was convinced she had never had an affair with a man, that she was, indeed, totally innocent in this respect. He'd come to respect this in her, and now as he looked at her as she sat at the table, he suddenly felt like he had been a boor. He sat down at the table cautiously and folded his hands in front of him. "I guess I forget," he said apologetically, "how this must look to anyone who's not used to the sea." He waved his hand toward the sea, saying, "This isn't really bad. There's no danger at all. I think it'll blow over tomorrow or the next day. Don't look for it to get any worse than this." He was ignoring her remark, but then he knew that that would not do. "I guess I did look pretty scary to you, and what I said could have meant something else."

Allyn knew at once that this was his apology. She accepted it for what it was. She said quietly, "It seems, Jason, you and I have the ability to say the wrong things to each other and—to do the wrong things. I'm sorry, too. I—I know I'm too sensitive."

She looked small and fragile as she sat there, which made Larrimore even more aware of the fact that he had behaved badly. "Well," he said, "I suppose that's right, but we're in a strange situation." He thought about it for a moment and said, "If we were lovers, it would be different."

Startled by his words, she looked at him, trying to see

what lay beneath the remark. She thought about it for a moment, then said, "What does that mean, Jason?"

"Why, when lovers have a quarrel, they know they've got to make up. No matter how bad the quarrel was, they don't have an option. Strangers can shrug and say good-bye, but not lovers."

It was an aspect Allyn had never considered, and she gave him a sudden surprised glance. *Not many men would think of a thing like that to say.* She thought about what he said, then added to it, "Then you mean, married people don't have the freedom to leave each other—so they have to learn to get along?"

"Exactly. Divorce isn't very popular. When a man or woman goes through that, they say good-bye to a lot of things."

Allyn was intrigued by his thinking. "I've never thought of it like that, but I didn't know anybody that was divorced in New Orleans. We heard about it, but it was mostly high-society people who had money and influence."

"Money always makes a difference, but it shouldn't. I always thought," he said slowly, forming his thoughts and stating them rather flatly, "that some problems you have with people are somewhat like the flu—it hurts pretty bad at the time, but you get over it and later it's almost as if it never happened. But a divorce wouldn't be like that." He clasped his big hands together and studied them, thoughts running through him. Finally, he looked up at her and said, "I'd think when a man and woman are married and love each other, if they ever did separate and get a divorce, it would be more like a—well—like losing a leg. That's not like the flu! You never forget losing a leg. You might get an artificial leg and learn to use it, but you'd limp around the rest of your life with it."

Allyn's features grew soft, and she stared at him, fascinated by what he'd just said. She had not suspected such insights to rest within this big rough man. "I never expected to hear you say anything like that," she murmured. "If you think marriage is that strong, why did you marry me?"

"I was a fool, and so were you," he said bluntly. "I knew it beforehand, but like most fools, all I could think of was what I wanted at the moment. I guess that's the way most troubles come to us. We jump into things, give everything to get something we want—then repent at leisure."

Allyn said quietly, "We could get a divorce, Jason, if that's what you want. I won't hold you."

"On what grounds?" he shot back. "Adultery is the only grounds most courts will listen to. One of us would have to give the other an excuse."

"I can't do that," she said at once.

The wind whistled through the cracks of the door as if it were a wild beast seeking to get in. The ship rolled sideways, falling into the trough, recovered, then the engines beat more steadily. "It may come to that," he said. "I've been lying awake at night, thinking about us. We made a bad mistake, Allyn." He wanted to say more but could not think of any way to frame the thoughts within him. They were a mixture of disappointment, anger at his own foolishness, and bewilderment concerning this beautiful woman who sat across from him. He was restless and unhappy and did not know how to fight it, and he could not say these things to her. Suddenly he rose and said, "I've got to get back to the wheel."

After he left, Allyn thought, *He's as unhappy as I am—and that's saying a lot.* She, too, was feeling depressed, and all of the happiness she had hoped for when she had left New Orleans had vanished. "When I get back, I'll take care of my father, as long as he lives. That's something," she said. But as she rose and went back to her cabin, the grayness of the sky reflected what was in her spirit.

★ ★ ★

"Look, Captain!" the first lieutenant called out, lifting his voice above the keening of the wind. "There she is! I knew I saw a ship!"

Capt. Ernest Webb of the United States Navy held onto the rail, narrowing his eyes. Darkness was falling fast, and the sharper eyes of young Lt. James Troy had picked up something that he had not been able to see. But now, just a glimmer of movement came to him that was not of the waves. "Full speed ahead, Lieutenant," he said, "and we'll see what it is."

The USS *Cormorant's* engines stepped up their speed, and the gunboat plunged forward through the rolling waves. As they drew nearer, Lt. Troy shouted, "It's a blockade-runner, Captain! See the lines of her?"

"I believe you're right, Lieutenant. Have the crew man the guns."

"We won't be able to hit much with the ship tossing around like this," Lt. Troy said, his face falling. Then he lifted his eyes and said with determination, "We'll do the best she can."

"You won't get much of a chance. But I don't think she spotted us yet," the captain said. "I expect she can outrun us from the looks of her, so the best we can hope for is to get in a broadside that would knock her sticks down or dismantle her engine."

"Aye, sir, I'll have every gun ready."

"I'll pull up as close as I can, then when she starts running away from us, we'll turn the ship to port. That'll give your starboard guns one good shot at her."

"Aye, sir, I'll have the guns loaded and run out."

The young lieutenant raced through the ship, screaming orders, and the crew, startled, at once caught his fervor. Falling out of their bunks, they scrambled toward the guns, where the bo'sun and gunnery captains began screaming their orders, which were almost drowned out by the sound of the whistling wind. Soon the guns were loaded, and Lt. Troy stood along the line of cannon calling out, "You're only going to get one shot. It's dark and we're pitching like a chip in Niagara, so make it count, men!" He stood there waiting, feeling the roll of the ship, and soon he felt the ship begin to turn to port.

"Ready to fire," he called out, his brain racing. He could not fire her broadside, letting all the cannons go off on one side all at the same time, but knew that he had to trust the individual gunners to place their shots on the small target as it presented itself. *Not much chance at a hit,* he thought grimly, *but there's such a thing as luck!*

He was caught off guard when one of the cannons suddenly roared out, filling the small confined space with the tremendous explosion. Then, another down the line. One by one the cannons went off, not in order, but spasmodically.

Up on the bridge, Capt. Webb had his glass out. Even with it, he had only intermittent views of the small ship. It was low in the water and obviously had spotted them. "He's getting away, blast it!" Webb muttered. He saw one of the cannonballs strike a hundred yards behind the ship and shook his head in despair. "No platform for shooting," he muttered. But he watched hopefully, for it only took one shot to knock down a mast, which might give them just the edge they needed to catch up with the blockade-runner.

He heard a clatter and glanced around to see Lt. Troy, his eyes alive with excitement, come barreling into the pilothouse. "Did we hit her?" he cried.

"No," Webb said shortly, "she keeps pulling away from us."

Lt. Troy let out a blasphemous curse, for which the captain rebuked him. "Well, sir, it just ain't right," he muttered. "Here we had him right in our hands, and now we've lost him."

"We'll follow, and perhaps we'll see him again." But the captain knew that was not likely. The captains of these blockade-runners were as wily as foxes and as hard to catch. In his mind he said good-bye to a lost chance and said, "Back engines, Lieutenant, we'll continue our patrol."

But Capt. Webb had been wrong. All of the shot had

missed *The Last Chance* except one—and that one had been an explosive shell that had pierced the thin hull of the blockade-runner. By chance it had passed through the cabin next to the one Allyn occupied. It had exploded, demolishing that cabin and sending fragments of wood and iron through the thin walls that made up the other three sides. One small fragment had struck Allyn as she sat on her bunk. She had been trying to read by the light of the flickering oil lamp, having no idea that they were under fire, for the sound of the crashing waves and the screaming wind blotted out the cries of the seamen. She felt something strike her back and at first thought something had fallen off the wall. But then, falling forward, she was struck by a terrible pain that ran through her nerves and exploded in a blinding flash of white. She thought as she fell, *I've been struck by lightning!* Then she knew no more.

★ ★ ★

"Captain! Captain Larrimore!"

Jason whirled to see the master-at-arms, who had come crashing through the door of the pilothouse. "What's wrong, Simms?" he demanded.

"Sir, it's your wife." Simms, a short, rotund individual, shook his head. "You'd better come to her cabin."

Jason stared at him only for a moment, then said, "Take the wheel, Malcolm," and dashed out of the hatchway with Simms following close behind. "What's wrong, Simms?"

"I was passing by her door, and I heard her moaning, Captain." Simms gasped as he scurried along the soaking deck. "I knocked on the door but didn't get no answer. Finally, I opened it up, and there she was, sir."

"What do you mean?"

"A shell, sir, it must have come from that ironclad. It went off in that cabin next to hers and—well, sir, she got hit."

Jason's jaw clenched, and he scrambled over the deck and plunged down into the hatchway. When he reached the cabin door, he leaped inside and saw Allyn lying face down, her back wet with crimson blood.

"Help me get her on the bunk." The two men placed her face down on the bunk, and Jason put his hand on her wrist, feeling for a pulse. He felt it beating and gave a sigh of relief. "She's alive," he said. "Go get the first officer, Simms."

"Aye, sir."

Taking his knife from his pocket, Jason carefully slit the material of the dress, peeling it back, and his heart sank when he saw the jagged wound that was pulsing with a flow of blood. He whipped out his handkerchief and held it on the wound. *She could bleed to death like that,* he thought, his mind racing wildly, *and no doctor on board.*

Almost at once it seemed, Malcolm came to the door, his eyes troubled. He looked down at Allyn, asking, "How bad is it?"

"I don't know. I wanted you to take a look." Jason lifted the blood-soaked handkerchief, and Malcolm drew a sharp breath. "I hope it missed the lung," he said. The wound was high on Allyn's back, in the vicinity of the shoulder blade. "If it went straight in," he said slowly, "I'm afraid it's trouble. Could be close to the heart—but maybe it hit at an angle. You can't tell with a wound like this."

"What will we do?" Jason demanded. He himself had no skill with such things, but Malcolm had served some time working on a hospital ship and knew considerably more.

The first officer's eyes were grave as he said, "That's got to come out, Jason. I wish we had a doctor here."

"Can you take it out, Malcolm?"

Davis hesitated. He knew it was no job for an amateur, but there was no other choice. "I'll do my best, Jason. No promises. God will have to help."

Usually Jason smiled at such statements. He knew that the thickset officer believed that God was in control of all things. He felt no such assurance. But now, as the ship tossed and he looked down at the gaping, ragged wound that marred the smoothness of his wife's skin, he said, "Tell me what to do."

★ ★ ★

Malcolm was standing over Allyn, looking down at her face. His own face was pale and his hands were not quite steady. They had been steady enough as he had extracted the fragment of shell that had penetrated Allyn's flesh. "It's a good thing it went in at an angle or we'd have lost her, I think."

Jason looked down at Allyn's pale face. He had stood by while Davis had probed for the metal, and at one point he had thought he would vomit. It was one thing to suffer a wound himself, but another to see the big hands of the first officer probing with the pliers that would pull the metal fragment out. It had been a bloody affair, and now as he stood there he was surprised to find himself unsteady, his knees suddenly weak.

Davis looked around at him. "Here, sit down, Jason." He pushed the big man into a chair and smiled at him faintly. "It takes you that way sometimes, but she's going to be all right, I think. The Lord was with us."

"What—what do we do now?" Jason said, taking out a handkerchief and mopping his brow.

"She'll be out for a while. I had to overdose her because I didn't want her jarring around while I was trying to get at that piece of shell. I think one of us ought to sit with her."

"I'll do that," Jason said quickly.

"All right, I'll go see to the ship."

"Davis." Jason reached out and caught the smaller man's arm as he moved toward the door, and when the officer turned to look down at him, he said, "Thanks, Malcolm. If it hadn't been for you, I—I don't know what I'd have done!"

Malcolm Davis had never seen the big man so shaken. *He must think more of her than I thought.* He put his hand on

Jason's shoulder and squeezed it. "She'll be all right. Just give God the glory."

"I do," Jason said shortly and pressed his lips together. He sat there with a preoccupied manner, hearing the door slam, and looked down at Allyn. She was still lying on her stomach, the left side of her face visible. Carefully he wrung out a rag and dabbed at her forehead, not knowing anything else to do. He was shocked at the ragged torrent of emotions that had shaken him down to the very core of his being. He had been through hard things before, but the sight of her still face and the thoughts of the gaping wound had taken something out of him. Drawing a deep breath, he expelled it—then he looked down at his hands and saw that they were trembling. "I didn't think anything in the world could do that to me!" he muttered. He clasped them together and leaned forward, his eyes fixed on her face. She was breathing lightly, her back rising regularly, and he pulled the sheet higher around her neck, tucked it in around her shoulders. For a long time he sat there, looking down on her and noticing the incredible length of the lashes that lay on her cheek, the perfect bow of her lips, and the smoothness of her complexion.

The ship plunged on, and still he sat there. Malcolm came back an hour later to change the dressing on the wound. "I'll spell you, Jason."

"No," he said quickly. "I want to be here. Do you think she looks all right?"

Malcolm looked at her, put his hand on her forehead, and nodded. "Aye, she looks good. The danger, of course, is infection from the wound. That's what kills most people."

"What can we do?"

"Pray," Malcolm said simply. "I know you haven't been much of one for that," he said, "but it's different now, isn't it?" He had seen the agitation in the movements of Jason Larrimore and felt that this was the time God was going to speak to the big man. "Things like this make us realize how helpless we are, Jason," he said gently. "That's when we have to learn that a man needs strength that comes from outside himself. That can only be from God." He could have said more but felt that that was enough. "I'll be back after a while and spell you."

Jason remained beside Allyn for four hours. Malcolm came back several times, but each time Jason had simply shaken his head. He felt that he was on duty and could not leave. As the hours went by, more and more he felt the strangeness of his feeling for this girl. She was his wife, and yet, not his wife. Finally he put his hand on her hair, smoothing it with a gentle motion, and as he did her eye moved and opened. At once he knelt by the bed so she would see him and whispered, "Allyn—Allyn, can you hear me?"

The long eyelashes fluttered, then her eyes opened all the way. She looked at him with confusion, licked her lips, and said, "What happened to me?" Her speech was thick, and she spoke slowly. She tried to prop herself up on her elbows, but the pain was too great.

Jason kept his hand on her hair and reached out and pressed her hand, which had fallen back to her side. "You had an accident, Allyn," he said, "but you're all right now. Just lie still."

She looked up at him, and he saw her eyes clear. She studied his face carefully and looked down and saw that he was holding her hand. "How long have you been here?" she whispered.

"It doesn't matter," he said. "Can I get you anything? Is the pain bad?"

"Some water—"

Quickly he put her hand down and moved to fill a glass, then turned back to her. "Try just to lift your head." He put the glass to her lips, and she managed a small sip at first.

Allyn was still lost in half-consciousness. It was like a dream to her. The pain gnawed at her, but she was more conscious of Jason's face in front of hers as she sipped at the water thirstily.

309

When she finished drinking, she whispered, "What happened?"

"A shell went off in the cabin next door. You took a bit of fragment," he said. "It was Malcolm who took it out. But you're going to be all right, now."

She felt sleep coming back and with it fear that she might never wake. Instinctively, she held up her hand, and instantly it was grasped by his. "Jason?" she whispered, her voice frail.

"Yes, what is it, Allyn?"

"Stay with me . . . !"

She drifted off to sleep, her hand nestled in his, and he whispered tenderly, "I'll stay with you, Allyn."

★ ★ ★

The Last Chance had touched a tiny spot in the Bahamas called Nassau. The ship's crew had worked hard jury-rigging the hull for the return trip, loading the supplies that had been waiting and replenishing the food and the water. Then, without pause, once all the tasks were accomplished, the engines started, and the ship moved out of the harbor, heading back for the mainland.

All day they sailed, and Jason had said, "Malcolm, the Federals know we come to Nassau to pick up supplies. I wouldn't be surprised to see a fleet of gunboats around here."

Well might he think it, for the United States Navy was aware of the part that Nassau played in the economy of the South. Salt, which was worth $6.50 a ton in Nassau, brought $1,700 in the South, and coffee selling for $249 a ton in Nassau commanded $5,500 Confederate on the Southern market. A successful ship captain might make as much as $5,000 on a single run. But profit was not on the mind of the captain of *The Last Chance*. As the ship plowed along, he stayed on the deck for two hours looking for enemy gunboats, then finally drew a sigh of relief. "Take the wheel, Malcolm, I'm going to see to my wife."

"She's doing fine," Davis said. He waited for one moment, then said, "Hope you know it was God's doing."

"You had a part in it, Malcolm."

"Oh, God uses men, no doubt. But still, it's God. As the Scripture says, 'The lot is cast into the lap, but the disposal thereof is of the Lord.'"

"What does *that* mean?" Jason demanded.

"Why, it just means that a man does what he can, but in the last event, it's God that's in control."

"Well, I've been thankful to God that he had you on this ship. I don't think Allyn would have made it if I'd have had to take care of her. I could never have gotten that fragment out."

"I'm glad I was here. You're a fortunate man, Jason Larrimore. I hope you know that."

Jason gave him an odd glance and nodded shortly. "I'm beginning to learn it, Malcolm." He turned then and left the wheelhouse.

He went at once to the galley and obtained a pitcher of fresh juice, then went down to Allyn's cabin. He knocked on the door, and she said, "Come in."

He entered and saw that she was sitting up. "You're looking very fine indeed, Mrs. Larrimore," he said. He sat down on the bunk, poured a glass of fresh juice, and said, "Here. Doctor's orders."

She drank it thirstily and said, "That's good!"

She was wearing a thin blue robe of silk that he had bought at Nassau, and he asked, "How does the robe feel?"

"Oh, wonderful." Her eyes were bright and clear, and she ran her free hand over the material. "It's so light. The only one I have is so hot."

"I'm glad you like it," he said. "If they'd had one big enough, I'd have got one for myself."

She drank some more of the juice and inquired, "Where are we, Jason?"

"On the way home. The hard part lies ahead, getting through the enemy fleet. But we'll make it. We'll stay out and go in after dark. They don't have anything that can catch us. We'll be all right."

They sat there, and he explained the maneuvers necessary to get through the enemy fleet. When she had finished the juice, he said, "Let's have a look at that wound."

"It's all right," she said.

"Don't argue with the doctor." He stood up and pulled her to her feet. "Is there much pain?" he asked as she turned around.

"It hurts a little, but I don't want to take any more of that medicine. It makes me feel like my mind's wrapped in a blanket." She hesitated, then loosened the robe, turned her back, and let it drop to midback while she held the front of the robe closely to her chest.

He lifted the bandage and studied the wound carefully. "I want to change this bandage." He had learned to do this from Malcolm, who had told him the best thing that could be done was to keep the wound clean. "You're going to have a little scar," he said.

She felt strange standing there half-naked before him and whispered, "That's—that's all right. It won't show."

Carefully he reached over, got a cloth, cleansed the wound carefully, then retied the bandage. Pulling her robe up, he said, "You can fasten that now." She pulled the robe together, tied it, and when she turned around she was blushing but did not comment.

"Feel like talking a little bit?" he asked.

"Yes," she said quickly. "I get lonesome down here, although I know you're busy." She added quickly, "I'm not complaining."

"You never do," he said. This was true. Most women, he had decided, would have complained considerably, but she had never uttered one word of complaint. As they talked, he thought about when she was first wounded. "Do you remember much about the first night after you were wounded?"

"I remember you and Malcolm and a lot of pain," she said.

"You had us pretty worried," Jason said. He leaned back and shoved his hand through his crisp blond hair. "I don't want to go through that again."

"What was it like? How did he get that piece out? I didn't know he had that kind of skill."

"I think Malcolm's just about the best man I know for things like that. He can do anything on a ship. Thank God he was here." He sat there quietly thinking about what he had said. "You know, that's true. I've been going along most of my life without even thinking about God, but that night, I did. I thought you were going to die and—"

He broke off suddenly and bit his lip. She looked at him curiously. "I wouldn't think you'd be afraid of anything."

"Well, I thought I had my share of nerve, but you were so—so *helpless*," he said. "There was nothing I could do. I found myself calling on God and asking him to do something." He smiled suddenly and said, "And he did."

His smile broke something loose inside Allyn, and she put her hand out saying, "Thank you, Jason. I know this hasn't been easy for you."

He held her hand for a moment, then asked, "Do you remember talking that night after the operation, after Malcolm dug that steel out?"

"No," she said in surprise. "I don't remember anything."

He turned her hand, noticing the fine shape of the fingers, the nails, then released it. Leaning back, he hesitated and said, "You had some bad dreams, I guess. You talked about when you were a little girl. I guess those were bad times for you."

Allyn dropped her eyes. "They weren't very good. I hope I didn't say anything—"

"Oh, just mumbling, mostly." He hesitated, not knowing whether to say anything more or not. Finally, he said, "You did say one thing. I don't know if you want to hear it or not."

313

Her curiosity rose at once, and she said, "I hope it was nothing that I'd be ashamed of."

"You might think so," he said. When he saw her eyes widen, he shook his head. "I don't know—just one sentence, and I may have heard you wrong, but you said, 'Jason, don't leave me.'"

Allyn bit her lip and looked down. Then she looked up at him and said gently, "I've always been afraid of being left alone. I guess you were all I had, Jason. And you didn't leave me, did you?"

"No—and I won't," he said. "This is no time to speak of it, I suppose, but I want you to know, Allyn, that our arrangement may have been just a bargain, a business matter, but I don't look on it like that anymore. I'd like us to be more. It's not possible for a man and a woman to be just items on a ledger. Mark wanted more than that for you."

"Yes, he did." Now it was Allyn's turn to hesitate. After a moment she said, "That's why he wanted me to come on this trip with you." She saw his surprise and smiled. "He thought we could get to know each other better on a cruise."

"He didn't know much about blockade-running," Jason said. He looked at her and admired the clean sweep of her jaw, the fine set of her eyes, and said gently, "Anyway, what I wanted to say was, I don't want you to worry. I'm not much, but I've never broken my word. I promised Mark I'd take care of you, and I will, Allyn." Suddenly he arose, as if he had said too much. "I don't want to come on too strong," he said. "I've already done that, haven't I?"

"Yes," she said. But when she looked at him, there was a smile in her eyes, and she said, "It's good to hear, though."

★ ★ ★

At midnight, Jason handed the wheel over to Davis and said, "So far, so good. We'll be in day after tomorrow, I think. We'll wait till dusk or maybe even midnight, and we can thread our way in."

"There won't be much moon," Davis warned. "We don't want to pile 'er up."

Jason clapped him on the shoulder. "Why, I've got the best night runner in the business. You won't do that. Good night." He left and went down below, as was his habit, stopping at Allyn's cabin. He didn't want to awaken her, so he opened the door softly and stopped, for he saw that she was tossing and throwing her arms around.

Quickly he stepped inside and moved over to her. He knelt beside her, ignoring the chair, whispering, "Allyn, are you all right?"

Then he was shocked to see that she was crying. He saw, also, that she had a slight fever, which alarmed him. She had had it before, and Davis told him it went with the shell wound, but now alarm ran through him. He knew wounds could go bad. He whispered, "Allyn, are you all right?"

She opened her eyes, and he saw fear in them.

"I had bad dreams," she said.

"You're all right," he said. He was kneeling awkwardly beside her, holding her hands, and said, "Let me bathe your face."

Quickly he dipped a cloth in the basin beside the bed and began to bathe her face and neck. "Is that better?" he asked.

"Yes," she whispered.

But he saw that she was still disturbed. Putting down the cloth, he said to Allyn, "What's troubling you? Is it the old days?"

"No, I had a dream about—I don't know what it was, but I was somewhere, and I was all alone."

He knew her fear of being alone, for she had mentioned it more than once. He said quickly, "You won't be alone. I'm right here. I'll stay here. You can go back to sleep. I won't leave you."

"Won't you, Jason?"

"No, I promise."

She lay there quietly, and he reached out and put his hand

on her hair. "You have such beautiful hair," he whispered, "the most beautiful I've ever seen."

The pressure of his hand on her head seemed to give her peace, and she lay there looking up at him. Then the memory of the dream came, and she stirred uneasily. "I dreamed I was in some kind of a big room, and I looked down and I saw that my hands were wrinkled. And there was a mirror. I looked in it and, Jason, I saw I was old. I tried to get out of the room and couldn't."

"It was just a bad dream," he insisted. "Don't think about it."

But she could not leave it alone. "The worst thing was, not being old, but being alone. It frightens me, Jason!"

She looked very fragile and vulnerable, and he wanted to comfort her. Carefully, he reached over, put his left arm under her, lifted her slightly, and held her in the crook of his arm. "Don't worry," he said quietly, "you'll never be in a room like that alone. I'll be with you." He looked down at her and saw that her eyes were enormous. They caught the light of the yellow flame of the candle, and he saw that her lips were trembling. Suddenly, all the things that he had thought, the doubts and the fears, agonizing over the situation with this woman, seemed to rise up in him. He groaned suddenly. "Allyn, I've been a fool."

She reached up tentatively and touched his cheek. "No, you've been wonderful," she said. Then she pulled his head down and kissed him on the lips. A shock ran through him, for her lips were even softer than he remembered. There was a gentleness and a vulnerability in her as he put his other arm around her, being careful of her wound. He held her gently and held the kiss. Her lips moved slightly beneath his, and there was a sweetness and a gentleness such as he'd never dreamed. This was not like the other times when he was demanding. He was giving this time, and as he held her, savoring the wild sweetness, he thought, *Why, this is what I always wanted!*

Allyn rested in his arms, and a sense of well-being and

safety came to her. His arms were strong and hard beneath her, and she thought, *He would never let anything harm me.* She held him tightly, pulling him ever closer. There was a strength and a cleanness in his lips that she needed, and she held him, clinging to him with all the strength in her arms.

Finally she moved her head back, and the kiss ended. He whispered, "Allyn, I love you."

Those simple words seemed to set off some kind of signal in her, and she felt the tears run down her cheeks. All her life she'd wanted someone to say that simply and plainly.

"I love you too, Jason," she whispered and then pulled his head down again.

He held her for a long time and said finally, "Allyn, don't ever think you'll be alone. We've come a long hard way, but I love you as I never loved anyone."

She lay there and knew that she had found what she had been searching for all of her life.

CHAPTER TWENTY-THREE
A Desperate Venture

The two men who had approached the hulk of Libby Prison stopped, the smaller one putting out his hand. He was dressed in the uniform of a Confederate captain and spoke to the other, who was wearing the uniform of a private.

"Have you got it straight now, Bing?" Noel demanded. He looked up at the sky and said, "I think we've got it timed about right. It'll be pretty dark by the time we get on the streets—if this thing works."

Bing glanced up and nodded. "It'll be dark enough, all right." He held a musket in his right hand, and underneath his uniform overcoat, he had a heavy navy .44 revolver fully loaded. A worried look crossed his face. "I been hearing about this Maj. Turner, the commandant here. He's a pretty tough hombre, so they say. What if you can't talk him into letting Col. Rocklin go?"

Noel smiled. "I forgot to tell you. That's part of the plan, Bing. Turner won't be here."

"Won't be here? Where will he be?"

"I found out that he goes to inspect Belle Isle every Thursday. That's the other prison he's in charge of. He leaves a lieutenant in charge of Libby. I figured we could handle a lieutenant easier than we could a tough major in the regulars." He looked at Bing thoughtfully. "Don't say any more than you have to. Just one word could give either one of us away."

"Don't worry. I've got it all down. Let's do it."

"All right." Noel marched ahead, and they approached the guard, who at once said, "You have a pass?"

Noel snapped, "I have to see Maj. Turner. I've got an order here from the War Department."

The guard looked at his fellow guard, who shrugged and said, "Maj. Turner ain't here. He's gone to Belle Isle like he always does every Thursday."

"Who's in charge?" Noel demanded.

"That'd be Lt. Bates."

"Well, I'll see him then."

"Yes, sir." The first guard opened the door and called out, "Cpl. Helleman—officer here to see Lt. Bates."

An older man, wearing a rather worn uniform, came and peered at Noel, and then at Bing. "Have to see your pass, sir."

Noel held up the sealed envelope and said, "This is straight from the War Department. I need to see Lt. Bates at once."

The guard gave it a careless look and said, "Yes, sir. Right this way." He moved along the corridors to a door at the end of the hall, then opened it. "Lt. Bates, there's a captain here to see you."

"Have him come in." Lt. Bates was sitting at a desk, and he glanced up curiously at the two men who entered. "What can I do for you, Captain?" he asked. He was young and stood to his feet rather nervously.

"I have an order here from the secretary of war," Noel said rather loudly. "It's rather urgent. I had expected to speak to Maj. Turner."

"He won't be back until the morning, Captain. Can it wait until then?"

"The secretary says no. I expect you'd better take care of it, Lieutenant."

Lt. Bates took the envelope, opened it, and read it quickly.

"Why, I can't release a prisoner, Captain! You'll have to wait until tomorrow for Maj. Turner."

Noel had anticipated this. "You want me to return that answer to the secretary of war? That Lt. Bates refuses to obey a direct order?"

"Oh no, you can't do that, Captain!" Bates raked his hand through his thin blond hair frantically. He looked at the order again and said, "Very well, I'll get the prisoner. I'll send a squad along with you."

"I brought a guard with me," Noel said diligently. "That won't be necessary."

"Oh, it's regulations, Captain. You understand, three guards have to go with every prisoner that's transferred. I couldn't release him otherwise."

"Very well," Noel said in a bored tone. "Hurry it along, will you? The secretary is an impatient man, as you probably know."

Lt. Bates did not know, firsthand, although he had heard. He at once dashed out the door. Noel waited tensely for a few moments listening to the commands being called, then the lieutenant entered. "I'm having the colonel brought in." He looked at the order again and said, "I don't quite understand. How long will the prisoner be there?"

"Well, the secretary hasn't let me in on all his plans, you understand, Lieutenant. I think he wants to interrogate several of the officers. Col. Rocklin will be the first. He'll probably keep him overnight."

"You'll have to send the guards back and then send for them when he is to be transferred again. I'm short of men," he complained.

"Yes, I'll take care of that."

Noel stood there, chatting with the lieutenant, putting on an air of impersonal boredom. Inside he was tense as a steel wire. All that had to happen was for one officer to challenge his identity. He had no papers, no proof, nothing except the uniform he wore. He was relieved when a knock at the door sounded, and the corporal said, "Prisoner's ready, sir."

"Very well, Captain. I'll turn the colonel over to you."

"Thank you, Lieutenant. I'll mention to the secretary that you are doing a good job here."

The remark pleased the harried young lieutenant, and he said, "Thank you, sir."

There was a tense moment when Noel stepped outside, for Gideon Rocklin was waiting, dressed in his tattered uniform. Noel's eyes met his, and for one minute he was afraid that Gideon would give them away. But he saw at once he need have no fear. "Col. Rocklin, I'm Capt. Hagan. You're going to have a short interview with the secretary of war."

Gideon had been aroused from a nap and simply told he was making a short trip. He had quickly become alert, suspecting that Noel and Bing were at the bottom of it. Now he nodded and said, "I'm glad to know you, Captain."

"Come this way." Noel led the way outside, where he found three guards already there waiting, with Bing standing to one side.

The corporal said, "Have to put the prisoner in that ambulance. That's the way we always transfer them."

"Very well, Corporal." Noel nodded and watched as Gideon climbed inside. "Suppose it'll be all right for me to ride with the driver?"

"Why yes, sir, that'll be fine. Here, Clyde, you drive this ambulance over. Bring it back in one piece, you hear me!" Then the corporal turned to the other two and said, "You two mind your manners." He gave Bing a sharp glance and said, "You go along, too, I guess."

Noel climbed up on the seat and sat down by the private named Clyde and said, "Let's go, Private."

"Yes, sir." The soldier slapped the horse with the line, and the ambulance moved off down the street. Out of the corner of his eye Noel saw that the two guards were ambling along behind the ambulance and that Bing had joined them.

"Going to be dark pretty soon," he observed. "Do you know your way to the War Department, Private?"

322

"Oh yes, sir, I know how to get there."

The skies grew darker, but not dark enough to suit Noel and Bing. Both of them were wishing that it was pitch black, but the timing had been hard to figure. What Noel had wanted was to pass through the streets in that interval between the time darkness fell and the streetlamps were lighted. He thought to himself, *I believe we've got it about right. Maybe a little early, but no help for that.*

The ambulance moved slowly through the streets, and Noel carefully watched, seeing that the streets at this hour were fairly empty. He knew it would have been impossible to carry out the plan during the busy hours, but he had studied it carefully. This was the one time when there was almost no one stirring. He knew that he couldn't count on that, so he waited until they got to a street in one of the more seedy elements of town and said, "I know a short cut. Go down this street, Private."

"Sir? I don't think—"

"Do what I tell you, Private!" Noel snapped. "I don't have time to argue with you. We're in a hurry."

"Well, all right. If you say so, sir."

The driver turned the horse's head down the narrow street, which was really an alley more than anything else. It led between two factories, both of them built of red brick and neither in operation at the moment. It was a long block, and the two buildings cut off most of the light. Uneasily the ambulance driver asked, "Are you sure this is the way, sir?"

"Yes." This was the critical part of the plan. Noel glanced back, seeing the forms of the men plodding along behind. Suddenly he gasped and bent over. "Oh!" he said, crying out as if in pain.

The driver stared at him. "What is it, Captain?"

"I took a wound at Seven Pines," he gasped. "It gives me problems." He leaned forward and said, "Stop! Stop the ambulance, Private!"

At once the private pulled up the horse and sat there, not knowing what to do. "Can I help you, Captain?"

Noel was not an actor, but so much depended on it that he threw himself into it. He began to cough and cry out saying, "Oh, it's terrible! I can't stand it! Help me!"

"What can I do, sir?"

"Help me down to the ground—I've got to lie down for a moment!"

Instantly the private fastened the lines and leaped to the ground. He ran around the wagon, saying, "Here, you guards! Help me get him down."

The two men came forward, and one of them said, "What's wrong?"

"Officer's sick! Help me! Put him on the ground there."

The two guards leaned their muskets up against the wagon—which was exactly what Noel had hoped for—and he resisted as much as he could, saying, "Oh, be careful, it hurts!" Soon all three of them were struggling to get him on the ground. He glanced over the shoulder of one and saw that Bing had put his musket down, too, and had drawn the .44. As the three eased him to the ground, Noel reached under his overcoat and pulled out the heavy pistol he had stuck in his belt. He pulled the hammer back, and it made a resounding click in the darkness. He shoved it under the chin of the private who had been driving the ambulance and said, "Just stand still, soldier—don't move!"

At once the other two guards reared back. One of them turned to make a grab at his musket and found himself staring into the muzzle of a heavy revolver. The big soldier who had said not a word, now spoke, "You two scratch for it. Put your hands up, or I'll let a hole in you!"

"What is this?" the driver gasped. "What are you doing?"

"We're taking a little detour," Noel said. "Stand aside." He shoved the driver aside and reached up and unlocked the padlock on the outside of the door. Opening it, he said, "You can come out now, Colonel."

Gideon looked out, saw the situation, and at once climbed to the ground. He didn't say a word, but his eyes glowed in the growing darkness. Noel flashed him a quick smile, then became sober.

"Into that ambulance—you three."

"What are you going to do with us?" one of the guards protested.

"Just gonna take you for a little ride. You won't get hurt if you do what we say. Now, get in there."

As they climbed in, Bing grabbed one of them, pulled his head back, and laid the muzzle against his temple. "I hope you have a full life, sonny," he said. "But if you make one peep in there, I'll have to see that you don't." He shoved the man inside and slammed the door, fastening the lock. "Let's go," he said quickly.

Noel climbed up on the seat, followed by Gideon. He spoke to the horse and said, "Giddup," then turned to see that Bing had taken position slightly to the rear, but close enough to get to the door if any of the prisoners acted up.

Gideon clapped him on the shoulder saying, "I never was so glad to see anyone in my life! How'd you arrange this?"

"I'll tell you all about it, but we're not out of the woods, yet. Are you all right?"

"I'm feeling better every second." Gideon took a deep breath and said, "That fresh air's the best thing I ever smelled in my life!"

Noel nodded, then drove the team down to the end of the alley. He took a sharp right, went two blocks, and Gideon saw they had come to a large open space. A pasture had been left, a small one, with a barn to one side. "I think they keep the horses here for some of the members of the cabinet who live in town," Noel said. "Anyway, that's where we're headed." Gideon looked up and saw, as they approached, there were no houses anywhere near, only the barn. Noel pulled up, and as he did a door opened and a voice called, "Noel?"

"Yes, it's us, Deborah. Open the doors."

Gideon got down and watched as the doors opened.

When Noel drove the ambulance inside, he moved forward and put out his hand, saying, "Deborah?"

She came to him at once and gave him a hug. "Uncle Gid!"

She hugged him tightly, and then Bing came up to say, "You can save that for later. We still ain't safe."

Stepping inside the barn, Noel stopped beside the door and said, "You fellows in there keep quiet. I don't want to hear a peep out of you."

He came over hurriedly and said, "Col. Rocklin, you've got to change clothes. Where are they, Deborah?"

"Right here." Deborah swiftly moved over to pick up a package and said, "You wouldn't get far in that uniform, Uncle Gid. Change quick as you can."

Gid ducked into a stall, shucked off the worn uniform, and slipped into the black suit with matching boots. There was even a hat to go with it, and he pulled it down. It was a little too large, but that caused it to fall over his face, hiding it a little more effectively. Stepping outside, he said, "Well, good-bye to the uniform. What now?"

"We've got to get out of Richmond," Noel said. "I've got passes for two men on the train that leaves in an hour. "You and I'll be on it."

"What about Bing and Deborah?"

"Bing will stay here and keep these fellows company until we've had plenty of time for the train to get out of town. Then, he can fade away. They won't be looking for him once he gets out of that uniform. And Deborah will just go back North as soon as possible, since she was just here visiting relatives."

"I wish we could all go together," Gid said. He looked over at Bing, who was watching with a broad grin on his face, stepped closer and put out his hand. "I understand this is all your idea, Bing," he said. "Can't tell you how much it means to me."

"Well," Bing said, embarrassed, "I ain't much of a soldier, Colonel. You know that, but I'm glad I could do this for you. Feels like I'm really doing something." He laughed aloud, "Maybe I could make a habit of busting prisoners out of Confederate jails."

"I don't think you could work this twice." Gideon smiled back at him. He held on to the man's thick hand and squeezed it saying, "God bless you, my boy. My family and I will be eternally in your debt."

"We better go, Colonel," Noel said. "I want to be at the train station just kind of out of sight. We'll get on the train just before it pulls out. They won't have time to look at the pass very carefully."

"All right," Gid said. He reached out and hugged Deborah and whispered against her ear. "You paid for your raising this time, youngun," he said. He held her tightly and said huskily, "Hang on to that young man. He's worth keeping." Then he released her and said, "All right, I'm ready, Noel."

Noel moved forward, kissed Deborah, and said, "Go as quick as you can."

She kissed him back and said, "I will."

Then Noel turned to Bing and hit him lightly on the chest. "You big sucker, I owe you one for this! When you get back, we'll go out and have the finest steak in the city."

"Yeah, you bet we'll do that," Bing agreed heartily. Then the two faded away into the darkness. Bing watched them go, then he turned to Deborah. He put the pistol in his belt and smiled at her. "Well, we done good, didn't we, Deborah?"

"Yes," Deborah said proudly, "we done real good, Bing."

CHAPTER TWENTY-FOUR
Homecoming

As Allyn looked down at the dock to stare at the crowd that had gathered to greet *The Last Chance*, it seemed that every available foot was taken. She whispered to Jason, who stood closely beside her, "I never saw anything like this, even in New Orleans at the docks."

"The people in New Orleans were never hurting for supplies as bad as the people of Richmond," Jason answered. He stood close to her and looked down at her asking, "How do you feel? Are you sure you're able to make this kind of a move? I can have an ambulance, if you like."

"Oh, don't be foolish," she said, smiling up at him.

They had been forced to lie outside the sea-lanes for almost a week. The weather was beautiful: the sun shining and the winds still, which was not to their advantage. She had been surprised when Jason had said, "I'd rather have a typhoon. Easier to dodge the patrol boats that way." Then she remembered he had smiled and said, "We'll just have a little pleasure cruise while you heal up."

They had cruised twenty miles off shore, keeping a careful look for the ships that maintained the blockade, and they had seen several. During those days, Allyn and Jason had spent much time together. His duties were light, amounting only to giving a few orders. The two of them had sat for long hours in the galley, which he had fixed up with a comfortable chair, padding it with mattress pads. He had discovered her desire to learn how to play chess, and she had developed, under his tutelage, into a surprisingly good player. During the milder periods of the day, he had walked her around the deck, his arm around her much of the time, although she protested she didn't need it. "Still a little swelled here," he had said. "Mind your doctor's orders."

Now as they stood at the rail, she thought of those times and turned to him. "These last few days, they've been—" She started to say *wonderful,* then changed her mind. That sounded too exotic. "They've been very good for me, Jason."

"Have they? I'm glad to hear that."

"Yes, I needed some sort of assurance, I guess. That night that you held me and told me you'd never leave me, ever since then I felt—well, secure." She hesitated again, and a slight flush touched her cheeks, which was not brought on by the sharpness of the wind. "I guess being sick makes you want to know you're wanted." A thought struck her. "I guess that's the way my father feels."

"I think maybe it is." He looked down on her and smiled. "We'll make him feel wanted when we get to Twelve Trees. Come along."

He called out to Davis, "First, you're in charge of the ship. Get all you can out of these folks. We need to make money to pay for this ship."

"Right you are! Where will ye be headed, Captain?"

"I'll be taking Mrs. Larrimore to Twelve Trees. I'll stay there for a while. When everything's done, you come out. We've got a room for you. We'll talk about the next run."

"Yes sir. I'll be there."

Jason led Allyn down the gangplank and waved to a carriage. He helped her in and then said to the driver, "You've got a long fare this time, but I'll make it worth your while. Go out the North Road."

"Yes, sir," the carriage driver beamed. "Yes, sir, Captain. It'll be a good trip."

It was a good trip, the wind brisk, but the November sun shone down, shedding pale beams over the seared landscape. He had the carriage stop twice to let her get down and walk a little so she wouldn't stiffen up. She had laughed at him. "Why, I'm fine, Jason," she had said, but that he was worried about her had pleased her. When they had pulled up in front of Twelve Trees, she said, "Come along, I'm anxious to see how Father is."

They moved across the yard. As they went up the steps he said, "Don't move so fast. You might get that wound to bleeding."

"No, I'm fine," she said. "Come along." She reached out and took his hand and started up the steps. When they reached the landing, both of them stopped. Allyn said, "Why, Susanna!" and then she asked quickly, "Is it Father? Is he worse?"

Susanna Rocklin held the door open and said, "Come in. He's not been doing too well. I thought I would come over and help until you got back."

The two of them entered, and Susanna had not missed the fact that Jason had been holding Allyn's hand. That pleased her, and she said, "Did you have a good trip, Jason?"

Jason removed his hat and bowed his head. "Why, yes, Susanna, we did—except for her."

Susanna shot a quick look at Allyn and said, "What's wrong?"

"Oh, she got hit with a cannon shell." Jason's eyes were gleaming as he saw her startled expression. "She's all right. Just has to take it easy. She'll tell you all about it, I'm sure."

"Oh, it's nothing. I'm fine. What about Father?"

"Dr. Maxwell was by yesterday," Susanna said. "He wasn't very optimistic, but then he never is. Come along, I know Mark'll be anxious to see you."

The pair followed Susanna down the hall, and when she opened the door they all entered. Mark was lying in bed, his eyes open. As soon as he saw them, he said quickly, "Allyn! Jason! How was the trip?" He struggled to sit up, and Allyn ran over and helped him into a sitting position.

She saw at once that he was much weaker, that the wound had drained him, but she said nothing of this. "We had good fortune," she said. "Come along, Jason, sit down on the other side."

Jason moved over and took the chair, reached out his hand, took the thin one Mark held up to him. "Well, I brought her back, almost whole," he said. When Mark lifted his eyebrow, he said, "Tell them about your adventure, Wife."

At the use of the word *wife*, Mark shot a quick glance at Allyn, and she looked flustered, but she immediately plunged into her story. When she finished, she said, "Ever since I got hurt, Jason's been treating me like a piece of fragile china."

"You should have gotten shot earlier," Mark said with a smile on his lips. "That's a good way to get sympathy."

"Oh, don't be foolish!" Susanna said. "Now, I'll leave you here, but don't tell all the story. I just want to go get your rooms ready."

She left the room, and at once Mark asked, "Now, how was it?"

"Well, I guess I can retell it later to Susanna," Allyn said, and she began telling of her adventure. Mark sat there quietly, watching the excitement in her eyes. He sensed there was a difference in her. He studied her face and the animation that was there, the liveliness in her eyes, and the fact that more than once she looked over at Jason for some detail. There was a freedom between the two that had not been there when they left.

Maybe, he thought, *I've done the right thing for once. They look at peace, as if they had fought their battles out.*

Finally, Allyn said, "It was so exciting. I'm going to go again the next time Jason goes." She glanced at Mark and said, "As soon as you get better, that is."

"You don't have my permission for that," Jason said. "The next trip might not go as easy as this one did—and that was no picnic at times. You never know when you're going to run into these gunboats." He leaned back and nodded. "We made plenty of money this time, Mark. Enough to pay the boat off, I think—so at least we start even the next time we make a trip."

"What did you bring back?" Mark asked.

For a while the three sat there talking about the voyage, and finally the visitors saw Mark was getting tired. Allyn said, "I'm tired. Let me go lie down a little, Father, and I'll come back after I've had a little rest."

Mark said at once, "Yes, I want to hear more about all of this."

Allyn left the room, and Mark looked at Jason. "She seems happy, Jason," he observed.

"Well, we had a few misunderstandings, but things are better now."

"I'm glad to hear that." Mark said no more and felt weakness creeping up. He put out his hand, and when Jason took it, he said, "Thank you. I know it's going to be all right." Then he dropped off to sleep.

Quietly Jason got up and left the room. He found Susanna and Allyn talking about the patient, and he said, "He doesn't look good at all."

"No, he's not," Susanna said. She bit her lip and shook her head. "He could go at any time. Dr. Maxwell thinks his heart's been affected by all of this, and it's very erratic."

"Can't something be done?" Allyn whispered. "I mean, I've just found him. I can't lose him now!"

"We'll pray, but somehow in my spirit I feel that he'll be taken soon." She saw the hurt look in Allyn's eyes and said, "But just think what he's done, Allyn! He's found you and made a home for you here." She looked at Jason and smiled. "He's seen you married. That was what worried him most." She saw that Jason looked uncomfortable at this, so she passed on over it to add, "And he's found God. That's the most important thing of all."

"It's so hard," Allyn said.

"Why, yes, it's hard not to get to see the ones we love, but it's something we all come to. And if we're right with God, we know that those separations are only for a little while."

Susanna stood there quietly watching their faces. She sensed that both of them had reached some sort of crossroads or a fork in the road. She knew that God was working on them, and she prayed, *Oh, God, bring them in! Bring them in!*

★ ★ ★

Mark Rocklin lingered for three days after the return of Allyn and Jason. Most of the time he slept peaceably. During the times when he was awake he was very content, they could all see. The pair stayed very close beside him, and when he was awake, he seemed happy just to have them there. They did not talk much, though more than once he would look at them and say, "God has been good to me." He did not speak much, for the effort seemed to tire him.

There was only one end to this, of course, and it was Susanna who came to awaken Allyn in the middle of the night. Upon seeing her aunt standing in the doorway, she said, "Is he going?"

"Yes, put on a robe and come quickly, Allyn."

Allyn pulled on the wool robe that lay beside her bed, stepped her feet into the house shoes, and without even giving her hair a touch followed the older woman. They moved down the hall, and she saw that Jason was there. Pain was in his face, but he said nothing.

When they entered, Flossie had been standing over to one side. "He done been callin' for you, Miz Allyn," she said, tears running down her face. She was an emotional woman, and although she had not known Mark Rocklin long, she had grown to respect him greatly. She moved back into the shadows and stood there silently watching, her ebony face full of grief.

Allyn moved quickly to the bed, and Jason went to the other side. Leaning over, Allyn whispered, "Father, are you awake?"

His eyes opened, and Mark studied her carefully. There was a peacefulness about him, a calmness that she had never associated with death. She did not know whether this happened often or not, but when he lifted his hand, she took it and held it. She could not hold the tears back, and as the hot drops fell on his hand, he said with some surprise, "Why, Daughter, you mustn't cry!"

"I can't bear to lose you," she said and fell against him, holding him tightly.

His free arm came over her and he held her shaking shoulders. A smile came to his thin lips, and he said nothing for a while. Finally he whispered, "The pain, it's all gone now. The first time since I was wounded—all gone."

Allyn pulled back, lifted her head, and could not speak, her throat was so tight. Mark seemed to be falling asleep again, but he opened his eyes and saw Jason sitting silently beside him. He reached out his free hand, and Jason took it at once. "Jason—my friend," he whispered, "faithful are the wounds of a friend. You've been good to me, Jason."

Tears stung Jason's eyes. He was not a crying man, nor could he remember the last time he had wept—but he knew he was losing something very precious. He held the fragile hand in his, thinking back to the time when that hand was as strong as his own. Now his throat grew full as he said, "I'll miss you, Mark."

Mark's eyes fastened on him, and his frail hand tightened its grip. "You must not miss the greatest thing there is," he whispered. "Jesus is the only answer. I want you to trust in him, Jason."

Jason had heard about Jesus from Mark, Malcolm, and others, but no one had really asked him directly if he would trust God and accept Jesus as Lord. He thought about what the others had told him about Jesus, and how he'd called out to God when Allyn was wounded. Now that he was asked to decide one way or the other, he found he couldn't refuse. Jason swallowed hard, then nodded his head shortly.

Susanna came and placed her hand on his shoulder, tears running down her cheeks, and she could not speak, except to say, "Praise God!"

"It doesn't take a lot—just ask him. Would you do that, Jason? It would make me feel good if you would."

Thus it was that Jason Larrimore, who had never asked anything of any man, bowed his head and simply called on the name of Jesus as he held the fragile hand in his. Finally he lifted his eyes and whispered, "It's done. I'll serve God all my life, Mark, all my life."

A great happiness came over Mark, and he turned his head. His voice was weaker, and he said, "Now, Daughter, can you do that? Jesus loves you so much."

Allyn was weeping fully now, tears rolling down her cheeks. She looked up at her father with diamonds in her eyes and said, "I've already done it. I prayed while Jason did. I'll serve God as long as I live!"

Mark looked over at Susanna and said, "Susanna—" She came over and bent over beside him, touching his cheek. She kissed him, and he whispered, "You've been faithful—I couldn't have made it without you. Now, the circle's unbroken. They're all in God's house."

"Yes, Mark, they're all home now." Her face was transfused with a joy that went beyond anything this world had to offer as she said, "I'm so *proud* of you, Mark."

Mark Rocklin held onto them for a few moments, but they could see that life was leaving him. Five minutes later, he straightened out on the bed, looked around the room, and smiled. He did not speak again except to say "Lord Jesus," then he took a deep breath, held it for a moment, and relaxed. His eyes were closed as he lay there, and they all knew that Mark Rocklin had gone to be with God.

★ ★ ★

The funeral had been difficult for Jason. There were many branches of the Rocklin family, and all of these Southern branches came, but it had taken two days for them all to gather. Jason had kept to himself most of that time. It was hard; he had never been in a house where there was a loss. People came and went, he ate when Flossie or Susanna or Allyn urged it upon him, but there was something in his spirit such as he had never sensed in all of his life. It was more than the loss of Mark Rocklin, he knew. As the body of his friend was lowered into the grave, he had felt a tremendous sense of loss—but then a sudden sense of certainty came upon him, and it was almost as if a voice said, "You will see him again."

Since that moment he had kept more or less to himself. Allyn, he knew, was worried about him, but his new commitment to God occupied his mind. He went for long walks, and on this day he had gone to the woods and stayed out all day and into the night.

He was sitting by a pond, thinking of what had happened, and marveling at the peace that had come into his heart. He was startled when a slight noise attracted his attention. He was a man who had spent his life in dangerous situations, and when he heard twigs snap behind him, he spun around and jumped to his feet. "Stop! Hold it right there! Who is it?"

The form moved into a shaft of moonlight that poked through the trees, and he could see that it was Allyn. "What's wrong? Are you all right?"

Yes, I'm fine," she said. "I just thought a walk would be nice. He came to her, and she put her hands out. He grasped them and held them. He felt strange in the darkness, wondering all sorts of things, but they said nothing for a time.

"Allyn, your hands are freezing," he said finally, not thinking of anything better to say.

"Really? I hadn't noticed." Her voice was low, so low he had to lean forward to hear it—and when he did, he smelled the scent of lilacs very faintly. He had smelled it before. It was the scent that had come to remind him of her no matter where he smelled it. The moon passed behind the cloud, then emerged and bathed them again in silver, as if a spotlight in the wilderness.

"Jason," she said quietly. "Jason—!" She suddenly put her hands around his neck as she had done once before and pulled his head down. He put his arms around her and drew her close. She let her lips linger on his and then she moved her head back, the moonlight dancing in her eyes.

"Jason—I'm your wife," she whispered.

His nerves tingled as he realized what she was saying. He held her in his arms and for one moment could not believe what was happening. "And, Allyn," he said deliberately, "I'm your husband."

"I love you, Jason," she said at once. Her voice was not quite steady, and he could feel that she was trembling.

"Mark would be so happy to see us out here, saying what we're saying. But," Jason mused, "maybe he is watching us, smiling down from heaven." He gazed into her eyes. "Shall we return to our home, Wife?"

She took his hand, and they began walking back toward Seven Pines. As the house came into view, Allyn stopped, kissed Jason on the cheek, and whispered faintly, "I feel like I've come home at last."

"We both have," agreed Jason. Without a word, they walked hand in hand to start their lives together truly as man and wife.

GILBERT MORRIS is the author of many best-selling books, including the popular House of Winslow series and the Reno Western Saga.

He spent ten years as a pastor before becoming professor of English at Ouachita Baptist University in Arkansas and earning a Ph.D. at the University of Arkansas. Morris has had more than twenty-five scholarly articles and two hundred poems published. Currently, he is writing full-time.

His family includes three grown children, and he and his wife live in Orange Beach, Alabama.

In addition to this series . . .

THE APPOMATTOX SAGA

#1 A Covenant of Love   0-8423-5497-2
#2 Gate of His Enemies   0-8423-1069-X
#3 Where Honor Dwells   0-8423-6799-X
#4 Land of the Shadow   0-8423-5742-4
#5 Out of the Whirlwind   0-8423-1658-2
#6 The Shadow of His Wings   0-8423-5987-7

. . . look for more captivating historical fiction from Gilbert Morris!

THE WAKEFIELD DYNASTY

This sweeping saga follows the lives of two English families from the time of Henry VIII through four centuries of English history.

#1 The Sword of Truth   0-8423-6228-2
#2 The Winds of God   0-8423-7953-3
#3 The Shield of Honor (New! Spring 1995)   0-8423-5930-3

RENO WESTERN SAGA

A Civil War drifter faces the challenges of the frontier, searching for a deeper sense of meaning in his life.

#1 Reno   0-8423-1058-4
#2 Rimrock   0-8423-1059-2
#3 Ride of the Wild River   0-8423-5795-5
#4 Boomtown   0-8423-7789-1
#5 Valley Justice (New! Spring 1995)   0-4823-7756-5

Just for kids

THE OZARK ADVENTURES

Barney Buck and his brothers learn about spiritual values and faith in God through outrageous capers in the back hills of the Ozarks.

#1 The Bucks of Goober Holler   0-8423-4392-X
#2 The Rustlers of Panther Gap   0-8423-4393-8
#3 The Phantom of the Circus   0-8423-5097-7